ZURABIA

ZU by *PETER DASH* RABIA

iUniverse, Inc.
Bloomington

ZURABIA

iUniverse books may be ordered through booksellers or by contacting:

iUniverse
1663 Liberty Drive
Bloomington, IN 47403
www.iuniverse.com
1-800-Authors (1-800-288-4677)

ISBN: 978-1-4620-4879-3 (sc)
ISBN: 978-1-4620-4878-6 (hc)
ISBN: 978-1-4620-4877-9 (ebk)

Library of Congress Control Number: 2011915552

Printed in the United States of America

iUniverse rev. date: 10/25/2011

DEDICATIONS

To my parents, Ruth and Philip Dash, for their enduring

love and support. And to Lower Canada College including

its incredible teachers and the remarkable Class of '74.

Never to be forgotten.

ACKNOWLEDGMENTS

A special thank you to Dr. Thelma Baer-Stein for the initial editing work and for making helpful suggestions, and to the staff of my publisher, including the editorial evaluation and final editing teams. Their expertise and timely help have been highly appreciated.

ONE

The Zentrum district that Friday evening had the vibrancy of a Van Gogh wrapped in mysticism. Street streams of lit-up bistros, cafés, and shops were casting their gentle shadows onto the cobblestone running up and down the lanes. Above, bloodred geraniums in flower boxes were twirling out their senses in the light breeze. There was only one major problem with this enchanting scene that early evening. It was being lost on faceless financial figures marching down Bahnhofstrasse, the corridor to temples of global banking power.

As these bankers hurried through the shadows on the way to their trains, they remained oblivious to a more decipherable stone face of a free-spirited noble lady. She was babbling water and looking down at a wounded, snarling dragon. No one seemed to notice her spears in the bubbling fountain of the square as they quickly passed her by.

Throughout the city, the church steeples stabbed too, but into a fading woolen blue sky. The tower protectors of a cathedral seemed to project onto walls of wooded hills in embracing parks. Farther afield south to southeast, the snowy pointed peaks of the Bernese Alps appeared like ramparts to the city's outer defenses. Closer by, the moatlike river waterways gave a feel of inner security. Altogether, a near perfect collage of quaint edifice snuggled into the bosoms of Nature's ecstasies.

To many global investors and bankers, the city was more than a lovely setting. It was a serene financial fortress to an upside-down world that was increasingly sending its gold bullion to the city for safekeeping. A growing number of fiscally failed governments evermore at financial war, or even violent war, were making desperate grabs for private wealth that was escaping them into this tax haven. The succeeding waves of mass austerity, new taxes, and restructuring of sovereign debt had led

1

to large-scale protests. Terror and economic fear seemed to be spreading almost everywhere but here.

Despite such growing threats, the town still remained the *Big Comfy*, as if nothing could ever disturb it. It was a name that had been derisively used by American investment bankers, such as Rich Fole, the Chief Executive Officer of Ripman Brodie. Fole was a man who had been brought up in New York street gangs and dilapidated tenement housing. He was a carnivorous male who liked to rapaciously attack his bloody rare steak and even his staff, rather than visit this European city known for its cultural pleasures.

However, the leading headline in the American media that May day was whether certain Wall Street financiers, with their London collaborators, would be turned into Swiss refugees. Would the Foles be forced to suffer those softer *delectables,* such as Swiss fondue with Gruyere cheese? So intense was the US Justice Department's scrutiny and so antibanker had become the American populace that there was almost a feel of mob rule and revenge in the spring air. It seemed doubtful, nevertheless, that these bank executives would ever leave, or be allowed to.

After all, many of the senior US bankers subpoenaed by a congressional committee on financial mismanagement were still too glued to their modern, glass-and-cement towers. They still enjoyed the "in your face" urban-spread culture of Manhattan, along with her red-hot lips that stirred their blood juices. New York, with its primeval energy for making big, fast deals, would keep them away from the gentle refuge of sipping softly and talking reflectively on Picasso and piano, while slowly cultivating mistresses.

And what about often-forgotten Chicago, the Midwest dynamo, looking as if it were about to go into financial seizure? According to activists, some of its investment houses of retail "slaughter" had replaced the real meat markets in importance, but not so much in nature. This criticism of greedy investment bankers and stock brokers was more politely stated on the website of a group of Dutch tulip farmers, who had been warmly welcomed into US commodity futures with no future. And less politely stated by insanely angry hordes that had stormed or firebombed their way through banks in Michigan, New York, and Ontario, Canada.

Then there was London, so full of young financiers who had been enraptured by American banking hyperprofit and collapse, like junkies on and off heroin—or cocaine, in some of their cases. Their careers had accelerated and decelerated as fast as their repossessed Maseratis.

But at the end of the day, the *Big Comfy* seemed just too dull and even a bit too cozily regulated for American and London manic bankers. For all I cared, you could have called it the *Big Sleepy* or *Camp Golden Pond*. However you embraced it, however you despised it, this was Zürich: pristine, attractive, and smug right down to its superior wealth and false sense of security. Right down to its haute cuisine, outer sophistication, and smooth, precise manners. And on time to the exact minute, and even its very last big ticks.

Into one of Zürich's more cuddly banks—or "slaughterhouses," if you had a penchant for US antibanking terminology—I had truly descended. There I had met its head fund manager, known as the Baron. Or pardon me, "head butcher" in the meat-market, hyperparlance of the new Chicago school of anarchism and antimonetarism. Where indeed had these vocal protesters refined their vocabulary vitriol? Likely during the foreclosures on their houses or in the broadening unemployment lines—or in the near collapse of their investment portfolios.

Yet as a Swiss banker, the Baron was truly a misnomer. For he was a principal officer of an American bank in Delaware that was more secretive than a Burmese dictator. The Delaware bank was essentially a subsidiary to a main Wall Street bank. His small private Swiss bank provided his vaulted temporary office and served a correspondent function to the same Wall Street bank.

On both sides of the Atlantic, he had had shady underground dealings with questionable customers, some of whom could be well described as wanting to radiate global ill will. Some of them, he killed simply for personal profit.

He had used his title widely and tidily among the rich, ripped-off widows of Wilmington, Palm Beach, and New York. There, he had tried to feign a more charming profile. He was a true delight for these American ladies who loved to lap up anything with the taste of royalty. Especially if it was packaged with tax savings, and packaged carefully.

In Delaware, this half-blooded American, who had dumped near-worthless mortgage securities onto collapsing Icelandic, Irish, and regional US and German banks, would set up accounts for dubious clients to funnel their laundered money into onshore/offshore secretive US accounts. But in Zürich, he had kept a lower public profile. There, he internally wielded his own saw of cutting costs and generating high revenues from staff and traders. His slicing away, though, had also included polishing off some of his customers as well as his steak tartar with their own silver.

To his bank bunker, he would take uncooperative customers who did not want to pay exorbitant fees under blackmail. He would force-feed them bottom-up with their own gold or silver until they spat out everything but the metal. Soon after their receiving the deadly shining booty, their raw inner linings would be stuffed with rough diamonds. Then the "packages" would be smuggled off by the help of an old, charming ex-Nazi. The elderly Alsatian would ensure the corpses would be delivered to their scheming widows. "*Sehr effektiv und sehr gut*," he would say in satisfaction as he sent off the next body and collected his payment.

The silver that was left in the poor sods was neither magnetic nor detectable to customs. Nor for that matter were many of the shenanigans of this banker. He was a financier who liked to play around with the wives of the deceased-to-be or the widows of those who already had mercifully joined the hereafter.

In fact, some of that body booty had found itself into a nice set of steak knives. It had nostalgically been bestowed to the Baron *for a job well done* by one of his favorite Leuvenstein widows. Well, that was what the silver embossed thank you card out of New York had stated from one of society's finest.

After finishing my meeting with him in his deep underground vault, soundproof to all except the well-stacked gold bars, I felt relieved to come up in his secret private elevator. Given its old mechanics and shiny brass accordion door, it seemed like it was a hundred years old. Fittingly, the bank, which was older, had a pungent fungal air, as if what was below was more mortuary than depositary, more monetary crypt than modern vault.

On the other side of the bank, up the long winding stairs, was the reception hallway, considerably more uplifting. There, just several paces from the entrance, was the bank's "guardian angel." She wore a long brown tweedy skirt and white blouse without frills, along with an expression that promised absolutely no thrills. She wore thick-framed, silver-rimmed designer glasses while seated at a long, narrow, fashionable black table that allowed a perspective on her legs as you came up the entrance stairs.

In fact, it was a view without a chair, so as not to impair the message that you were to be quickly swept away in one direction or another. No matter how much you liked the legs—or even if you had preferred the table—you knew you would not be seeing her beyond a few snappy clicks of her clock.

After getting past this stiff sentry on the way out, as fast as my own legs could escape past her mahogany ones, I decided to go for a stroll. I wanted to get as far away in thought as possible from the Baron's disgusting packing operations. The walk, at first, had been good for my health.

After rounding the train station square, I passed over the bridge spanning the Limmat with its fast, vibrating, turquoise spring flow. With a deafening roar at that time of year, the river invigoratingly cut through the Alstadt, known as the old town. It had almost cleansed me from the sordid residues I had taken with me from the bunker. But I had a different destination in mind to provide for more peace and solace.

It was the far tower of the Grossmunster that had been my real destination. I arrived there after about ten minutes of a somewhat brisk and relieving walk. It was a tall and enigmatic, twin-towered cathedral largely built in the Dark Ages. Inside the first tower, the spiraling narrow steps made for a long, ponderous climb, which allowed me to think about whether I would ever be forgiven for the sinister forces that I had succumbed to. Curiously, the other tower stairs were boarded up.

These medieval symbolic titans of past absolute faith and inspiration for secret orders were more inspiring nowadays for adding aesthetic charm for passerby tourists. They were relics to when religion and state had been practically one and the same. Relics to when much of faith had been intolerant and dominant throughout the continent.

I looked up through the sliver openings. It gave me the shivers. I could see a steeple that was eerily lit up toward its heaven-piercing tip to ghostly effect. Overall, the atmosphere was Gothic cold and creepy, and it somehow made me think of inquisitors through the ages ruling with severity. And of newer castles and temples. Of newer crusaders and newer inquisitors, too.

At the top of the tower, I still managed to enjoy the better part of the fainting scenery in the broad panorama of the Alps that rolled their pastured foothills down to the shores of Zürich Zee. The lake then seemed to carry forth the motion of the mountains as it waved in the wind up to the rooftop of the opera house. It was a pure illusion of undulating, telescoping horizons. There, the percussive rhythms of waving winds and strings of landscapes orchestrated with the escaping voices of sopranos and coloraturas. Those voices seemed to call out to the Baroque angels moored in masonry to sing out Nature's praises. But what could one expect of the unfeeling, stone-deaf statues cemented to their lofty perches, irrespective of their designs to look like rising angels?

After taking in this "concert" in air, I walked down the tower's steep stairway, which from its great height to its very bottom seemed to take an eternity of steps, as if each foot had felt one decade following another. Centuries, even millennia, were seemingly in the dust that I disturbed in the shafts of light that were broken by dark stained-glass images and by my passing body. Would this brick and mortar eventually pass into dust too? I morosely wondered.

I left through the Romanesque archway, recalling the physically transient and the transformed. According to legend, this was a church built over the graves of three saints discovered by Emperor Charlemagne. It was erected in sight of where a Roman fortress had once stood, now replaced by a Masonic lodge. Decades ago, some of the Roman subterranean passageways from the lodge to the cathedral had been secretly converted into a vast network of gold vaults of some of the largest banks in the world. What a divine evolution. And what goose bumps.

After a short while, I felt a bit nauseated. I needed to stop along the crusader pathway known as the Limmatquai that hugged the river. There, the restless warblers sang their own opera. But it was an opera that portended darkness or ill weather.

It was at the foot of the Rathaus bridge that all went wrong. Melancholy was met massively with violence, and I found out how foolish I was to think that the very change in time and being in a sacred place would give me the real peace that I had desperately sought.

Instead of being cuddled by the end of the day's soft light that had couched the nearby holy sanctuary, my body was savagely bludgeoned. The subtle hues and pleasures made for soft canvas were suddenly severed to red all over. It was as if the sunset had decided to pour out its anger. As if the piercing, inflexible spires of surrounding faith had drawn blood.

For that moment, my sad, screaming, and broken body had become a metaphor for the violation of the first commandment. In the unwritten book of executions, there was no space for public killings or a maiming. A professional would have made it a lot quicker and more painless. He would have understood what it meant to kill in Zürich—the need to make it quick, hidden, and above everything else, clean. Certainly well away from the tourist crowd, who expected everything to be postcard perfect.

The unseemly public disturbance had unfortunately included my own blood flowing down eyes and chin. It felt like I had been crashed into by a runaway manifestation of the Swiss Bundesbahn. As if a locomotive feeding on some electricity of hatred had plowed into me. But if it had, I might have puckered up for that baby, given my occasional love for wreckage.

But the trains, like so much in the city, were so coldly dependable that they were even fined if they were not on time. As further proof of that orderliness, the city had the world's largest clock face on a church. Its massive timepiece was so oversized on the St. Peter Kirche that it looked as if it could have taken out time itself if it had somehow collapsed. That might have meant the end of the Swiss universe. And not to forget, the railway timetable.

The possible reward for my own bad timing in letting my inner defenses collapse seemed to be reflected on the river waters in the form of a fragmented head. I had prayed that I was simply hallucinating onto the gentle, swaying, and *neoned* waves. That I had been mesmerized and hypnotized by magical reflections. Yes, the Limmat River had become my opiate. Though I had not been consumed by it, it had helped me through tortuous pain that meandered in and out as much as the river's trajectory.

There had been additional compensation for my struggles to stay dry and avoid the watery siren appeal of complete defeat. It was to have the bejesus further beaten out of me; my short shouts of agony were followed by more fists, kicks, and other protuberances. It was like an imagined canvas of *Starry Lights Out* that Van Gogh might have painted with his last brushstroke before he shot himself into eternity. It was like everyone's final and empty portrait snuffing out the confused swirling themes of life, no matter how distinctive I had felt that my own death should be. God, the pain of it, the futility as the final darkness descended on me.

* * *

As somber darkness and stillness began to wrap around the city, one Maurice Strange was given what seemed to be unusual instructions: *Go to Hanger 25 quickly. And quietly move a shipment of cargo of faulty radiation units of hospital X-ray machinery.* He was further told to handle the consignment carefully given the low-level residual radiation, which he was protected against by lead and titanium inner encasings. He was to deliver it to a basement apartment office of the DBAM Trading Company on Richterstrasse.

Maurice Strange was a shipper originally out of Strasbourg. He had grown up in the days when the *Führerprinzip* had very much been in vogue in the Nazi German *Reich*. That principle meant an order was an order and was to be faithfully executed, no question about it. As Strange had been in the Hitler Youth, he especially knew how to ingratiate himself with authority. That explained why he had been well chosen for this deadly assignment. Besides, he had been known to be desperate for money, as the French government could no longer afford to pay a decent pension.

What Maurice Strange—expediter nonextraordinaire—did not know was that the small but heavy shipment containing fifty-six kilograms of nuclear-enriched uranium was about to meet its destiny with several pieces of trigger devices and metal castings in a nearby crating. Maurice Strange was unwittingly becoming a conspirator in putting an atomic bomb right downtown in a city of half a million people.

The history behind this delivery had very curious origins. Dr. Khalid Al Boom of Waristan, famed nuclear bomb maker, had been denied something very special from his Swiss bankers that no such banker would ever wish to be publicly accused of. Something no banker would have wanted to do against such a man of influence as Boom, unless his life and probably that of his loved ones, as well as his livelihood, had been put into serious jeopardy. All of which would suggest that any such responsible, survival-seeking banker would have to change jobs, houses, continents, and probably identity.

The problem with the doctor, a.k.a. *K-Boom* by his enemies in the US Pentagon and State Department, was that he could not access his money. To be more precise about it, his millions had evaporated into thin air, as well as any explanations as to why it had happened. To say that the bad doctor was miffed would be to say that a bull in a ring watching a fast-waving red flag was a very passive beast. It was all of the "bull" he was getting from the bank's low-level account managers that made him see explosive red.

His lawyer, Peter M. Baum, already in the shithouse for defending Nazi war criminals and neo-Nazis, could not even find out why Boom's normally reliable Swiss bankers had basically stolen his client's money. The bankers had denied that his client had ever even had an account with their bank, Julien and Company, out of Geneva and Zürich.

The bank's spokesperson, a Ms. Kalichek, went even further. She stated that any such charges by Boom would be seen as an attempt to defame Julien and Company. If necessary, their lawyer would see him in court. Along with a warning that he might soon be put under house arrest by his own government if he did not shut up, this made him wonder. Had the president of Waristan made a deal with the devil?

In fact, the doctor had fathered his own country's nuclear bomb program several years earlier, as well as assisting Nubia and Tyrania with their uranium enrichment work. He believed that he was being punished by the West mainly because of what he referred to as his distinct, nuclear leadership. Whatever the exact reason, he did not have one single centime of a Swiss franc equivalent in any one of his five Swiss bank accounts, denominated in several currencies, to show for his atomic efforts.

His financial troubles had been discovered just before he lost Internet access through his special satellite hookup system with highly advanced encryption. Everything had been done to make it impossible for his communication traffic to be penetrated by even the National Security Agency's high powered decryption computers at Fort George G. Meade, Maryland. So he had thought.

Unknown to K-Boom, there had been staggering threats to ensure he would have no access to his Swiss money. These included possible removal of Julien and Company's banking licenses in the United States, as well as the implied incarceration—or even liquidation—of the relevant bankers themselves. But nothing less than the hand of the CIA and two-faced gutless bankers would explain his problems as far as he was concerned.

Until the last few years, he had generally trusted the Swiss not to bend excessively to the Americans. But now, what was he to think of a country that he had once thought treated its neutrality with the same vigor as a nun protecting her virginity, despite having been surrounded by NATO troop-serving whorehouses? The mad doctor was livid about what had happened to his beloved Switzerland, which he had previously referred to as his beautiful *Jungfrau,* meaning *virgin* in German. He even romanticized about the country's purity of purpose when he looked up at the towering snow white peak with the same name. He should have realized that practically next to it was a peak called "The Ogre."

For breaking what almost had seemed to be a financial blood oath sealed in geopolitical impartiality, he would demand payback—and with a premium. That gift of returned compliments would be well on its way. *Someone was going to definitely pay dearly for this deceit*, he had said to himself.

A unique storage area would eventually house his special *Gift*—a word which incidentally in German means *poison*. It was fitting to him that the final depositary for the bomb present had historical connections to the dreaded crusaders. He profanely accused today's Western soldiers of being more modern crusaders. He was incensed that they still circulated in the caves of his homeland, looking for whom he called the heroes of the Al Quomini Brotherhood.

He had the additional "brilliant" idea to stuff those specifically responsible for his financial hardships into the depositary alive. Their bodies would be incinerated worse than if they had been burned at the stake. They would be told of their destiny hours before doomsday arrived to extract the maximum amount of mental suffering. More importantly, they would be tortured to get any useful confessions that would help him find the whole gang responsible for his enormous bank losses.

K-Boom would also be delivering a present to his jihadist brothers by generously letting them get full credit for the humongous blast. Meanwhile, he would take what was left of his "measly" million or so at Banco San Diego in Panama and financially leverage the money to benefit from the coming of all mothers of explosions. Surely, he could still count on Banco San Diego not to thieve his remaining money. Or could he?

In the disguise of a veiled woman, he had walked down the road from his house to an Internet café, making sure that his escape through the toilet of a restaurant had not been noticed. He had to risk using a public computer. Yes, the money was still there in Panama. Yes, he thought, Allah was not only great, but far greater than the false idol of money that the West had prostrated itself to. *We pray continuously; they watch TV commercials all day*, he further scoffed to himself.

The infidels of the West, he believed, would see the results of not being on the true path. They would feel the destruction for pressing their hedonism, consummate licentiousness, and decadence through the Holy Lands. Then, with that last judgment, he erased the history of his surfing with the toolbar. Immediately after, he uploaded a special program from his

USB portable drive. The virus in it would make it impossible for anyone to use the computer or find where he had been surfing—for weeks.

That the doctor demanded millions for his work was never seen by him as a religious contradiction, for about a 5 percent portion had gone to so-called charity—what Islamic law demanded in the form of *zakah*, obligatory donations to good causes. They would continue to be used to protect the Brotherhood and its web of terrorism.

Ironically, his last payment, which had gotten used for what he thought might be his grand nuclear finale, had come through a Swiss bank, with which his friend Baron Schmidt was associated. Thankfully he had suggested that it be transferred to Panama.

The Baron had previously warned him of some skulduggery from Julien and Company against certain Arabs and Muslims not in the good books with the US government. K-Boom had not listened at first. He had more than a few reservations with the Baron, an occasional though important financial advisor, especially in distributing his charity to Al Quomini.

Boom's concerns were that the "fine" aristocratic fellow had wanted to charge much higher commissions than the average Swiss bank for managing his money and gold. And further, that any potential confusions or disagreements with the terms of agreement could lead to K-Boom's own severe chastisement. There was a grimmer possibility of which he was unaware: his body would be plugged up with hot gold or silver and sent off for a sacrilegious burial if he truly ticked off this banker.

The doctor's frugality, gained from years of living in Scotland as a university student and researcher, combined with his fear of Schmidt seemed to have cost him dearly. *But it would cost the West much more*, he thought as he prostrated himself for prayer in the direction of Mecca while practically screaming out *Allah Akbar*. Boom did not realize that his praying was in line with a city he intended to ruin. It was a line of prayer that made sense though to the Waristan cabinet, for it ran all the way to their CIA deposits in Zürich containing Boom's money.

TWO

Miraculously, I came to. There must have been an angel looking over me and not merely taking in the views or castigating me for my own sins. No, it was a well-dressed flabby lady with flapping, department store bags in both hands. *How relieving*, I had thought, *that there was so much shopping in the hereafter.* I was surely delusional or a member of the wrong belief.

"Are you all right, *mein Herr*? What has happened?" she asked with the sympathetic voice of concern of a Good Samaritan, or a good nun under the influence of a saint and too much *Schnapps*. Or under the influence of a saint of fashion, Yves St. Laurent, that is, as I got a better view of her. She had certainly nicely filled out her haute couture with her fill of *Kaffee und Kuchen* at the local *Konditorei*—loosely translated into English as the coffee and cake shop.

"What do you think?" I croaked out hoarsely. I waved her away in disgust, but not so much disgust with her. There must have been dozens of other flapping people who had gotten a glimpse of what had happened to me. And one of those morons who had done nothing had been me.

"I'll get you some help," she said, looking damn worried as I hopelessly looked up but then got half up. I said not to worry. She moved on as I sarcastically waved good-bye saying, *"Alles gut und in Ordnung,"* when little was good and I was definitely out of order. I was suspicious that she would take me home and nurse me into becoming another contented shopper.

My body in whatever its state was functioning. And what was left of it felt like it had gone through a kind of resurrection. It was amazing how much hitting one could take without becoming a total invertebrate. How appropriate, as this undercover work had definitely made me feel spineless at times. This pulverizing had gained me a new appreciation for living.

Yes, it was beautiful to still be alive even in my pseudo-gelatinous state. To feel the cool, fresh air going through a nostril, what was left of the blood still pumping, and the exhilaration of exhaling. Then the hellish pain hit me.

That pain reminded me of being continually a major disappointment to others. The proof was that those who had tried to put me over the edge had actually failed, despite all the odds in their favor. Put it this way. If some undesirables in the local banking community had placed a massive credit default swap against me hoping for a drowning, I would have wrecked their entire business. Given my views on some of these merchants like the Baron and their questionable financial dealings, I would have come back from the dead even if the custodians of hell had tried to prevent me. Then I would have personally delivered the notarized letter saying they were out of business, and how would they like their bullet? I, indeed, had an unhealthy feeling about some bankers. I had reason to.

Though badly bruised all around, I managed to fully gather myself up from the quay after the parade had moved well on. Things were looking up. My head seemed to have moved off the water and back into its socket. I had been hit so hard that I was just between a cosmic void and being pulled back to Earth.

Foolishly, I had thought nothing much about the caravan of youth and laughter that had approached me along the quay behind the Rathaus, the old city hall that was just off Limmatquai. They were mostly well-dressed college kids, nice cuts to the hair, though clothed all over in black Gothic style. One was doing pirouettes; another was clowning and egging a friend on to do what I did not know then. They had seemed like party time looking for nothing much else. I had let down my guard and written them off as simply playful, slightly sloshed youth. It had cost me big-time.

Of time, I had no damn idea. My eyes were blurry to the clocks on the church towers and steeples that seemed to be everywhere and nowhere. They were heavy with bells tolling an undecipherable cacophony. Then my head swung down like a chime. My own timer of a large Swiss military watch seemed to have shrunk and gone into another dimension. Even though worried as to what else might come out of the dark, I knew I would have to try and scramble back, or more like hobble back to the hotel to prepare for an important gathering of the esteemed Order.

Good, then something went right. Finally, my human headlights had come back on, though dimmed. I made out that narrow bleak street of

Saracenstrasse. It was named after Moorish invaders who had taken a good part of Switzerland with ease many centuries ago. Too bad that it wasn't on anybody's map except mine. It had been recently changed to something or another *strasse* that was no doubt a bit more romantic and less threatening according to members of the tourism commission.

I moved my sluggish carcass of gelatin over there. I stopped for a moment on that avenue of despair while reflecting in a squeaky, smooth, and shiny window of a closed bookstore. A window so large with unobtrusive wooden framing and so spanking clean that it could have attracted a convention of narcissists. A gathering that might have included some financiers I had been investigating, who might have had to stare harder to see their own reflections.

What I saw in that window that evening I did not like at all, but at least there was a clear reflection. It was ugly. It was shameful and downright disgusting. It was sadly mostly me. Good ol' macho-tough me grounded down by a bunch of punks. The bookstore backdrop was the Old Testament, the Koran, and the Torah. It was a religious shop with guides that spelled out not only the way to peace, but also traditional Abrahamic revenge. I should have probably taken the whole set. But it wasn't my kind of burglary.

Yes, I might have also gotten a bit of a clue as to who had been my attackers. There was a lightning form of a tattoo under one of their collars, which I had clung to when trying to brace myself for a heavy fall—though in my battered, losing-consciousness state, I might have been deluded. After all, back at the quay, I had thought for a moment that I had seen in the river my decapitated head. Evidently, it had just been a mirage, as any *Zürcher* local worth his salt and *Schnitzel* would have stopped me if I had been so disassembled.

There also had been a reflection on the water of a lightly veiled, happy lady with a crossbow and an arrow. Satisfaction in brutality was not really my kind of thing, though perhaps my subconscious was saying otherwise given all of my hallucinations. However you looked at it, there was nothing to smile about at all. There was certainly nothing to smile about being clanged with a god-awful weapon.

But as a professor, I kind of felt a moral duty to give firm lessons on alternative lifestyles to those youths who had clanged me. Right, as a modern instructor to be also a bit more spiritual, a bit touchier feely and forgiving. No, as a simple, everyday male mortal, I had almost wanted to kill them and mentor them into their own oblivion. How sad that revenge could be so stimulating even for the scholarly and the academic. How had I gotten a PhD in youth studies at Harvard's Kennedy Center?

It all made me feel meaner than when I had had a class of lazy buggers who would not have done their work even if you had beaten them in public at Beatenplatz. Actually, I had wondered for ages about the name behind that Zürich square. It had been rumored to be where they had burned witches, for which Switzerland just about had the world's record. As an aside, I wondered if the ladies of the Order knew this. I thought that probably it was better that they didn't. About the record, that is.

Thinking of such women, no, of just regular women, I must have appeared as a pathetic male form trying to regain stature through vulgar anger. I was indeed a Cro-Magnon delight and exhibit number one in the feminist cause, including the ones who couldn't get enough equality out of a beaten-down man. Unfortunately, I was probably more than a bit deserving, though certainly not of the part about being superior even when beaten.

Then something swung around to refocus me further on more useful aspects of life, like my own survival. What in God's name was over there? I had had enough of happy trails.

Was I seeing right? A short distance beyond Rathausbrücke that I had crossed and in the shadows of the Augustiner Kirche, I sensed a seedy-looking, wrinkled entity. Was he a man? Certainly not a mouse, though he could have been a rat. Was he tailing me, and were there others? I turned fully around as smoothly as a rusting gate blown open from a gust of a southerly Sirocco wind. Well, that was one way to make my mild arthritis sound enchanting.

He looked beastly and beady-eyed, irrespective of what kind of a critter he could be. There was also one problem to the theory that he might have been the mopping-up executioner. I was very much full of theories, as a university faculty member who got paid handsomely, more than occasionally, for outlandish ideas. But the simple problem was that I could not see fully straight, which was even slightly beyond my normal academic predicament. For all I knew, he could have been a dwarf giraffe who had escaped from a decadent zoo. That was a nice theory, too.

It was all getting to be too much. No wonder I had felt a lump move down from head to stomach so big it could have been the bump on my head. Yet it stimulated me at the time to fumble around in my upstairs faculty filing cabinet and retrieve a page salient to the moment. "Look here, the standard treatise of the *Art of Peace* by Zen," I said to myself. "When in doubt of survival in a public place, scream rudely and act like a gangster."

"Hey, you. *Wanna* take a swing at me? I'll scream so loud I'll break your *fuckin'* face, you piece of shit," I swilled out. However, my further insults and yells went short along with my height. I was at risk of fully returning to glowing eloquence. It was just too difficult to role-play gangster-nouveau, as my vocabulary was *thuggedly* short on good common *thuggery*. Well, at least I vibrated impotence and pain poetically.

Then out of those very shadows he emerged—goatee bearded, with a swarthy complexion, and in a long white Islamic robe called a *thobe* in Arabic. As well, with a desert headdress of a *smug* and an Arabian sword that glittered for gore. Was I seeing a Moorish ghost? Had I passed through some time portal in Saracenstrasse in all of my imploding? The easier answer, I feared, was that I had simply gone completely crackers.

He said in a thick accent, so thick it would have weighed down morning spring fog, "I am sorry to see so much violence in such a quiet town as Zürich. I'm but a Muslim tourist passerby of some renown researching nocturnal activities. Please carry on."

"Carry on? Can't you see I am bleeding? What are you, some kind of voyeur of viciousness? Are you going to call somebody?" I adamantly demanded assistance, though not wanting any.

"Would that be the police?" he said rather coolly and detached as he lit up what looked like a Galois, the cigarette, that is. I was desperately hoping that he was not spoiling for a fight with something bordering on the geometry of a pretzel. In my confused mind, the Zürich snack bars with their stacks of pretzels seemed to inspire contortions in my neck—and arms, back, and legs too.

"Thanks but no thanks," I said with all the nervousness of a walking twisted corpse-to-be. It was actually quite sad that my last beer pint and pretzel had prejudiced my imagination.

"Very strange for a beaten man, but you are seemingly very much alive," he said with the smallest grin. A surprise! The man, in fact, was not very wrinkled except in the face, which seemed to have been sandblasted right down to his long, snooty, high-profile nose as well as his elevated neck. Yes, indeed, a giraffe of a man, so to speak from lower latitudes. Theory had successfully met reality. How nice.

"You're really strange. Are you screwed in the head, man?" I punctuated that with spit-out blood droppings—all patterned, no doubt, to complement a Dada ambiance.

After looking at him more carefully, I should have probably capitulated and aimed for an armistice by saying he looked dapper. But I was usually just too straightforward to the all-mighty and powerful even when *pretzeled*. The story of my beaten-up life.

Then it all went silent . . . eerie silent. My heartbeat pounded into my bruises. The lull before the jackhammer and jackboot kicking of another onslaught, I feared. Or possibly, I had made too good of a scare with my impression of a vampire ready for seconds.

Whether fact or fiction, he evaporated back into the shadows. It might have made a lovely chase even if he had not existed. A chase that I dreamed of having ended in primal scream therapy—at him, my salary, my job—in fact, at the whole blasted world. Unfortunately, the follow-up would have been less enticing with me all in white and further twisted.

Then I came to in a small church. I had fainted and been out for some time, but still I didn't know the exact time. What a nightmare.

There had been a clear solution to my troubles. A hotel with a good defense of dull stone and shiny iron that was desperately needed. It would be better than lying prostrate on the ground; certainly better than a hospital bed, where too many intrusions would be made into my extrusions, old and freshly new.

Worse, if I had been picked up by an ambulance, they might have eventually made a full investigation of my teaching, which had made some of my Sarabian students run and hide in their Lamborghinis. It had produced so much remorse in me. Well, for the time it took them to rush out and start their engines.

After leaving the church and walking a few blocks, I saw then that I was approaching my preferred sanctuary at the end of Bahnhofstrasse, Zürich's main thoroughfare. I had turned onto this runway to safety near the Augustinian church. Thankfully, as I limped down the street, I had gotten nearer to my hotel. Or should I say, my symbolic final defense and sanatorium? Though it is happily not a real madhouse, which is where so many in my shadowy profession are eventually headed if they have not already gotten there.

The assassination trade is what I am mostly referring to. Though certainly more than a few professors I know could have benefited from having a reservation there, if they could have afforded it and the perceived indignity of being classified as being partly or totally insane. I know some of them whose students would have even paid for their stay. In my case, it was a wonder that I could hold down both kinds of jobs, and survive and stay out of one of those fine, Swiss, cuckoo houses. But I was a hard-ass that put people there, rather than went there. Yeah, I was a regular sweet-heart assassin.

Now, the Hotel Schotland, Zürich am Zee facing majestically out onto the lake was truly grand like a stylish dowager, but reincarnated in its interiors with a youthful spirit of Zen, zest, and vitality. It was built in what they called the "Belle Époque" before World War I. It was a golden epoch, which had poured out its wealth into the creative architecture of the lakeside hotels that even today look like extended Swiss castles of hospitality. In their heyday, they had been often serviced by new railway expansions. They were also the ultimate playgrounds for the rich, particularly those looking for fresher air and fresher health and sometimes fresher women, too.

Some of the most famous hotels created during the early twentieth century, such as the Kempinski aux Bains at San Moritz, had benefited from thermal baths generated from nearby hot springs. My bath that night was to be different, but the clients of today were still the same in some ways to those of that older period. Too damn wealthy and pretending to be so clean that they sounded like they were almost beyond the need of even a mild soapy dip. The ladies of the Order might have been described similarly, and could have easily fit into that period for the kind of luxury services they demanded.

Outside, the Schotland was gabled with a few gargoyles that seemed to stare down from their lofty perches ready to strike down onto the uninvited, or even perhaps, some of the less refined and invited. The Medusas seemed to be also working successfully at those less-than-inspiring guests who walked around stiffly with false heirs. These stone creatures had not managed to stop the alpine spring and winter winds from seeping in. The gusts would occasionally roar across the lake and make guests more than slightly shiver and almost turn into stone. All possibly making poor Medusa so jealous of the competition, whether the wind or the walking kind.

Higher up, the loft windows bulged eagle-eyed to all that was around. The platinum blue slate wig to a tall bulbous roof over the entrance to the lobby, along with the cast iron corset of a fence, only added to its Edgar Allen Poe flavor. What a lady.

As I stepped into the lobby and reached out, he rushed forth. I was then holding onto his shoulder, looking like death. Nicholas, the trusted concierge, could not predict nor believe his sight, nor my words as I temporarily crumpled into his arms. More believable was my understated delivery. That night's version had nasty black and blue stamps all over it.

"Excuse me, I have had a little accident," I forced out with a wobble at the time.

"*Herr Zand, mein Gott*, what has happened to you? Let me summon the house doctor," he implored.

"I ran into one too many objects, Nic, and maybe a ghost too. Some of them were quite moving, but unfortunately I didn't move enough."

"Really, what can I do? Something, surely."

"A first aid kit with something to suture me up." My words, like my body, had practically expired like a balloon being squeezed out of its last gas.

"If I may, you sound a little confused, my *Herrn*. Those cuts on your head. And your skull. Looks very, very bad. Please, I insist, let me get some help."

"Nic, I am doing fine. I even found the hotel in my darkness." With my handkerchief I waved away his concerns, but probably should have used it as a sign of surrender to his advice.

"Right away, I'll get what you need. *Furchtbar*. This is terrible. Whether we report it is, of course, up to you, sir."

"This is just a silly matter, not for the police. A bad and stupid accident. Let me get to my room *tout de suite*. Perhaps tomorrow, I'll see the doctor."

"Yes, of course, sir, but . . ."

"I'm fine, really. And my room key. Yes, a sewing kit, first aid kit, or whatever you have for sewing—enough strong thread if you can . . . Throw in a bandage while you're at it. Oh yes—and a vodka martini."

"Of course, sir. Here it is. Room 911, is it not?"

We had worked out this precaution with the hotel to ensure my identification and that my key would not be given to the wrong person, whoever the concierge on duty.

"No, it is Room 119, I believe," I quickly retorted. The correction was the password.

"Oh *natürlich*, here it is," responded Nic as per instruction.

"*Danke.*" I was more thankful than ever. A key to a secure hotel room that night was even better than my third passport to a tax haven without extradition. Money couldn't always buy happiness. But it did get me into this slavishly lavish lodging, where I did not have to explain how everything had to be or should be. What a pleasant relief to so many of life's little traumas. What a pleasant relief to the holiday inns of America.

And of Nic, I never knew whether to use French or German. He was a complete Swiss bilingual, French-speaking mother and German-speaking father. He could connect both ways and in English. Indeed trilingual, I suppose. Like so many Swiss professionals, truly adapted to so many foreigners. The hotel personnel, including Nic, had to provide high quality services given the nightly fare of between three hundred to eight hundred US dollars per room.

For all the money it brought to Switzerland, English should have been called the *lingua Swiss franca*. However, the Swiss would have spoken Malagasy if it could have made them the billions that English had. They were a dedicated lot, internationally speaking.

There was almost no other country with such consistency of high-quality hotel service, including not going fully gaga when one of its clients came bent over looking like dead or having won the Nobel Prize for peace. Or both, as sometimes the latter demanded the former.

As for Nic, he was the best of this Swiss hospitality tradition *par excellence*. And as a bonus for these parts, he was quite friendly, with a great wide smile and sense of humor. I could have loved him.

Nic had attended to me faithfully over many stays. That one face of loyalty was all that counted. It seemed like it was the only warmth on the inside away from an outside of that evening's chaotic violence, mayhem, and the empty cold void and meaningless of it all.

I then went upstairs hoping to avoid the further glances of the hotel guests. Some of them had looked at me like I was some sort of agent from doomsday. And I was certainly a nasty inconvenience to these guests, given the steep price they had paid for absolute peace and tranquility, and elegance, which I was definitely not.

It was a dizzying and tiring ascent, but one that let me put behind the gasping and uncomfortable faces I had left bouncing on the lobby floor. A close-up encounter in the elevator with these prissies was not preferred. A close-up encounter with the police was definitely not what was needed.

There would have been too many expletive *inexplicables*—or was that *explicable* expletives?—that would have gone said or unsaid. The Swiss police would have preferred polite and tidy formal English, particularly from their foreign visitors. But it was not really in my personality to provide much of any.

It might have been a one-floor climb, but it felt like I had hiked up to the last bench near the top of the Matterhorn by the time I arrived at my room. I had climbed up much of that towering citadel of granitelike gneiss before practically collapsing, but somehow this seemed like my worst ascent. Was I losing it? I was turning toward fifty. "Just open that door," I said out loud to myself—"I surely can handle that."

To my great comfort, I had a room with four picture windows, which by all dimensions could have fit a true Swiss locomotive. Though it might have been a little tight on the snout of a TGV express to Paris. Even the bathroom could have fitted all of my clients and have had a bit of space left over for the Mardi Gras.

It had a separate shower with a decorative, transparent glass door, all the rage in designer hotels. Along with it was a deep cast iron and porcelain bathtub that had not gone out of style with the passing of Art Nouveau—or was that Deco?

In that bathtub surrounded by marble tiling, except for a lit bit of fakery in the trimmings around the toilet, I sank into the hot waters of my soreness seeking to forget the pummeling. I sought to rejuvenate all my internal systems, as obviously this hotel had successfully done with its new plumbing. By a watery transformational osmosis, I hoped to come out all clean and shiny marble, with all valves and taps working smartly. But I was a one-star body in a five-star hotel.

As I sank into what seemed like it would be my watery grave, I tried to think nice thoughts. Rehabilitating ones. After all, I had come out of the day's tragedies with a deal of a room for an unprincely Swiss sum of about three hundred francs. Some consolation prize, but certainly not the trophy. That was to be left for a European football cup tournament that had used up all the regular puny-size rooms, leaving only this huge one available.

Sadly for the hotel, they had overbooked, and I had been somewhat late in checking in. The thought that soccer hooligans or just raw, unwashed fans might have made this suite affordable was a small compensation for the roughhouse antics at the quay.

I still could not help wondering as my brain found its place whether those young pit bulls were really just a bunch of pissed-off or pissed-up hooligans. Whether they had picked on me because some blond, British, iconic lout on grass paid millions couldn't get it up for the afternoon's soccer match.

Hell, what did I have against Buckhart, the midfield striker whom I had seen in the lobby? He was a lot more handsome and richer, and would have probably been a lot more agile with those muggers. He would have made great company whatever his incomprehensible Yorkshire slang or his own drunken rants. And impressively, he had not looked like he was complaining after seeing me bleeding. He was truly a champion in my books. After all, he was used to seeing so much blood, and causing it.

The world indeed could be a raw and unlucky place, both on and off the field. Whether one had descended down from the holy lights of the Etons or some more practical down-to-earth *peda-druggery* as Buckhart did, life could go bad . . . very bad. For that evening, though, we had become invisibly bonded together and socially leveled. We were both sore losers, whatever our pitch.

I went to sleep finally, trying not to feel too alone in my extreme downtrodden glory. Trying not to think of the new dangers that might emerge because of my association with the Order. Thankfully, hours free of worries seemed to pass, as I drifted in and out of my throbbing pains.

THREE

Eleven o'clock, it read. Oh shit, had I overslept into the morning? Curtains pulled back. Thank goodness—darkness. After a half hour or so, I literally dragged my bedraggled self from bed. But all bathed, sutured, and made up, I set off to the fashionable Rothirsh Café near the Storcher Hotel for another mandatory midnight meeting of the Order. I would somehow manage to keep face by reading into my *Neue Zürcher Zeitung*. Hopefully, no one would notice that Madame Tussauds's wax work of Frankenstein had just escaped. Its recent edition, that is, with read-all-about-it headlines on my forehead.

Despite these disfigurements, I did not booze up, well, not right away. There was always the outside possibility that the runaway train of teenage horror or their real *Führer* might have decided to track me down. Or could I look to the whole incident as excessive youthful exuberance and pure blind poor luck? Did the answer just lie in their being on too much testosterone and booze? It was a potentially dangerous triple combination—like a Molotov mixture for a human explosion. Why couldn't they have simply stuck to lemonade? I seemed to have conveniently forgotten my own adolescence.

I was still guessing on the motivation behind the attack and was desperate for answers. But I was getting worse at it. I thought that my meanest rugby-playing friends might have described the evening's activities as a bit over the top of a youthful roughhouse spirit. A liveliness that we often wanted to recapture with our pickup games, short of course of crowbars and hate-fed hits to the groin and elsewhere. Well, short of crowbars.

Yes, how philosophical. How deep about wanting to recapture lost youth. No, instead, that night I feared that I had just wanted to murder it . . . with bourbon, rum, whisky, or just the whole lot. I was definitely menopausal . . . or manic. What the diff?

It was certainly time to try and relax, if I could forget how old and decrepit my body had gotten. There, a nice comfy café chair for the old gentleman, near the edge of the river, in which I unceremoniously *geplunked* myself. And would hopefully behave myself.

I felt consoled then that I was both alive and middle-aged. Not so bad, a nice package deal. To recognize my coming to my age, I had gotten eye-drunk on watching these elegant women across from me all so well cloaked in Christian Dior. I had strangely envisaged that they were partaking in some form of absolutional ritual. It could have been because of the clothes. Or, perhaps, something else.

Surely they had more reason, I thought, to look for forgiveness. My lingering suspicion was that in some way they might have been the reason for my summary execution from the conscious and a throbbing that felt like a beheading. They were trouble, but they were my trouble. So I needed to stop the whining even if I could still hear the clanging.

I then reflected more profoundly on the concept of pain, not fully warmed up at the moment to the nearby female company and still too much into my head like the good academic that I could be. I suppose, as Dr. Guillotin was reported to have said to King Louis XVI of France, no one could really tell anyone how a beheading felt. I thought that conceivably I had been in the nearest best shape to describe that indescribable moment that poor Louis was never able to share, before or after his execution during the French Revolution. Indeed, kings too could be vulnerable to the swift edge of history. And to so much pain and defeat.

Why had my thoughts somehow turned to kings and revolutions? Was it because I had also sensed that I might be under threat like some unlucky head of state to become a political victim for disposal by some manipulated mob? So nice that I had elevated my status. Though certainly no guillotines or swords were nearby last time anybody checked. At best, a lovely assortment of Swiss army knives for gutting a small fish or showing off to your girlfriend was in a plethora of close-by shops. It all made one wonder as to what kind of tourists the Swiss were attracting.

Yes, given the surroundings, any real chance of revolution here stank to high heavens; the whole idea to the well-off Swiss and their upscale visitors would have been putrid. But for Sarabia, that was another matter. There, a guillotine could have many friends. There, a Swiss knife just wouldn't make it. There, a Swiss tourist could become . . . well . . . just dead.

With those thoughts, some relief was definitely now very much needed. I waved to the waiter. He marched over. "A Pernod, please," I said rather gently. For some reason, I felt too broken up for a Crown Royal whisky or a Royal Salute. Too fragile to ask with a hard snap of commanding German known to be common in these parts when asking for something from a supposed subordinate.

"Certainly, sir, anything else?" the waiter responded in turn kindly.

"*Ein Mineralwasser mit Kohlensäure*," I said.

"Of course," he said obediently, but with a slight questioning rise of the eyebrow. I hoped it would dull my pain—aniseed-based alcohol added to sparkling water.

"Did you know," I said to the waiter, "I even convinced an elite French family with a *grande maison* in the Loire countryside that it was an acceptable mix?"

"Really, *mein Herr*, very droll; you must be a very persuasive person."

"Yes indeed. They had made a few pleas that this could not be—only regular water would acceptably go with it."

"*Mein Herr*, we Swiss would not argue. We would have better things to do; no slight to our neighbors, of course."

"No, of course not."

"But if it is not too forward, are not you Americans very good in promotion? Ah, you are an American? I should first ask. As I suppose you could be a Canadian."

"Hmm . . . I think I am a little too forward and opinionated for a Canadian. But thank you for that thought."

"So sorry for any possible confusion," he said as he so politely retracted his mild faux pas, but less politely than if he had been a Canadian.

I laughed and said, "Not to worry. I have been mistaken for much worse." I added, "I suppose we Americans are pretty good at promotion now that I think of it. Yes, that French family was quite persuaded after a lot of resistance to accept that bizarre concoction of a drink."

"I hope that you very much have a nice time visiting our country. And good health to you. I will be back shortly," he said with a pleasant, sympathetic wink.

I wondered why. Possibly he sensed a common link: we were both servers to the high and mighty European clients. And feeling like we deserved a higher calling, despite our somewhat less refined ways. Or maybe, he had the *hots* for me.

"Thank you from the bottom of my . . . bruises." He had completely turned away before I finished my sentence. It was better that way. I think I had confused the poor man enough. Probably sickened his stomach by what he was about to serve.

But with the right confidence and a good argument, one could also reinvent the wine carte in France even as an American. In fact, an American had: Roger Tannenschmecker, of New York, was his name. A man who was now considered as one of the premier wine connoisseurs in the world. An important lesson of sorts to the apologists who traverse France feeling like they are some subspecies because they are North American.

It made me think that sometimes, we so-called culturally deficient North Americans needed to proverbially kick the butt out of uptight old Europe. But that would have been in poor form. And my Canadian friends would have been reluctant, though finally compliant. However, some of my European friends would have been cheering me on as poor old Europe screamed.

I was beginning to sound like a hard-talking, Daniel Ruffield conservative; how sickening. "Bring it on," I said to myself as I requested a second sip. All in remembrance of the former US military secretary whose ship had sunk off France's Bay of Dismay along with his rigid ideology.

Not surprisingly, because of the jingoistic and high profile reputations of US politicians like Ruffield, it was increasingly difficult as an American to feel fully welcomed almost anywhere outside of stateside. Especially on the continent, even if you had a few manners. Or it could have just been my hard-boiled personality. Okay, well, so what, and where was I going with all of these thoughts?

I was digressing and wandering laterally, like so much talk tends to zig and zag in Sarabia, my ol' home desert country. A crack to the head probably didn't help either. So, was I becoming a good Sarabian? Well, probably not, but it might have been better than being a good, predictable, stiff piece of human clockwork.

These constant reminders of an intense mechanization of life here in Zürich made me feel an occasionally crushing need to avoid the linear thinking in the upper-crust city bar scene frequented by academics, highbrow intellectuals, and technocrats. I didn't much like the Cartesian square heads either, who were all about in the fashionable make-believe

Bohemian drunk tanks of the pseudo-*Untergrund* in the Altstadt. They would punctually go back to their posh banks with their rigid, white collars rebuttoned.

You could even sense their starch in the perfume of their expensive, metrosexual colognes. They were a peculiar kind of X-generation antirevolutionaries trying to look revolutionary. They were dull and as exciting as molten plastic in some of the contemporary art galleries they frequented. They made me like most of my Sarabian students—a lot. They, in fact, kind of made me sick.

Most certainly, after my future returns to Sarabia, linear life would be left way behind. Europe, well, much of northern Europe, just got too pretentiously rational and intellectual at times even over a brewskie or after one. Funny, I still liked it in a strange way. Europe, that is. Why? Who knew? Who really cared? Yeah, I wasn't always too rational. Too bad.

But that night's knockout experience made me wonder whether times were a *changin'* in good old Europe. Dark and nasty emotionalism seemed to be on the rise and looking to be the new in. No wonder that in response, the Dada art style had come back home to a country still largely the blessed land of neutrality and peace. Well, Switzerland had been generally quiet and without guns being shot off or bombs going off. It was almost a macabre quiet.

Dadaism had first started as a Zürich-based protest movement to World War I. Not completely surprising given the spreading bloodshed and anarchy throughout the current world, it had come full circle to its origins. There was, though, an increasing rejection of this surrealism movement for peace among the rising number of warmongers and religious terrorists, as well as crusader nuts that were outside the country. Or conceivably, they were about, but in disguise or on vacation. A lot of them liked the peace and quiet in Zürich when they were not planting or dropping their bombs.

Sadly, for that evening, my body had approached a form of Dada's, modern artistic antiviolence expression—hammered and bronzed. Though too raw and rough to be a museum piece, nor fit for a pedestal. What went there would be decided by the likes of the high-society ladies of the Order, grand patrons of the arts. What went there would definitely not be the "crude" likes of me.

Fortunately and more favorably, there was the comfortable distraction of these fine . . . well, refined ladies. However, they remained frivolous to my pains even if they were just across from me. I suppose they were so caught up with themselves that my slightly rearranged face had not registered. What did I need to do—fill in a form?

Instead, they had chosen better. They were swallowing cold café latté made with water from the glacially fed Limmat—all between elevated gossips that lowered my attention span. It made me feel distant from them by hundreds of leagues. And they seemed additionally hundreds of years away from my churning desert past.

It was a past that gave me considerable insights into Sarabia and its fanatics, who were of burning interest to the ladies of their sacred Order. But it was a past that could not really tell me for now who the hell had hit me, nor why.

FOUR

It was presently the twenty-first century according to the Christian-based calendar in the West. However, currently, it was also the fifteenth century according to the Islamic calendar in Sarabia where I worked for most of the year. Coincidentally, the fifteenth century in the Christian datebook was not such a marvelous year. It would have been about when the Turks had begun to overrun the Byzantine Empire controlled by the Christian Greeks. It would have been when the Spanish Inquisition was getting warmed up. For some, though, parts of humankind had never really left behind those religiously dark brutal ages.

Sarabia overall seemed to be one of those modern anachronisms left over from that period, but with some exceptions, such as having SUVs and satellite TVs. It, indeed, had the feel of the fifteenth century, especially in the outer provinces. It also had a special feeling of being one of the world's last absolute monarchies married to rigid religion, which disallowed many female freedoms basic to the West. It even allowed stoning of women for so-called illicit sex outside of marriage.

In the capital, Raddah, it was sometimes just about as interesting as the dusty provincial cities, though its outward appearance looked modern if measured by the smooth, wide highways on which Burger King and McDonald's had gone forth and multiplied. Along with other franchise accoutrements from the West, it had the distinctly avant-garde skyscrapers of Sarabian Sovereign Holdings (SSH) and Banque Pan-Arab-Swiss (PARABS).

One of these skyscrapers had a loop in it at the top that made it look like the pull handle to some modern giant grenade. The other looked like a very tall and narrow, aluminum pyramid. Overall, Raddah was a dull place, as in capital D for dull. Even the king's favorite great-grandson told me that he did not like it that much.

Yet in any necessary exposé of Sarabia, there were more useful personal experiences that I felt had to be brought to the Order's attention, so that they could do their work there more effectively and possibly more prudently. Yes, indeed, my observations and occasional analysis for the Order were well beyond the overarching symbols of so much wealth for which Sarabia was so famous, well past the golden palaces and palatial houses that put Beverly Hills to shame—that is, in size and decorative gold only. These prefabricated white and brown massifs had cavernous rooms with high chandeliered ceilings, which were hidden inside the homes, in turn hidden inside the compounds, and finally, hidden well behind the towering walls. That was a lot of *hiddenness* for a society. There was occasionally a lot of hideousness behind it, as well.

First, a real primer on Sarabia was incomplete without talking about traffic. Why traffic? It was an allegory for some of the male madness in the country. Simply speaking, too many drivers drove fatally, as if whatever happened at 160 miles per hour, Allah would deliver them to the Promised Land even if they took out a few innocents along the way.

That driving chaos helped to put things into perspective, particularly for the capital city. It could make one believe that it was the real terrorism and biggest problem of public safety—at least according to a good number of expatriates who were less impressed by all the headlines in much of the Western press that practically put a terrorist on each block in Raddah.

One had to also say that many foreigners were equally unimpressed by some of their embassies that said, "Your next walk in the nearby desert might be your last." Such well-thought-out travel warnings from certain overpaid diplomatic stars never ceased to amaze one. The worst of them might have been better off to have gotten into their military helicopters and given traffic advisories—or just kept on going.

But how could one rate diplomats in Sarabia objectively? The whole profession, with some important exceptions, reeked of excessive subordination and flattery so alien to my essence. I broke out in hives when I saw them. Most, though not all, would be next to useless in the ladies' pursuits given this group's limited insights and dedication to risk avoidance. They talked the good talk on female rights to the Sarabians. Then they simply ate their sweet dates and drank Arab coffee.

In so many ways, the ladies were a potential plague to foreign relations between the West and their largest petroleum purveyors, of which Sarabia was the number one producer. In fact, the ladies' own Western embassies might have contemplated putting out a hit order on them to prevent any possibility of the ladies' good works from slowing down these fossil fuel conveyor belts to growth and global financial glory. But no, diplomats did not do the actual killing. People like me did it for them.

Yes, instead of being run down by a Toyota Camry with or without a faulty accelerator or a camel on the loose, which were much greater risks than being rubbed out by terrorists, I had been severely affected in other ways by living there. I had simply been psychologically overrun in Raddah by *burkas, niqabs,* and other facial veils and *abayas* covering women head to toe and all jet black. And there were no single women to talk to, even at the Jewish-owned Starbucks. That is, if one did not want to go to jail courtesy of the Islamic religious police, the *Mootawa.* Traffic and *Mootawa*—now those were two things that could be hazardous at a minimum to your mental health.

Indeed, some of the *Mootawa* wanted to gobble up globalization and retain as much as possible the segregation of the sexes. How nice. I kind of wished them well in their *gobble-ization,* as I would not have wanted many of them as exports. Yet some had gotten through US customs and earned doctorates at American universities paid for by taxpayers, according to a student in one of my classes who was from the Sarabian religious establishment. I take this moment to thank Mohammed externally.

"Professor Sands, we have some very good *Mootawa,* and only a few of them act dishonorably," Mohammed said to me with total conviction while he was one of my students.

"What about the business lady who got picked up by the *Mootawa* because she was simply meeting one of her male customers in a Starbucks?" I retorted this in a Sarabian critical thinking class that certain professors in the West had described to me as being an oxymoron.

I took pride in my ability to teach in such an atmosphere of contradictions. When I told this to these Western academics, they looked at me like I was a lunatic or a glorified missionary. I preferred the former, as the latter would have gotten me put away in a Sarabian prison or simply expelled on a "good" Friday.

Mohammed patiently continued, "Why was she in such suspicious company? Very unladylike for a Sarabian."

"Her office air-conditioner broke down, and it was 120 degrees that day, Mohammed."

"Mr. Sands, she should have known the rules. She was acting superior in trying to break them. Our religion teaches us more humility. Are you so sure she was really there just for business?"

"That's what a student told me whose friend was the son of the arrested lady. That's what it also said in the international press."

"Please do not believe what the international media says about Sarabia. Our censors occasionally have to rip out whole pages given the propaganda in them."

"I don't always believe them, but what about the friend?" I added, "By the way, that sounds like a lot of ripping for the poor fellows who must do it, Mohammed."

"Very sad. It must have been embarrassing to her husband and family. It might have been shameful, whatever the reason for doing it. Now, as far as the ripping goes, it is done under the supervision of the *Mootawa,* who oversee it with joy and pride at no expense. Our Bangladeshi Muslim brother workers, for example, do it at little cost."

There was no serious arguing on many devout matters with many of my students who represented a number of the most progressive elements in the country. As well as being the richest, they were very religiously and politically connected. And despite so many being Western influenced and travelled, quite a few were still mad as hell that America was pressing too strongly in their view for more freedoms for Sarabian women. Where had I gone wrong with my teachings? Given where these so-called progressives of the powerful stood, could the Order's initiatives really have any effect on an overall changing of the Sarabian male mind-set? I doubted it.

One student's interesting opinion in favor of the black *abaya* was that he found traditional female dress to be useful against the lone jackass teenage stalkers that I was almost pleased to say the *Mootawa* had largely banned from the many spacious malls. After all, he contended that many Sarabian youth were still in the salivating stage if they saw a pretty woman without a facial covering or an *abaya* in public. As an academic, I would have hoped that such a description was bordering on being a gross stereotype. But quite a few of my students insisted on it. However one looked at Sarabian dress with its own hidden virtues, the kingdom was largely visual saltpeter to the Western male eye and libido.

The place was so dry for fun that if the mental cacophony from my bruises had been expressed musically, it might have been banned in Sarabia, whether done in full chanting harmony or beyond. And with my poor vocals, as I said to my Sarabian students, it was lucky for them that public music and singing had been largely forbidden. Otherwise they might have been exposed to my "strangled" singing in classroom musical activities. Happily, they were too busy with their Blackberries and iPods to have cared. A few of them were going gaga, too, over MP3 video feeds of Lady Gaga.

Despite such threads of modernization, in a classroom debate on Sarabian females being allowed to drive, those who objected to it had won the day, though certainly more than a few were for it. One of the arguments was that male drivers would gawk at women drivers, see them as harlots, and then attack them if they, the male drivers, had not already been distracted into having accidents. It was a fascinating perspective. In my attempts at being a fair-minded individual and educator, I tried to appreciate their perspective. Actually, I failed to understand it even after gymnastics—intellectual ones too.

For those on the other side of the debate, they kept on stumbling about mentally trying to substantiate the unusual idea that women should be allowed to have a chance at the steering wheel. Stopping women from driving would have hit a giant intellectual roadblock in America in any similar debate. But in Sarabia, even a woman on a bicycle would have caused too much grief for too many men. Yes, there was a lifetime of work for the Order and their allies in Sarabia.

One stark incident reminded me, however, of my Sarabian college being part of this tiny oasis of reform, irrespective of the student body being fairly conservative by Western standards. Our college did not always escape the persistent and darkened forces against being a movement of change, which it very much represented in Sarabia, if not America.

After all, our college was led by our illustrious president—a man of prestige educated at a top US institution specializing in postmodernism, a philosophy that almost says that anything goes. It was a fascinating injection into a conservative Islamic country. And so was he, even though he himself was pure Sarabian.

"Good evening, *Salam Alikam*, may the peace of the Prophet be with you," said this always-hopeful college leader at the time. "Tonight our beloved institution is going to present the play called the 'Tug Away from Strife.' It is an insight into the tugs between modernization and traditions, achieving a balance and avoiding extremism."

The president, Dr. Akeem, gleeful with satisfaction, was quite beside himself. If he had been any more chipper, a few in the *Mootawa* might have jailed him for being too charismatic. He had every reason to be pleased, for he had personally underwritten the cost of the production and been the chief adviser.

"As your president, I want to thank our kind students for all of their great efforts and courage to put on this play. This is truly unprecedented, and another great achievement for our forward-thinking school. I hope, *Insha'Allah*, you all enjoy it. I will now turn the microphone over to your new student council head. Please enjoy yourselves, and do not be alarmed if one of our glorious and brave policemen makes any security requests of you tonight. I am sure you will comply and understand. *Shuk-ran.*"

The student council head stepped forward and said, "Good evening to you, President Akeem, and all honored guests and students. Let me thank you, fellow students, for electing the first student council anywhere in Sarabia. This, along with the presentation of the play, is another new accomplishment, as you have already heard. Our greatly respected leader president has sponsored the play with all his conviction and heart for a better Sarabia. We, the student youth of Sarabia, commend him for his great talent and courage. He represents all of what we have wished for in leadership."

What would be considered by some in the West as sycophantic behavior and excessive compliments to one's superior was just good form in Sarabia. That style did not do a lot for my American digestion, but so be it. After all, one had to remember that Sarabia had come out of slavery not so long ago, and was still somewhat immersed in what the West would consider as a form of medieval feudalism: a full joining of religious institutions and state under monarchical dictate.

At times, Sarabia reminded me in ways of the Dark Age historical references I had made surrounding the Grossmunster in Zürich during that unforgettable Friday walk when I had been savagely beaten. Thankfully, the president was trying to break the thinking in his country that supported that old mold . . . I think. Ah well, he was charming and trying.

Swoosh, smack, slam, was what I heard from the back of the spacious hall as a small parade of long-bearded conservatively dressed men in long white *thobes* pushed forward before the play started. If their beards had been any longer, they would have been grounded. Their intensity and raw lack of dexterity resulted in the crash of the door and the toppling of the welcome sign. What they were shrill about I could not hear at first. Then, unfortunately, I did.

"Stop this play," one shrieked out. "In the name of Prophet, peace be upon him, you cannot show it. All theater is blasphemous. Your message condemning pious Sarabians is deceitful. We will put a stop to it if you do not. A thousand lashings to all who further partake in this. It will be done."

The president's eyes were glowing like red embers. His reform efforts had been put into jeopardy by a roving band of self-appointed inquisitorial jackals looking to feast on Sarabia's green shoots of change.

He belted out his displeasure against the threat of the lash. "Who are you? Your presence is not welcomed! You must leave right away, immediately, or we shall have you thrown out. You are a disgrace!"

Dr. Akeem had become so alien to his usual permanent smiley self that almost no one could recognize him. He was showing anger so intense that it seemed to have risen up from the very depths of his bowels. He looked like a human atomizer, jawing back and forth spraying out verbal bile. He had been totally pissed off. But he was most impressive.

Meanwhile, the actors on stage looked at each other with fear. But the fright soon turned to defiance as the president barked out his disgust with the interruptions. Just in front of the stage, the student council head moved to prevent enraged actors from climbing down to take on the invaders. Others yelled out, "Murderers and shame!"

There were a few other slogans slapped around in the fouling air that night. The American-style curriculum the students followed had profanely widened their sense of individual verbal empowerment and their willingness to be critical. And altogether, it had gotten critically fucking ugly.

Waving their hands and arms briskly to cut through the crowd, punching the air with their fists, the fundamentalists looked increasingly agitated.

Their leader said, "We will not be spoken to by the young this way. President, you have corrupted our youth away from the great principles of respect for their elders. From the most basic principles of the Koran. Your play cannot proceed. I accuse you of treason against the holiest of Holy Lands. We demand you be put into custody through the *Mootawa*. We shall see to your arrest."

"No, see to his jailing," someone yelled out from the crowd.

It was clear that not all of the students were enamored with Dr. Akeem, a man steadfast to pushing American-style educational standards that many students could neither fathom nor work hard enough to meet. It was payback time for a vociferous cabal that had been asking for his head for a long time, a group that had even rammed into his parked car when he had refused to alter his policies or their marks. And they had enough influence to make Akeem feel the singe of their words. It was evident that his safety was at stake, not simply his Mercedes.

There was also another reason for heightened concern by security. After all, a number of Sarabian swords, as well as a gun, had been found in a few students' lockers weeks before. Would such weapons all of a sudden reappear? It would have been an atmosphere conducive to their use if things had further gotten out of hand.

This was a college that many in the local community considered as being full of trouble and way too westernized. Amazingly, no one had shut us down or blown us up . . . yet. Could we have been too tiny for almost anyone to have really cared? Probably. Yet, pressure had been mounting for months like a boiler being continuously heated up with a blocked release valve. Something had to go. And in this case, it was to be Dr. Akeem

Almost as miraculous as Moses' parting of the nearby Red Sea, two wall barriers of protective students and internal security personnel formed around the college chief. A volunteer student security captain and assistant then carried Dr. Akeem off. He was gone in a flash like a human fly, arms flaying about like wings. Once again, he had avoided the "swatter."

One swatter he just barely avoided was the Sarabian SWAT team that had arrived from a nearby army base. Unfortunately, they added to the chaos that had seemed impossible to become worse. One member of the SWAT team came down so hard for order that after he jumped off the stage, he fired into the air! Bull's-eye! He had bagged himself a chandelier. He was that evening's last attempt, thankfully, at spontaneous human combustion, as the fundamentalists exited, threatening to pulverize the college.

It had been a complete madhouse even before the arrival of the commandos, with almost everyone ending up on stage. If it had been a play, its name would have been "Pandemonium." The extremists were not just intent on upsetting the actors. They had ripped away the props, which they used as battering rams to clobber things.

They hit students, while in a bizarre dance of death that more reminded one of Whirling Dervish apprentices still working on their one, two, and three. A good number of students returned the compliments, but with more of a smooth waltz, yet with no less passion. In the end, it was all theater and no play. And a whole lot of ambulances.

It was also my first direct experience and a visible warning while working in Sarabia as to how deep the cleavages were between the reformists and the fundamentalists. It was a lesson I would continue to keep in mind during my occasional advice to the Order concerning their efforts to undermine the extremists, but with a minimum amount of backlash.

The image of Akeem flaying about as the fundamentalists tried to descend on him would stay in my mind forever. It was pathetic to see how such a learned and civilized agent of change could be driven out by such fanatical madness. This was not just the college's story. It had evidently been too often Sarabia's larger story.

Very worrying was the question of how these livid religious zealots had gotten past the college security gates. It was near mystifying, as attendance was by invitation only. Though a few extra open invitations had been given to important princes living in Raddah as a matter of protocol. One of whom, incidentally, the Order now had its eye on.

In a way, an innocent effort at a rather small college, heroically trying to promote moderate Islam synthesized with American educational values, ended with such a lack of moderation. It was a possible warning of how a more intense operation at reform would be dealt with by the opposition.

It was an opposition that considered a woman's place as being behind veils, or behind walls. And those who protested against it too loudly could find themselves behind bars. This opposition would find the very existence of the Order to be poisonous down to their very last Western female atom, especially if they ever truly found out about the Order's complete mission.

On the other hand, Mohammed, who had returned in bandages after defending the theater group from the attack, like so many of my students, provided me much instruction on all things noble about so many Sarabians. If he had been with me in Zürich, he would have simply chopped out the asses of my attackers. Mohammed, I missed you.

Mohammed had specifically reminded me that there was still value in the West trying to connect with understanding Sarabian ruling class challenges. We tried through conversations we had on desert picnics, important social happenings, and poetry readings that were so popular during the Sarabian winter, if you could call it that.

The winter ended in March, when the near ninety degree Fahrenheit temperatures began to come back in the last days of the month. Certainly, the seventy degree temperatures in late afternoon during winter months were more bearable. And as an aside, I had never experienced such chills running through my body as when I was laid out before the nighttime desert fire.

There, late into night before our outdoor hearths of rugs and cushions, we gossiped worse than old hags. There, some of my Sarabian hosts almost insisted that I drink a detestable Lebanese-based moonshine that had practically put me into convulsions. Convulsions that also went with drinking camel's milk, which seemed to have unusual bacteria in it that had made me continuously puke after I had drunk it. Yes, modernization had its value at times, such as pasteurization, notwithstanding a whole lot of French cheese.

"Professor Sands," Mohammed added with sincerity during our desert picnic, "what do you think of our government and leadership now that we are out here before a fire, speaking plainly as man to man?"

"Mohammed, I think they are very conservative and struggling to bring an old society into the modern age."

"No, Professor. We are struggling to keep all the darkness from the modern age from polluting our wells of knowledge, too. I fear that our university has become too contaminated. And once a well is poisoned, it becomes no good for a long time. To those who do the polluting, there are consequences."

"What might these be, Mohammad?"

"It is difficult to exactly say. But our leadership will act to maintain that balance so as to keep the fanatics from growing."

"Really, Mohammed, you really think that our university is too liberal? I can't believe it. You saw the students still adhere to women not driving and generally staying under the veil and being subordinate."

Mohammed was one of a small handful of students that I could still have a fully frank and open conversation with and who would allow me a few sips of the forbidden waters when in the desert.

"Look, Professor, with all respect, you are missing the main points, like so many Westerners."

"How so? I am always willing to listen, unlike one of my bosses who . . ."

"Yes, listening is important, but please also respect your boss. Very important!"

"Yes. Sorry about that. I shouldn't involve you in faculty politics and management. We American professors rudely complain about that too often. Respect of authority is not always our best attribute. My mistake."

"The minor peculiarities of a lot of our culture should not be considered to be so important, as well. What you need to know is that the radical fundamentalists are absent from the establishment. We consider them as crude embarrassments, or at best, excessive enthusiasts who have lost their bearings, if not their minds."

"Lost their bearings? They killed thousands of innocent people in New York and many other places. Interesting you think the establishment is completely free of them."

"Remember, your people killed thousands of innocents in Iraq and other parts of our region. So, some say we have two groups of fanatics to deal with. How many innocents have lost their lives because of what we Sarabians have done? Many fewer. And without our help, these fanatics as you call them could have killed a lot more in the West. We sometimes worry about your fanatics who want to impose everything American, even though there are still many things to admire about your country."

"That's because in killing your enemies, which are ours too, innocent people have been killed as collateral damage. Very unfortunate, Mohammed."

"Professor Sands! There have been a lot of indiscriminate killings, and some sanctions have wreaked havoc on the lives of Waristanis. And drones have been sent in, blowing up innocents. Our establishment has paid a heavy price for not criticizing your people more severely. For letting your airplanes still fly off from our soil. For letting thousands of your countrymen who are not Muslims to work in our country, which our king and most of us consider to be one large Islamic shrine."

"I understand how sacred Sarabia is, but not even one Christian church is allowed. Look at Syria and Turkey and many other Muslim states where Christians are allowed to practice—though I would say it's no picnic to be an Orthodox Christian or Jew in parts of Syria. Tolerance and mutual respect are crucial. Is that not what the Koran says?"

"As I said, Professor Sands, our country is a very special one. Would you let Muslims practice Islam in your church? Think of our country as one large mosque, as the homeland worshipping structure for all the world's Muslims. Do you let Muslims pray to Allah at the Vatican? Please have some perspective."

"Mohammed, I do, and so do many Muslims in other countries who successfully allow for more religious and cultural freedoms. But I respect your genuine, well-held views, and the difficulties of managing such a large country with well-ingrained traditions."

"Thank you, Professor Sands. You are an honorable man, I think."

Yes, despite what seemed like the sterile madness of Raddah's culture, it had to be also remembered that not all Arabia was Sarabia. Plenty of other Arabs and Muslims considered a fair number of Sarabians and their Tyranian sister neighbors' interpretation of Islam as being just short of being from another planet or another galaxy. Like the dark one to which I thought I had gotten close that destructive night in Zürich. A vast expanse of blindness to a variety of enjoyment and social possibilities. A cultural crippling and staggering of sorts for a lot of outsiders. This all was, of course, irrespective of the great hospitality Sarabians like Mohammed offered over camel milk, Sarabian coffee, and dates . . . the fruit, that is.

"Whatever you think of us, I swear on my uncle's grave that I and those in my family will do everything to protect you from harm's way. For you are my teacher and friend. For us, we are honor and duty bound to our tribe and those with special connections to us. Would you die to protect me? We would for you, and leave our rewards to Allah. No, we and many other Arabs have already sacrificed our lives many times for you and to protect your civilization."

It was touching to see Mohammed's loyalty to me, and his dignity. I hoped it all might be highly useful in the future. But who could say? After all, I was still an infidel to so many in the kingdom. A religious and spiritual adolescent at best, in need of being converted to save my soul. In another way, it was patronizingly annoying. So annoying that it felt like a sharp intrusion into my whole well-being and sense of modern, open self. Yet, I needed to reach out and try to understand the Sarabian perspective, just as the Order needed similarly to open their hearts and minds to this distinct desert culture.

There was yet another perspective I needed to consider. Could I have sometimes been too irritated about a desert culture I did not understand?

Was I just a tough ass, jaded American bigot, not adaptable to quaint ideas like kamikaze jihadists, religious police who used the lash, no single critical word or drawing against the prophets or changing religion without the threat of death, and no mixing with the girls, especially by single me—besides all the other completely unusual social strictures? And was the Order just a bunch of naive do-gooders who would prove the expression that "the way to Hell is paved with the best intentions" if they seriously tried to push for reforms in this society?

Right, I was just getting warmed up with my own self-flagellation. Yes, I was also a real rotter, and a Yank at that. I was damn evil and glad there were so many to remind me of it in case I got arrogant and intoxicated with our national might. And I was sometimes recklessly sarcastic to boot. Yeah, definitely reckless. And shame on me, if only I could have been a Canadian instead of being equated with Satan. After such ironic thoughts, I felt fully expunged. Better than an exorcism or an enema—unless the Baron was administering it. I was now a proud American, again. Well, sort of.

More seriously, I thought, shame to those who were just too polite about all the crazy religious meanness and backwardness, especially in the outer parts of Sarabia, where there were now chockablock executions of those who had not followed strict Sarabian religious law and practices. The Sarabians had largely wanted me to more than turn the other cheek, to completely look the other way. I had been there, but the Order would have more bravery to go elsewhere. They would need all of it, and more than likely, some of the wisdom I had gained from Mohammed in the desert.

FIVE

I continued to keep a watchful eye on the ladies of the Order at the Rothirsh in and out of my reflections on Sarabia. They would increasingly need my protection, so I thought. My contacts in intelligence had told me that these ladies were beginning to get increasing attention from potentially hostile elements connected to Sarabia and Tyrania. That was all that I needed to complement my adventure-applauding bruises, which no one wanted to take ownership of, at least openly.

However, whatever the Sarabian religious extremists actually thought of what they probably considered these "wild," controlling, and decadent women (mostly of the West) and their feminist liberation theology, certain facts remained incontestable. These ladies of the Order remained quintessentially the powerful *establishmentina* attached to the other powerful global "religion," worldwide private wealth and mass consumption. And they and their money were not going to go away, despite whatever threats the extremists might plan for them. That was predicated, of course, on them not being murdered and atomized, with me not letting it happen. Simply speaking, they were hypothetically the most politically dangerous ad lib organization that I knew of.

But there was a difference between them and many independent political movements that I had encountered in and out of jungles and deserts. Notwithstanding an acceleration of investment rot from within, overexposure to hedge fund rip-offs, and subprime imbroglios within their husbands' banks, the ladies of the Order were financially set for life. Only a worldwide depression would dent their consummate habits of high luxury consumption.

However you looked at these new emerging heights of power, they were loaded, which meant they could make a major difference to change in Sarabia. Or a major mess to a volatile region if their plans did not work out. Nor did they need to rob a bank, like one of their principal terrorist enemies, to get enough finances for what they intended to do. They were the bank. Well, next to it.

In fact, these ladies considered Zürich their protected parish, if you will, a quiet cool, central to their "caliphate," of a special kind of fashionable feminism and chic spending fundamentalism. These wives were the grand priestesses of the arts and opera, who organized charity balls even for struggling artists, social causes, or even the insanely gifted eccentrics their husbands would not touch. If Van Gogh had been living today, they would have likely made him a hero and cut off his critics before he even thought about cutting off his own ear. And nobody ever told these ladies to shut up or what or whom they were not allowed to support.

Yes indeed, much of the world was at their command and beckoning. They had the networks to make a strong campaign for increasing support to the women of Sarabia. After all, media, well-endowed foundations, literati, prime ministers and presidents, cabinet ministers, cardinals, courtiers, and princes were all available to them—though they might find it difficult to get an audience from time to time from those immediately close to them.

Indeed, their husband bankers seemed to have gone missing in nonaction. They had come down with the extended seven-year itch, or twelve years plus with a "witch," or maybe what they thought was simply a fifty-year-or-so-old bitch. The ladies were highly educated, opinionated—oh yes—and potentially quite destructive whether they knew it well enough or not. They had plenty to be mad about the old boys' club of senior bankers, who had shown no interest, or quite little, in their next major charity event connected to an art exposition.

The proceeds from this event were to go to a fund for a free speech and religious freedom activist referred to in the promotional brochure as the unknown activist who was—or was that had been—also an artist. Unknown? Was the guy—or sorry, was that a woman—buried or what, I reflected, as I tried to read through what seemed to be humanistic trivia to most of the beautiful people on the by-invitation-only list of star-studded frivolities.

The brochure essentially promised a visual extravaganza and a time bomb about female human rights abuses. The country or countries or other details were not given in the literature, but presumably would be at the event, though in what exact form almost nobody knew.

The invitees, the list of which Frau Stihl had showed me, looked at best more like voyeurs of other people's gross miseries than real mobilized troops to the ladies' social and political causes. Meanwhile, more serious sponsoring groups, including Amnesty International, Human Rights Watch, and Pens without Borders, had stuck their reputations out on the line by pushing for more serious freedoms in some of the darkest places in the Middle East and beyond. And largely on a volunteer basis, and in the field of fire.

There was hopefully still fairness shining through a crack here or there, though certainly not for a million dollar banker bonus or a stock option plan. But cracks often seemed to close fast due to the cold hard calculations of the stone deaf and the unfeeling looking down with a sense of remote superiority and false self-righteousness. They demanded limited scrutiny, if any at all, from those they oppressed below or ripped off. To whom, I wondered, was I referring—extremist ayatollahs, fanatical sheiks, and a variety of crooked Western politicians working with certain corrupt Western bankers, for instance? Luckily, they had not gotten together. But, I corrected myself, they had. Though they would certainly not be appearing jointly at this coming event associated with the exhibit.

Instead, the majority support for this Van Gogh exhibition was indeed more from the cocktail crowd, who had their own remoteness, too. Some of their fashionable, unaccomplished works were far from being called art. In fact, sadly, a few of their own miseries were to be their own art on display—well removed, thankfully, from the main Van Gogh Ex. I would have hated to be the fund-raiser who had come with that amateur bait to the true artistic connoisseur.

However you looked at the preparations for what would be Zürich's stellar social event of the year, it was all getting to be a little overwhelming, if not mysterious—a human rights homage and possible epitaph, and a Van Gogh show to boot. What a peculiar package it all seemed to be. So surrealistic, given how divorced these beautiful and socially registered people had been from Sarabia, torture, any real thorough suffering, or even a brief visitation to this hermit kingdom.

Oh my, I remonstrated against the artistic supporting classes' true social commitment or issue awareness about what Sarabia was really all about. Where was my assassin conscience? Where was my sense for this important artistic moment soon to be in the next few weeks?

These so-called frivolities on the invitation list had been major donors even to the Zeel Foundation, which neither I nor they were supposed to know was a major arm to the Council under which Z5 had been established and funded to do things that more official spy agencies could not or would not do.

Maybe these social butterflies and artists had their worth after all, even if I thought that a lot of their art didn't. But who was I to criticize? After all, my central role to the Order was as a kind of sophisticated bodyguard, a muscle man galore. And a killer if I had to be. Definitely, who was I to criticize those who would be paying part of my paycheck through their contributions to the Zeel Foundation? How grateful and balanced I could be when exercising the kind of critical thinking that I was largely unsuccessful in imbuing my Sarabian students with! And it all certainly helped me to remember that the foundation—indirectly—kept me in more than Gucci.

I came back to the immediate moment from my distractions, and looked up at the ladies across from my table of social subtraction. There, peeking out beyond the platterlike presentation of her breasts, was the gilded and jilted Frau Stihl, who led the conversation as usual with a putdown of someone or something. Happily, she seemingly had enough good taste to put down intermittently her glass of Chateau du Chasselas.

It was of such high quality it would have received five stars in the Swiss wine system. The best in wines that the Swiss could ever have, according to people like Tannenschmecker, who generally tried to avoid them. Instead, he would usually settle for a lowly Premier Cru, Saint Émilion—two hundred dollars more a bottle out of Bordeaux, France.

Sometimes, both Tannenschmecker and I thought the Swiss could be very provincial with their palettes. But then, I could be dreadfully jaded as an overexperienced traveling assassin who more than occasionally had quite an expense account—and a fatalistic attitude at quickly gobbling up the very best. But when I ran low on money, I would be happy to polish off a cheap rosé that was good enough to lap up off the table. Or leave all over the table in a drunken, sad fit after staging another act of unfeeling liquidation.

Meanwhile, Frau Stihl was still purring, or whatever larger cats do when so delighted. I was truly happy for her. Like anyone who had a "tiny" tiger as a pet, she probably needed to do a lot of loud purring so as not to be mistaken for prey. The wilder the pet, the bigger the paranoia, and the bigger the visible false bravado of its master or mistress had been my experience. Animal rights activists especially did not much like her. Could it have been because her fur was still alive and was not protesting?

"The exhibition is going to be marvelous. But with no presence of Banque Swiss. Oh well, no one ever heard of the portrait called 'The Banker,'" Stihl further bubbled and snubbed.

This was a woman who definitely was not getting enough attention. I wondered why. She flowed so intensely that I thought I saw bubbles emanating out of her so-smacking-thick and lovely elongated lips. They were so well wrapped around her smooth facial canvas, which was only touched by the strokes of eyeliner paint. The plastic surgeons and makeup artists had done well, though it was hard to separate out each other's work. She was in a sense her own work of art, which would have been excellent for a bust at the Louvre. Facially, she was more beautiful than the best of Rodin. But she was no great thinker.

Meanwhile, Baroness Schwartz, a woman of great noble restraint, could not help but buckle up her chuckle. Outside of her esteemed company, I visualized her preferring to let herself go emotionally, at least in the more reserved and less judgmental company of an empty locked room. Husband Fritz was emotionally as good as one, as I had ascertained through a brief encounter with him at an upper-crust bar for picking up unsavory, but expensive and discreet, women. Yes, it was embarrassing to admit my occasional association with this banker. And he himself had been all too often embarrassed by what he felt to be his wife's emotional outpourings—even if demonstrated infrequently—and bizarre passionate interests. He had the heart of stone that seemed to be only transformed by large-size deposits of his customers, which sometimes even hardened his other organ.

From my reading of his files from Z5, he had more to be embarrassed by his own very naughty behavior—but comparatively more of the leashed kind. He was an amateur pornographer to go with his flagellating habits. Some tiger, too.

Perhaps these ladies' husbands should have all been put into the bank vault. Well, at least their ridiculous sexual habits, if not their unending lust for greed and perversion. Baroness Schwartz alluded to this when she said, "If only a man's bad character, if not his entire self-centered self, could be separated as such and locked away!"

They almost all laughed. Frau Stihl thought it was funny, but not that funny. And Baroness Schwartz gave her usual nod as a substitute for a smile, and a smile for a laugh. I had always wondered how one could get a hoot out of her. It stretched my imagination so much that it hurt my head.

Another wife, Frau Smuts, a displaced flying Hollander, jetting into the Zürich scene when it suited her, seemed to add to the conversation on art and culture with only the authority the Dutch elite can have over all things Dutch. Or was this just a branch misinterpretation of arrogance of the well-educated, European, feminine elites, Dutch or not? Possibly they were simply well informed, assertive with a confident sophistication and elegance that would intimidate more than a few of my fellow male Americans. Though I knew there would be quite a few of the very forgiving, if they had known about her mounting anxieties.

Her connections to a major Van Gogh collection in Amsterdam had proved very productive. As chairwoman of the board of the Van der Roos, she was able to get the authorities there to lend many brilliant masterpieces to the Order's wingding. It was unprecedented to all that so many pieces were to be lent to a human rights funding event. She was one of the most resourceful women that I had ever known and the organizational and logistical brains behind many important operations of the Order. She could have been a chief operating officer for a Fortune 500 company, and still had enough passion left over for planning a dozen bar mitzvahs.

No one knew exactly how she had been so convincing in moving what amounted to half a billion dollars in paintings. It was a security nightmare. However, her marketing savvy could be overwhelming, particularly given the positive connections she could make with her most difficult contacts. She read a person as fast as she could read a book, which was equally impressive with her photographic memory. And what of importance could not be read, she actually felt until it released the essentials.

"Well, at least Van Gogh would not have touched a banking subject even during his worst fits of insanity," Smuts said with the expertise of an eminent historian of Dutch Impressionism. "The banks had treated him terribly. Some said they had made him go insane when they refused to accept not even one of his paintings as collateral. He had temporarily run out of paints and other materials because of it. Left only with a gun as his last artistic medium."

"Unbelievable bastards," interjected Schmidt as if she had had quite a fight with her husband the previous evening and had decided to do a little indirect venting against him.

"And surely a banker in an impressionistic painting simply did not make a good enough impression whatever an artist's mood," said Smuts as she threw in her verbal dagger with a bit of fashionably incisional condescension, to go along with the public collective mood on big financial institutions. That was about as populist as she got, for her own husband was the head of a Dutch financial insurance company bailed out by a few Western governments.

I really enjoyed Frau Smuts, not only for her ability to cut down her own establishment in an odd moment, but also for her attractive staccato and prance for logic at times. However, occasionally those moments got a little too thick for me. But I imagined that her quick business-like thinking and intelligible monosyllabic utterings had helped her leap onto both the boards of the Zürich opera and ballet societies.

Not surprisingly, while the ladies might have been loaded, they also shared one characteristic tendency with their husbands. They did not want to appear frivolous in public with their money, whether it was theirs or not. Very Swiss or Dutch indeed? And no nouveau-riche wannabes here, I mused, throwing money around *villly-nilly*, as the ladies would say with their Dutch or German accents. Not surprisingly, this made for a lenient and welcoming group of ladies, who permitted Baroness Schmidt to get her money's worth of words in. If she did not, she would probably take it out on everyone by not fully paying her share of the bill. I had been the *disenfranced* victim on occasion. But tonight, she was going to be a real star to get her two francs worth in. She squeezed the words out like toothpaste in a bind, being punched rather than squeezed.

"A traditional Swiss banker . . . in front of a true artiste . . . might cause a revolt—of the paintbrushes," she stammered. She glowed while waiting for appreciation.

"I believe you are right," said Baroness Schwartz. "And a Wall Street banker might very well evaporate the palette, as well as a canvas or two."

There was consoling laughter. Schmidt had finally triumphed. However, no encores had been requested, or she would have been stuck with the entire bill.

I fear if their husbands had entered the scene and Van Gogh had been painting, "Swirling Lights Gone Out" might have been the scene's name.

And it could equally be said that the lights had gone out years ago for so many of the wives, when it came to starry bedroom with twinkling husband.

Nevertheless, there was good reason to believe that as far as their sex lives were concerned, things had not got dimmer. There was always a chance for a revival—indeed, a sexual epiphany, if not a supernova—for these middle-age ladies. I sympathized as a member of the supporting cast.

Yes, I had the insane lane on that one, and a fast track no doubt to a very bad inquisition from worse than an incensed imam if I were not to keep my mouth shut in Sarabia about my "extramarital" social life—even if not so much recently. I ponied up on more of my own false liquid absolution as I reminisced about these beauties more fit for a touch from Rubens than Van Gogh. These ladies' affections could be overpowering. Their husbands must have been sexually dead not to have more frequently responded.

This Dianesis Order, as the wives called their special discreet get-togethers, was to provide a form of feminist reverence to their patron heroine, Diana. The word *Dianesis* was a synthesis of *Diana* and the word *genesis* to imply a new dawn for women worldwide through applying the values Diana represented. They celebrated their membership on their rings, which were in the shape of a finely emerald D with a cameo outline of this female deity of the woods. And with a capital U, her moon sign and symbol of femininity, finely painted just inside the D. In fact, their Order was an obscure female Masonic lodge with ancient roots.

Every year, they would book the statue wing of the Louvre, where the most incredible representations in the world were of Diana, the "Greekified" goddess huntress, famed not only for pure spirit, but also for strength, beauty, and—oh yes—penetrating spears and arrows! In a number of myths, she was even a virgin, Amazonlike creature. There was a colossal collection of rooms, which I recall had the most convoluted maze of exits and entry points for some reason. They would raise millions for the Zeel Foundation, an indirect secret source of funds also to the Order.

All of these events and their activism were publicly stated as focused to help the Foundation support oppressed and maligned women around the world. There was no public mandate to focus largely on highly conservative Islamic countries, or any other type of country for that matter. The Order's agenda was largely unknown.

For all the public knew, these women through the Zeel Foundation were faithful to battered, tied-up women in Japan, as much as to extremists' injustices perpetrated on women in Sarabia. And their public profile was reduced to a few social columns in a newspaper here or there, not indicating that they were that engaged in activities more fit for a spy ring of committed political dissidents.

I had to wonder, though, whether they were all politically and socially mad in the head given that they seemed almost willing to go head-to-head with Muslim extremists, even if they were content to believe that it was being done all undercover. Everyone remembered what had happened to Salman Rushdie and a coterie of female authors and journalists who protested loudly against Islamic radicals. And did they not read all the headlines about the bombing of banks by jihadists? What planet were they on? And such cultlike theatrics, too, to celebrate their bonds and commitment.

Possibly I had become too skeptical about so many movements celebrated by rich wives that ended as simply dilettantish exuberance. Play toys to keep the spoiled entertained and out of the booze. Or could I have just needed a bit of cheering up from the famous Dr. Kardiac, a psychiatrist and brother-in-law to one of the husbands? A doctor, though, who would likely need his own psychiatric help shortly.

It is hard to be happy in the presence of so many of the rich when your cash account at the end of the month can run down to eleven cents. All due to even a lower-level lavish lifestyle than that of the Order's, including only occasional visits to Europe that involved checking my poorly performing investments at places like Banque Suisse. The balance was courtesy of no other than Baroness Schmidt's husband. He still managed to get healthy commissions from managing my portfolios. I felt like a sucker in so many ways after my many visits to his bank bunker or this café.

But more importantly that night, under the surface of celebrations, there was portending tension in their emotions in a frigid air. And all I could do was to feel like a sophist on Sarabia—or just plain sophomoric, especially with the previous run-in with the punks. Why me to see them through the day—through their hunts, or more to the point, through their being hunted?

What could I really do to help, given how badly I had let my guard down and given the willingness of my employer, Z5, to let just about every dangerous development in the Order play itself out? Yet, out of no personal choice, it was time to change the subject, for something more pressing had come to mind with such a thought. It was a headache, a splitting one.

I went for some Advil that had been shaking around in its pillbox that day. Telling me to live a better life, or that it would be gunning for me. That I was out of rhythm, as my Zodiac had confirmed with the stars. Yes, indeed, there was a celestial anvil of mythical proportions bearing down on me from those piercing constellations that I was wise not to stare at too much. Or was it just a big arrow from a cold, quivering sky that I could not get out of my head? No . . . I think it might have been a crowbar from a few German teen folk.

And then there was Isolde, a constellation of her own, sparkling, shining—apart and yet part of this coterie of wives, though single certainly by nature. I was to keep a special eye on her, too. It was easy, with her extraordinarily ravishing looks, slimness, and perkiness, ready to strike down and peck your eyes out with her bedazzling form and piercing personality and intellect.

She was surely the grand huntress. The chaste, the chase, and the prize of the group. Well, two out of the three. She was a knockout whatever her disposition, whatever your math. A beautiful outsider on the inside with élan and cool, contradictory contempt for Zürich's Teutonic orderliness and conservatism. These were very strong currents that still ran through the cool veins of many a burgher, particularly the aristocratic and older kind. In Zürich's *haute societé,* Isolde's free spirit had made her largely immune to these deadening forces that could make Zürich rather gray.

But even to Isolde, *von und zu* Leuvenstein, it was still her city despite obvious limitations. It reeked of quiet stylishness, coolness, and smugness wrapped in mystery, and a sort of outward piety. And despite Zürich's architectural inertness at times and bland financiers, she fancied the city right down to her little Gucci boots, Ferrari, and I.V.L. embroidered and customized scarves by Armani. And not to forget, her complementary stony personality to the culturally unwashed.

Sadly, I could still feel through the rawness and dark stubble of my scarred chin, and it all hurt. I was a muscular *enfant terrible* and elegant ruffian to the ladies. A kind of sophisticated "catch-her-in-the-rye" and keep them out of the rye, and especially any other trouble. And to Isolde . . . harder to say. I thought at least that I could wear more openly my raw persona, wounded pride, and intellect, all of course stacked up against me by my more than military mercenary tendencies.

Isolde, in that smooth graceful way that some women can do with such ease, had floated over to me. She could have been the lady in the river walking on water and between the neon reflections, given how magical she was. She lit up a Marlboro in her equally graceful cigarette holder. Happily she was off cigars—or was it cigarillos that she liked? Even with cigarillos or cigars, or if it had been a brick between her lips, she was stunningly feminine. I felt a twinge of remorse for the antismoking lobby. And the anti-Masons, too.

"Jean-Claude," as she beckoned lightly to me and looked away at the same time, "you look a little bruised tonight." She said it with a caring remoteness that only she could pull off so well. She was so good at it that I had nicknamed her the Royal Coldness *Contradictori*.

"Thank you, Isolde, for your heartfelt care. By the way, you didn't have anything to do with those nine punks that had mistaken themselves for engine number nine from the Bahnhof, did you? Oh sorry, they were only about five; cross-eyed vision must have affected my final head count. And one of them must have been but half a man, if my math is correct."

I decided I would knock her off her smug perch but realized I had been less than gallant and not very sensible in bringing her into my confidence about the incident. At least she quixotically laughed.

"*Vat* do you mean? You confuse me, darling, but very amusing your slang and colorful descriptions. Some young people, maybe a dwarf, you had problems with. *Nicht*?"

She seemed to punctuate chunks of her words as if they were strobe lights that had gotten out of her throat. In return, I was a vision of a throbbing multicolored light of anger as I levered in with penetrating eyes. We should have done disco.

"I was beaten up by a bunch of teenagers if that makes you feel better, and just wondered who might have done it," I said with a full bout of wounded pride. "Of course, I don't think you and the ladies were behind it. But . . ."

"Why then the question? Why ask for what you already have the answer to?" said Isolde as she seemed to peck at me with her logic. But framed against her incredibly soft-looking skin and feign of innocence, I was all mush ready to be swept down from my investigatory heights like a melting Swiss glacier hit by napalm. How the heck could I stay sane on this assignment?

Tonight, we were together in the eye of the storm, but never to be, it would seem, even at the same table. The tranquility and closeness were only momentary, and the illusions as fleeting as her brief conversation with me. There was a wall of social class, the need for distance due to my work, and then the impenetrable thicket of her emotional defenses harder than the iron railing around the Schotland.

Isolde had the good grace to move on, so as not to break my cover. She gave that cute, quirky smile that I hoped said, "Come hither at another time." That time had certainly not come, and would it ever? I was probably fooling myself (what cover). I might as well have got cuddly with Baroness Schmidt over an exquisite Chateau du Chasselas 57. Possibly not. Definitely not. Where was my mind? Definitely dented.

Looking at Isolde and the wives in particular, I thought indeed that the "cobblestones" in the old twisting streets of Zürich had magically risen up smartly after many centuries of relative inertia and fashion cruelty. In recent decades, they had become the stylish international elite of the world. There was no question that these modern women and the social movements the ladies wanted to orchestrate were excessively open-minded for too many old-style males who lorded over Zürich's dark financial havens and thrones of financial power.

Taming enough of the shrewd and senior Swiss financiers into supporting the progressive would be more than a challenge. At a minimum, it was necessary to keep them out of the way from interfering with the ladies' good works. The only thing easier for me to imagine doing for the ladies would be to put a Sarabian imam into a gay musical. No problem at all. I was here to do it all.

Meanwhile, Baroness Schmidt had moved over to Isolde. She said in an eerie voice, "Isolde, I could not but help overhear what Jean-Claude said tonight. He was attacked. Why?"

Isolde's normal coolness looked frayed. Her true feelings were possibly beginning to come through, which she had previously found difficult to express to me. She knew something else that she had not wanted to tell me.

Schwartz said, "I cannot think why a bunch of teenagers would attack him. And frankly, it is a little worrisome that he let them."

Schmidt looked confused and interjected, "You mean he had them do it? Trying to prove that we are in need of security?"

"Gertrude," Isolde looked stern. "If you do not mind me saying, but that is a preposterous idea. I have had J. C. recommended to us by no other than Frau Smuts."

Frau Smuts subtly nodded and added jadedly, "I have had him fully checked out." She nearly protested.

I mused, I smiled and I chuckled, I self-flattered, but above all, I remembered how I had come across to Frau Smuts. I remembered very well when we had made love. But only a one-night stand and a memory that Frau Smuts had put aside when she checked out my "authentic" inauthentic credentials. She had also fully inspected my body, and deemed it satisfactorily powerful enough that she had asked little about my character and intelligence skills. On the two latter, I think she had given me barely a pass. I truly wished I had her good instincts that permitted such impeccable standards in judging the mental fitness of an organization's security personnel with such little work—and with so much pleasure.

I wondered whether she would put me to a more severe test another time. It was a brief fling with a briefing: I really had to know it was over and could not allow it to last. I could not get emotionally involved with any of these ladies, at least in theory, during this assignment. Yes, boudoir theory was always fascinating. I lived in a theoretical world of all shapes and sizes—and even of the written form, too. I continued to listen and be unfulfilled in my social journeys at that moment by simply listening to the frowning Frau Schmidt.

"You know, Isolde, I am wondering whether our activist on the inside of Sarabia is going to bring out or have couriered out more film on the executions."

My ears definitely perked up. What was this?

"We are also trying to get various cell phone quick clips smuggled out of the country showing severe lashings of women victimized by Sarabian justice," stated Isolde. She then looked around in too much discomfort, in a way that I thought was more fit for a member of the hunted than a huntress. "I understand something much bigger is in his focus," she added.

I felt my ears grow as big as hares, and even the hairs on the back of my head stirring and becoming all ears as I listened to Isolde.

"The visuals of these horrid punishments of victims of rape would be central to our cause. It would further embarrass those fundamentalist jurists of the regime who seem to have recently got stronger. But trust me; one of our activist friends seems to have gotten possession of more vital information, secret papers that will make all the rest small . . . out of Prince Bashard's office, that is all I can say for now."

Schmidt could not believe the words she was hearing. "Really, Bashard's office. You don't say. Amazing!"

Isolde continued, "Priceless information, hopefully that will put into jeopardy a number of rotten extremists in the regime and their chauvinist fanatical friends. Share this with no one except the inner circle of the Order."

"Certainly," responded Schmidt, with the honest commitment to inaction of a manicurist holding a bomb about to explode and turn her well-polished nails into lethal cluster fragments in her salon. Schwartz moved closer and further joined the conversation.

Despite their full pledge to the Order, at the meetings the ladies sometimes liked to circulate around, taking in the nightly sights across and around the river. As if they were bundles of nervous, unfulfilled energy, feeling that body and river kinetics could replace the lack of movement at times toward their goals or fulfilling their sexuality.

The Limmat was no more than sixty to seventy meters or so at its widest point and seemed almost subterranean, given how dark it was below at night and how quietly it flowed outside of the spring run. The ancient pedestrian crossings had been there for centuries, weathering the floods, plagues, and convulsive ages. They would weather much more.

Did getting closer to the river's edge, as they caught the stiff breeze coming off the water give them a sense of Zürich's shadowy history? Those chills in whatever form did not seem to greatly bother them. The church towers or spires they did not seem to notice.

Isolde was sharing further with Schwartz the hot information on the Order's little clandestine operation in Sarabia, minus all the details about any Bashard connection. Meanwhile, the Baroness plumped herself down as only a Swiss lady over a hundred kilos could do, with the finesse and radiating charm of a badly docking battleship. And battle-ready Schwartz had a *Rubensesque* body that was not completely without its enjoyments.

Again perplexed and unsettled, Schmidt queried aggressively, "Bashard is one of the good guys, isn't he?" Schmidt still needed to be more prudent even if she was one of Isolde's main confidantes. In fact, Schmidt and her husband had been Bashard's favored guest couple on more than one occasion. I wondered if Isolde knew that useful tidbit of information. I pondered if she had any idea about the character of the Baroness's sadistic husband with his silver touch. And what he could do if the Baroness opened up to her spouse about too many of the details of the operations of the Dianesis Order. Fat chance, I thought, given the not-too-positive relationship these two generally had with each other. And given her husband's multiple dalliances and multiple orgasms with other partners, besides being consumed with business and travel.

Isolde was hesitant to say anything further. I could easily figure it out. She tried to act less interested, to cool down the nervous chatter that was getting out of hand. Though the pinching of her eyebrow muscles surely gave away her discomfort that Bashard was now more fully on screen. Why the heck had she mentioned his name? What was the point? Had she been aware of her apparent blunder? Or had she been testing the Baroness's loyalty in a strange way that was beyond my understanding? If so, it seemed very risky.

Everyone knew that Bashard was truly powerful, a cousin to the Sarabian king and head of a range of important Sarabian sovereign wealth funds. He was not to be meddled with. He was essentially the chief Sarabian financier and responsible for overseeing the fourth largest sum of debt owed by the US government to a foreign government. And, oh yes, a manager of significant shareholdings of US enterprises, including the Manhattan City and Trust Corporation (MANCITC), the second largest bank in America. Interestingly, his cousin, Prince Waheed, owned privately almost as much of the same bank. Were they sparring? Its near collapse had demanded restructuring, and they had very different views on how to do it.

So powerful was Bashard that a number of biographical and business books that had been critical of him had been killed even by Western publishing houses, such as Ziminons and Schacter, owned by pro-German interests. The empire he oversaw was so big it was as if he had ownership of every CCTV and telephone and communication network—or at a minimum, a major stake in them. He had even paid for part of the sponsorship of the Louvre's statue wing at the behest of his cousin. It contained the most expensive statue of the Goddess Diana made in white marble, which Prince Waheed had donated. Nobody fooled around with

Bashard. Or if they did, no one in his social and business circles could remember where they were employed, lived, clubbed, or even ate a burger. He was well known for his efforts at blacklisting troublemakers who got under his skin.

There were rumors of late, however, that Bashard was seemingly reaffirming his strong conservative Islamic Wadi sect faith that he had moved away from when a college student at the Eastern Texas State University. He was coincidentally selling off various luxury items, including his gargantuan personal train carriage on the Trans-Arabian express, with a bar, tennis court, and helicopter.

The bar, of course by decree, was only for nonalcoholic drinks like Sarabian champagne, a concoction of sparkling mineral water and apple juice. There were other nonalcoholic specialties with alcoholic-sounding names, but definitely no Bloody Mary. For the (Virgin) Mary was the only woman referred to in the Koran, and a misuse of her name could be near fatal, especially in Sarabia. That included calling her a virgin, which Islam did not hold to be true.

That's about as exciting as it got officially on his trestle mansion. However, there were other stories well beyond Sarabian champagne and veiled, staid, and dignified conversation across sexes. There had been stories about wild sex with the weirdest instruments borrowed from the "torture" chambers of the Ministry of Virtue. They were only stories, but so was this book that I was writing on all my fascinating experiences in Sarabia and with the Order.

While it was observed by Z5 that more than a few imams had visited Bashard recently—a number of whom were known not to be too friendly to the West—this could have been an effort simply to soak up more money for his funds from conservative elements. Such imams, the prayer directors and moral leaders of the mosques, could provide their blessings, ideal in encouraging financial contributions that needed to be managed according to strict Islamic Sharia law. Or . . . there was another possibility. Could they have visited him to give him a warning about his behavior, or even those of others closely associated with him?

It was all beginning to sound worrisome, and Isolde looked rightfully concerned about Bashard. But who really knew if it meant anything until solid evidence was presented and scrutinized? So far, there was too little, except a small fact recently discovered that one of his associates had given invitations to the storming fundamentalists to the theatrical imbroglio at my college in Sarabia. That was not a determining proof that he was up to any serious trouble, but it did give me an uneasy feeling. It would be far better if Bashard himself was out of the equation as far as the Order's work was concerned.

I shook my head. It had been quite the evening. What in God's name had this Order gotten mixed up with? If they unnecessarily screwed around with Bashard, all hell would break lose. I could see ambassadors being pulled out, Switzerland without gas or oil, and billions being pulled out of banks. Dead bodies possibly turning up in nice and not-so-nice hotels. And then pinning the blame on donkey me for not preventing it.

But then, of course, there had been my mugging. What connection could there be to events around Bashard, if any? These punks appeared to be German-speaking, nihilistic zealots, with SS Nazi-style tattoos. Not certain Arabs with religious fundamentalism on their minds. Though there was the guy with the goatee. Was he a reality or just distorted into something else in my dreams? Had he been a friend of Bashard sent to warn me to find another vocation? Could it all be coincidental?

I was of the more traditional school, those who looked at major happenstances with all the scrutiny they deserved. Plausible, unconfirmed paranoia had its value at times, even if disguised in self-doubting sanity. And this seemed to be one occasion, especially given my line of work, to be very concerned that enormous trouble was brewing. But there were still too many dots that were missing or unconnected. I had thought that I would be able to connect them up once my own brain had become fully reconnected. Could someone have been hoping that I, or even the Order, could not—or would not—after my licking?

SIX

More disturbing than my college's dazzling theater of the absurd was something horrific that had taken place that day that reminded us of the deadly importance of the Order's mission. Something that definitely had the potential to seriously blacken Sarabia's image more profoundly and fan the flames of religiously inspired violence. That made our school incident look like pure pabulum. That combined with so many dangerous events to make me almost shudder.

It had been reported on the café's radio at the time, to all of our horror, that poisonous Zyklon-B gas, followed with petrol gas, had been released into the Berlin Holocaust Memorial Centre. Canisters rumored to be left over from the days of gas-oven extermination at Nazi-run concentration camps had mysteriously been recovered, with their deadly, fume-releasing "pellets" being fed into the center's air intakes.

The guard had been decapitated and the doors locked, turning the museum into a veritable gas chamber, after which it was torched. Three figures, completely veiled and with *abayas,* had been captured on the remote TV cameras before they had been short circuited. The terrorists had thrown off their *abayas* and escaped in all the smoke and chaos.

No surprise that it had completely exploded, leaving one big black hole in the center of the city. It even blew up into the air some of the thousands of square tablets, to remind the public of the huge numbers of concentration camp deaths. It was like the world's worst mass despoiling of a Jewish graveyard, to go along with the killing of the hundreds of visitors to this memorial. It took all of the fire trucks and most of the city's ambulances to deal with it.

The rancid smell of burning human flesh would dominate the downtown air for days. Three Sarabian swords, each blood-soaked, had been used to bar the doors to the underground subway through which the terrorists had escaped into the blinding smoke. The carnage had been timed with the Sarabian festival of Eid Al Fakir and a Jewish holiday celebration. Was there an additional message in the attack? That the perpetrators felt that never these two Semitic cultures should ever meet?

There remained a burning question in my mind as to whether the Sarabian government was being framed. Both extreme right-wing media and Internet blogs seemed only too happy to blame Sarabian authorities, even if they had nothing to do with executing the attack, so it would seem. It almost appeared like a gloating and orchestrated media propaganda campaign from the far right.

A national week of mourning was later declared, and the German chancellor emerged defiant, declaring that no stone would be left unturned until the perpetrators were found. Essentially, martial law had been declared, with frightened Holocaust survivors alluding back to the fire in Hitler's Reichstag parliament in 1933, which had been used as a pretense for a fascist takeover and pogroms against anti-Nazis. There were a lot of nervous political dissidents in the city that day, too. There were a lot of plain, tense people wondering what might be next.

The Sarabian king completely denounced it, and none of the Arab or Western intelligence organizations had any evidence that the terrorists had originated out of the Middle East. If not radical elements from Sarabia or other parts of that region, then who could have done it? The very same question I still faced about my mugging. And there was still the question as to who was behind those who had attacked the college. There weren't even big enough dots to connect, other than the fact that these incidents had occurred in the same month, coinciding with the heightened rise of fanaticism in the outer Sarabian provinces during Eid Al Fakir.

Now, could anyone be surprised that for a growing minority, the newer Berlin still smelled like the old one, even though the government was doing its best to allay people's fear in their new crackdown on terrorism? Europe, not only Germany, still had more than an infrequent gang of neo-Nazi punks and extreme right-wing political movements to deal with, as the embers steamed in the fresh killing fields of the innocent. I thought it all stunk, including part of the new world order that was supposed to be our salvation after the Berlin Wall was torn down.

The world, indeed, was in a turmoil that almost made the Cold War between the West and the Soviet Union look tame. Southern Asia and most of sub-Saharan Africa were aflame. The Gulf countries, with the exception of Qatar and the Emirates, were engulfed in breakouts of fanatics or numerous bombings—or in some cases, civil wars. Mounting neoauthoritarian populist movements in a good portion of Europe, especially in the PIGS countries of Portugal, Italy, Greece, and Spain, had been rejuvenated after some of these countries' governments had defaulted on their bonds or had essentially gone bankrupt.

The army had to be brought into certain US city centers where the tax base had crumbled due to all the high debt payments, leading to a strong law-and-order right-wing revival. In short, the world was a political mess, with widening battlefronts between the haves and have-nots, the secular radicals and nonsecular extremists, and those with totalitarian impulses to find quick solutions. Those with undemocratic, antiminority tendencies were gaining the upper hand. They were eroding the powers of those who wanted to bring about reform within the framework of current or developing democratic institutions.

There was another worrisome thought, better put as a confusing question. Could a new movement of Islamic extremist women in *abayas* (homegrown in Europe) be connected to burning down a Holocaust memorial in what was formerly the capital of the Nazis? It did not make a heap of sense. Other targets might have had a more profound impact. And not many women could be up to a so-called *Kill Bill* performance of chopping heads off. But then maybe I was just demonstrating again my simple male mind.

There was another thought that perhaps the extremists were trying to open old sores between the Germans and the rest of the West, a divide-and-conquer strategy, while invoking fear in the public about the price of Germany staying in Orficestan and meddling in nearby Waristan. Or perhaps it had been done to stir up further opposition to the *burka* or *niqabs* in the dress code that had caused a polarizing debate between the Muslim and non-Muslim communities, especially in Europe. Or was there something even more sinister that I had missed? It was at times all very confusing.

There was, of course, little way to identify the assailants, who did not even have defined silhouettes, given how well the *abayas* and veils had hidden so much. It was easy to see how political leaders on the continent's calls for the banning of traditional Sarabian dress were strengthened by the terrorist incident. The French even established a law forbidding such dress in public buildings. And soon they were about to ban traditional Muslin dress altogether.

This degenerating political environment at their home base in Europe could very well make the Order's work in Sarabia seem hopeless and wrongheaded to even the mainstream of Western women. Even in their homelands, where a good number were downright disgusted with the status of women in Sarabia, and certain other Middle East countries, there was a growing view to simply focus on internal problems.

In a way, it was a moot point to worry about the Western general opinion of the Order. There was no intention to let the pubic really know much of what this organization had been up to, and certainly not what they would be doing. This ladies' society was not an open-door, democratic movement inviting wide-scale membership. Even I could not exactly figure out how its members had been constituted, given how secret its whole structure was, including its founding fathers—or was that mothers? I was neither privy to its rumored book of rituals nor its complete list of members. I was not even sure as to who were its arch deaconesses.

Some Europeans who were panicking about these increasingly explosive developments in Berlin seemed simply hell-bent to erect a new wall. A wall to ban further immigration of Muslims. A wall to prevent any Muslim states from ever joining the European Union—ever. Strangely, one wall had come down in Berlin decades ago. How ironic. That's history for you—largely forgotten.

One just needed to look at the Tyranian leadership, who did not recognize the existence of the Jewish Holocaust, to see how history could be so easily and conveniently forgotten—or manipulated. The decaying life of critical lessons from history made enriched uranium look permanently stable. But at the same time, more threatening by the day—both that regime and its pile of nuclear bomb-making fuel.

Meanwhile, in Sarabia, not all trends were regressive or excessively restrictive, which should have given hope to the Western mainstream and the Order. King Abdul of Sarabia, a gentleman of the old school, was moving reforms forward. This was not always well received by either the West or within his own country. Even allowing for another hundred satellite channels had led to outright local revolts in some of the provinces, headed up by a minor sheik. He had been killed by the police for refusing to abandon his call to arms against the spread of satellite television. He had made an impression, though, as Sarabia, under pressure from the religious clerics, was now going to set up its own Wadi-sect satellite TV system in twenty languages, targeted to 101 countries.

There was another potentially aggravating internal problem at the highest reaches. Some of the younger princes who had been in my classes were not as accommodating with the West, and America in particular. The young royalty also had had just about enough of seeing their country being vilified as simply a den of religious fanatics and bombers. They would put all their money in Asia and the near region if they weren't going to be respected by the West. They would kill the American dollar and conceivably even the euro by a thousand cuts by investing in Zürich gold, Swiss francs, Singapore and Hong Kong dollars, and Chinese renminbi.

These princes wanted the respect they felt their country and Muslim immigrants were well due, but which had been stolen away by the actions of a few fanatics. And a small, vocal minority of hotheads within the right-wing Tea Party Republicans were beginning to dominate the new president's party on issues of religion and immigration. This did not impress the Sarabian princes either.

Despite some of my sympathies with Sarabia's own tug-of-wars, even within the royal family, I had to still ask my student Mohammed, whose father was also a chief advisor to the king, why he thought that Sarabian women were still veiled and "locked" into *abayas* and *burkas*. Occasionally, it all reminded me of parallels with chastity belts in the days of medieval European monarchy. This was part of our continued conversation of student and professor. I joked that it was equally for my own education as a student, if not a believer, of Sarabia's interpretation of Islam.

"Look, Professor Sands," Mohammed tried to explain, "we have to understand the human condition, as our religious leaders and the Koran have so well explained. Men are overly charged up on hormones, and certain thoughts come into them if they see uncovered parts of a lady. Women not related to these men that are improperly clad are then shamed. And a man can get very upset if any one of his wives is stared at, especially any uncovered part. This can upset peace in the community and generate mad jealousy. Peace is so central to us that it is even in our words of hello."

"But, Mohammed, in many societies, men generally restrain themselves when seeing a woman's full face, hair, or legs. How is that?"

"Professor Sands, I do not want to be impolite, but I think rape, prostitution, pornography, and divorce are rampant in your society.

Though I think where necessary, divorce should be permitted. Protecting our women and promoting marriage more seriously and family values are more important here. You need to better honor your women and elders and the family as a whole. The veil and the *abaya* have been helpful."

"Mohammed, do you think rape, prostitution, pornography, and high levels of divorce do not exist in Sarabia, even in a veiled society? I heard that even near some shrines . . . right, I should not discuss that. And what about those young men displaying themselves on the corner in some very bad neighborhoods, who some of my students showed me at a distance? What in hell is that all about?"

"Please, Professor Sands! I have tried to be polite. I am telling the truth. I am sure you do not want to tell lies. That, of course, is not to say that we have become a perfect society. And any degeneracy, if it existed, would be mostly because of the influence from the West."

There were so many red lines to discussion that I feared my intellectual sincerity about Sarabian women and sexuality would get me into very hot water and even cause my expulsion from the country. If you wanted to talk, for instance, about the significant amount of homosexuality in the country, you might as well have fallen on a Sarabian sword. You might as well have been inside the Holocaust Memorial when it had been torched.

Sometimes I forgot that my Western concepts of free expression could be lighter fluid to a proverbial kind of self-immolation. What was I supposed to do as an American associate from Harvard on loan to Sarabia? Just always stew in my juices and contribute almost nothing of my values and culture? Too often, they wanted my paper credentials, but not my ideas. How brilliant!

Now, if the Sarabians had known that I was also working freelance for Z5, an intelligence agency, one that would never admit to my membership, I would have been buried in the desert, probably alive. It would not have mattered how honorable the Order's intentions were or that I was effectively representing the quality of my intellectual arguments against blind rigid faith. If I was not careful enough, I would make American diplomats' warnings about walks in the desert look relevant.

I needed to get the conversation back to a more deferential and genteel feel. "Yes, Mohammed, we must keep our discussions sincere, but respectful and polite. And none of us must make ourselves appear superior. I've much to learn from your culture."

"Of course, Professor Sands, for Allah does not reveal all to us at any time. We humans must therefore be humble and hope for his mercy and continued guidance whenever or whoever we are. Modesty includes that our clothes not be too flashy and luxurious."

It was then that I looked at my one-thousand-dollar Bäumler jacket and Armani pants and Brook Brothers tie with increasing trepidation. Mohammed was reminding me of my station. In fact, the Hadiths, sacred Islamic writings, had effectively banned even the silk that my tie and part of my jacket were made of. How, indeed, could I stay out of trouble?

Garments could take on so much loaded symbolism. And Sarabian public clothes, despite how modest, simple, and humble that most were, had become symbols for Western discontent with Islam, especially the more conservative forms. We definitely could learn from each other about some of the occasional mutual poison we held over each other's thoughts by way of the world of fashion.

Some modifications, for example, to the Sarabian female dress code were taking place. In the not very distant future, who could guess if the black *abaya* would be the rave in Paris? Even if it was currently in popular retreat. After all, there had been enough outrageous haute couture on the catwalks that made various ladies look like they were from Mars. Surely, there was room for forms of traditional Sarabian dress here or there in Paris, the "city of rights."

I wondered, with the West's dedication to "letting it all hang out," would the *abaya* be adapted with a slit running down one leg if it eventually came into vogue? Or with a famous rock singer wearing one on her next album cover, or a top fashion runway model? A fashion designer would be slit if he or she tried! Or the album cover designer. And the runway model would be turned into a runaway. However, I couldn't see members of the Order breaking out in Victoria Secret *abayas* anytime soon. Though it was a mad world out there, the Paris fashion world seemed sometimes to be even madder.

Nevertheless, serious amounts of Sarabian money were being shunted into international haute-couture by Princess Fatima, whom they called the Pink Princess. Along with her enthusiasm, there was a growing view that inevitably there would be wide-scale Arab influences in European clothes unless there were an expulsion of France's six million Muslims, which was not going to happen. Unless there were an expulsion of a lot of oil from France, which could very well happen if France overly reacted to Muslim clothing and immigrant influences. There was good reason for balance and dialogue on these matters, as I further underscored with the Order during those few moments when they seemed to want to be too aggressive with their attacks against the veil and *abaya*.

I remembered telling that august body how a good many Sarabian women could be very chic. I recalled almost to their jealousy, how so many Sarabian ladies had the most beautiful skin and the best makeup almost beyond what France had to offer. I told them how some were like Lady Oréal, compared to a number of my Western girlfriends, who were more like plain dried-out Oreos. They did not like to hear it. They were almost pouting in their wishful jealous disbelief.

Surely, revealing ignorance could have its whining price that might get one chopped to pieces in a number of places. But I could get away with it that night. After all, we were not in any of the hot spots that were burning too brightly with so much intense ignorance, violence, and hatred. Instead, we would wallow in our comforts in the *Big Compfy*—at least for that moment. And in our freedom of fashion, no matter how badly we could look to either the fashion designers of Paris or fashion killers of Sarabia.

SEVEN

Her Royal Highness, Princess Fatima bint Waheed Al Sarab, was a progressive, and one of Sarabia's finest. She was well-known for her canvasses that lit up the desert, with old Bedouin-style buildings and tents with panache and pastel colors. She seemed to add her charms and radiant personality to her art, which she worked on between Paris and Raddah. She had also added her distinct presence at a very special gala at the Louvre in Paris that I had attended, along with the Order. Coincidentally, some political and financial notable friends from my school days had been there, though not the husbands of the ladies of the Order—almost thankfully.

Speaking of a beautiful canvas, to her face Princess Fatima applied her brush one might say even better than to her art, and with gentler and softer tones with a few exceptions. She had unbelievable highlighters that made her smooth skin shine like a baby. Lipstick that was glossy without being cheap, but of a metal chrome tint that made me feel that she was so modern. She could have been an advertisement in *Vogue* magazine if her culture had permitted it. Bland-looking, conservatively dressed Sarabians of the female persuasion? Not this one.

For some reason, a veil had meant to me that the dull restraint it represented would be even worse than the face behind it. That was almost a monumental mistake to believe. After I had seen so many Sarabian women without one, I definitely changed my initial view about their being unattractive.

Those Sarabian delights of the "harem" I had to ashamedly admit included the gorgeous ones I had seen illegally, peeking at from a boudoir closet in Raddah. Or, should I add, from the more open views from a deep underground cathouse reserved for the specially connected? That den of iniquity should have been made stronger than the Baron's bunker, given how nuclear the anger would have been had the *Mootawa* found it—and with sexed-up, infidel Western professors in it. But then, one of its best customers had been the Minister of Virtue! What a protection racket. And what hypocrisy.

Despite her own high status and exceptional attractiveness, the princess simply and humbly introduced herself at the fund-raiser by saying, "I'm Fatima. I am studying art part-time here in Paris."

"Oh, really?" said starstruck me, not knowing what to say at first. Thinking—or was that worrying—that most Sarabian princesses, if single as she was, would be chaperoned by a brother or other relative. There were none in the vicinity that I could see at the time. However, I took a good, long, prudent look. Never could so much beauty be so frightening to me. Never to be even slightly touched if I did not want to see the sword or get the axe.

"Do you follow art much, Mr . . . . ?"

"Ah, Ah," I nervously stammered in response. I was speechless and almost felt like I had gone dumb. Yeah, mostly dumb, with a contradictory fear. Finally, I relaxed and became discernible.

"Call me Jean-Claude, if you wish. That's Jean-Claude Carterone. Mr. Carterone is okay, too." This was, after all, a Sarabian royal princess, who should be left with a formal option on how to address me if she wanted to be naturally a bit aloof.

"Oh, I'm sorry, are you French? I'll switch to French, though somewhat poor even after all those tutors, I am embarrassed to say."

She was fashionably humble. Well, humble to describe her impeccable French as being remotely inferior.

"No, actually Franco-American. Probably your French is better than mine, though I did pick up a few words when stationed in France, and even in Quebec."

"Quebec, you don't say. My father has a hotel there. Yes, how did you get up there? I hear it's a fascinating place."

"Oh my parents wanted me to learn French, but not be too far away from them in New York. So I went to school in Montreal. In fact, my mother was brought up in Quebec before immigrating to America."

"That's very interesting. They were forward looking with your schooling. Yes, parents need to help and encourage their children to get a global education."

"Yes, that's a very good point. I keep an interest in the education field." That was the understatement of the year by me. Fortunately, she didn't ask me to explain it. Fortunately, I still had small diplomatic talk left in me when the occasion demanded it, and certainly if the lady before me was radiant enough. But I still felt out of my skin at these stiff social functions.

"Oh, well good," she continued. "How did you find school there?"

"A little stuffy and overly exclusive. I was sent to one of those private schools. A kind of Eton of the far north—Oxford—and McGill University-educated teachers. The best education overall a young man could hope for, I suppose. But unfortunately, I have to say a few of the grads, especially senior bankers, are over the top, at times, for grabbing as many dollars as possible for themselves. Some of them even becoming bagmen."

"You don't say. Sounds overall like an impressive place. Though nowhere is perfect, I suppose," said the princess, evermore staying very diplomatic and polite.

She was, however, in a way, testing my nerves. I was increasingly getting the shakes as I was pressed to push my limit with speaking *diplomatese*. Worse, I was beginning to get back to my favorite language—direct *Americanese*. I continued on despite my linguistic handicaps.

"Meanwhile, I became simply a security consultant, so to speak. I'm sorry if I sound a little forward. I don't know why I am confessing all this to you. Do you normally have such an effect?" I genuinely asked this angelic-looking lady with soft, sympathetic eyes that made me gush and go wobbly.

"I am sure, not so simple," she said as she bashfully avoided answering my question at the end of my rant; I did not know what had possessed me to make it.

"You know, speaking of financiers, we in Sarabia have Islamic banking that, in many ways, makes it more difficult to charge usury fees. In fact, it is usually forbidden to charge interest."

"Right," I said as I tried to be so agreeable while finding the straitjacket of reception talk increasingly stifling. Given her magnetism, she would have kept me fascinated even if she had talked about the manufacturing processes of Islamic-approved Ping-Pong balls.

"And, oh yes, advertising is controlled with the greatest sense of good taste in mind. No sexual exploitation in images. But bagmen, you said earlier? . . . Oh yes, I understand now."

It was a little hard for someone from an absolute monarchy to understand a person with a permanent role of "grubbing" about for money for a political party.

Sarabian royalty was generally above needing such fund-raisers, at least at the highest levels. They had pretty well all the power, so they did not generally need to beg for money or bow down too much to sleazy bankers or politicians in their own country. In fact, no Wall Street-type lobby was really needed. The Sarabian royalty was, in fact, the bank and insurance companies, half of downtown Raddah—hell, half of the decent land of all of Sarabia. And not to forget, a large percentage of MANCITC Bank.

I continued, "Yes, I heard. No banks in Sarabia can questionably bundle off mortgages. And they can't avoid losses on the loans they initiated. No banking meltdown happened in Sarabia, if I understand correctly."

"Yes, that's right, Jean-Claude."

"Right, something positive." If I didn't watch it, she would convince me that her country was the road to paradise, so infectious was her charm.

She laughed a little about my further comments about corrupt political and financial machinery in parts of the West. It was a bit of a touchy subject, and like a princess, she smoothly diverted the discussion to something a bit more neutral.

I was also glad that she got me off the subject of Western politics and finance, because it pained me a little to think that one of my classmates, who had been standing not far behind me at the reception, had become a six-million-dollar-a-year man partly by financing a number of environmentally questionable projects. As a professional assassin and environmentally conscious hunter, I appreciated clean workmanship, and not deviating from school values that emphasized cleanliness and tidiness.

However, Galen Nickeroff, CEO of Real Holdings of Canada (RHC), had been a smooth, careful financial operator. He had neither flogged nor bought billions of dollars of questionable mortgage-backed loans. He, along with other Canadians and even the Chinese, Russians, and Indians, not to forget the Australians, had bought up American banks as they were increasingly put up for auction.

We Americans represented one giant welcome wagon of a country, especially after our first major economic meltdown of this century. I was one of the growing legions of exceptional Americans exceptionally dependent on foreigners. It was kind of a sad statement on where America was headed, as Galen and his fellow Canadian and foreign bankers picked up Wall Street's broken pieces at deep discount. But maybe we deserved it, given how badly most of our politicians and regulators had managed the banking system.

Somehow, I could not initially seem to rise out of that new American feeling of a kicked-down status. And to further get it into my head to say that teaching was more rewarding, as Gal and my rich students had told me to soothe my bruised ego, no doubt, and my bruised wallet. And neither my Sarabian students with their expensive Maseratis and Lamborghinis, nor the senior Western bankers with their just plain Bentleys and Lexuses, paid school taxes, or any other taxes for that matter of any relative consequence. Yes, there was no justice for the scholarly or the very learned. How sad that the teaching profession had descended to such perceived status lows, and my occasional sense of it.

But I was behaving shamefully, waddling in my pool of largely self-deceiving despair. There was still the sporadically well-paying killing business I was running—the other side of my work. Such work, indeed, had raised my bankable value.

"I have to ask you, Jean-Claude, what do you know of the Zeel Foundation? I'm very new in learning about it," inquired the princess, looking genuine as she turned back to me after a lapse in talking to one of her flunkies who had briefly shown up and interrupted us.

"Not much information on it, I have to say. A nice charity to help women. And hopefully we'll raise a lot of money for it tonight," I lied. Well, about not knowing about this financial arm to the Order's clandestine activities. That bit of information was even beyond top secret.

"So, how did you get into the gala?" she further inquired, almost looking puckish.

"A long story," I said.

The princess smiled a little too easily, and did not probe further. Was she being royally careful and coy? Or did she know more? My instinct was the latter. But intuition was more in the realm of the female, I thought simplemindedly. And my simple mind thought plenty enough. My tingles signaled that I should be very careful, including being conscious about anyone overhearing our conversation.

It was a nice try to think she was alone and to have all the male fantasies this beauty would entertain in my wicked, little, yes, simple male mind. She was definitely not alone. In fact, she was guarded practically day and night by the patriot guard of the king, as her father, the king's cousin, had requested.

Instead of *thobes*, the princess's guardians were in inconspicuous suits that night. And trying not to look like they were hovering over her, so as to prevent stereotyped media and social column reports about her being too cocooned—for various members of the Western media had gotten into the gala.

Their thoughts about Sarabia could be simpleminded, too, though of a very different nature compared to mine, at least for that moment. I wanted visual pleasure and preferred carnal thoughts. They sometimes wanted petty scandal and to stir up hatred.

I would tread carefully, especially around any journalists, and say simply, "Good night, Princess Fatima." I bowed and exited without showing my back or looking back. I would have turned to male molten if I had stayed in her presence much longer, given how delightfully charming and supremely beautiful she was. I might have also ended up in a photo of the *Internet Inquirer (II)* if I had stayed too long.

Being tracked down by an assassin over the paparazzi (or paper-rat's-eye, if you will, if one was big on puns and metaphors relating them to rats) was almost preferable. It certainly seemed to have been true for Princess Diana, who some believe was killed—not far away from where the gala took place—due to their hounding of her. I had another theory on her murder. I later learned about a story of the princess's death with a Middle East, macabre twist.

Prince Waheed, a paper-rat's-eye favorite and a billionaire, had known Princess Diana well. He had established a whole new wing on Middle East art and fashion at the Louvre and at the Berlin National Museum. It was no coincidence that the gala that night had been held in Paris, which was Fatima's and her father's favorite haunt.

Speaking of Waheed, he was, indeed, a forward thinker in finance and politics. It was, thus, easy to wonder how long he would last, given how politically violent and tumultuous his homeland had become. Not surprisingly, his bodyguards protected him day and night—right down to testing every bit of his food, and even the air quality of his hotel rooms, including radiation levels for some reason. These tests were not only made in his hotel chambers, which were often in premises that he outright owned. They also included the whole Hotel Cinq Robes de Pierre near the Champs Élysées, where his cousin, Prince Bashard, preferred to stay when in town.

Meanwhile, quite apart from the princess, were the ladies of the Order, who were in attendance and mingling throughout the crowds of the glitterati. They included such worthies as the French Prime Minister Mignon-Filleton, a master genius of domestic diplomacy. His British wife was impeccable for her manners and discretion, though possibly a bit beefy.

In fact, Mignon-Filleton had been talking to the US ambassador, a fellow alumnus of Yale. He had been an offshoot descendant of the famous Morton family, now of Montreal and Wyoming, who had made their second or third fortune secretly dragging beer across the Canadian border into the United States during Prohibition. Then there were the other, newer kind of rich families who had done it with hard liquor and the help of the Kennedys. They were my kind, at least their liquor, but sadly had gone to the other school across town, leaving me holding only "dreadful" Canadian beer for free instead of pure Scotch whisky. I had really wished that the whisky-distilling Bronfmans had been in my senior class.

The Mortons also had a bit of a nasty WASP (White Anglo-Saxon Protestant), old family establishment tendency to act a little too smug about the cleanliness of their fortunes and their moderate, politically correct, suave nature, and I suppose about their Canadian beer, too. They visited Switzerland every year, along with a tad sum of their smooth bull while they checked out their bullion.

Not surprisingly, the Mortons knew about good ice hockey through a very successful Colorado team they sponsored. Though one of the Mortons had been extracted from my school for having been checked too hard into the boards of our hockey rink. I really had felt badly about it; I had dislocated my shoulder doing it. The Mortons, I had to admit, were great at charity giving—including their outstanding contributions to the school's new "green" hockey rink. They did not seem to like the old one that much. Neither did the scion of a local food empire that paid for most of the new facility and kept on comparing the old surface to his Swiss cheese.

There were loads of such beautiful people, but some with significantly worse manners, including a few other ambassadors who had essentially gotten their jobs by being major donors or "bagmen" to the governing parties. I feared a lot of them did not want to talk to me, as I sounded like I was just a hard-ass with a chip on my shoulder from a bad neighborhood, from the wrong side of the suburban tracks. A number of these Old Boys, moreover, disliked me for my penury when I had insisted they pay the bill at the tavern down the street from the school. I was less discriminating. I just did not like most of the massively inherited rich going Dutch on me. And I had no choice sometimes but to count my own pennies.

Well, they were right about me being tight and, in a way, about the tracks. But I had not figured that I had been brought up on the wrong side, as they practically ran directly through my bedroom window with locomotives shining light every night on what might be my future in the other world beyond the silver spoon. Yeah, I was a regular kind of guy looking for sympathy as I polished off my Chateauneuf-du-Pape, premium wine, looking around to see who else had shoes of mud. There were a few, but not too many. And my mud always seemed to look better.

The ladies were certainly not to be forgotten, as the gala was all about their projects for the most part. And I should not have even taken my eyes off of them for a moment, even for a delightful Sarabian princess or for my minor thoughts about my early life's destitution.

These ladies were definitely more assertive but no less sophisticated than Fatima. And not too bad in haute couture from Dame Vivienne Westwood, Yoltan Solomon, or Amina Al Jassim, who had moved mountains to make the ladies look shapely, desirable, and very fashionable. Though Isolde could have come in a loincloth and pulled it off.

Unlike the princess, who had few so-called Western vices, the ladies of the Order had many, if the Koran was your guide to good living. They might have even been a bit forgiven by sophisticated Muslim moderates like Fatima, but less by those in her bodyguard entourage. One of whom would be likely reporting back to the Grand Sheik to ensure there was no question about her behaving improperly while in the "City of Lights" and sin. One of whom would be reporting back to the king that the Grand Sheik knew that her behavior had been Koranic, but that she shouldn't talk too long with Western strange men, like me.

The royal family and the Sarabian Wadi religious-sect establishments were, indeed, inextricably interlinked. One could not survive without the other, and being well out of good graces with each other. It was a very powerful, old political and religious alliance. Fatima knew no matter how broad-minded she wanted to be, she could not afford to embarrass the religious sheiks. If she did, it could cost her head at worst, or at a minimum, her freedoms to go abroad if she even committed minor indiscretions.

And why did the Order really need to be absolved in the first place, by me or anyone for that matter? For the ladies of the Order, their sharp tongues and pecking of their husbands could be forgiven, ignored, or become liberating dowries of immense alimony in our society. In Sarabia, it could have gotten them buried. Was even a powerful princess like Fatima still a falcon under male master control? And with essentially much less freedom and power than the wife of even a small Swiss banker? Or was that my simple male Western mind acting up?

In my occasional deference to all things Sarabian, I also wondered, though in another way, whether these ladies of the Order were missing something very vital. The immaculate protection that Fatima was provided as a single woman, or that Sarabian wives had from their husbands—this protection was demanded by the Holy Book of the Koran.

No one said that Western modernity had it all, with singer Janus Julips' boobs hanging out at the Rose Bowl or certain rap music extolling violent crime. A few cheers for the Sarabians and their Tyranian "sidekicks" I thought of as a good show of Anglo Saxon fair play. Fair is fair. But who really wants to be? So much of the world today, in a nutshell. So many reasons as to why so much of the world was on fire. Oh yes, and bankrupt.

However you cut it, even with the West's own hypocrisy, macho arrogance, and bouts of decadence, Sarabia needed more than a cosmetic makeover and a time-out from the almost weekly rat-a-tat-tat of falling blades at chop-chop square. There, in the flat, stony, wide-open area before the Ministry of Virtue, the public got to view even victims' relatives taking a few swipes of the sword at the condemned. Occasionally, it got very messy.

Was the whole effort a dangling metaphor for state-sponsored torture? That was the view of various famous human rights activists, who owned no Sarabian oil futures. That was essentially the perspective of the Order, who couldn't care a damn about the future of oil over women. That was what, in part, the gala was all about. Bravo! Well, perhaps.

Meanwhile, in Tyrania, the government was acting like a kind of political *Tyrannosaurus rex*—increasingly rearing its ugly extremist head and chomping away at women's rights with its executional incisors.

That night, though, despite all my worries about these extremists and their sponsors (and my underfunded personal situation), I had hoped I could make the fear, anxiety, and dread connected to our work ahead go away with my own sense of dedicated liberalism, a progressive movement toward inebriation. I had hoped that I also could forget about the highly restricted life that I had been living in the desert kingdom, the sterility of the summer-oven heat, and the sterilization of my social life that went in tandem with the ovenlike weather.

I also desperately needed a good cause to defend, to take me out of my cesspool of cynicism as a ghoulish kind of operative. One that had seen too many parts of a crazy, unjust, violent, and dangerous world. To rehabilitate myself—given the way certain conservative elements of Sarabian authority and various Western subordinate henchmen had tried to make me feel so small and pushed down, at college and beyond. I also needed that "good cause" of the Order to compensate for seeing too many women so marginalized and kept in their place.

I still feared, despite all my escapist machinations, that we were all becoming a big fat target, Zürich or not. Possibly my paranoia was simply playing up from the timpani percussion section still drumming in my head or from my trumpeting bruises.

Meanwhile, over the hill of Zürichberg, these ladies' husbands, with extensive banking connections to Sarabia, Tyrania, and nearby parts, remained well away from politically inspired galas. They might have been neutral to human rights extravaganzas, but they were no pikers to the Swiss clothiers. They seemed branded together at times by the fashion cardinals of Armani, Bäumler, Cardin, and Versace, through which they threaded their financial allegiances.

Their tailoring helped them converse smoothly with a pattern of cashed-up, self-congratulations, no matter how devastating had been a number of their financial practices on the global economy or human rights. There were, however, other Swiss bankers who despised them. A new generation that avoided them altogether, mixed with the so-called enlightened group of older banker statesmen called the "Wise Men." But no one seemed to know their names. Or even whether they were that active. They generally seemed to be absent.

These husbands of the ladies of the Order were truly of their own dark brotherhood. A brotherhood of secrecy that seemed to zip their lips after each sip of cognac and cigars. They, unlike their wives, sequestered themselves more deeply in the shadows of smoky backroom parlors of luxury hotels, well beyond artists' canvases stroked in old Zürich. Well beyond the scrutiny that more public fund-raisers would expose them to.

They were also far removed from the non-banking side, including their wives' charity life—and certainly lacked much of a commitment to any real social life. You could simply say they were content in their own "ether-world" of making the next deal and having a few nice jackets and pants. But maybe, I've been painting too much of a one-dimensional caricature of these gentlemen. I could live with making that judgment of their character. So could they. Except possibly one or two of these very special Swiss bankers whom I got to know too well, one based out of Zürich and another from Delaware.

EIGHT

The grand husband to the wives of the Order was Johan Friedrich Stihl, Chief Risk Officer for Banque Suisse. He was the mastermind behind much banking for a diverse array of Sarabian higher-ups among an extensive list of world notables. To a host of rich Sarabians, Stihl in a sense was almost as important as their Sarabian king, a custodian of Islam's holiest shrines. For Stihl was the overseer of their "Mecca" of money. In short, he was the "Sheik of Zürich," holding court with a constant pilgrimage of secret account holders, flying in to perform their own ritual ceremonies to reinforce their faith in Swiss banking.

Once upon a time, Stihl used to frequently receive warm bundles of cash from tropical dictators, whom he would seem to kiss on all four cheeks. Gokar of Nubia, Borazza of the Central Equatorial Republic, Armin of Ougoobanda, and Foester of formerly Southeast Africa. And not to forget Stresser from Paramay and Sheik Mahmoud Al Sarab. With a few exceptions, candidates for the pantheon of world's most infamous butchers were all his monetarily.

However, due to changes in Swiss laws several years back, Stihl now pretended that any money horded away for corrupt dictators and politico-paths had been returned or been properly transferred to legitimate organizations. How nice. But not completely true. The money had simply been sent to Delaware, with its liberal banking laws toward receiving offshore funds. Or to Panama, if the US government were less friendly to his clients.

Where Switzerland had represented a tight vault of secrecy, Delaware was not only secretive, but comparatively off the map of US tax investigations or newspaper reporting of sinister, tax-haven banking. In fact, Wilmington, Wyoming, and western Florida were offshore favorites to several of the world's most hated. Even the Chinese used the US Virgin Islands for interesting tax avoidance and clandestine transactions.

I vividly remembered my conversations with Stihl as I played them back interjected by my own more up-to-date narratives, a number of which would no doubt find their way into my reports. A variety of which would not, as they would be seen by intelligence as excessive moralizing or irrelevant color commentary, more fit for a novel.

"J. C., your company is always appreciated. But the company of many brilliant, ruthless geniuses has not only been highly illuminating but highly profitable," said Stihl. Nevertheless, as he patted me paternally on the knee—he might have even bounced me if he could—he said in a slightly forlorn voice, "I really miss that son of a gun, Kardiac. In a way, it was a pity that he was locked up in a United Nations war crimes cell. Of course, these days, we Swiss bankers officially have nothing to do with political undesirables. Nothing to do at all," he stated with a Cheshire cat smile so wide that if it had gotten any broader, it might have chopped off his head.

"Of course," I added with a slight disbelieving shift of the eyes and rising winks and wrinkles of the forehead. I did not know what to say but that he had simply got under my skin. Even as a killer, I felt squeamish listening to banker Stihl often indulge in his nostalgia of dealing with the ethically reprehensible.

Naturally, bank secrecy never permitted him to state outright who were—or had been—his ugliest customers or certainly anything about how much they exactly had. But he had in a roundabout way. Though I still was left a little bit guessing, as he would only use coded names and talk of millions without the precise magnitudes and origins. I wondered if they were somehow close to the original family names and countries. I think I had wondered right.

However, I really had to also wonder why Z5 wanted me to keep such a close eye on him. He seemed at first blush to be just another member of those minorities of elegant and immoral Zürich bankers, overly plumped up on their own sense of self-importance, bonuses, and net worth. He might have been an important husband of a wife of the Order, but that was about all of a connection he had with it. He seemed to have no natural interest either in the political or social activities of his spouse—or any members of the Order.

As Stihl consistently and succinctly put it in layman's terms, "Ideology has no great appeal to me. Cash is cash." He made a very worthy case for being a financial neutralist, a case that ensured many more cases were opened—of money and investigations. He had also no problem expressing to me how grubby he was with getting money. He was definitely not a usual diplomatic and opinion-restrained Swiss banker. He was also just plain ruthless.

Meanwhile, the more timid regular bankers talked softly and more obliquely in public places, such as investment seminars, annual meetings, and the lounge of the Storcher Hotel that German tongue-tied Americans pronounced like Stalker. Bar none, it was the favorite haunt for deal making, especially by representatives of the American investment banking community in Zürich. They used so much coded terminology it was hard for eavesdroppers to know the financial parties to whom they were referring and other key details. It caused me no end of consternation when I got bored waiting for a banker or a friend to join me for coffee there. But I got over it, knowing the leaks that awaited me from Stihl or his equally dark friends.

The Storcher at least made a pretty good cup of café, full of enough caffeine to keep an army of deal makers or arms dealers awake late into the evening. It could have been sold over the table as ammunition. Any more caffeine, and they would have had to have sold it under the table as a weapon of mass destruction.

For the part about morals, Stihl sometimes felt that he had been indecently proportioned by activists as a sort of lowly camp commandant of a major branch of Banque Swiss gated onto Zürich's Bahnhofstrasse. Being described even by protesters as fairly far down the chain from his bank's CEO was almost humiliating. It did allow him to get around with a greater degree of political and physical immunity than his few superiors, though.

Whether he should never have had dealings in the past curating Nazi bank accounts, filled with money stolen from those put in concentration camps at Auschwitz, he would have preferred to have left to history—for which he had a fairly limited interest, incidentally. Whether he should have had bigger dealings for his own personal benefit was a better question that he would have preferred to have ruminated on. For Stihl, it was always hard to understand why so many of his customers had more money than he. He felt abused.

He had confided so much as one of my personal Swiss bankers and as a social acquaintance. It had not been easy to get into his outer, inner circle. It had been hell. It had taken almost a year of sycophantic endearment. However, the conversation got more substantive as we got past our first phase of business meetings and short café drinking sit-togethers at the Storcher. After all, German Swiss elites were very cagey and careful as to who got on their social roster. One could add doubly for Swiss bankers, especially given Stihl's background.

Nevertheless, our social connecting kept on progressing well. My prize for being a very good listener and a good boy was to be taken to his private clubs, gastronomically favored restaurants, sports clubs for executives, and even many an expensive bar sponsoring high-class company. Then there were a few less-than-acceptable members of civilized society I was sometimes forced to meet.

Finally, I felt secure that we could call it a relationship when he invited me out on his yacht. It had been nicknamed the *El-Dee,* which caught my curiosity. It was kind of Spanish or even Moorish sounding. Something about his wife having to do with its christening was his brief disinterested explanation. Or was it just simply *Dee,* representing D as in dough, for money. His lady sure spent heaps of it. Yeah, a yacht named after a wife and translated to mean "The Money." Why not, I smiled.

The *El-Dee* had a communication room that seemed equipped enough to monitor Russian submarines, with enough left over to act as a command and control center for more than the Swiss navy. Or at a minimum, what was left of it: steamers and all, floating out of Interlaken. However you looked at it, there was a lot of equipment for a pleasure boat. Stihl did not seem too content that I had gotten a glimpse of his communication *centrali.*

The steely blue-eyed banker loved to sail his craft on late Friday summer afternoons into the long body called the Zürich Zee. The cool, dark blue lake waters seemed to pour into his hardened pupils. Despite that hardness, no matter what the occasion, we both loved to shoot the breeze, as it cooled us off from the insanity and stress of our demanding lines of work. A bond of sorts, but one that bore me overall few social dividends.

It was rare for anyone, including his wife, not to experience the deep depths of his critical icy stare. It would almost make you shiver—like all of a sudden being plunged into a bottomless glacial lake with lead weights. His serious disagreements could indeed weigh heavy on one.

Playing Robin to financial Batman sometimes got a little thick, too. At times, I felt as if I were becoming one pupil too many. His cold blue eyes seemed to concur, especially when I did not agree with one of his central axioms explaining how the banking universe should be unfolding. Why he was one of the chosen financial rulers of the high temples of global banking, and why others could never be.

On the yacht, though, he would generally loosen up a bit, even philosophize about what he referred to as the natural flows of life. How good banking mimicked a good skipper in symbiosis with all currents—cross, forward, deep, above, and behind. How the perils of not respecting the natural order could lead one adrift or into shoals—or to the bottom.

God, based on these images, one would have had to conclude that a distinct number of his fellow bankers were like drunken sea captains. That they were floating about with their customers' wealth in nearly capsized wrecks, even with lovely paint jobs and beautifully framed certifications of seaworthiness from the Moody rating agency "nautical board of approval."

But at times, he would just look into the wind with a big comfortable smile, glancing around almost like he hoped for something short of a storm. When the clouds came with swirling hyperwinds to the force of near squall, he and his team were at their best at moving his launch around with dexterity, while others headed for the shore. It gave him sheer delight to see me bent over and seasick, while he seemingly crowed and strutted about like a master of the sea—well, of the *Zee*.

He was even more delighted when he recognized an adversary from a major competitor hurrying back to port. He especially liked it when his main German/American rivals at *Goldilock Aktion Gesellshaft* (GAG) capitulated, faced with the risky waters of their plight. In the end, everything was for Stihl a part of the evolution and survival of the fittest.

After sailing, we would go to the Storcher, where the conversation would get a little bit more *lattéd*. There, he had broken the ice in one of our first chats by defending his banker's credo.

"We bankers collect the money. We cannot be burdened nor have all the resources to wash out and sift through entirely all of the chaff, graft, and pure *Sheisse* of our clients." He enthusiastically added, "And, J. C., forget about figuring out who did or did not pay their taxes. I think that is what you call a laughter? *Stimmt?*"

"A laugh," I said. "Yes, no one pays a Swiss banker to study the depths of a customer's intestinal fortitude. The commissions would never be big enough. Right, Johan?"

"*Ya, Ya. Genau. Richtig.* Correct. But I can think of one case where one banker might have found a silver lining to such research." Stihl laughed diabolically.

He and fellow banker Schmidt had the propensity of adding value from just about anything they did. And Stihl had such a Midas touch that he probably could have even made money while riding a bicycle, if he physically could.

Beyond his dark humor, he still kept to his favorite treatise on social Darwinism and wealth. He had evidently been happy that I was lapping it up. He was on a roll, so he had to continue.

"There is a natural order as to why some men have so much money. It is the strength of commitment, built-in natural character, and talent. Not so open to compromising, only when absolutely necessary; striking down anyone who interferes with their advancement, their grandest plans. It is in the DNA, I think. Yes, *sicherlich* . . . surely, it all starts there."

"Interesting, Johan," I pleasantly concurred, as there was almost no way or good reason to stop this steamroller once he got on his favorite topic.

"Did not your coach of the famous team Greenbuck Puckers say nice guys come last? This is the last point if you actually want to succeed, especially with the people I am dealing with. And I am not simply talking about my sharp-toothy, so-called partners."

"You mean Green Bay Packers. And he not too long after sharing those pearls of wisdom, he died, I think." Stihl showed little sympathy or interest in my correction.

"Oh yes, Packers, Puckers, Greenbuck. Whatever. *Ya*, Green Bay," Stihl said with a chuckle, as if getting the name wrong of the famous Super Bowl champions was a very incidental faux pas, more of a Freudian slip. He was pissing me off as I loved that team and its city, which had good, honest, working-class integrity. A community spirit that had let a small community fund an NFL team that one expected only large cities like Chicago or New York to afford from their publicity-ventilating billionaires, possibly with their own offshore accounts at Stihl's bank.

I thought I could now understand why Stihl's attempts had failed to get National Football League teams, including the Nationalists, to open offshore accounts for some of their multimillionaire players. Stihl had an interest in American football about as much as I liked the bottom end of the Coca Cola soccer league in the United Kingdom when it was playing horridly.

I didn't know why he confided in me about his banking philosophy, or even his dark secrets. Maybe he felt that, as I was a teacher, I might find difficulties with his moral positions, so he could place me in a role of priestly confessor. Make me kind of a medium to the sanitation of guilt; an equivalent visit to the church for confessional or even beyond that. Perhaps subconsciously, he liked me leaking out a few of my scruples onto his social-order parchments, and staining those morals onto his paltry *apologetics*.

Or a stronger possibility was that he wanted to fully convert me, and enjoyed my continuous flattery of him by my willful loss to his arguments. A building of a new church with my bowing down and kissing of his ring, as its new pope, or maybe its chief cardinal.

Or was it all because he had a mild form of self-hatred that he had to share? Who knew? Possibly not even his wife or his masseuse knew. Yet I could not help but keep guessing. But did I actually care, except to know that this was one screwed-up banker that I had to be careful with? If I played psychiatrist any more as to what really ailed him, I would probably need my own.

It was convenient that Zürich and its environs were full of shrinks, and without coincidence, as a good sum of bankers and the big moneyed craved them. And their wives lapped them up faster than they absorbed their own hard liquor. Family medicine at its worst.

I thought I was being a little too hard on this fascinating city, as most of the patients were from abroad. Interestingly, quite a few were account holders to people like Stihl, who had robbed them of their dignity much more than their shrinks did. It seemed like a closed circle at times: psychiatrists and bankers almost looking like they were working in mutually reinforcing exploitative harmony. And then, of course, maybe the culture demanded psychiatry, all that running around under the threat of giant cuckoo clocks. If so, then we were probably all Swisslike and needed to be examined as neurotics under the heavy hands of Dr. Clock.

To get back from one of my many diversions that sometimes made me suspect my own mental state, Stihl was a man of great ambitions and overarching ones. Possibly Z5, after all, might have been right that I should watch him. Conceivably, the pope should have as well, though it was hard to see the Vatican being able ever to politically and economically compete satisfactorily with the likes of Zürich and its financial Templars.

Fancy another undisciplined diversionary thought disobedient to the tidy Teutonic orderly thought processes of the German Swiss banker. If my history is correct, the Church and a French king successfully conspired to wipe out the real Order of the Templars, Europe's top bankers during the Holy Crusades.

I also wondered while on the topic of religion, if the pope was including Zürich and Wall Street when he referred to the West as a "spiritual wasteland." It was a thought that evidently a much earlier pope had more vigorously interpreted to action against those in the financial community. That pope had simply burned those ancient Templar bankers at the stake for their greed, according to one ecclesiastical interpretation. They didn't fool around back then if you started figuring your money was bigger than the main public faith and the king. They especially did not fool around in today's Sarabia, either.

I had to also actually wonder in the end whether there was a tiny gilded conscience still left in the inner cold vaults of people like Lanny Zeroche, CEO of *Goldilock*, or Stihl. Whether they had left their good emotions there to keep from generally seeing the light of day. If they existed, they would seem hard to locate, even with an electronic microscope.

Was the general reality of today's super investment financiers and senior bankers so grim and attached to too much corruption and waste? One would hope not, but where was the contrary evidence, especially on Wall Street? Certainly not in Stihl, who like Zeroche was reported in inner global banking circles to be a top ten member of the "Masters of the Universe." Stihl, in fact, had been awarded the highest medal among this Masters League—Grand Knight of the Temple, with golden oak clusters and Sarabian swords.

However, one had to say Stihl was exceptionally aggressive, avaricious, and exaggerated for an average Swiss financier, especially while I was around him in private. It was so exaggerated that it was like a theatrical performance. Even Zeroche would have been put out, I think, by a number of Stihl's assertions and antics. While Zeroche was certainly overly forceful and brazen about taking risks, I wondered sometimes if Stihl was just crazy.

I could not help but weigh in against his Germanic *Uber*-confidence on occasion, to criticize the kind of banker Stihl was and the dangers it would bring. I challenged him, which was unusual for me when with most senior bankers.

However, I had a disinclination for being too bored or always so polite. This deviance included an occasional tendency to revolt against authority that I first developed at that exclusive private school in Montreal, where I had been a poor American kid with a scholarship that kept me there. A school that for my "plebeian" American tastes was sometimes a bit too steeped in Canadian political correctness, except for a whack or two to my derriere and its lust for British imperial lions as mascots. It was also seen by more than a few as a vestige of a dead empire. But a colonial empire in many ways looked moral compared to Stihl's concepts of global power, unless one was referring to the Belgian one that had run the Congo into a pool of genocide.

As a legacy from my confused rebellious youth, I had liked the uncomfortable reaction from more than a few of the excessively wealthy, *WASPy*, uptight students at that private school, as well as at Yale, where I had done my undergraduate work on a scholarship. Later in life, as a corollary, I even better liked to remind the esteemed powers that I was subsequently still here to irritate them. Yeah, it was a bit trite and mildly hypocritical, but it was me.

Too many silly bad habits were just too hard to get rid of. So unhappily, from time to time, even though under the threat of Z5 discipline, I had to interject a bit of my contempt for certain members of the sleazy wealthy and the incompetently well placed because of privilege. I continued in that vein. Yes, indeed, I had a lot of sad attitudes.

"Some of your clients are worrisome and dangerous. Couldn't they turn around and do to you as they have . . . you could become toast." I threw it all in like a wrench into a meat grinder to upset another member of the rich—a banker at that.

"But really, J. C . . . . you should think about . . ."

I jumped ahead before Stihl could get in another smug reply. I was now strongly making my point unambiguously, and further testing his supposed supreme confidence in his managing the accounts of the deadly. Oh yes, trying to bother someone who had ripped me off with high fees.

Now, with that last thought, I was actually getting mean—at least from the point of view of a banker.

"Kardiac is a killer . . . . Do you feel safe?"

"Oh yes, J. C., and their women too," he quickly replied with a face of patronizing pooh, pooh.

It was clearly better to act like a grown-up with him, and more importantly to go back to my full adult disguise. Just lie like you *like'm* if you *need'm*, because they are rich and powerful, even if you don't *like'm*. I returned to my airs of mature dignity. How swell.

I was surprised, though, by that remark about women. Which ones was he referring to? Bizarre, but I let it pass. I thought that perhaps his peevishness with his own wife was seeping out into a wide range of his worries. But his answer also demonstrated at the surface a kind of cavalier dismissive behavior. Could that have been a bit phony, too?

"Look, my good *Freund* J. C. That is the very reason they all do business with the Swiss. Reputation . . . reputation for quality delivered on time, total loyalty to the customer, and absolute secrecy. And our incurable ability to keep government noses out of their business."

"Yes, I have heard all that before, but a hundred percent secrecy, Johan? Are you sure? The Internal Revenue Service (IRS) of the US government had enough leverage and willpower to act like an acetylene torch cutting like butter through every defense the Swiss put up. Didn't it?"

"Now actually, J. C., I am surprised with your comments," said Stihl with a disregarding wave of his fingers.

"Wait a second. You were even forced to send part of the interest generated on American-owned accounts directly to the IRS. Sorry, Johan, just dealing with the facts—as you have previously emphasized is important."

"Now actually, J. C., our Swiss butter is known for its superiority even under the duress of great heat. Our buttermilk comes from iron maidens. And it is not so bad to take a little cream off the top and give it away for good global community relations. Very little, indeed."

"Only a little, Johan? That all sounds delicious. Pray tell me more." I was fully back to my regular self as far as Stihl was concerned, continuing to butter him up.

"Look, J. C., on top of that, whatever you hear about us going to shut down certain numbered bank accounts owned by Americans, it is more of a publicity show, don't you think?"

"What do you really mean, Johan? It's all in public now that it is practically impossible for tax cheats in rich countries to hide away money in Switzerland."

"Well, the media is always fascinating for its fantasies. We can shunt these accounts to other offshore locations or to Delaware. Report a number of customers with measly hundreds of thousands on which little additional taxes would have to be paid, if things really get bad. Or an obvious small criminal, so to speak, out of sorts even with his bosses could be thrown in to keep your sharks at bay."

"That's no publicity show, Johan. That's a big collection agency of Uncle Sam bearing down on Switzerland, along with a lot of other Western governments."

"Hah! A number of your biggest US senators are my best friends, especially from places like Delaware, Wyoming, Florida, and parts beyond. I could not say they were my customers. Just wait. If the US dollar further weakens and the US government introduces exchange controls, where are they going to hold their additional cash? It is quite possible that these US politicians are already asking these very questions to their Swiss or other offshore friends. Maybe US bankers will soon be doing the same." Stihl had one of the sliest and snidest expressions I have ever seen on his face.

"Really? Very interesting."

I was surely getting the inside goods, while the press generally made it look like Switzerland's financial glory days would be over soon. Could it all be a public charade? Or was he just dumping on me a lot of false bravado? What he was about to tell me made it more convincing.

"You understand my meaning. This, of course, is said in full confidence. But no matter."

I nodded like a good apprentice—with a gulp.

"Of course, we are not insensitive. We do try to be *ein bisten* sympathetic to important US politicians and their publics with our press releases and joint declarations. The IRS—lots of noise."

He looked like he was about to explode into me with a large jolly grin of seemingly paternalistic confidence, as if he were a father dispensing fundamental wisdom to his son. Or possibly, there was another reason.

"Well anyhow, J. C., it would still be very hard for, let's say, the more challenging customers to believe that a Swiss banker was 'screwing' them, as you say in American English, and giving any information away to any tax agency. Given their reputations, they would know that their banker knew that."

"Right. Yes, quite fascinating all this, Johan," I confirmed so he knew this layman of finance was following well. He sometimes chided me for my financial ignorance and wondered why those in the teaching profession seemed to know so little about money. I almost felt like he used this ignorance against me with respect to one of my portfolios, which he managed. If he had known that I was an assassin, he might have provided me with the premier services and returns that I normally got at a Hong Kong bank. And all without even having to threaten anyone with a bullet.

He continued after my own internal melodrama about banking services.

"All that publicity about giving account information to the IRS was meaningless. We also have our own pathetic Swiss courts that sometimes have the backbone to protect us. We'll keep working out nice public agreements with the American authorities. Ones that will certainly protect us from . . ."

He hesitated, restraining himself from stating the obvious. Stihl knew that he would be deader than dead if he messed up the finances of those whom he thought were a fascinating crowd of sometimes entertaining scoundrels. And giving any information on these "gentlemen's" accounts he held in his bank to any tax authority would result in very deadly sanctions for whomever was held responsible. Especially if they were given outside of official channels.

The last banker who had given such information was buried in the deep outback of Australia after friends of the banking community, so we shall say, tracked him down. He had been almost as long in disguise as Adolf Eichmann, one of Hitler's principal associates, who had escaped Germany after World War II. At least, Eichmann got a trial from the Israelis.

Those who revealed unpardonable secrets about certain Swiss accounts were more apt to get a stiletto from a hit man brokered out of the Italian-Swiss city of Locarno. In fact, for those who had died because of their indiscretions, a new word in the vocabulary had entered the banking dictionary. They were simply referred to as having been *Locarnettoed*.

The Mafia found the upscale town on Lago Maggiore to be highly pleasant to visit from time to time, especially during the hot southern

Italian summers, when the Calabrian heat of the Italian boot could be insufferable. Or was that more precisely the nasty toe? Oh yes, the film festival in Locarno was quite good too, with the hit squads especially enjoying the remakes of film noire like *Dillinger*. In a certain way, you could say their predecessors had inspired the reinvention of the genre.

The joke in the liquidation trade was that the festival provided training footage for the uninitiated in their first sortie to Zürich. No wonder the young apprentices used stilettos and cement blocks, or just plain good old hammers and crowbars. The Mafia dons used to lament that they got what they paid for with this inexperienced lot. They would only use these relatively uninitiated on small bankers, and usually at first for only threats.

It was also no surprise that the Swiss would end up repeatedly in court with various Western governments to protect certain account holders' privacy. It could be truly a matter of life and death. High-level Swiss bankers who are privy to much remain well aware of the Locarno sanctions that were primarily instituted by a number of their more unsavory customers. Even when being requested to divulge information due to pressure that had first come from their own police, they remained very canny and careful.

A full release of information about Swiss secret account holders could also be equally fatal to the Swiss economy. This included the indirect impact on government assets, which altogether represented only one fifth of the two main Zürich-based, publicly held banks. The Swiss banks were thus too big to be allowed to fail no matter what your view was on capitalism. Anything or anyone who put them in overall jeopardy was asking a lot—even for a lot. The whole employment and government tax base would crumble if these banks collapsed. And the chain effect on the global economy could prove to be devastating.

"I hope, Johan, you never get caught up in any trouble with these interesting gentlemen," I said with feigned concern. "Nor these tax authorities and other investigative US financial agencies."

"*Yawohl, verstehen Sie.* Don't even give it a thought. Everything is in order. The discussion on the risks of these matters is closed," he formally said with piqued irritation.

Stihl was looking a little less confident. It could be that the IRS was more serious a worry than he was pretending it to be. For a lot of Swiss bankers, this US agency was potentially more destructive than the Mafia.

While the Mafia might kill or maim a few of their colleagues from time to time, the IRS might one day kill the entire golden Swiss goose if the IRS got sloppy. That demise would partly be dependent on the work of the IRS's special investigative unit, run by a small "shock and awe" team of highly trained and veteran forensic accountants. In the tax monitoring trade, and even among the Mafia, these IRS "untouchables" were simply referred to as *unfuckable*.

There was, however, a new bet emerging in the liquidator leagues that the gloves would come off the Mafia against IRS investigators if they screwed around too much with the Mafia's Swiss accounts. The IRS collecting huge taxes off the accounts of professional assassins? Ouch! Or was that more like boom, boom? If they had touched my money, they would have been on their last good-bye.

On the other side of the ledger were the political do-gooders. Killing certain Swiss banks might just not be enough for certain activist prosecutors and regulators within the US government, or even among the left wing in political Bern, Switzerland's capital. After all, the Swiss parliament had sitting Communist members to go along with the ultraenvironmentalists. They were looking to gorge on the increased unpopularity among the public of certain bankers and banks.

The Swiss public was increasingly fed up with the dirty branding that a number of these financiers had given their country around the world. But they were even more upset with the wild attacks, by specific Western authorities, against what they knew was their bread and butter, number one industry for high value jobs. Almost perversely, these attacks on Swiss banks from abroad had resurrected the popularity of the Nationalist Populist Right (NPR).

America and Britain had their own offshore or even so-called onshore tax havens they protected while they went more vigorously against the Swiss. It was global capitalism and Western solidarity at its finest moment, and the extreme right NPR was going to exploit it to the fullest if they could. This Swiss right-wing upsurge surely just connected to a broader global one. Nevertheless, the NPR would laugh all the way to the "political bank" as American politicians and journalists stepped up their vitriol against Swiss private banking.

In various radical circles, there was even a neutron bomb mentality to banking reform: activists and a number of regulators were desirous of taking out the toxic senior bankers, but keeping the institutions alive.

That was very much in form in the United States. Stihl had a lot to say about the Swiss variety.

"You know, *mein Freund*, what really pisses me off are those irritatingly self-righteous members of the Swiss Federal Council. And not to forget, the very questionable elements in the rest of the parliament. They have been targeting bankers with their sanctimonious drivel," said the robust financier. "The Communists and Greens even want to set up a truth commission on us. *Unglaublich*—not to be believed."

"What do you mean?" I asked, as he seemed to either want to end his point there or pause for air. He was, after all, a mild asthmatic.

"Look, the Swiss economy would collapse if we were to work under their proposed rules for goody-goody banking. It would be like Switzerland's first civil war, with the bankers as the evil confederates. After the fallout, though, you would hear these activists screaming all the way to the bank, when their little salaries were cut as government revenues contracted."

"Sorry to hear you have so many political problems, Johan. Or should I say worries about them possibly becoming major ones."

Stihl was getting worked up and vexed, almost turning ruby red in the face. He looked like his head was about to pop.

"Why do we tolerate letting the government put one of those villains on our board if they are not going to shut up? It is truly bizarre."

"They are even on your board of directors?" I tried to sound like a sympathizing soul, as well as a surprised soul. "Oh, right, I remember now, the one on the front page . . . I think in the *Financial Times*. She made a big splash on banking and ethics."

"Oh, *mein Gott*! Don't mention her." Stihl seemed to want to go blind, with his hand over his eyes as if he wanted to delete thoroughly even her image.

"You mean Frau Steller, that crypto-feminist and *enviro-mental* case of the Green Today Party (GTP). Isn't she up for possible election to head the Federation Council? Which, I think is essentially the head of the Swiss government?" I hoped I sounded sympathetic enough to further firm up Stihl's trust.

"*Richtig*. Absolutely right, if someone doesn't stop her getting elected," Stihl added as he nervously took a big swallow of his beer suds, which conjured an image of him swimming unhappily in the Rhine after a major industrial leak had crippled its ecosystem. Which it had, and in which his bank was indirectly involved. And which had truly upset Frau Steller and had led to noisy but ineffective consumer boycotts of his bank and the polluting companies.

The campaign included putting anti-Banque Suisse slogans on the sidewalk in front of the bank's head office. The writings even quoted former trustbuster US President Teddy Roosevelt's warnings against banking barons like J. P. Morgan of the early twentieth century. (Interestingly, that Roosevelt was both a procapitalist and pronature conservationist, whose Harvard thesis had been on promoting women's rights.)

"Yes, Johan, and they are also pressuring your bosses to expunge suspect third world government money. And to return it to the countries of origin. Mostly African and Latin American countries, and Middle East ones, too. I think they believe they have evidence that you never did as promised all the way back to the 1990s, sorry to say, Johan."

With an odious face that looked like he had caught wind of that leak, Stihl said, "*Gott in Himmel*, this is as efficient as putting toothpaste back into the tube with diamonds. Or reversing falling bodies over the Rheinfeld Falls, and even reversing the falls themselves. Yes, it would be bloody unnatural." He said it almost like a physicist would explain to his freshmen students a basic law on dropping bodies, but with a bit more gravitas. Possibly he should have added the gravity of dropping industrial sludge into the river by a number of his customers, who were being protested against by what he referred to as the "stinking" Germans downriver.

Stihl suspected that those so-called "stinking" Germans wanted to essentially expropriate his bank's wealth by making big tax claims against Switzerland. They wanted to attract more business to the big German banking industry at Switzerland's expense—meaning at the expense of his bonuses. He considered that as being even a bigger stink for him and his banker confederates than any wanton excessive pollution put in anybody's river water.

Stihl shifted back to his sunny disposition. "Oh, of course, I do not mean all that stuff about falling bodies. That is just a thought," he said defensively with a more benign slight smile. "Just an analogy. We talk about falling profits these days. Any falling bodies would be Swiss bankers jumping if the IRS got its way."

"Ha . . . ha . . . ha," he laughed in disjointed mechanical synchrony and in blobs of laughter. They might have been offloaded as rejects if laughter had been produced in one of Switzerland's factories dedicated to quality. But somehow, the idea of that country fabricating laughter seemed incongruous to its bankers' principal missions.

Rather, Stihl's solution to the political discontent about the so-called dirty money was to have these activist Council and parliamentary members followed, garnering his own files on them. He remained worried that they might find out about the hidden embarrassing details of all his little sordid activities and capers, and spoil a number of his grandest projects on the table. He fretted that they wanted to turn anything they had on him and his banker friends into public display, for what he would have thought were simply cheap political points. Politicians made him sicker than effluent.

What I could garner from Z5's strangely thin files on him went all the way back to his school youth. Altogether, history and politics had been Stihl's worst courses at the famed schools in Neuchatel and College Philippe le Grand in Paris, where he had enjoyed intellectually and physically bullying every leftie who had irritated him. He had been sponsored by an unknown paternal entity known no more than by its now expired account number of MI611/11572011 of Landesbank Leuvenstein. What a way to live a life—fathered by a secret bank account.

He had taken a great deal of bullying in elementary school for being a pimpled orphan, rumored vaguely in leftist circles about being a son of a deceased German officer of the SS, Hitler's personal army. But there was little more than that in the file, and Stihl was never willing to talk about his youth to the media—or anyone for that matter.

As a result of this discrimination and hard, loveless childhood, he had built up enough nastiness to go all around, and a thick Hyde to go with his charming Jekyll when he found it to be useful. One of those he had bullied had even become prime minister of France. *Quel horreur*, as he tried to make the promotional cocktail rounds in the City of Lights bumping into Mignon-Filleton or his minions.

There was even a rumor, with reference in his file, of a banker's club for S and M (sadism and masochism) in which he might have been a member. It reportedly had been so rough that it had led to the death of one of its members who had been headed for Davos. It was all embarrassingly timed, not long before Stihl was to be on a minor joint panel with the murdered banker at that economic forum. In fact, the two had been archrivals. His counterpart had become a vocal proponent for clean banking and aggressive regulation. This included his willingness to turn over data on thousands of accounts to cooperating tax agencies around the world, including the IRS.

I looked at what the Mafia described as the pretty pictures of the murder. No, they weren't really pretty, nor were they meant to be. Possibly a Mafia warning. Who knows? He had had his head hammered into pieces and his body whipped raw, with dollar bill signs cut into his behind. He had been stuffed up his arse with a small bar of silver and a few silver-wrapped Lindt chocolate bars.

Yes, I had also become head-hammered, but luckily with head intact. I needed to give thoughts about Stihl and his decadent hobbies and possible wicked behavior a rest, as well as all that drink I had been enjoying while talking to him. After all, he was a lot of man, even for his bedsprings or whatever other helpless victims lay under him. But how could I relax and always be fully sober in the frequent presence of such a corrupt and greedy sadist? Was he saving something special for me?

He would never get me into his private apartment. That was one thing for sure. Nor would he get me into bed with his intimate friend, Lady Whip, who was sponsored by his close friend, Schmidt of Finanz Oberlander (FO). Yes, another unsavory financial figure hidden in the many shadows of the temples of Bahnhofstrasse—one of a number of streets that I now walked down with more care.

NINE

Isolde, the Countess *von und zu* Leuvenstein and Princess of the Grand Order of the Maltese Falconry (just a few of her titles from a long list of many), officially sounded like major establishment material. At least, at first glance in any party at the Leuvenstein Palace, where a waltz would be the most revolutionary demand that would have been asked of her by her late father.

However, even close members of her family, including her brother *Graf* Friedrich, were beginning to see her as taking on a dangerous aura of one of those famous revolutionary visitors to Switzerland. As far as the Swiss authorities were concerned, they were starting to refer to her whole family as being more tragic Austrian than placid Swiss, given their distaste for her politics.

As far as Isolde knew through her grandmother, one of the last princesses from prerevolutionary Russia, her family tree had started in Switzerland several hundred years ago in a town called Aagen. To a growing number of the staid Swiss establishment, despite her being a blue-eyed blonde bombshell of blue blood, Isolde was not looking like she represented a good return on their money as far as her activities with the Zeel Foundation were concerned. She had increasingly become public through this forum about the excessively male-dominated House of Leuvenstein and the need to put more money toward feminist causes. Even to change the laws of primogeniture that only permitted males to obtain the throne in the earldom.

The real problem with what she referred to as those "stuffy elements" of the old hierarchy was that they could not see the value in letting her cause and foundation pet projects prosper. Fortunately, they also could not see the huge potential for losses from her activities in the sister organizations to the Zeel Foundation, which were well beyond the view of her clan. In fact, they knew nothing about the Dianesis Order. It was far better that way.

After all, the current old elites were familiar with Swiss tourist tours, which they held in contempt, and included guided talks of revolutionaries' comings and goings and their not always so lovely impacts. Lenin, who brought in Soviet Communism, had lived just a bit up the hill on Spiegelgasse in Zürich. Rousseau, the exiled philosopher who expounded equality and shaped critical concepts behind the American and French Revolutions, had been a refugee out of France who was given Geneva citizenship. Who knows? Perhaps even the Swiss had given money to notable American revolutionary heroes.

Sadly for the Leuvensteins, many of these movements that Switzerland had sponsored had undermined the aristocracy and its role in the state. However they looked at such movements, there was no getting away from the fact that the Swiss establishment cash hand was almost everywhere there had been a major political movement, clash, or upheaval in the post-Renaissance period. The Swiss ruling classes always seemed to be well leveraged to power, whether existent or emerging. And the Leuvensteins, with their strong connections to Switzerland, wanted everyone to forget about it.

While Switzerland might have had a powerful world presence in politics and finance, its present elites did not especially like to be reminded of their ancestors' hands in a number of the failed movements. Especially if they had undermined their position and wealth and that of the old families of stature in other parts of the world—including the Romanoffs, who were exterminated in early postczarist Russia by Lenin's minions.

Apparently not without pure coincidence, there had also been many caravans of history and their political detonators that had passed through Switzerland well beyond Isolde and her friends—or even Lenin. These not only included those attached to the Russian Revolution, but also the African colonial devolution, the Nazi determination, and finally, the post-Cold War liberation. Not to forget the more obscure League of Nations disintegration, a precursor contribution to creating World War II.

The Swiss were also very much behind the United Nations, the successor to the League of Nations that had been based in Geneva. Not coincidentally, many of the UN's offices were located in Switzerland. None of these events or large global organizations could have happened in their fullness without important contributions or support from Swiss-based financial organizations. The Swiss and their banks were everywhere it counted. But so increasingly was the Order—on a possible collision course with the old order.

Many traditionalist Swiss leaders, aware of their country's history, would want to extinguish Isolde's "radical-type" movement rather than be blamed for generating another worldwide revolutionary fiasco. And given all the attention their banks were getting from Uncle Sam about tax evasion, this was a time when they especially wanted Switzerland to generally lower its head on the global stage, rather than get it financially or politically chopped off.

It had to also be remembered, despite whatever limited progress the ladies of the Order had achieved or the risks the local elites might perceive them to be, no revolution of significance had ever been actually allowed on Swiss lakeshores. This again demonstrated the Swiss dedication to internal peace.

A political upheaval in Switzerland was as possible as a dung heap in the center of Zürich. The town had a fetish for cleanliness, right down to daily getting rid of every cigarette butt on the street. Only Singapore, with its no gum-chewing laws, aspired to a higher level of outward cleanliness and order, as well as being a financial center and tax haven.

Keeping internal peace now was critical, particularly under the threat of historical revisionists, who had already caused their banks to be drained of Nazi victim money and so-called taxes owed to the American IRS. If the elites could have rolled up into an innocuous boulder in an alpine meadow while the world blasted itself away, it would have been dandy fine for many of them.

To further understand this near DNA priority to domestic staidness, one had to realize that the last Swiss revolution or war—an oxymoron, one might say—last took place all the way back in 1798, when Napoleon rode through and said hello to Heidi. However, the Swiss were not even going to share their chocolate, let alone be pushed out from beyond their chocolate-loving neutrality.

Around the very early 1800s, the conservative elites largely kicked out Frederick la Harpe's Napoleon-backed revolutionaries, even if France still maintained general control. *Vive la revolution* or the antirevolution, said the Swiss. Thank you very much, but no thanks to any important changes in their own social structures, including giving much more equality to women as Napoleon had done in France.

Napoleon, instead, would simply become the name of a too-sweet pastry. It was known for its chocolate icing as well as the need to be eaten quickly, so as not to spoil the excessive promise due to its good looks. It was, in a way, the best of the emperor's legacy to the Alp land. Since then, a lovely tranquility punctuated only with the opening of briefcases full of deposits had restored a sense of confidence and *raison d'être*.

Indeed, the Swiss were a tolerant lot, especially if you had a banker on your side—or an important connection to one. Isolde and the overall Order, in this respect, had gone more than one up on Lenin. That had certainly helped to dull her critics in a variety of the low-minded, high-level social circles.

But something was a little bit more lacking concretely in her manifesto and that of the Order compared to Lenin's. Much money without a well-developed and carried out scheme could spell an early and messy collapse, even with the best intentions. Z5, my intelligence agency employer, had proved correct to place me on the ladies' detail, despite my initial protests that I did not want to end up being a big babysitter to the irreverent and irrelevant rich.

Was Isolde's Order also satisfactorily sanctioned by even a key minority of the male Swiss establishment, as Lenin's had initially been? I very much doubted it, though my own Swiss-based organization of Z5 was not ordering me to stop her activities. Was I being set up for her Order's premature fall? Or worse, to get sandwiched into massive infighting between Western and Swiss intelligence and policing agencies? I drank up and kept the punch flowing.

Then again, there was what I sometimes referred to as the Dianesis manifesto of madness. Possibly a new genesis of mayhem despite all the great intentions and idealism if they didn't get it right. Baroness Schwartz had been the first to read it out.

"Women of the Order, we desperately need to make up for what our countries have done to the world, including not doing nearly enough for oppressed women in the Levant and beyond. We need to show strength in our movement, and make sure it is for global good against the tyrannies that support female oppression. To *unstain* the stains of our ancestors of the temples of Mammon, brutality, and even false justice, including all of the overseers in self-righteous forms. Muslim women have seen their blood and that of their loved ones carry down the gold and silver all the way to our banks. Gold and silver that could have done much more to raise their lot. We need to make a real movement for change, one that will free people up and make women equal and dignified. Only that will restore our countries' pride. Whatever it takes, we need to purge so many dark stains from our history. We, the honorable women of the Dianesis Order, are sworn to uphold this promise consistent to our Lady Patron's ideals."

I thought they were very nice words, all said fairly triumphantly but before any real major triumphs. ("Bravo!" I said to myself.) Yet, I would have had to put heavy red ink on any essay written by my students with this pabulum, I thought upon first reflection.

There was no real, well-thought-out plan, no strategy, and no critical thinking about backlash and overall logistics. There was little regard for the likely impossibility of the authorities in just about any country letting the Order get beyond hearing the starter gun to their mad dash against Islamic extremism. And there was no examination of the full economic fallout on all social strata (especially in their own countries) if they really sparked an unsuccessful Islamic-feminist revolution and were held chiefly responsible for it. There was also no consideration of the fact that a good bit of the entire banking system, even in places like Delaware to the Channel Islands, historically might need closer examination of its guilt to more than just Muslim women. They might even be effectively fingered for spending too much energy on women's issues in a place foreign to them, when a lot needed to be cleaned up at home or in the rest of Europe.

But was I underestimating these ladies and overestimating the near-term potential damage to themselves and their own countries? And why the heck was Z5 being generally passive every time the Order seemed to ratchet up the ante? And every time I had reported it! The ladies seemed on a collision course with history. Worse, they could even wind up starting World War III. Oh Christ! I felt like a deaf and dumb eunuch on my last ball.

Somewhere there was someone who had questioned it all. Baroness Schmidt seemed shocked at the time about the risks, which she characterized as seemingly naive college studentlike idealism that had been no stranger to her.

"People must know enough as to their place," she had said even during the heady revolutionary days as a student at ZIT—the famed Zürich

Institute of Technology. She had first met Isolde there many years ago. Isolde, on the other hand, had been a stylish retro-hippie.

Maybe Isolde's life had been too much under control in recent years. It could be that her revolutionary spirit was her elixir, her fountain of youth bubbling up for a nostalgic connection, a kind of hope for a more glorified future of future past and innocence lost. At forty-five or something, she had stopped counting, increasingly feeling the math was against her now. I never noticed. She was a nonaging immortal to me.

For Baroness Schmidt now, things seemed to have progressively changed from her days as the voice of restraint to Isolde's college days of political revolutionary spirit. She, too, though more bit by bit, was looking to recapture the energy and surrounding optimism of the young adult years, but seemed more reserved about making a major commitment to the movement at times.

As well, her husband had not been inspiring. He had become as dull as a dud—in fact, as attractive as someone she had seen in a bad cartoon. A "Mister Magoo," she affectionately called him, and no doubt something less attractive when her mood was less sympathetic. But I think she still had sporadic affection for her beast in her own strange way. And banker Schmidt was definitely a beast.

Altogether, most of the wives felt a social vacuum, especially after the nests had emptied—a need for a challenge and even a bit of danger. They thirsted for more excitement, as so many of these wives displayed by voracious energy in bed along with their ever-growing hunger to get involved in something that mattered, as in the Order.

The ladies had clapped with enthusiasm as the Baroness raised her glass with the rest of the ladies. "To the Dianesis Order, our sworn allegiance," she proudly exclaimed as she rose and stiffened her body like a sentinel. As they put on their rings, which they kissed, they further swore their complete loyalty to the actions of the Order until death, and to absolute secrecy. They would need that commitment, but would everyone keep true to it? History was full of quislings.

The clang of the glasses and the claps resonated to the point that a distant snooty waiter seemed to stare them down, making short work of their moment of joy. He was the only outsider allowed in the café that night, though at a distance. However, could I actually call myself an insider?

"We'll have to speak to Siegfried about the help here," said the Baroness, as she swooned to the democratic and human-right ideals that she was expounding on—all framed, of course, in the tidy Teutonic culture of Zürich's finest. The fomenting of important changes in societies of the oppressed would definitely not start with the dreary, confined, and penurious life of this male waiter. And this again made me wonder as to what I was to the ladies. Furniture *musculaire, solitaire*?

I was still in their employ, though who knew of any coming misfortunes of the waiter because of the critical gestures he had made during the wine toast? A good start, I thought, given my months with this crowd and my less-than-blue blood. A good start that they did not consider me finished, as I watched the chastised waiter looking around nervously, with his hands stiffly crossed between his legs. He was definitely out of pockets, and probably pocket change, too.

The ego, especially the bruised masculine one, needed sometimes to be kept under a restraining order, particularly before such commanding women as these Dianesis ones. Let them lead for now, and let me follow but swallow my pride will be my motto. It was simple, but seemingly alien to my DNA, as well as Switzerland's—or, for that matter, Sarabia's. An ego that was also under restraining orders from intelligence not to jump in and tell them they were all mad and to go back to knitting blue woolen sky patterns of how idyllic life should be. To remain protected against whatever would pierce those gentle skies.

No, I needed to be more encouraging and to check my watch to realize what century I was in, never mind the time of day. It was certainly time to let these feminine elites eventually dig up their own findings on the worst elements of the male bastions of the Swiss banking system, which had allowed some of these very conservative and even religiously meaner prosper and ruin the lives of so many of their own sisters. The ladies would be able to do it more efficiently, in a way, from their own lofty and overprivileged heights.

In fact, many of the wives lived in Swiss-style mansions on the mountain heights looking down on old Zürich. These somewhat towering palaces were slightly contradictory in their appearance of wealth by their preponderance to keep an architectural earthy, folksy, and country-style look. A good many were even made out of wood, occasionally with rounded sides to look like logs to give the feel of a giant chalet.

These earthy lodging behemoths had a touch of Renaissance here and Gothic there, as well as spires and towers. They were girdled with landscape artistry of neat flower beds. But with wide smiling sunflowers, to remind one more of the bucolic outer city surroundings, and with a hint of alpine meadow blooms. It reminded one further that the Swiss were still caught up with a romantic nature ideal—never that physically far away, given how small and burgherlike their cities.

And then there were the omniscient mountain landscapes, dominant and sometimes seeming to shadow almost every movement. They gave a geological sense that nature was not so unrestricted and that time and change could move at a glacial pace. That there were, indeed, strict boundaries, even when the land seemed to embrace so much physical freedom and God-given beauty.

There were also the ubiquitous forests. They were impeccably well protected and managed, and seemingly demanded so much affection from the Swiss that woodsy and forest-related names had been stamped onto street signs and other place names almost everywhere. It all unearthed a popular culture of not wanting to get too far away from their agricultural and natural roots. Not to glorify fast-paced change or to see it as so natural. It was the very message that much of Wall Street had so disdained that had led to the uprooting of entire beds of global finance. That had been carried over the shores by the likes of the Foles and Zeroches to Zürich and elsewhere, as they dumped their mortgage-backed loan contagion on the continent. That had made some of the Swiss financiers forget their very strong earthy roots and slower rhythms. At least, the more positive ones.

Fortunately, the Swiss sensibilities for law and order were applied to their love for nature, making uncontrolled and obnoxious development nearly impossible. Reminding one of the incredible legal creativity of certain cowboy elements of the Swiss banking system that, thankfully, had not been in charge of regulating conservation. Otherwise, there might have been clear-cut vistas, with few remaining reserves.

The district in which many of the ladies lived was known as the Walder, a word relating to "woods." In the nearby area, there were two very pricey hotels, given how superb the views were of the Zürich Zee (lake). One, called Chateau Walder, had rooms priced at eight hundred dollars a night, but it was the cheaper Forsthaus Hotel that had the most superb view of the snowcapped Alps. The difference between the two was that one had

Japanese marble and sushi and the other didn't. Whatever the insides, the views seemed to be permanently enraptured with virginal innocence, so white was the snow and so primeval the surrounding hills and forests.

However, the mountains could provide only so much protection in the globalized world of the twenty-first century. After all, a number of major Western governments had taken the country to the new tribunal at the United Nations International Tax Haven Agency (UNITHA) in The Hague. There, they requested an ostensible repatriation of one trillion dollars from all offshore tax havens for what they considered illegally begotten money through massive government and corporate corruption or tax fraud. It was going to be the case of the century.

While this bounty of nature had kept out the German Nazis, as Hitler's armies had found the mountain passes and cliffs to be impenetrable, would those defenses hold up in the modern interlinked world? Or against the prosecuting teams at The Hague and any eventual huge demands for restitution? Even extraditions of certain American bankers living in Zürich, who had been publicized as being equivalent to war criminals or financial terrorists by Chicago-based radical groups, had been requested by certain New York prosecutors looking for quick political fame. Would Switzerland's natural isolation and neutrality be used against it now to begin to pluck its wealth the way a farmer plucks a duck?

I had wondered why Stihl had been so dismissive of the case by The Hague against Swiss banks, not even mentioning it. Maybe it was too distant a worry given that these cases took ten to fifteen years to fully prosecute. Most legal experts knew that this UN tax tribunal would likely lose, and looked for a settlement of a few measly billions to go to third-world development projects. After all, many UN officials lived in Switzerland and would have to live with the consequences if Switzerland were bled dry. Indeed, Switzerland almost always, in the end, was well hedged against the many dangers to it or caused by it.

There was a swimming pool club in the Walder neighborhood near these bank executive homes noteworthy to Z5 activities. The local denizens, as well as hotel guests, were the principal users of this facility, which was at the Hotel Forsthaus. It seemed out of the 1960s, modern-cut metal and nondescript stone statues outside a wide exterior window. A little retro, so to speak. But the pool facilities had afforded me further cover for clandestine discussions, as they were generally unused. The light stained, modern wood panel of the sauna provided insulation not only for the heat, but for the not-so-reassuring private conversations in it.

There I would meet Zen, my Z5 controller, in the special circumstances when the cyber drop was not working or if the information was too hot. I could not completely fathom the choice of the venue or even all the reasons for such "teat-to-teat" talks. When need be, I had expressed instructions to go to this hotel the following day, at 4:30 in the afternoon, and pile into the sauna.

There I delivered verbally and simply to the controller's memory any important new developments—particularly if they were too sensitive to share electronically. There was no chance for any electronics or recordings in this sweat jungle. This was better than beating around the bush and dropping off envelopes behind park benches, as MI-6 used to do in the so-called golden age of Cold War espionage. Possibly, it was even better than drop-offs into private parts of a fountain.

I felt doubly relieved when these briefings were over. I also approved that it was hard for my controller to discern any evidence of increased palpitations or nervousness. The sweatbox gave nothing of this away. At around fifty degrees centigrade, how could the body language of looking for escape, as manifested in excessive outpouring from one's sweat glands, be noticed? Add another fifty degrees, and we would have been vaporized. Though Zen looked so cool that he seemed to have a higher personal boiling temperature.

To my chief controller, I had to pose the question as to whether Isolde and her friends would become a powerful force of instability. Was, indeed, the Van Gogh exhibition a crucial and major gauntlet to a rising storm of intensified confrontation between the West and certain Muslim communities, which were increasingly allying themselves with the rising tide of lunatics in Sarabia—or Tyrania? The same lunatics that the Sarabian monarchy was evermore having a difficult time of restraining, despite all their publicity agents indicating the opposite in the Western media or even in their own newspapers and on TV.

Zen listened at times intently, but with a benign smile that essentially signaled he was disinterested in whatever political analysis I wanted to add to my reports. However, he seemed to perk up upon my discussions about the Van Gogh exhibition and news about Bashard. I remember Zen's words that followed.

"Van Gogh was mad, wasn't he?" Zen smiled in a manner that I initially thought was mischievous or condescending. It was clearly rhetorical, or I thought he expected I would take it as such, so he continued during that dreary spring day.

"Yet sometimes, one's madness is genius or even holy faith for another. Sometimes, it is a matter of the context of time and place to switch from one judgment to another." Zen looked at me as if his statements were testing questions. I did not take any bait, because I couldn't even see for sure if there was any.

Rather, the thoughts of this professor were to act as a student of Zen. I knew that it was a good strategy to appreciate the "Analects of Confucianism," which encouraged good listening, especially from subordinates. Perhaps my rapture with this esteemed teacher/leader had even saved my job. But it had its limits. I wouldn't be learning Japanese or joining the local Buddhist temple or working hard to find a Swiss Shinto shrine, clapping around hoping to be respected.

Zen had no need to hesitate. He proceeded carefully in his methodical, slowly halting English, which made it fairly easy to understand. Even with his *Japanese-ized* English, which in the linguistic field was sometimes referred to as *Jinglish*, he was usually discernible. I just could not always understand the drift of where he was going. Inscrutable, mysterious. That was Zen to the core.

Zen continued in his deliberate and patriarchal manner. "We are not, however, interested in turning the religious clock back in our own countries, Swiss crafted or not. We do not accept that a time continuum, culturally speaking, over several hundred years can be fully applied in a globalized world. We have passed that phase. Let others cut off, cut up, or cut into bodies to spite or to revenge or to praise. We will fight this primitive, dark thought to the final end from even piercing into our smallest vein. You, my friend, are our glorious warrior on the battlefield in this precious mission, but also a peace protector against all the destruction that will come if that continuum does not universally move sufficiently forward. Though not chaotically or too quickly. That could prove to be implosive. You can choose to act like an honorable samurai, even if a lonely, solitary one that seems to provide few personal benefits. A noble cause demands sacrifice, and this is one of the noblest, I assure you your mission is. Even if you wonder whether the madness is on our side, as well. Stand fast and loyal through the many tests you will face, and the greatest rewards will eventually follow. We will overcome the enemies; we will spare our people huge tragedies . . . And your work is vital."

On such a fairly obtuse final note, he then left the sauna. The interview was over. I was left wondering whether I had passed the test of loyalty, instead of wondering whether he had fully understood the significance of my report. I was instructed not to follow. It would be difficult anyhow, as my head was left in a philosophical spin, trying to fully decipher his talk.

I was still sweating, even well after I had left what we referred to in our intelligence lingo as the *woodshed* or the *shack*. I had certainly been taken out to the "shed," but psychologically not too badly beaten, I think. I sweated away, wondering where this enigmatic Japanese man had come from. Where was he going? But more importantly, when would he be returning? He was so guarded that not even one of the well-connected wives knew of Zen; and even if they had known of him, there was nothing much to tell about Zen for certainty.

There were only rumors, vague ones, about his father being a very senior military man in Japanese-occupied Korea during World War II. Prestigious warrior ancestors? Believable, given his analogies to warriors and knights.

"Cut into bodies," what was that? An allusion to hari-kari? Glad he seemed to feel those kinds of requests were passé, as I felt any lack of success in any measurable way on my part might definitely lead to his own madness.

Zen was known for his dedication to having his agents perform impeccably on the job. He could have worked for the old Toyota before all the recalls. He was a killer for results, even if he left the blade alone. The Japanese had largely gotten beyond that kind of history, even if Sarabia had not. Even if Hollywood had not fully gotten over World War II, or the world of ninja and samurai scenes—of one hundred zillion and three times too many.

I had mentioned to Zen that Frau Smuts had a bee in her bonnet about promoting more rights within Islamic countries, especially women's rights. Her commitment was over and above most of the wives, and led to her central role in making the exhibition a happening. I could have been talking about the potential use of milk cartons in origami given Zen's lack of interest.

Smuts had been greatly affected by a story of one of her friends about the stoning of a Sarabian woman who had been raped and then left blind and for dead by a bevy of men who had caught her smooching with her boyfriend from a tribe and religious sect opposite to her own. That woman had been directly related to one of her personal friends, an immigrant in Holland. A very short segment of a video of the stoning had been secretly whisked out, by whom no one knows.

Yet it had been largely erased, supposedly accidentally, by a Swiss custom official after temporary confiscation. I had mentioned to Zen at the time that I knew something might be coming over the border soon. Could he have had anything to do with its interception and censoring? Was this just another piece of evidence of a cat-and-mouse game between Zen and the ladies, not to forget poor me? Was it to create tension against the extremist Islamists, but not enough to let a calamity take place?

Who knows? Going through the further screening of any new video clips could be just about as gory as what I had heard about viewing certain Nazi horrors caught on film in Auschwitz. Would they show them at the Van Gogh exhibition? I was wondering theoretically how this film would be appreciated by museumgoers, who would likely be more intent on simply viewing the madness of Van Gogh than the whip-lashers of Sarabia.

To conservative establishments, Isolde would probably be seen eventually as a provocateur, and the main one. Would she and her Order end up being remembered by the Swiss and German banking establishments in the same negative light as they held Lenin and his mobs? Would these ladies "blow up" their business in the Middle East theocracies and dictatorships?

Whatever Isolde and the wives' next move would be, it could very likely turn them into hot targets in a shooting gallery of disdain and hatred, borne on the hot winds from the south. However, there was still time before the blast from the south might even become more forceful than the Sirocco winds coming from Arab countries by way of Italy. Of current and serious news was that Isolde would likely get that "tail-burning" feeling from her upcoming travels to Central America and the Caribbean. This knowledge had come to me after my talk with Zen in the sweat chamber. Conceivably, he had been preparing me for it.

By the time Isolde got back for the closing of the Van Gogh exhibition, I sensed there would be very hot fireworks and that I would be in some panic, if not hyperventilation. I prayed to the heavens that nothing more would come down on my head or the Order's. But first, I had another date with the Baron.

TEN

Julius Wolfgang Schmidt, Baron *von* Braunaese, came from lower Swiss nobility. That was not the only lower thing about this gaunt, thin, but full-cheek banker with round glass spectacles and a cold glare—all combined with an equally taciturn personality to anyone except his most intimates. While he had pride in being an aristocrat, it also made him rather bored, given the size of his inheritance. This was his greatest self-criticism, which gave him no end of irritation. He worked hard to overcome his ennui. He did it by having a worldly, though very hollow, cause: he grabbed much more money through using anyone he needed, dead or alive, in between his sadism and debauchery.

Probably this overarching cause of his *raison d'être* made him receptive to receiving a number of the same notorious clients as Stihl had, and going to even greater lengths to manage their affairs. As these customers often felt uncomfortable on overly relying on one bank, there was no point for Stihl not to share them with one of his favorite bankers along the Bahnhofstrasse, in almost frightening sight of each other. It was a mutual pact that had proved profitable, if not ennobling. It allowed Stihl to further his important network to counter troubling, bubbling cauldrons of forces against his perverted use of the Swiss banking system. You could say that it was a pact made in blood.

Stihl had glowingly introduced me to Schmidt at a rather respectable bar. It was frequented by various muscular women. These young women were really after "the treasure" of these two outwardly staid banking gentlemen, whom they seemed to know quite well. Eventually, I went along to firm a bond with Schmidt by looking like I had taken one of them to my hotel. In fact, I had dumped her a few days before my clobbering, which made me wonder if she had undermined my position with the Baron.

"What are you, a kind of sissy?" she seemed to have spat out at the time, but with a silver ring on her tongue that would never follow her dripping saliva. Saliva that seemed to hang down her chin and into the air as long as her insults. She was still of the human animal kingdom, but definitely more amphibian than mammal. If I had taken her for a full taxi fare, I would have left her at the Tiergarten, Zürich's zoo, providing I had survived her. She had not taken too kindly to my fairly swift rejection of her.

"Look, my dear. I have had a change in heart. I would rather be with a baboon than you," I said as I let her out, laughing to myself about how much she might have disturbed the zoo's animal life—and have even caused the real baboons to run away in full flight. She had been another dark Swiss entity that had bent my mind.

"Why make a choice?" she had finally said with a snide laugh, as she simultaneously farted and bubbled up her gum that she blew up in my face. "I can arrange a baboon, no problem."

Her body coiled. I began to better realize her true origin and evolution of species. She was a particular chameleon, looking to move up the chain into being a viper. For myself, I would have just enjoyed a moment of lesser devolution: it would have been my turning into a giant mongoose and swallowing her whole, of course, after she had first passed through a sanitizer. Indeed, she had released my predatory instincts. Was this what made Madam Ugliest (her nickname) so attractive to these two bankers? Was this the feature creature of the evening that fired up the bankers' animal spirits for their next big deal in the morning?

Instead, I did my own constricting well away from her and bid her a goodnight.

She said at the time, "I won't tell Wolf that you're just a straight puppy. You know we eat them."

She laughed a witch's cackle. I didn't know how those so-called staid bankers could ever deal with such a woman. She was all poison and domination, wild and incredibly ill-mannered. Perhaps that was the attraction. Maybe that's why she simply made me feel ill. Yeah, maybe she was right that I was a sissy. At least I wasn't her sister. I almost went unhinged after she slammed the door so hard.

I felt that despite all the wealth that Schmidt had cornered, he must have had a deep-down complex that in a sense, he was just not much more than an over puffed-up and boring accountant. He was fighting hard to counter it through his more-than-infrequent visits with the depths of depravity and his grandstanding on his connections with the truly odious.

That tape on Schmidt I had attached to his file from Z5 surely should have gone to Harvard's psychiatry faculty. Or been used as part of the central plot in the first horror movie on Swiss banking. There were a lot of weird people among some of the ranks of the nobility. There were a lot of weird bankers in Zürich, too.

After this operation, I would have to randomly look quite a few Swiss bankers up in the Yellow Pages. And interview them all, so as to fully reestablish my overall faith in the sanity of Swiss finance. In fact, I had started doing so many months before as a kind of professional therapy. One vice president had not looked too impressed with my thin references; he threw me out because he did not like being introduced through the vehicle of a telephone directory. At least the lady banker at my first exposure to Banque Suisse, due to my yellow page follies with my finger, had simply said to come back with more money. All before she rushed me out and before I could gulp a ton of free Earl Grey tea and Tobbler. Or foolishly try and hold the door for what seemed to be Banque Suisse's first feminist.

For some reason, a good number of the banking weirdest seemed to have been introduced to me or assigned to me by Z5. My visitations by way of the public directory were beginning to make me believe that not all were so bad in this industry. What was my problem, or what was the common thread in getting to know so well the dysfunctional and the insane in this financial community or the over-the-top political do-gooders as in the Order? Why me? I usually stayed away from the massively greedy, those in S and M sex, or the politically discontented. I had been just a regular bloody boy scout for an executioner.

But Zen would not allow me to get away from these people or their pets. I must have had bad karma. Did he think that I deserved punishment as a consequence of something or other? Yet, he wanted my full loyalty in the face of having to deal with so many awful people. I couldn't figure it out. Could I have been his bad banker in his past life? Buddhist bankers—that was one idea that definitely needed a bit of a rest.

But Schmidt had truly warmed up to me over liquor and cigars; such was the effect of Stihl's high regard and references for me. He mowed through one too many compromising brandies and opened himself up to me about a number of his sad business relations, but almost always with that superior tone and vocabulary that did not let me forget his social status.

"I had the most civil conversations with Kardiac on Freud and Jung, and the relation of asset accumulation and war to the Oedipus complex," Schmidt had proudly recounted unknowingly into my little receiver. He had asked that I check all of my electronics at the reception desk of the Walder, his favorite comfy hotel with individual rooms for discretion. Unfortunately, he didn't know that I had a few things hidden up my sleeve, and he was too Swiss a banker to frisk me. Interestingly, Stihl had not asked me to remove my phones and other bells and whistles, but this guy had.

"*Und nicht vergesssen* my unforgettable visits to Joddah in Sarabia, where I would meet Armin, who had converted to a strict, possibly dangerous version of Islam," added this demented banker.

"Interesting." What else could I have said to keep in his good books, even if one could say it was difficult for me to do so consistently with the depraved?

"Not so dull for a banker, *nicht*, J. C? You need a lot of stomach to do our job, though. Our jobs are not so colorless and gray. Stihl, however, looks like he has more of a stomach for this dangerous work from what you have told me." Schmidt said it almost disappointedly, not knowing that he should have used the words *guts,* as he did not have his own generous stomach to pull in. Schmidt had drunk so much during that occasion—like he had swallowed the entire bottle. Glass and all.

This *Uber*-banker seemed to have more than a drunken glee in his eyes, while rubbing his hands more like a kid about to get long-wanted delicious candy, but with the naughty face of the undeserving. He didn't need candy. It was sweet enough just to eat up his words to himself. Or he was putting on a good con.

"Yes, what about Armin, the Butcher from Campallah?" I said a bit shockingly. Schmidt had been talking about no other than the famous African leader who chopped his enemies up right down to their livers. And then ate them. The livers, that is.

"Amazing you know such people!" I said.

"Yes, that one," Schmidt retorted, trying all of a sudden to act nonchalant and more restrained in his excitement to tell tales about his customer *horribles*. He had been mildly shocked by my less-than-excessive shock of horror.

"*Unglaublich*, he had an immense open and welcoming presence in Sarabia on the Joddah corniche. Yes, just about to everyone . . . at least at first.

"You can't mean everyone, Baron."

"*Bitte*, J. C., call me Wolf."

"Certainly, my pleasure." For a Swiss banker to let you call him by his informal name so early in a relationship was impressive—or he was too drunk. Or he was brought up partly in America, or you were an American widower in drag and loaded with a lot of money. Or all of the above. Or none of the above. Why did I even care if he allowed me to call him Popeye or Mister or even Monster? Yeah, the last one would have been good.

"*Ya*, J. C.," he said with all the due reverence for me that I would want from him. "I mean it seemed like nearly everyone used to pass Armin and he would say hello. Even to the seemingly inconsequential."

"Really? Like who, for example?" I had to keep him talking, even if it meant going through dull small talk and *drunkenese*.

"*Stimmt. Ya.* There was a hard-up British teacher with the scruffiest dark purple sweater, to whom he would throw a few pounds. Or the small merchant returning from Salah prayer with whom he occasionally prayed on Friday—Sarabia's Sabbath, so to speak."

"Nice to see he was actually so sociable. I remember, Wolf, that there was talk that he had quite a friendship with a chauffeur."

"Oh yes, the chauffeur he would invite for a quick coffee and a quickie." Schmidt twinkled on the last word.

"That one was purported to have had sympathies with the minions of the Al Quomini Brotherhood," I stated in a manner that made even Schmidt look surprised about my depth of knowledge about Armin. Or possibly, he was astonished for a different reason. I continued, "He was reportedly blown up with a whole compound of Lebanese and his minister's limousine. It was also recounted that he did deliveries for a variety of embassies—including the American one. Running state secrets, I think, Wolf."

"Such rubbish, J. C. In fact, he ran an alcohol smuggling operation for American ex-pats, teachers, technicians, and engineers—no diplomats—run out of the Morannian embassy."

"Wasn't it reported that he himself had taken the car from the ministerial motor pool to the bombing site for a fee?"

"*Nein, nein, nein!*" The Baron was slurring his speech but managed to continue. "He did it because he was blackmailed about his homosexuality." Schmidt looked very uncomfortable when he made the last point and looked deeply into my eyes when he said it. He looked nervous and angry at the same time.

"Oh yes, given the death sentence laws in Sarabia against homosexuals, the Brotherhood would have had a strong hold on him."

"Quite so, J. C. After he brought the car, he was betrayed and dumped in it, rather than being made to personally drive in the bomb and leave it there. It looked like an insider suicide to some, but it wasn't. He was thoroughly used in an effort to implicate the minister of police, whom he worked for."

"How did you get all this information? Extraordinary!" I said.

"No matter, we all have our contacts."

"Quite so, Wolf."

"As a matter of record, he was a low-level spy for Sarabian security. A sleeper who was never much activated."

"You mean Armin," I said.

"*Nein, nein,* the chauffeur. Though Armin had been rumored to be working on African intelligence matters for the Sarabians. Well, from time to time."

"Armin was doing that? I'm astonished to know that. Yes, no wonder they allowed him to stay in Sarabia, beyond the fact he had spurred the conversions of millions in his homeland to Islam. Though he was far from being the only ex-dictator who found Sarabia to be one of the best escape destinations."

"Anyway, J. C., there were a few funny stories, too. Armin's appetites were large in charming the many, or the menu. And his anger was so famous that once, I thought he was going to eat the menu—if not the waiter!"

Hearing all of this, I almost fell off my soft cushioned seat in the restrained clubby atmosphere of our plush surroundings. It would have been unconscionable in such a noble and high class setting. Even the muscular ladies behaved here. Yet, Schmidt, the top Zürich banker and aristocrat, could not help but laugh himself silly like a juvenile prankster. He finally continued after a lot of coughing. He was warming up to the punch line.

"When they asked him whether he would take liver since they had run out of steak, he almost went homicidal. This was *sicherlich* a man not to refuse good meat to. Steak tartar was his favorite, though I did not have the stomach to eat any kind of meat with him, as he looked wildly into my eyes like I was his next item on the menu." Schmidt then almost collapsed into a puddle of further laughter along with his coughing, before he returned to his upright position of looking dignified.

"Amazing," I confirmed with an ingratiating tone to show my appreciation for letting me into such interesting insights, even if some were anecdotal expansions on what had already been largely covered in the Western press about the Butcher. Such insights might have left the anti-banking, glib, Chicago-based anarchists pale for critical terminology to describe either Schmidt or Armin, his big Ougoobandan friend. In reality, I could have vomited.

"Unbelievable he could so openly greet the public even after his reputation of massacring thousands of innocent civilians," I added.

"Yes, J. C, though his open presence did not last, even if the Sarabian press censors under the police minister's influence kept all information about Armin out of the regional press, and his severe critics out of the country. Sadly, due to security concerns, he essentially locked himself up in his suite. Thereafter, he ate breakfast in a salon cordoned off from the hotel regulars. It was hard for Stihl and me to see him after that, and carry out our lucrative business with him."

Now I knew why Schmidt didn't want me to have anything that resembled a recording device on me. This information was sizzling. Even if revealed in partially fictional form without the precise name and locations, its holder could find himself or herself being tracked down by God knows who, possibly a half dozen intelligence agencies at a minimum, who had collaborated with Armin.

God knows as well what other weighty matters he was going to burden me with, as he seemed to unburden himself like it was good therapy. I felt like a poor substitute for the shrink he should have had, and very poorly remunerated for it. He needed to talk with somebody, and I was stuck with it. I was just every bad banker's conversation buddy. How lovely!

I nodded and said, "Oh yes, I remember pictures of Armin. Huge, big, bulging eyes and seeming to be in a constant heavy sweat."

"*Ya*. Quite a guy, J. C. *Sehr gross*. Big as a Buddha. Though comparing him one day to that got me a long lecture from him on how Buddhism was a decadent religion, because it centered on idolatry and a tolerance for a loose sexual lifestyle. Yes, quite the convert. But terribly nonfactual about important details about Buddhism."

"Yes, that's sometimes a problem with the newly converted: they can get carried away with their new religion. Overly trying to demonstrate their devotion."

"Rightly so," said Schmidt, whose very own idea of religion seemed to be communion with the wealthy and hoping for the largest possible deposits from the people of the prayers—or even people without a prayer.

I further added, "Armin was lucky not to have permanently ended up in a war crime cell, like Kardiac."

"Quite so, J. C. He had divine protection. Don't we all?" Schmidt seemed to get a kick out of his last remark, though only tepidly chuckling about it. Was he talking about the inherent protection he thought he might have from the religiously well-connected, Sarabian establishment? It had all probably gone over my head, but he seemed to have quite enjoyed his own joke. He was at least entertaining to himself.

From his dossier at Z5, I understood that Schmidt, along with Stihl, had run a collection agency for Armin's money gained from human smuggling and sex slave traffic through Joddah. The police minister had known about it, but the crown prince, now king, had not. I certainly wondered about that minister from all of my intelligence work in Sarabia—if they would ever let him out of the country for completely blowing intelligence work on some major terrorist events. And for having very strange political bedfellows.

The minister also had the effrontery to blame some Western alcoholic for a spate of bombings and for being a spy for the West. Some even thought he or his kin from the outer provinces had been behind letting the bombings happen to test the stability of the new crown. After all, the police minister's own tribe from the south had had reservations about the new king.

Fomenting clandestinely or even letting pass a small revolution in Sarabia would just have strengthened his hand. He would have likely crushed it for a high price from the monarchical court. That prize might have been the promise from King Abdul of becoming the crown prince and heir successor. That would never happen if Prince Waheed's father, Prince Tahmimi, had anything to do with it. He would have burned his own house down to prevent it if he had to, given his complete contempt for whom he kept on referring to in his own household as the *Dungster*.

When the police minister's car was blown up, it was a double signal from the Al Quomini Brotherhood. Their logic went like this at the time: "We can get you anytime or even implicate you, so be careful about coming after us." However, after 10/11, that effort to blackmail or frighten the minister and others in the so-called cabinet became very secondary to the necessity of the royal family to survive bigger wraths, like that of a fully mobilized CIA.

As far as the poor jailed alcoholic sod was concerned, who was forced to take the rap for the spate of bombings, we used to refer to the martini-drinking rebel as he rotted away year after year as "shackled but stirring." He was abandoned by his own embassy until he made it spectacularly into the Dutch newspaper front pages. I found it interesting that it happened just before a very brutal assassination of a famous Dutch artist by an Islamic extremist. Why the Dutch covered the story at first was anyone's guess.

His first act out of jail was to throw a James Bond-style, Grey Goose vodka-based martini in the face of the Canadian ambassador at a cocktail party to celebrate his release. Only, of course, after he had gotten plastered walking down the meridian on a main street in Raddah, telling everyone they were shit in his usual insubordinate manner. And then on Valentine's Day, he had given out valentines, which was totally illegal to do. He had passed them to anyone without a smile, including those whom he referred to as the long-bearded ones. The *Mootawa* had not been amused.

Interestingly, the next day, he gave giant red tulips with one of the cards to the deputy ambassador at the Dutch embassy; he used to listen to jazz with her.

He had wondered at the time why the price of the flowers imported from Holland had doubled since he went to jail. A Chicago hedge fund connected to GAG had gone massively long and cornered the tulip market. It was all done with money raised from the tulip shorts it had sold to a large cooperative of Dutch tulip farmers. They, in turn, had eventually lost their shirts with their shorts. All were advised by the hedge fund to hold onto their shorts, well after the hedge fund had gone long and had started to make a killing. However, the deputy ambassador had been well worth the expensive bouquet, as he considered her to be a very lovely lady, though a little too preoccupied with espionage infiltration. And with a small, lovely, little, yapping dog that needed more than penetration.

The Dutch put on a marvelous jazz festival every year with a full open bar. Their patrons were courageous, knowing that the *Mootawa* was lurking not too far away for any emerging Sarabians or Westerners who might come staggering forth. There was one emerging Westerner who had gotten so drunk that he finally fell flat on his face; they put him in handcuffs and leg irons at the local police station. All that for a piece of jazz and an open bar. Sarabia sometimes demanded sacrifices if you wanted to have a tiny bit of fun.

Then there was Schmidt again, choking for air and interrupting me from my pleasant reflections so clearly recorded. His gasping at times was a sound in my mind not from his breathing difficulties, nor from getting too excited over all of the money that he had vacuumed from third world corrupt dictators; rather, it reminded me of the bipedal and backstabbing leech that he was.

A further major concern of Schmidt, well beyond his customer or network *horribles,* was his worries about his wife. He released his words on this subject as if getting physical relief from letting out a large fart. But it was ignoble to use such a metaphor, as Schmidt was after all a baron who was fartless in public by nature, even if he delved too much into the intestinal weaknesses of some of his pitiable customers. All done, in fact, with a World War I gas mask left over from the gas attacks at the Battle of Ypres. Yeah, it would have made great Dada art if what he had done with it had not been so sick.

Schmidt said with a worried brow, "You know my own wife is my greatest sorrow at times, well beyond all these stressful though interesting deal makings I have told you about. Do you know what I mean, J. C? Armin . . . Borazza, the whole lot I have been able to deal with. But my wife. Do you understand me?"

"No, Wolf, if you remember I never married."

"J. C., if you knew my wife, you might abolish marriage altogether!"

"What's the problem?"

"She is not only testing my credit limits, which I am kind of used to. But her social causes are really unbelievable. I believe *weird* is the correct Americanism . . . or . . ."

"Oh, yes," I interjected. "That female society. Kind of worshiping a Greek Goddess and all that, along with mild interest in charity and the arts. At least, I think it is kind of religious and artsy. Just strange; not consequential."

I lied with a big sliver of truth to make it sound good. He was a man who fittingly I was giving silver linings to my lies about his wife, who should have told him to get stuffed, like his victims, years ago.

"Are you sure? If that were the end of it, I would be overjoyed," said the slightly sweaty banker.

Schmidt had been listening to somewhat questionable sources about his wife, which he very much had to listen to if not accept. I suspected that a number of them might have come through by way of contacts at Interpol, or simply from the Swiss police. I was instructed by intelligence to squash rumors from those sources, which I did as best as possible.

Schmidt had subsequently met me in one of his bank's vaults to ask me to watch over his wife on that fateful day when I had been viciously mugged. He specifically asked me to gather useful evidence to "facilitate an inexpensive divorce from her," to quote his own words. But I gather that he was paranoid about her discovering information that would severely compromise him in any alimony negotiations. It was only a bit of an add-on to my more legitimate watching of the Order. It was a good ruse and gave me additional cover, as well as additional money. But I knew if I ever told him what she had been actually doing for the Order, she would become the next victim, well beyond the help of the proctologists and psychologists that she frequently visited.

Yes, there was too much evidence all around that Schmidt had very nasty anal and S and M fixations, first picked up at his notorious school of Kleinmunster. So read his Z5 file, reviewed by the psychiatry directorate, which had even been sickened by his ghastly behavior. A real severe commentary on Schmidt's extremism, as the reviewing doctors had also been private school Old Boys—though certainly not from Kleinmunster—and so preferred not to make his school an issue.

The funny thing was that Schmidt could reroute billions away from prying regulatory eyes, but could not somehow get his wife to behave the way he wanted her to. Which would have been to simply work for Red Cross charities and idle her way in café gossip. Specifically, he was beginning to get too much information about her views and interests to stem Islamic radicalism. It was better to downplay it than try to completely dismiss it or say it was a fulsome lie.

"Look, if you are worried about this human rights stuff, she'll probably get over it like a bad flu. It's all out of her league or real interest, I am sure. Maybe she's bored. Needs more attention—whatever. She seems more interested in the art aspect of social life anyway," I said with feigned sympathy.

"I am bloody bored of her. I just wish she would disappear, sometimes." In the context of it all, his "I" had been heavily capitalized. Her spending habits had made it especially easy to extend extra intonation to the word "bloody," but less easy to extend her credit lines. In all that uncharacteristic emotional bloodletting, I was further wondering how really noble Schmidt was. Was his title a fraud? Or was I insensitive to the trials and tribulations of rich and married, aristocratic couples?

He told his complaints to me like I was his surrogate doctor. You could tell he was certifiable just by the way he talked about his wife like a baying hound with a smell of the fox on the tip of the nose, but frustrated by not being unleashed. It was an analogy that he might have very well appreciated. As well, he had a nose that looked as if it was whipped and inflamed, along with his fattish wobbling cheeks, while he practically screamed out how he could not take it anymore from her.

No, Schmidt had not returned from an S and M session. He had simply had too much to drink, or too much of something else, like his wife. The publicly conservative banker had also had too much of keeping it all bottled up. I sadly concluded I was one of the best friends that he thought he had.

Some men make friends badly. And Schmidt had to rate in the champion's league on that one. Maybe his self-centeredness catered to it, or his generally well-reserved self above ground. Or his vanity or worry about being turned in by others in his league of base bankers. But for now, I would have to smile along and seem like a bona fide and sympathetic confidant. A kind of bromide to a pal. However, it was increasingly looking more like running tail to a human garbage truck, hopefully soon to be at the end of its days.

ELEVEN

Isolde, whom I had first met by way of Smuts, had hired me for her personal security detail. Yet even after quite a few encounters dating back several months, Isolde remained quite a mystery—including her new deadly assignment. My own layers, though, were definitely peeling away to her and the Order, sometimes more than was prudent. And worse, I would now have to lay bare a number of my own secrets and those of the Order to Friegel, my contact with the Swiss police.

That mystery of Isolde's character and her general worth to operations were definitely occasionally very puzzling. There still seemed to be so many remaining walls that they were almost as infinite as the security checkpoints at an asylum for the criminally insane, or a main gold depositary in a Zürich private bank for the certified greedy. An interesting juxtaposition, no doubt, only possibly lost on official psychiatry. But not on the fact that Isolde was almost making me criminally insane and feeling like I would need to be put away if she didn't reach out to me more.

I was trying to look like more of an open book without being too much so. I was a freelancer, formerly of the French Foreign Legion, with questionable discharge for occasional excessive drunkenness and insubordination, all nicely packaged in a mercenary past history, so my file said. I came cheap, as the military no longer wanted me. But in the files, the planted references said I was highly disciplined and mission-centered when a major operation began. And evidently, I had convinced the ladies that I was.

Being a professor in recent years might have also helped me convince Smuts that I was now sufficiently tame to enter their very civilized society. Smuts was the only one of the Order to know all about the details of my academic past and how I desperately appreciated the money they were paying me. What none of them knew, so I had thought at the time, was that I was also a part-time assassin, who, under the right conditions, would put them all away with a bullet or a sledgehammer. It bothered me that in the end, I might not be able to choose between my deadly work and a potential sweetheart. No, in fact, my grim trade was my sweetheart. "How lovely," was what some old codgers might have responded at Britain's MI5. But probably less so in the Sicilian Mafia—who likely had more feelings about murdering a loved one.

I was further a soldier's perfect anti-authoritarian, known for my disgust with all things political, but not good gastronomy, elegant clothes, and the right hotels and cafés—that is, only when off the battlefield. Not to forget the women who came in and out of my life, as they consumed me as if I were their sausages. Nice file, anyway, that Z5 had somehow slipped to Smuts through a third party, no doubt. I still was unsure how this was delicately done. However, I had strangely once seen both Smuts and Zen coming out of the Hotel Cinq Robes de Pierre in Paris almost right after one another. I had returned to the hotel for my dark sunglasses. It was fortunate that I found bright light to be bothersome.

I had to take a bit of credit, too, in getting this job. I had surely worked hard to make myself sound responsible enough to Isolde over and above the bad boy image that had been so well documented. I also appreciated Smut's work ethic in convincing Isolde of my worth.

In my vane-less duplicity at times and sense for the singular-fee style, I could easily identify with Isolde's exterior of social judgment-free philosophy, together with a Swiss priority for financial self-interest, high style, and general liberalism among the younger or more progressive. I fully appreciated that no one was going to close down her felinelike love for freedoms that had been so jealously and hard fought for in Switzerland. Isolde was a product of that better part of Swiss society that had helped to improve women's rights. That was one side of her character that had been increasingly easier to read and admire.

As an historical aside, the Swiss had given women the vote by the 1960s, while Sarabia had abandoned slavery in the same decade. From Isolde's point of view, never the two chauvinistic temperaments should meet to extinguish the Order's passions to change the world positively for women, if she had something to do with it along with her coterie of influential wives. And the police and the military still remained with her and on the wives' list as excessively male bastions. Ones that could irritatingly interfere with their noble activities if they did not maneuver correctly.

I tried to feel grateful that they even let me watch over them, given what they perceived as my membership in a very male club known for its vulgar machismo. Perhaps the fact that I had shown a detachment to following orders from my male superiors, all pumped up on enough testosterone to disqualify them from the Tour de France, had put me on the ladies' good list.

However, the ever-so-polite, nosey Swiss police liked their cobblestones to generally stay in place or not to rise too far up even if so stylish or well connected. That definitely included any proper women of important bankers or close connection to. That especially included visitors like me.

Speaking of the Isolde cobblestone, not so nicely in place for the Swiss police, she would rise up in not quite the ladylike manner, given what she was to bring back from Panama. Something very vital. Something one could say in a way was very vile.

There would be within her traveling case what the Swiss establishment would never like to see comfortably fit into one of those wonderful, regular-size deposit boxes. Something that might even lead to more disturbing outcomes than what Napoleon had manifested on Switzerland. An item that could turn Zürich into a political and financial ground zero, the very antipathy its burghers strove for, and that I feared for some time.

Yet in her hands for eventual Swiss bank safekeeping, according to Zen, would soon be a Pandora's Box with the deadliest elements. A possible global contagion of sorts for some, and for others a possible salvation. She was not only the courier to bring it at first to Z5 through the associated bank of the Zürich-based Zeel Foundation. She was effectively the only one who knew who had penetrated the inner sanctum of a most important representative of the Sarabian establishment so as to obtain it.

There was no possibility for its electronic transfer by any means, given either the state in which it came or given its level of confidentiality, so I was initially told. And no further information about it was to be given to me. I was simply told that the initial courier could not or would not be allowed to enter any Western country, not even one of the embassies. That there was a trusted person in Switzerland who could bring it back. But that same person who had fairly easy access to Sarabia was beginning to get too much on the Sarabian intelligence radar.

I suspected that person to whom Zen was referring for such an assignment could only be one person. That person must have been me! That further created an eerie feeling that indeed the Order was beginning to get too much attention from potentially threatening people.

The contact person would come through Africa and South America on the way to Panama, buying tickets at each stop so as not to attract attention. The Sarabians were to think that he was simply going on a vacation to Kootoomba in Nubia. While he backtracked through South America and Africa after depositing the deadly package abroad, Isolde with me would do our own backtracking after picking up his "gift" in Panama, where he left it off. We would do this by way of Miami and Barbados and transit through London's Heathrow to Zürich. I would act as a kind of air marshal in second class to Isolde, who would happily be in first class. We would make no contact in the flight unless security demanded it.

The package would be left in a Panamanian bank by our mystery spy. I presumed it could not be left there too long for a few reasons. First, Panamanian banks, while fairly dependable, were still known in a number of cases to be a bit too nosey about their customers, especially new foreigners largely unknown to them from countries not on the US favorite list.

Also, a number of these bankers still had one too many connections with a variety of international mafia, from Italy to Las Vegas and beyond, who could be quite inquisitive in reviewing details on any customers who they thought could be leveraged to their benefit. The appearance of unusual foreign customers could distinctly draw their attention, including the man from Kootoomba with his Sarabian passport. His interesting variety of tourist visas could get more than the usual consideration.

Finally, there was no way that Z5 would contract out to Panamanian intelligence whatever work needed to be done in dealing with such an important package. There was still too much of an issue of corruption, not to mention incompetence. That was the popular view about Panama, though possibly dated. Nevertheless, Z5 could not contact them, as Z5 didn't officially exist. And Interpol could not be fully counted on at this stage for such a delicate task, as it was full of member countries, which could not be guaranteed to be discreet and on our side at this juncture.

If the package made it to Zürich, it would be an odyssey, if not of mythic proportions, certainly one that would bring immense danger not only to Isolde but her associates as well. Those who might follow her and track her down represented another untidy package that the local Swiss authorities really did not want, nor did I. There was no getting around it. I would have to be her backup and support at a safe distance. But it still seemed highly risky just with the two of us. It had to be. Until we reached Zürich.

There would also be no way to keep the information about the general importance of her travels away from the Swiss police. We would need our own back-up from them—and even my own eventual protection, once we got off the plane at Zürich. Z5 did not have competent or available muscle if things got violent. As the package got closer to intelligence's custody, those desperate to get it back could become deadlier and more focused—especially once we got out of any airport terminal.

That, of course, did not mean that I had to tell a lot to the Swiss police. I would still stay in character of being skimpy on giving much to them, which was safer. And what did I actually know? Just that Isolde would be bringing in a package, which Zen later described as one of the most important of this century to Western civilization. He added a list of other metaphors and hints that further underscored how critical it was to deliver it to Z5 fully intact and not tampered with.

My good "friend," Inspector Friegel of Swiss police, feared already that like Napoleon and Lenin, people such as Isolde and her followers were going to unleash either a very bad hello or a finger or two on the way out. I understood from the reports on the Order that were beginning to seep in from Interpol and elsewhere that the ladies of the Order were beginning to more than annoy them.

There had even been less than well-documented speculation by a low-level Canadian RCMP corporal on loan to Interpol. He had offered the possibility that the ladies might be a diamond-smuggling operation for their husbands' efforts to repatriate money to tax-avoiding customers. How trite and how silly, I thought. Smuggling paintings would have been my off-the-wall guess if I had been in that corporal's shoes. Interestingly, he had nasty, bright red, undercover heels that he would have clicked more often if he had not had so much of a drag.

In fact, he used to dance very well with one of Mossad's ex-finest from Israel, who had also been a successful transvestite liking to dress up in a large cabinet. Finally, this Mossad agent had successfully made it into the upper reaches of the Canadian political executive. The agent was outed only by the security service's prowess and controversial new program of looking into all government members and officials with dual citizenship.

Friegel had called me for organizing a meeting just before the planned trip. The Panama leg would definitely go unsaid. And by Friegel's less-than-charming demand for a get-together, I knew from my past dealings with him that he might very well have quite a few broken answers to the many questions he would broker aggressively to me.

I had already planted a question on him as to why Isolde was making such an important trip to Miami. He seemed baffled that I had asked it. It was my opening gambit to get him on our side and see what he might know, and to check how leaky our contacts were at Interpol, which provided my cover to the Swiss police. But it was a risky one, especially since I had kept Zen out of the picture about the exact extent of my liaison with one of Switzerland's finest.

The question in its second part went like this as far as Friegel was concerned. Was he going to also end up in his own good-bye, as in out of a job, if he did not manage this big headache called Isolde and friends? He was not fully sure what they were up to, but Interpol had given him enough of their communication traffic to ensure that certain instinctual indigestion that something was not too kosher.

Friegel probably felt mousy after I had told him about Isolde's trip. Isolde was not on a priority watch list, but her presence and importance had been acknowledged by certain discreet but important bigwigs at Interpol, who felt it was unwise to completely bury all their efforts from those who might eventually have to know.

Sadly for our mission, a number of member states to Interpol were less-than-savory or not fully cooperative member regimes, including an associate status with Sarabia. At the Interpol secretariat and its branches throughout Europe, all efforts were made to hive away key security secrets from such countries. But they could only go so far for so long. Z5 had at least their own spotter at the Interpol headquarters in Lyon, France—a woman referred to as the quarantine master.

The QM was a busybody rendering to no end to downplay the importance of Isolde's crew to the Sarabian delegation and various states partially or fully friendly to Islamic-fundamentalists or to any overly inquiring local or national police forces. From what I heard, she had done well to convince these state security apparatuses that the wives were generally a nutty club of political amateurs not that serious about much of anything. Yes, the amateurs I hoped they would not mimic, given my view how dangerous and messy things would likely get with such people. Given the residual gelatinous state that I was still in because of the action of so-called juvenile nonprofessionals.

My relation with Friegel would hopefully be helpful in keeping everyone in the Order out of someone's jail or interrogation chamber, or at least out of general harm's way from both the Western intelligence and enforcement authorities—not only the Islamic radicals. The radicals had taken third place for a while as being the most compromising opposition. Snooping journalists could blow everything wide open, further lighting up our operations for a knockout. The police might not even be able to protect us if everything hit the front pages. But they would have to at least provide final bodily insurance from a massive onslaught of the violent enemies, who might do everything to stop the package from getting delivered.

These extremist elements and their easily contracted assassins were potentially in Switzerland, given the strong presence of unfriendly elements, such as the Tyranian delegations or those in axis with such countries. As well, there were dozens of international organization missions in Switzerland, with many of the attached Sarabian and Tyranian personnel accorded diplomatic immunity. They could have shot you and left the country without even a disturbance to their handkerchiefs. Fortunately, there were few of them in Panama.

Switzerland was so clustered with spies and posh criminal elements that it seemed to be almost too crowded for any serious espionage. Panama was no supreme safe haven either, just usually quieter for our purposes. But importantly, Panama was distinctly and thankfully more removed geographically from Middle Eastern radicals. That in the end was a key determining factor for making the initial exchange over there, I had gathered. And it would ensure the best possible safety for both sides involved in the exchange.

As I gave it all a worrisome thought, I felt a sudden rush of vertigo—a most uncomfortable feeling to have in this country of crevasses. I then looked down at my feet, which were normally more distant. I had fallen down my own precipice, and sadly, I could no longer climb back up it. Again, the pressure was getting to me. I had avalanched onto myself and had become human rubble.

Was there really much left of the ex-mercenary in me—or was I more like just a bag of aging jelly? I thought sadly and pathetically as to how I had gotten here. And how much lower things could get. Like six feet under or lower.

The taxi came not too soon. I had been wobbly, and I knew if I stayed any longer I would become pebbly. I would become detritus to the cobblestones or smacked again by a few on my way down. I was not gaining stature with this work.

Out of the corner of my closing eye, I could see that the Mercedes stretch limousine had departed with the Order. In a way, so had I left before I had even gotten into my own, the scaled-down version limousine with the meter. I could not even read it in my stupor, even by a stretch of my cramped body on the backseat. My terribly throbbing bruises were beginning to revisit me—and badly. I was out like a flash.

TWELVE

I woke up with the knowledge that penetrating arrows do not come out of the celestial skies. Rather, sledgehammers do. At least, my taxi driver was very personal—he had even tucked me in. Or somebody had. Maybe it had been Nic. Yeah, it had to be.

Taxi drivers were never let beyond the elevators at the Schotland. That wouldn't have been too classy for such a Swiss hotel. It would have been fine with me if he had been shown the red carpet and given the presidential suite. For what I had deposited in his backseat had been ugly. Not even Schmidt's vault would have held that in storage, evidence to my growing discomfort with all the discomforts of the job and the increasingly difficult police, all washed down with liquid fear that I might not be able to protect the Order from death and destruction. How had I gotten myself into this hell?

No matter how pure or royal the Scotch whisky, I had concluded my drinking with the intent to render a form of amnesia—but there was always tomorrow, a worse one the way I figured it. I put on the pot—of coffee, that is—and remembered "Orangina" was so good in the meantime. A Scots friend had recommended this thick grapefruit or tangerine mix with soda, or whatever citrus delights it was made of, to fix the worst hangovers. It was called a *Limonade* in the German language for being a pop, which further made me feel juvenile as I swallowed it. How sweet.

It was no less than a soccer hooligan, even a fan of Buckhart, his hero, who had recommended this beverage. What was good enough for the drunken rabid soccer fans—or even the champion of drunken *ranters*—would be good enough for me after that night's liquid violence. Soccer hooliganism could have its value, at least if it was on my side. I wondered, if I had used them instead of the police to defend us, could the odds of our protection have been improved? With such a thought, I actually knew how bad a hangover I had.

It was then time to get focused on my dossiers and plan out the next step. First, I had to divert Friegel from showing his own hand too quickly in his attempt to demonstrate Swiss police efficiency as I brought him more closely to what was going on. Or maybe I didn't need be too concerned with him.

We also did not want the ladies and Isolde to move shop and go underground in an obscure place. We needed to keep this "harem" of new feminist and political consciousness so uncomfortable to many in the Swiss police, not completely in their law enforcement spotlights. But we also needed to give Friegel enough so he would not get impolite by being too much out of the loop, and so he would not be too unprepared to help if we needed to call in his cavalry.

I wondered why I kept on using the "we." Did I think I was royalty? Did I think I was really part of a team, who were really fully engaged in protecting the Order—or taking care of me, if I was in my own distress? The only royalty around were some of the ladies. The only muscle around, and definitely no royalty at that, was little ole me!

Speaking of Friegel, I knew him well, or at least as well as any foreigner could be allowed to know a Swiss detective. It was also my job to know which police were handling the Dianesis dossier and to get a little, but not too, friendly with them under my cover as an Interpol agent working on VIP protection detail.

Zen probably thought I would use this cover simply to keep an eye on Friegel's progress or, preferably, lack of it. But not to make any actual use of my Interpol ruse in providing information, and certainly not to divulge anything of importance. It is nice sometimes to keep a few surprises from the boss, though from this one you definitely wanted to keep it to a small number.

Meanwhile, I thought I might as well have been preparing for the Venice Carnival given how farcical it was getting with so many different disguises. Adrian Sands, Harvard Associate on leave in Sarabia; Jean-Claude Carterone, bodyguard *enfant terrible, extraordinaire;* and finally, Pol Martin, an American Interpol interloper. And then there would be another one for Panama and Barbados. Confusing? No, just your average everyday mole.

Hopefully, Martin should never meet his professional compass opposite J. C. Carterone, ex of the Legion. Think what people might say.

A fraudster, a schizophrenic, or both. It was a gamble that Friegel's stooges would never be in the same room with any of the ladies of the Order or my hotel staff contacts or anyone I might get to know in Panama. Such a room would be too small even if it had enough space to hold Napoleon's invading cavalry, which had been to Bern and back to Paris. Was it completely a reasonable gamble that my actions would not leave an impression of a multiple personality disorder? I hoped for the best, but I was probably well on my way to becoming a *schizo*.

For Friegel, a lot of tax-avoiding foreigners using his country's banks showed a kind of duplicity by nature, if not by insanity. He was likely not surprised that so many of them were also in Switzerland for psychiatric treatment. Worse, they lacked protocol and appreciation of the very firm Swiss legal framework, which in his mind was worse than being psychologically troubled. Such visitors could be rather invasive in their own manner or without many manners altogether—to put it mildly. That was very upsetting to the tidy and orderly Swiss, as Friegel truly was.

An American having a range of disguises to go along with a variety of passports would not be all that new for him. That was definitely consoling, and I needed soothing when preparing to deal with the Swiss police. There was a sort of grudging acceptance by Friegel of a certain degree of deception from American financiers and depositors with the darker kind of past, but especially for those from the so-called new Europe, such as Russia or the Ukraine. I mentioned the latter so as not to show any prejudice to the former. The joke had been lost on Friegel when I first uttered it in my ironic chastisement of his criticisms of Eastern Europeans.

Poor Friegel. Poor Switzerland. Switzerland was so full of new world and less-than-transparent, new rich crazy foreigners. I remember on meeting him for the first time, that he turned abruptly around to his sidekick, Sergeant Schultz, to whom he murmured, "Our banks are going to be our temples of doom. And the doomsters are certain questionable foreign residents or depositors."

Schultz, as Friegel's subordinate, was very dutifully dull and very Swiss. So he had nothing to say when Friegel was giving color commentary about his challenges to protect the Holy Grail of his nation's wealth and prosperity from these so-called evil foreigners.

It was better for Schultz not to be overly inquisitive as a Swiss subservient, and yet not to demonstrate an overbearing lack of mental agility in understanding important though inconvenient details. In other words, silence to superiors was golden, but stupidity was unforgivable. Yes, indeed, I would try to turn the chief inspector into my own Sergeant Schultz, but a bit of a more sophisticated and thoughtful variety. I would fail rather miserably at it.

On that thought, the bell rang. Had those last thoughts won me a prize like on a game show? No, they had not, and I should not have expected it as I had never won anything, including a door prize. Speak of the devil, it was Friegel. I had indeed won something—an awkward surprise. That was as good as my winnings would probably get, including at the Baden casino.

"So, Martin, are you going to be the solution to our problem?" said Inspector Friegel with the irritating authority of a schoolmaster about to chastise a difficult private schoolboy. He was moody and looked weighted down with all the seriousness of someone looking like they were about to give a death notice or go on a crash diet. But then Friegel was a detective. And Friegel was very Swiss, and looking more and more larger than life. And it was very Sunday and very much the morning, without me in my Sunday best and certainly looking more like my past Saturday worst.

Friegel was so serious that his words weighed like lead that could have held down a fighting, screaming corpse refusing to be one, but that was headed down to the bottom of the Zürich Zee. To cheer him up and make him feel that he was not alone, I decided I would need to be a bit enlightening and unburden myself of my own lead weights before somebody might add their own. Like into my gut or tied around it. And oh yes, to hand him an Orangina *Limonade* and hope he would be a good boy too and lighten up.

I reminded myself, though, that dead is dead, no matter how you go. With or without lead. If Friegel could help save us, so be it, even if I had to embarrass myself. Even if I had to slightly grovel, and more importantly at that moment, give him the last of my Orangina. But then it was Sunday, a day for kneeling and giving, which inevitably had to follow some heeling—in this case, my own shoes in my face, as I had collapsed in such a twisted way that previous evening.

"Please come in. Make yourself at home," I said graciously.

"This is my home, Mr. Martin. Please remember it. But yes, thank you for asking. Sorry not to say hello. I am feeling all business right now."

Friegel had not even taken his hat or coat off as he sank into the chair, looking like a man who had run three overlapping shifts with no meals and not much of a shave. I could count on it that, as a Swiss detective, he had at least taken a full shower and even used a bit of dental floss.

"Look, Friegel, we know, like you, that this wives' club, whatever plaything they call themselves, are amateurs, even if they seem to be stirring up a bit of a bee's nest among Sarabian politics. They just need to be watched closely enough to prevent them from accidentally stepping on some mines, or other figurative explosives."

"You don't say," Friegel said sarcastically, like I was playing him as a dummy.

"And, of course, in the unusual circumstances that they do, we would appreciate a few hands from your department—even a few to greet one of its members on her return from abroad." I was trying to be modest in request, not only appearances. But I might as well have been pretending to be overdressed—like one of those widows who had opened her drawers to Schmidt.

Friegel looked all too unhappy. He had also seen enough of my disheveled body—and, oh yes, the suite, equally disheveled.

"Really, Martin." Friegel punctuated the stale atmosphere with his highbrow head movements. "We have to be cautious and even presume the worst. We need a lot more information before making any summary judgments whether or not they are at serious risk. And then, we can decide on the dimensions of the security detail for your welcoming committee. On your return from . . . what was it, Barbados?"

"That's quite right," I said quite defensively, waiting for the next shoe to fall off or proverbially, to be thrown or stuck to my face. I had told him nothing about Barbados—the trip there was supposed to be absolutely secret. Only maybe about Miami.

Friegel continued, almost not noting what I had said. He looked like he wanted another Schultz, and only temporarily could I provide him with another one. If I ever had to take on such a personality permanently, I would have preferred the only alternative—suicide. How did those Swiss police supremo subordinates do it?

"So you actually think you deserve a detachment on her arrival back in Zürich? By the way, that is no simple lady. That is Countess Isolde *von und zu* Leuvenstein. Just in case she is . . ."

"Really? Leuvenstein? Where is that—next to Liechtenstein?" I said with mild surprise. Oops, I was out of my Schultzlike character and being plain too noisy and too dumb. I had not known at first that she had a major title, though I had known that she had interesting aristocratic ancestors.

"Look, Pol, I am not here to discuss at length her breeding, and clearly the fact is that we know a few useful things that you do not know. Just the point that we have extra reason not to want anything to happen to her. My superiors would be, let us say to use your American banter, would be 'trashed' if anything did and we were held at fault. So let's have a bit more cooperation so we can be helpful. And of course, there may be a lot more over and above just protecting the Countess."

"Sure, sure, Friegel, peace and goodwill between all law enforcement agencies. How else will we continue to ensure humanity's survival and be successful against fighting terrorists?" My Schultzlike scraping before authority had completely ended. It had lasted all of five minutes, a record for me, excluding Swiss bankers who, for some reason, I couldn't stop bowing down to. Perhaps it was because they still held my investment portfolios, which was as good as holding my balls. That was one way to get respect even from a sometimes insubordinate assassin.

Friegel looked a little uncomfortable. He was also under the collar, underfed, and underpaid, for the weekend, that is. He was also a bit too lost in his own country on one of the most important cases that had come his way. He was trying to act like he knew something important that he largely did not. He was at a loss for even a juicy tidbit.

The coarse American he perceived me to be was not going to provide the full proper support, he uncomfortably sensed. On the other hand, if I did not share enough, he might keep me out of his own loop. Furthermore, he might start to give the Order uncoordinated attention that surely Zen did not want to see from the Swiss police. However, I kind of doubted it. I think I just needed to convince him that I was enough on his side and would not overly compromise him and his department.

"Okay, I'll come fully clean. Look, Friegel, I am already quietly inside the case. I have been able to penetrate this ladies' society by convincing them through one of the ladies to hire me as their security detail. I am acting in a loose way as an Interpol operative—deep undercover, known almost to none at HQ. You could say I am intimately connected and very well trusted by them. The ladies, that is."

Friegel knew the Americans had a lot of initiative, not always of the respect-of-the-rules kind. He probably wondered whether I was another raw, off the farm or reservation type involved in clandestine activity that was going to cause a putrid reaction from his superiors. Another freelance American laying waste to charming, quiet Switzerland.

Maybe he thought we would even eventually fuck his perfect cows, given how he and his countrymen had begun to feel about all the financial, criminal, and political disasters of recent years with an American element to them. Of course, only after milking completely their big financial teats would the Americans and other foreigners leave the Swiss to their peace. So went the cynical Swiss scenario. That was probably what Friegel worried about, along with the whole screwy banker crowd that was his responsibility, too.

It was an old song on a broken record. Tiny Switzerland and not so tiny Friegel could play the good victim when it suited them, as they rapidly counted up the "dirty" money as the belabored script went. If not with a long smile or a flash of one, then with more than basic accounting contentment.

Though to be fair about it, with the exception of my banker friends, Switzerland had increasingly cleaned up a lot of the skulduggery and laundering with the help of people like Friegel, overweight and underpaid, with a lot of flatulence and not much flattery from his chiefs. However, he still stuck to those lamentable lines of that hackneyed script and continued in that vein of a paragon of self-righteous, cool self-pity.

"Look, Martin, where in hell—pardon my language—did you get the authority to run operations in Switzerland without our permission? That is well beyond Interpol's mandate in the international cooperation agreement. You were to let us observe the ladies, but now you've been so deep undercover with them . . . I really don't know what to say. You've broken every rule in the book, running around just about naked and a finger in our face," said poor done-in Friegel.

It was time, however, to slap Friegel around. His sanctimonious anti-Americanisms and holier-than-thou protections of his sacred *milch* cows were getting to me.

"I don't like your innuendo. You know Interpol has the right to do research at an operational level," I belligerently belted out. I would have just rather belted him instead. But this was Switzerland. Oh yes, and he was of the police. I smacked him anyhow with my blazing eyebrows. He fired back highbrow criticisms. How sadly restrained we were, like two misfits in an asylum, straitjacketed and muzzled, trying to communicate anger. I suppose regular Swiss-like, or was that northern European politeness?

Then, he took a turn for the better with his tone—or was that not better for the German Swiss—as he began to show a little passion.

"Research!" said Friegel in a rather loud voice. "We have procedures, and something tells me you are not telling us enough. What research?"

"Okay, okay, all right, I'll come fully clean, but don't ask me to do a 'full Monty.'"

"A what?"

"To strip."

"Oh."

"I am Jean-Claude Carterone, ex-Foreign Legion, a bit of a drunkard and womanizer but excellent ex-mercenary to boot, who kept the famous mercenary Frank Derenard out of trouble and alive. That saved Anglo-Schweitz, the Swiss mining company, more than a pretty copper penny."

"*Fantastish*," said Friegel. "I don't believe it."

"Don't screw with me. I am basically making sure these women do not unnecessarily attract extremists due to what is largely a dog and pony show to improve women's rights in Sarabia. I am fed up with your anti-American moralizing. I and a lot of my colleagues are protecting your holier-than-thou, white cross backsides with our tedious constant watching over the spoiled rich Swiss bitches. They are probably more dangerous to themselves. Probably exaggerating the importance of the package. Remember, they are your women, not ours. So cut me a little slack."

I thought I was nicely faking it to Friegel, making it sound like the Order was a covenant of bitches just to solicit a bit of empathy. Well, not totally faking it.

"Package? Okay, okay, not so touchy," said Friegel, who looked increasingly more unnatural to the surroundings, more like he was in foreign and unfriendly territory without papers. Or with papers like the ones that pups use when they are training. Yeah, Friegel at least looked like he could have wet himself with anxiety if he had been a young canine. But after that crude analogy, it was rude to add in my anger that he was looking for a leg up in life when he should have done his own better job in scrubbing about for correct details. But at least, he then thankfully adopted a holier tone that was more difficult to refuse.

"Okay, Pol, okay. But what can you share with me? I need to know more," said Friegel as he began to look as benign and thoughtful as a Benedictine monk looking for the ultimate answers. Certainly an improvement over his previous incarnation.

"Okay," I responded informally and casually to lighten the holy truths I was about to deliver. And to get him further out of his mad, barking rut.

"They have lucked into a variety of documentation, I gather, that I will get from them to pass onto Interpol when Isolde returns from the Caribbean."

"Okay, go on." Friegel looked like he thought that I might just get nervous feet, so he blocked the door so I would not skedaddle. He should have figured differently, as if being a member of the senior police made him own my hotel suite. I was simply getting nervous in calculating whether what I now wanted to say was a bright move.

"*Herr* Friegel, the higher-ups at Interpol with whom I am in contact will then give the package to you after they have digested it, if that is the appropriate action as it no doubt would be. I'll put in a good word for you, so there may be more chance of you getting a promotion, if not the documentation too. Feeling better?"

I lied a bit, but it was probably a lie that Friegel could deal with, as it more or less represented a kind of return to proper procedures and protocols. And he probably had mixed feelings about getting his hands on the package if it was that hot. We would never let the Swiss or Interpol get those papers. Not in a million years and not for a zillion dollars, I had thought at the time. He now only knew that his people would be in some serious danger, not stationed in the airport for a whim.

"Are you really this J. C. fellow?" said Friegel sheepishly, with a goatlike grin through his goatee.

"Sure am," I said in a mauled southern drawl to show him that I was not totally ticked off. I added, "And a few other people, especially if my mood is downright ugly or I am trying to explain my multiple personalities to my Swiss psychiatrist—or a Swiss detective."

I laughed all the way. We both laughed so hard that if our laughs had been ice sprinters, they would have got gold at the winter Olympics in San Moritz. We would have only slowed and stopped laughing by the time we got to Austria. The Austrians would have insisted.

I had told Friegel about my cover, with a few embellishments, and he did not believe it at first as it sounded so fantastical—at least the part about being a former mercenary in aid of the Swiss. It was, in fact, the

Swiss who had a long history of providing mercenaries, even including those to the Vatican, now simply the Pope's guards. But then Friegel had something to report to his inquiring supervisors if need be, and a further excuse to keep a distance from what he knew instinctively the Order to be—a lot of trouble, best mostly left to the supranational authorities like Interpol.

He would just quietly check out my story with Interpol in the loosest way so as not to create too much of a fuss that might feed back to his command. And he would present the information to his bosses only when everything was solved, or just before everything went to hell. Then he could take his disproportionate credit. Or if chaos broke out, he would arrange for his bosses to be so distant from the case that he would be able to shove blame onto Interpol for not initially briefing the Swiss police sufficiently into having taken enough preventative action. Oh yes, and accuse us of failing to describe the contents of the package (which even I didn't know much about at the time) if he ever found such a protest to be useful.

The Swiss police bureaucrat Friegel would come out shiny. He would have fulfilled his ultimate task: he would protect his above-chain in command. It didn't matter how the situation exactly evolved as long as that important principle was maintained. It seemed like a particularly Swiss tradition to make sure you win no matter which side loses. As an American, who knew nothing about neutrality (though a bit about isolationism), it all made me want to puke.

Even Heinrich (Henry) Metternich, the famous former US Secretary of the Interior and leading foreign affairs expert and pragmatist, was more than occasionally offended by Swiss political diffidence on so many global issues. But not without having a Swiss bank account, too.

I was counting on Friegel as being a low-risk pragmatist. I was happy to have him believe that the document would get to a legitimate law enforcement agency safely, such as Interpol, even if it was not part and parcel of his own organization. And I would still be able to keep him completely unaware of Z5, given his lessened curiosity to want to figure out more about me. Z5 would have been unforgiving if I did not keep Friegel from knowing who actually employed me.

To any agent who revealed the nature of Z5 to those who were not on the need-to-know, there was a simple answer for such a blunder. They knew they would be terminated summarily, and possibly so would those who had been informed of its existence. It was as clear as daylight when one signed on that one's loyalty was well beyond a regular nondisclosure agreement.

One thing for sure, though. I was not going to let myself look uncooperative to the police if chaos broke loose with something untoward happening to a member of the Order. I wasn't going to be the last little-known-about man standing with a pitchfork on any homicide crime scene, trying to say that I was just there for the ride. Getting Friegel on my side would help get me further in the good books with the Swiss police and provide added protection against future problems. Or would it?

However you looked at it, Zen would not get me to be a patsy for a total mess-up—or the police, a fall guy if things got too messy. At least, not if I had anything to say about it. For all I knew, Zen had standing orders under seal and delay to terminate the entire Order if things really went bad—perish the thought—and blame it on sucker me. Somebody else would have to play that role of being responsible for a giant screwup or blowup from whatever side it came. However, Friegel's attitude, and the usual distance that Zen and Interpol had kept from me and the Order, were reminders that there were not any enthusiastic volunteers around to be held accountable for a major calamity. That was the worry.

THIRTEEN

Prince Bashard had a lot to say to his own Wall Street princes. His mood was like a dust devil—the swirling hot and abrasive tornadolike winds of the desert, gyrating sometimes so violently that they looked like they could lift a car. This one went across the room in the form of harsh words in a twister of hostile harangue.

"I do not understand how a mainstream Manhattan bank in which Sarabia has invested fifteen billion American dollars is almost ready to be taken over by the Federal Deposit Insurance Corporation (FDIC). And possibly in weeks."

"We're kind of confused too," said one of his downcast business lieutenants.

"Even after an original bailout by the American government in partnership with Sarabian Sovereign Holdings a number of years back. This will not only render our investment into nothing. It will make me the laughingstock of my kingdom."

His executives looked further downcast, as if they were preparing for a Sarabian-style execution on the block. They would have never thought in their lives that they would be so humbled by a foreign owner from a nation once equated in the American media as being a "sand-dune collective" with jumped-up Bedouin herders who had more money than sense. And an owner from a country that was almost on the hate list of a lot of the American public. Yes, his American lieutenants had sunk very low in so many ways in their own eyes.

"You are a disgrace!" Bashard nearly screamed out. "My cousins, as well as no lesser than the king himself, were encouraged to put huge sums into this institution. And based on your analysis of the bank's inordinate potential for growth!"

"We are truly sorry about how things have worked out," the two bayed and sweated before the master. "But . . ."

Bashard was having little to do with excuses, so he interrupted. "And I gave them my personal assurances at the very desert tent, the sacred ground on which our family prays. Where we make our most solemn promises. I'm screwed. Practically a dead man, unless we can turn this around."

Chad Pincer, Chief Executive Officer, MANCITC Bank, did not know what to say further. He had done everything to raise additional capital through new rights offerings, and cut the legs out from under the short sellers who had fomented panic on the bank's stock. Finally, he had even cut staff by the thousands—more than ever done in the bank's history. All of this despite high-powered senators from New York begging him to delay such decisions. One of them had powerful friends on the board of the FDIC, which already did not much like the idea of so much Sarabian interest in MANCITC. Senator Brenda Fether of Westchester County, a former Madison Avenue executive, seemed out for MANCITC executive blood, and was already sick of their lack of progress in hiring more women executives, which she blamed on Bashard.

The second crisis (or was that the third major economic one?) had been partly brought on by the 10/11 terrorist bombing, which had taken place years after the 9/11 catastrophe. That economic meltdown had generated outrageous levels of unemployment. The US government statistics bureau had kept on fudging the figures to try to placate the growing mobs, who wanted the heads of bankers like Chad. And especially politicians like Fether, times two, who seemed powerless to get the bankers to clean up their act. Wall Street's loss math was turning highly ugly again on those who had already bailed it out for amounts nearing almost trillions of dollars by way of the so-called good senator from New York.

"Yes, of course," stated Pincer, who initially tried to divert responsibility. "We are flabbergasted at how badly the economy has been managed by the US federal government. We apologize for not fully recognizing the extent and implications of this second, and now a coming third, meltdown. We certainly thought everything was looking much better after a good number of quarters of growth, a rise in the stock market, and a major recapitalization. Just about everybody thought things were looking much better. Except that perennial doomster lady, Meribeth Wesler, and that eccentric academic Raul Bimi. But who would have ever thought they really knew? . . . But yes, we accept responsibility."

The best way to a Sarabian ruler's heart after a major screwup, even if largely created by the same ruler, is through massive confessionals by a subordinate for the whole imbroglio. Pincer, having worked for the Prince for a long time, knew this assuaging groveling tactic well, and had almost mastered it to refinement in order to prevent his early retirement on more than one occasion.

"Yes, we all screwed up, except of course, M. W., whom we refer to as that 'angry lady.' Sorry, we thought she had a weird fixation against male bankers. We just assumed that she got lucky on calling the first bank meltdown. So, we dismissed her."

The Prince more calmly responded now that he could play the position of being nobly humble by assuming the guilt of his team. He slowed his finger motions down, visibly sliding along his worry beads, those traditional soothers that many Sarabian businessmen carried with them everywhere, especially when unsettled. Though they had been explained to me as a positive exercise instrument and nothing else when I had asked my students about them.

"Okay, Chad, what do we do now?" asked Bashard, looking more glum than when learning recently of the passing away of his brother in a terrorist attack in the south. A loss of a brother was a terrible thing, but MANCITC dead could lead to the loss of the kingdom to the fanatics who had despised every last dollar the Sarabian government invested in America. Who had also protested every single *hallal* (equivalent to a quarter cent of a US dollar) put into American stocks. Given the repercussions of the bank's demise, Bashard could not appear that he was not going to go down fighting for MANCITC's survival—at least at this stage. It could draw too much suspicion to his more important agenda.

These desert extremists despised the monarchy to the point that what the Russian Revolution had done to the Romanoffs would look petite compared to what they envisaged for the Sarabs, the family after which the kingdom had been named. And a collapse of the kingdom's economy because of such poor investments in the West, including too many holdings in fast-depreciating American dollars, would fan the political flames as social programs and *zakah* (charity) were cut from the lesser well-off. The junior princes, who listed in the thousands, would be boiling over if their stipends were sliced even slightly due to such financial blunders made in the land of the so-called infidels.

"Prince Bashard, this is critical. Unless we come up with up to twenty-five billion dollars, we cannot be sure that another more thorough meltdown crisis in the market and the economy will not wipe out our shareholders, and other creditors too. We are looking through the gates of Armageddon to a tsunami of massive economic collapse. The real one this time."

"Right, Chad," said the Prince, who tried to seem sympathetic, knowing that there was only so much his people could be responsible for and predicting. "There are a good number of friends, including you, with major stakes; and *Insha'Allah,* we can do something."

"Yes, timing is critical, Prince," Chad continued. "The new US administration is full of monetary hawks, who blame the previous administration for throwing so much money around that they created impending stagflation. The banking bailout fund won't be renewed this time by the government."

"Chad, how much time before the bank goes down the tube? What about the FDIC? What's their true present position?"

"The FDIC is threatening us with near imminent takeover, and Treasury basically wants us to sell off the most profitable remaining parts. If we did, then we might as well be a Canadian beaver under attack."

"What do you mean?" The Prince lightened up a slight bit to what he saw as a bizarre analogy promising interesting and well-timed comic relief. He would be rewarded.

"They eat their balls to assuage their predators."

Prince Waheed almost fell off his chair. Once again, Chad had delivered his delightful ballsy humor known so well by Texans, which the Prince had learned to appreciate in his college days in the Lone Star state.

"And Jesus—excuse my language!"

"That's okay, Chad. We're friends here."

"The congressional hawks are not going to allow major FDIC deposit protection for wealthy accounts. Our best customers are jumping ship by the boatloads."

"That's very bad news. I wonder how long before it becomes widely public." Bashard's beads were being twisted back and forth violently as he spoke.

The diminished but not surrendering CEO responded, "I think we still have a bit of time on this. It's a massive warning shot across the bow. The FDIC with their time line is trying to speed us to action. Not destroy us—I hope!"

"Right, I understand." Bashard was now trying to look wiser, reflective, and more under control.

Chad elaborated. "The US government actually wants us to come through with additional reserves against any future disasters as well as this immediate one. They are worried that if we fall, we might set off a domino collapse of the economy. Too many undefined counterparties, too many worries about massive amounts of unknown trillion dollars of derivatives wrongly positioned in which we have participated. Even sovereign wealth funds and, unbelievably, the US Treasury are on the wrong side to an extent. The new banking legislation has not had enough of a positive effect on stopping the bleeding."

"Okay, Chad. I know all this. These highly leveraged funds can bankrupt holders or issuers of them within days if anything negative happens too quickly. Yes, I believe a great wise investor in the United States referred to them as financial weapons of mass destruction. And to think my country has been more worried by Israeli nukes or Tyranian and Waristani ones. Ha, that financial wizard, Louis de Cyro, was right about derivatives being more dangerous than Israel on the brink! And we are still holding huge amounts of the wrong ones."

"Prince, let me reiterate that there are no more bullets from the government and no more political capital left to bail out a major Wall Street bank," said the increasingly sweaty Pincer.

"This is really worse than I thought. I've got to tell the king to buy a lot more gold than I recommended."

"I don't know about that, Prince."

"No, that wouldn't make up for this mountain of shit shares of MANCITC. But if our bank goes down, we're all screwed, even in much of the Middle East. We've got four hundred and fifty billion dollars of reserves still left in US dollars that we haven't or can't dump. And China's got much more. There will be a run on the dollar. What the heck is wrong with those political hawks? They're the real fanatics!"

"There's another problem in figuring out our time line."

"Go on, Chad. It's all right. My heart can take it even if not my wallet."

Bashard knew the Americans, for now, had a few aces in the trenches to ensure the Sarabians and their neighbors would remain interested in digging them out of the hole. Like the military protection that prevented invasions from their neighbors, such as the Tyranians, who had a much more massive army than Sarabia's.

"Having any extra time also depends on there not being an accelerated run on the bank's deposits, particularly from our larger clients. Though the very big money is not in current account deposits, so they can't liquidate their holdings immediately in a good number of cases. We have thirty days on a number of those."

The Prince looked reflectively to the ceiling, but he would have likely preferred to have been outside his tent looking at the stars for an answer. Finally he said, "Sounds like the end of the world if Sarabia doesn't come to the rescue. Ironic, isn't it? We, the chastised evildoers because a few terrorists from our country bombed Americans. And twice, believe it or not. Now we're in a position to be the saviors. Well, at least, maybe."

"So the upshot, Prince, is if we can come up with a sizable chunk of money, we could buy ourselves additional time until the economy takes better hold. Without it, we're all doomed. One view is that not even the IMF could pull America out of this hole with all its existing obligations once MANCITC goes down," added Pincer.

Bashard paced nervously up and down. The best of his plans were turning into a giant quicksand hole. It reminded him of the way so many of his kids and their friends' SUVs had been swallowed up in the red desert sands, not far outside Raddah. Brazen confidence that the natural dangers were for others, not in their time. It was infantile, or at least like irresponsible teenager behavior, like an indulgence that reminded him of his grandfather, who had lost three hundred million dollars one night at a casino in Macau without even having bought it before he placed his mammoth bets. Fortunately, Bashard had obtained the casino instead, thereby saving the kingdom zillions and saving the monarchy, for which he was rewarded well afterward in becoming a high-level steward of the country's funds. But maybe his bet on MANCITC would become a greater folly of a venture. It could make his grandfather look like a piker of a gambler compared to Bashard. And there would be no one to bail him out, but more likely someone to chop his head off.

At another time, he would have practically wished such a financial curse on America. His ancestors centuries before had fought off murderous Western crusaders, who had butchered his people with as much compunction as an ant exterminator. Now, again, he felt a certain kind of defeat, but this time by the hands and weapons of Wall Street. The short sellers and speculative hoards—a good number of whom had financed Israel against his fellow Arabs—were not going to play him as a patsy. But possibly, he eventually would have a big lesson to give them that was still up his sleeve. However, it was not quite yet ready to be implemented. MANCITC sinking right away could be a disaster to his plans and his power base. But in weeks, maybe days, it might be his so-called pleasure.

"Look, gentlemen," he said, with a slight turn of his cunning lips that he tried to suppress. "To restore confidence in the bank, a major investment will have to be made. No doubt about that one, Chad."

"Clearly," said Chad, with his fellow bank executive, Jock, too full of canapés to say anything. Yet, he was quite able to get in a nod of approval that seemed larger than usual with his cheeks puffed up with food. In the Prince's eye for detail, that represented the final subordination.

"Look, those regulators at Treasury and the Securities and Exchange Commission got on me and my cousin's tail last time when we tried to initially own no more than about 10 percent of the stock. Not only that, but they made it abundantly clear that they did not want the Sarabians to have too much control of American banks."

"I think times are a *changin*—probably they won't be so paranoid given their desperation."

Jock and Chad were down to their last financial pail of American pride, and so was the US government if it was not very careful as to how it handled this emergency.

"I hope so," said Bashard. "These bastards set both the FBI and CIA on me, and practically put me on the terrorist list. And pretty damn close on the no-fly list. However, Chad, I think it may be the time that I will be able to increase our sovereign holdings in MANCITC by a worthwhile level, where I can begin to exercise more control over our investments. What do you think, Jock? You're our Chief Financial Officer. You surely have some idea?"

"Prince, the dollar is so banged up and so few will touch the banks, not even the insurance companies that backed them up in the past with credit default swaps. I think regulators will probably acquiesce, as long as you don't replace the board with all of your own people. Especially from Sarabia or thereabout."

Jock coughed nervously. The last point was bordering on being indelicate, and also a further reinforcement of the discrimination that Bashard had continuously faced as he tried to increase his control and presence on corporate boards in America.

"Right, gentlemen, I'm not sure they are going to let Sarabia—or should I say, Sarabian Sovereign Holdings, along with other Sarabians—directly take control of the second largest US bank. I say this even if your country were at risk of turning into camel dung."

"Okay," said Chad, earnestly broadening his torso with the bravado of an old matador wondering whether he still had the magic to stay in the ring and drive the bulls his way, and survive. "We were also thinking that we could set up a foundation in Panama under the apparent control of a big-time American investor, who will be strictly under your orders through a number of secret, but legal, protocols. We would provide the money."

"You mean Sarabia, or through Sarabia, will have the real control and provide the money?" The Prince was reinforcing his position and making clear that no money was to go directly to a third party without control of the voting shares being put into Sarabian-controlled structures that would effectively override what appeared to be a secret kind of so-called blind trust.

"Yes, of course, Prince. We can also communicate in various codes so as to reduce any risks. You already effectively own a Panamanian bank, where such trusts could be set up," stated Jock.

"That's Banco San Diego, isn't it?" Bashard occasionally had a few problems remembering all the exact names of the assets he controlled, given their huge numbers and sprawl.

"Yes, San Diego," Jock confirmed.

"But what about a *Stiftung in* Leuvenstein?" added the Prince.

"You remember the bank employee who sold the list of secret accounts at Leuvenstein Landesbank to the German government and disappeared?"

"Oh, right. Yes, I see what you mean, Jock. Excellent point."

"Right!" said Chad as he took back control of the conversation. "Management is dependable there at San Diego. Unfortunately, there was some scandal recently about a missing package of one of their depositors . . ."

"But . . . Chad, let's move on from that one," interjected Bashard. "It is being satisfactorily taken care of from what I heard. Not an important matter, and I insist you forget about it so that we can focus on more important things."

Bashard said it with a very relaxed and quick smirk. But his overall body language was less relaxed. He knew of the great gravity of the thefts at Banco San Diego if the whole matter were made public. And he knew his own people had run the thieves to the safety deposit box, not too good publicity for a bank. Not very good at all.

"Yes, sorry about all that," Bashard further continued. "Yes, let's move on. I'm sure large money transfers with all the proper records can be handled by Diego. But I had better personally make sure of the details, and the execution of the transfers."

Jock intervened, partly to defend his territory and to reinforce to the Prince how indispensable he was. Chad had even indicated that his presence at the meeting was not that necessary. That was a signal that he was on a slippery slope to career irrelevancy at the bank, especially with all the turmoil in the market and staff cuts. It was now his magic moment to intervene, Jock thought.

"Chad, that sounds great about moving new funds, but given the amount of funds, I think we had better move them in smaller multimillion-dollar bundles from a diversity of offshore accounts and locations. Maybe we need a lot of foundations, so as to make people think there are not too many shares concentrated in one institutional holder's hands, as they get rapidly soaked up on the market. So we'll need more than one third party, so to speak, as vehicles for secretly buying the shares."

"Right, but Jock, are you sure? I suppose our legal people would probably advise it. I'll see what they say but . . . What would your opinion be, Prince?"

Chad was the CEO for a reason. He had feigned support for his CFO, who had been a longtime competitor for the top job. He had known that Jock would come up with something that was too legally complex for an emergency. He then turned to the Prince, who he knew hated bureaucratic processes and lawyers, not necessarily in that order.

"Oh, for Heaven's sake, leave the lawyers out of any major decisions on this one. Or at least limit their involvement. We'll never get it done by the time they identify all the risks and carry out the full paperwork."

"If that's what you think best . . . but we should protect ourselves," said Jock.

"You mean protect yourselves. I have diplomatic immunity, and last time I checked, there were no extradition treaties between Sarabia and the United States—except for certain terrorists."

Chad and Jock looked stony-faced and depressed. They had already seen two friends of theirs in close banking circles go to jail for advising the use of tax havens in very fishy ways, to permit foreign control of certain major US corporations and to avoid huge taxes. And more importantly, to ensure their own institutions' survival. Pretty tame punishments were carried out on their friends of a less than a year in jail and hundred thousand dollar fines, compared to judgments on similar crimes taking place after the "Big Meltdown"—also referred to as the *Big Melty* of 2008. That wasn't exactly a parallel situation, but it had the smell of it. And the media could add a charge of greed and unpatriotic selfishness to Chad and Jock, even if they were not charged initially by the authorities for doing anything wrong.

The American public was in no mood to support any smell of illegal dealings from Wall Street bankers on behalf of any of their Sarabian friends—or anyone for that matter. GAG (the New York investment bank), famous for its financial overreach referred to as "Goldilocks' follies," was a living, breathing example of how public hate would make legal protection of a bank irrelevant. And eventually cause executive terminations, or even lead a number of their executives to flee from America, by using second passports they had obtained from nonextradition countries.

"Relax, gentlemen, I'm just joking. I'm Sarabian. We don't leave our friends hung out to dry in the middle of the desert. We're not two-faced Anglo Saxons. Besides, where would we find the trees to do it with? *Insha'Allah*, I'd smuggle you out in my executive jet and put you in my compound. Just before the closing of the embassy. And what an exciting life you would live in exile given our impeccable hospitality. No, I would be human, let you get off in the *Big Comfy* in Zürich!"

Everyone laughed, but it was a muffled chuckle that seemed to eat away at Chad's and Jock's insides, though a bit more color had come back to their faces. The Prince was occasionally a bit of a bully playing on his employees' prejudices against Sarabia.

"I can see the panic in the short sellers' faces," said Jock, "when the new money comes in massively to buy up the new share offerings and existing floating shares at a premium."

"Jock, who do we deal with in Panama to pretend to front the money?" asked Bashard, already knowing the answer but looking for confirmation.

"Barney Rob in Panama would be our principal man. I gather he will be one of our fronts whom they will eventually—I mean in months, if not a year's time—find out. How about a little PR with Chad and me pleading to him what a fine investment MANCITC is for his organization and how the bank has been grateful for his idea of coordinating the rescue with the cash? These media people will eventually get the story, but with a big bad twist added to it if we're not proactive." Jock had unknowingly once again given somewhat questionable advice.

"Right," continued Chad, trying to look as if he were being cooperative with his CFO. "That's after he goes beyond the SEC 3 percent limit, when he will be essentially forced to declare that it is himself making a huge infusion into MANCITC. Legally, a Panamanian foundation could be structured without anyone knowing who the owners are. But practically and functionally forget it."

Jock added, "Yes, a nosey freelance journalist wanting to turn himself into a Bob Woodward would find out. And if the US government wasn't told, they could put a monkey wrench into everything. Though who knows? Under the pressure of revealing the true ownership against the deadline of saving the bank, we might not have to say anything. Including that it was essentially Sarabia upping its stake and almost completely taking over the bank for now. Anyway, not the kind of brinkmanship to be played for too long. At a certain critical point, the real change in ownership will have to be known."

"Thanks for that, Jock, but any public announcement of a pact with Barney would just inject too much suspicion at this point," said the Prince, with a negative reflex action against any unnecessary publicity of himself in America. A reflex action like a child who had once placed its whole hand on the burner and got stuck with the whole apparatus, and did not want to have a repeated experience.

"Chad," said Bashard, "I think it might be better to lowball these investments, and slowly build up market momentum to a point that others will create additional market force, with the shorts running for cover. It would save Sarabia a good deal of money, as well. Then, possibly we wouldn't have to let the nice Mr. Rob get too much control of MANCITC, even if he was just holding proxy votes so to speak. And ones we couldn't immediately grab back, if we didn't want to risk making a big public stink if Barney got any bright ideas to play God with all that pretend new control. I think, though, he would not do that to an old fellow ranch hand like me. You get my overall drift?"

"Plenty enough. Yeah, I suppose Rob could vote in a lot of his own directors theoretically, but I don't think he would want to. He might get his head sliced off," stated Chad.

Bashard laughed. "Now you're talking my kind of turkey." Everybody chuckled, but Chad's and Jock's bodies didn't. They were on the corporate chopping block if anything went wrong with this massive deal that would put any financier on edge. No wonder their bodies were erect, but that was all that would be for quite some time as the deal was nervously played out. Neither their Viagra nor their wives' best lingerie would help them reduce the stress over such crises.

However, Chad generally loved these strategy sessions with Bashard, who was a brilliant maneuverer. As generally a no-frill Texan, he loved seeing the smooth Ivy League, Harvard-*MBAed* Wall Street executives being interrupted for prayers by the Prince, who took his prayer carpet everywhere he went. Chad and Jock were religious men, too. But they tried to keep it to Sunday church between rounds of golf or a rodeo roundup. If they didn't make money for the Prince, they knew it didn't matter which God they bowed to.

Bashard added his timely, sharp, clear views, which demonstrated his lateral thinking, at least financially. "I would also suggest you invest in Baldson, Diamond Jamison Trust, Fifty-Philth, Goldilock, Nomoore Bank, Zioness, and other prominent Wall Street banks, as there will likely be spillover from these new MANCITC investments. Hopefully, no meltdown potential with those, except possibly Nomoore. Keep it below the threshold 3 percent, to keep regulators and the market at bay from snooping around and putting the dots together. I don't think they'll be able to pin insider trading on us. We'll put those secondary share purchases through my cousins in Hong Kong and Singapore, where regulators would again ask fewer questions about Sarabian investment intentions. New York is becoming just too regulated. And London is getting very bad press recently—even threatened with jihad, I heard from a sheik in the Pharoahsan Islands. Strangely, also a part-time herder of dwarf antelope."

While Jock and Chad saw a lot of new red for the Prince, Bashard thought he could see his new longer-term vision unwinding to his benefit due to the current MANCITC calamity being deferred and synchronized with a wide swath of dramatic, future negative disasters. He had always been a master of taking chaos and turning it into new capital, financial or otherwise. If Sarabia was not now thoroughly controlling Wall Street, it would eventually be in a premier position to provide enormous leverage for any coming projects in America, he would tell the council of Sarabian elders. Bashard would be sure that they got full credit for the new investments in the bank, and at the right time.

The elders were dedicated to building many new mosques in the big cities like Chicago, Houston, Los Angeles, and New York, for which the king had given his blessing—albeit with the provision that it be done with full sensitivity to local interests, as well as to larger concerns by the American establishment. With these new deals, Sarabian-based elements would eventually become almost integral parts of the American establishment. Even if the establishment would not know of it, at least until it was too late.

Yes, something good could come out of this mess after all, Bashard thought to himself. At a minimum, taking control of MANCITC and its expressed resulting benefits would be sold to the king and his advisors this way, as further insurance against America turning Sarabia into an Iraq or worse. The king would appreciate the discrete and steady way in which it would be done with low risk. He would appreciate that the Americans would likely not refuse the deal, even if it came out in the open, given the current economic crisis.

Texas would be next as a hotbed for ramping up Sarabian sovereign fund presence in America and Sarabian political involvement. The Prince enjoyed such a thought, as he was almost committed to a variety of Texan hospitality—the ones well removed from the downtowns, the prancing ballerinas, and the nouveau riche-new museum galas. How he detested the pretentious new Texan wealthy, who would not know an oil well from a colt nor have an iota of an idea how to tame both of them if they were wild. As Bashard reflected, it all reminded him of the younger generation in his own family, who had gotten sloppy and, indeed, had turned into slobs in certain cases. Occasionally, he felt a greater kinship with those of his age or older who lived off the plains of Texas than with some of his own younger, westernized kin.

Prince Bashard would have to draw up the instructions for the operations of the Panamanian foundation in what was referred to as "Code One." It was only known to his most trusted advisers, his most inner Sarabian financial circles. Now, he would have to share it with Rob's inner group. No matter, he must have thought to himself, as events of more earth-shattering proportions would soon be set in motion. They would be moving so quickly that such ciphers would be rendered moot and unimportant in a few months. In fact, Code One was in the southern Arabian dialect of his mother's mother, who had secretly taught it to him when he was a young boy. Even admitting knowing or teaching it would have got one branded as a heretic in the old days.

"Okay, we'll deal with Barney Rob to get things going," said Chad in his Texan drawl, a drawl that the Prince himself had also picked up in his stint working for a Texan oil company and taking studies at Eastern Texas State, where all his friends would joke with him and call him "Bastard." Now, it was mostly his politician and businessmen enemies who called him that—a long list, but which would be getting shorter, Bashard thought to himself with all smiles.

There were old grudges he carried from his college days. He still had a list of them mixed in with other targets. They would have to ask for his mercy, the ones that would be unlucky enough to still be alive and would be summoned before the tent that he would moor just outside Dallas when the time was right.

The weekend warrior boozing, the anti-Arab sentiment, and just plain racism had driven him crazy at times at Eastern Texas. Only the intervention of his uncle, ambassador to the United States, along with his rancher friends had made him stay until his English was good enough to even impress the people he liked the most, the ranch hands and ranchers. They had been damn impressed with the way he could ride a wild stallion better than anybody on the spread.

In fact, no one except himself had been able to deal with the wild spirits of the free-spirited horses. A few ranchers said that his eyes looked wilder than those of the horses he had broken in. Especially to the ones that seemed hell-bent to stay unconverted to his lashings with his reins and digging in with his boots in a strange manner, intermixed with praise when the horses gave way to what seemed to be more like bizarre punishment than good ridership. None of the Texans exactly understood his methods, but there was full agreement that they worked.

These cowboys had taken affection to Bashard, even as they cursed how Sarabia as an oil cartel coleader had effectively made gasoline prices ridiculously expensive. But the ranchers forgave him and his country for those price spikes, because oil was the economic lifeblood of Texas. High oil prices made for the state having one of the lowest state taxes. Bashard teased them mercilessly and called their governor a "*taxaholic*." He reminded them that Sarabia had no income tax. That impressed the hell out of his rancher friends, too.

What really impressed Bashard was that his friends liked to quote the Old Testament and refer back to Abraham and his sense of justice—whom his faith referred to as Ibrahim, a main prophet. Good old Ibrahim had built his temple on the holy land of Sarabia where the giant black square *Kaaba* stood, around which millions of Muslims exclusively did their circumambulations. Bashard never let his rancher friends forget that, too.

When a new execution was ordered in Texas for a serial killer, they would look with mutual satisfaction, knowing that Texas was also the land of Abraham. Bashard's Texas rancher friends never bothered him one iota about Sarabia's human rights policies. After he carried out his wider plan, he wondered whether almost anyone would, in America, at least of those who counted in power. Yes, Texas and a number of Texans would be useful in his new holy campaign, he hoped. But first, he had other advance troops in his broader sinister scheme that would make the purchase of MANCITC bank look *piddly*.

FOURTEEN

In Panama, William von Drax was to be my disguise number three—no, correction, number four. I was getting so confused to the point that I thought for a moment, under influence of a good Corona, that I had no real name anymore—stripped of having my own personality other than what Z5 thought convenient for the job. Such professional dedication was mostly known to Hollywood actors. Of particular interest were those who had played Mafia dons, but who still were lost in their past roles as they ordered an execution of their new directors. I would need to have my own act fully together, though, to deal with our own coming adventures.

There were definitely dangers with such a reduced level of personal identity as a result of being absorbed with one's own special vocation—in my case, as an assassin. I was getting to be a full house even for a psychiatrist specializing in personality disorder. Wouldn't that be nice, if I found my life had been simply a dream of too many occupants in the house of human fantasy? How long, I wondered, could I maintain control with this kind of lifestyle? And if I lost it, I feared I would put Isolde and the Order in jeopardy, especially if we were in a life-and-death struggle.

However, I had been reassured by Zeel Foundation's Biggart that nothing was beyond the good therapy of Dr. Heimlich, Banque Suisse's resident psychiatrist for its customers who Z5 had under secret contract.

Unfortunately, Heimlich was considered a bit of a standing joke in the profession, as having overly backward methods for BS's sore, money-losing clients. They had choked upon seeing their full losses, and no therapy seemed to be enough to calm them regarding their new status in finances. Heimlich had simply told me to go on a long vacation. Hopefully, that had not meant he thought I was a hopeless case.

Nevertheless, the flight from Zürich had been on schedule. The change in itinerary to have us come through this US transit point on the way to Panama City had been late in the planning. Of course, there was actually no transit in the United States. All the bags and passengers had to come off and be reprocessed through security and customs. A real pain in the butt and especially other parts of the body being used to move heavy luggage, making the United States one of the few big countries insisting on welcoming all, including those who had no interest in staying.

For Isolde, this unique inconvenience was almost made up for by having experienced the best first-class service that the Swiss airlines' double-decker provided her in the upper section: champagne, Michelin star-rated food, Internet, and a lot of recent movie releases, which had just come into American theaters. And a first-class suite with access to showers and a spa, as well as a private lounge.

Meanwhile, in the lower deck, I had elbowed around a very large brute of a passenger, who reminded me of one of the frontliners of the Nationalist football team. The food was generally okay, but the champagne was unavailable along with the Internet. I was too happy to get off the long flight; I knew then what it was to be a sardine escaped from a can. In fact, I think I had happily escaped eating a rather sad one in my salad. Yeah, the fish that had gotten away, me and him, though at least I was still alive, though barely, after my experience with flight economy.

We had been booked into one of those resorts that were blocked off from fishmongers and hawkers to the slums, not so far down from central Panama City. Or it was supposed to be choked off, but there was a whole lazy, sultry, and disconsolate feeling about this area. It was as if the divisions between the so-called uncivilized destitute and the rich could not be so easily separated, given the overwhelming amount of poverty and social desperation. Or possibly, not so easily detached, given that some of the rich were nouveau riche, whose wealth came from local or international *gangstering* that they had not been so long away from. Whose poorer associates from past days were not so willing to be left behind.

Those nasty things like tax avoidance scamming and public theft had become sanitized into tax management and private wealth enhancement at the heavenly and divine *bancos* of the San Diego that were favorites for this new up-and-coming establishment. Yes, it was certainly hard to separate the dirt and the sleaze of a number of those in the penthouse apartments from those in the gutter. No, maybe the gutter was better than being associated with this upwardly ignoble lot. Well, when you didn't have to sleep in it, as I had to when I had refused a hand up from a bagman. He had wanted a political contribution that I found to be too high—one cent or more. And strangely, he had wanted much more.

On the very lower side of the social ledger were the very destitute: they were descendants of tribes from the western highlands who had migrated into urban squalor. Then there were the great lumps of white "trash," including more of the organized gangs, more of the ruthless kind. They needed money badly, and they knew where the money was. They would get it even if they had to use a pole vault into your stomach, or overhead to leap buildings and every kind of fence.

Not all the guards were so diligent in keeping these kinds of desperadoes away from the kind of luxury hotels at which Isolde and I would stay. They sometimes had a stake in it. If they did not cooperate in letting certain criminals in, they might be accidentally put into a police cell and beaten, because they breathed on a copper on the beat or had not tied their shoes straight. Or other phony excuses that also made up for not filling their monthly police quotas on reported misdemeanors or crimes, because real police work had been too up the chain of intelligence for some of these dropouts.

However, Panama was also a country that always had a sense of great promise and much old heritage relative to the Americas, along with enormous diversity of wildlife, emerald water, and jeweled beaches of smooth coral sand. A stunning beauty in places, above the grime and grease of excessive urban poverty and more than occasional corruption.

The Casa Viejo, a very old and quaint elegant quarter, was one of those splendors. A true classic gem anywhere in Latin America. Its cathedrals were put up centuries ago, with the full Spanish colonial stamp of towering and muscular neo-Gothic structures. Dark, shadowy, and sometimes dirtied by fungal decay, they also had subtle Moorish crenate lines and decorations in their architectural touches.

After all, the Moors had occupied Europe, though primarily settling through Spain and southern France. They maintained control in parts of the main continent up to the very late 1400s, leaving an architectural legacy as well as a cultural and linguistic one. They had finally been driven out of Europe and replaced with a supposedly devout royalty-Roman Catholic alliance. That alliance had established one of the most vicious and unjust religious tribunals in the annals of history, known as the Spanish Inquisition. Sadly, it had made it to the colonies, too.

It had been a time when church spires represented to the heathen the fires on which they were burned at the stake, all with the tribunal blessings that their souls would be cleansed through the Pyrrhic processes. It had been a frightening period for both Islam and Judaism, both more moderate and tolerant than much of Christendom in those times. At least according to many liberal scholars of religion.

Interestingly, the church belfries in one of the cathedrals in the Viejo had been imported all the way from Toledo, the capital city of the inquisitors. That city was famous for the gloomy, omnipresent, and somber dark canvas by El Greco, painted during the peak days of ecclesiastical torture. The church's large Panamanian bells were also inlaid with pearl and cast in gold alloy so as to affect a soft chime. That softness must have been lost on the burning unfaithful.

Speaking of gold, those were also the days of the great Panamanian, Peruvian, and Mexican silver and gold transfers that were never to be replicated again for their dominance in the holds of ships leaving Latin America. Even today's US federal reserves do not currently contain the amount of gold that came out of Latin America in those religiously fundamentalist days. All these precious metals from Latin America would have outweighed the silver stored in the vaults below present-day Zürich.

It was argued by a number of activist researchers at Stafford University's economic crime history program that at least 5 to 10 percent of all Swiss gold and silver had their origins in sixteenth—to nineteenth-century Latin America. These findings were supported by a Central American charity funded by the Zeel Foundation. The Costa Rica-based Mother Lode Society was looking into the political and legal means to restoring this Swiss-held wealth to the original natives, who were living today in grinding poverty. This was another headache that Stihl, my banker, had groaned to me about in a quest for his own victimhood.

It was also said by certain Panamanian mediums, including Hector Vizioni, that Aztec spirits roamed those very underground golden corridors of Banque Suisse and other Zürich banks. And that one day the Aztec curse would somehow wreak its vengeance on those depositories. One Zürich banker I knew had actually brought in a Mexican shaman, given how worried his wife's psychic was about impending doom. But months after that warning, all seemed to be calm in the city. Or was it simply the lull before the doom?

Panamanian and other Latin American banks, in a sense, were precursors to the Swiss as recipients of a gross infamy of huge wealth, a stripping away of the Incan, Mayan, and Aztec gold and silver heritage by the hundreds of tons and thousands of delicately engraved works of art. These ancient indigenous civilizations had been ravished by the conquistadors and nearly completely destroyed in the name of religious fanatics with the blessings of European money interests. And not to forget that certain members of the Spanish royalty had been coconspirators. Though the current crowned heads had given generously to the Mother Lode Society as an attempt at partial restitution.

Yet Latin American banks had not been, and likely would never be, seriously requested to return wealth the way their Swiss brethren had been officially convinced to do in the case of Jewish money in dormant Swiss accounts, owned by those killed in concentration camps—or money stolen from Jews by the Nazis and deposited in Zürich. The indigenous people of Panama and the nearby region would need to become more empowered. The records of theft clearer. The beneficiaries more visibly defined. And a global outrage more profound.

*   *   *

Against this interesting but sometimes sweltering and sleazy history of grand thefts, massacres, and current social decay, I was supposed to meet Isolde at the Boaco Loco luxury hotel. I was to act like a high-flyer playboy looking for wealthy women. I remember my silly line, "We beach bums should play together, even the aristocratic ones." My deadpan face on its utterance received at first only a chilly welcome. She had not recognized me under my elegant and broad-rimmed Panama hat, as well as large-frame Ray-Ban glasses.

My Hawaiian-style shirt, with seahorses on the open seas pulling no other than the British queen in a floating chariot, was enough to make me as attractive to Isolde as a British colonial lout with fashion gout. I should have instead checked in with one of those famous Panamanian tailors and come out a new man. This shirt's redeeming feature was due to the great height of its previous occupant; it nicely hid the buttresses creeping out from my near-invisible Speedo. It was something my aristocratic friend had grabbed at the last minute off one of those racks, a prêt-a-porter. Brought to me by the same pal who had also lent me his title for this trip.

He was out of York, England. It had been a Norman title. One that was happily a relatively obscure one, at least that's what I had thought. It had only been authenticated as belonging to my friend's ancestors after lost papers in the Caribbean had come recently to his attention—from a dragged-up pirate ship. Too bad it had been authenticated that his ancestors were also associates of Captain Morgan, one of the bloodiest cutthroats and brigands of the Spanish Main.

As my friend put it, these were niceties not to be spoken about by gentlemen, unless they were dead-drunk in private at the Carrington Club with fellow aristocrats like those of London's Lord Mayor, another pleasant scoundrel. Though that one had gone to Haberdasher, while Morgan had briefly ransacked Winchester as a student and torn up his tailor. Enough money was gathered in the process to pay for a ship. Such a show of early academic promise, well at least entrepreneurship, had put him in good standing with the governor of Jamaica, also a Winchester school dropout.

Interestingly, Morgan had thoroughly ransacked Panamanian cities. His reputation was so foul that when the denizens heard he was on his way, they put all valuables into carts and went off to the highlands to bury them and themselves in caves until the last of his fleet left. I thought as an aside that the Internal Revenue Service could have done well with someone like him. Morgan had been put under contract to the British government to plunder its enemies and to split the booty. That included the Spanish banks, the money ones. The only things Morgan split were heads.

Back to Isolde. She had been in some fear when I first approached her on the beach. But that fright was soon replaced with laughter, as I could not but feel the absurdity of my introduction as a count, given my gaudy, absurd clothes.

"And what title might that be?" she aspired to know.

I decided to avoid giving Isolde a direct answer, as I was without the foggiest idea about anything impressive about this aristocratic name that I now carried. Rather, I was reduced to fast-food repartee, serving up a quick need to shift her away from explaining any further what I could not explain—my title.

"You will need to at least let me buy you *a chien chaud et pommes frites*," I added impishly in French to make a hot dog and French fries sound like a culinary delight and to playfully see if she knew who I was, given Isolde's knowledge that this was one of my favorite dishes. At that moment, she let out a long laugh. Too late, I realized my faux pas and poor manners. Around the back was her little dachshund.

"You should show more feeling for my dog, General Ripper." And then I ripped out my own laugh, as no dog of that size and dimension deserved such a name as it growled in tune and tone fit for a triple muffled Rottweiler.

"Please tell your dog that my interests are more elementary than alimentary." She recognized the code word alimentary and looked less relaxed, yet with a hospitality that made the real toy boys on the beach look jealous. She grabbed me by my arm and looked to take me for much more than a stroll. She now knew beyond any doubt that I was her beach contact, as well as her overall protection.

I too was uneasy, for those toy boys looked too greasy and dangerous to have just regular sex on their mind for pay. The guards must have also been fairly well compensated to have let them in, perhaps paid in full with baron of beef rather than steak—probably as close to anything with a noble name that they would get to, present company excluded. Or these thugs might have been invited in because their owners were so powerful a criminal patriarchy from which the management or the guards did not want any trouble.

Whoever these degenerates were, things looked very bad. They looked decidedly more like rape. And three or four centuries back, they would have looked positively *Morganic*, especially if they had furnished a rapier for a deadly twist rather than just their increasingly tense fists.

They were becoming Isolde's and my own bookends to the beach. And the library was closing in by what additionally looked like a band of illiterates, who would only get close to a book if it meant using it as a projectile in an attack.

They had been schooled on the backstreets, and ripping into us would only go down officially in the short police reports greased by corruption as "death by misadventure." Their better half that could not have made it as *banditos* had largely joined the police or the priesthood—or a bank. Everyone in this small country seemed like they were in each other's pocket or church or hood. But then again, that could have been my simple mind wrapped in acting-up paranoia and discrimination, based on hackneyed stereotypes.

Isolde, on the other hand, trying to demonstrate cool detachment, had put her hair in a bun and quipped, "The neighborhood is going to the dogs, of a kind with which I do not want my poor General Ripper to be associated."

Bald, scarred, and militarily tattooed were the most attractive descriptions I could make of those who were approaching. I then calmly spoke out to Isolde and said, "Beware; a new beast is among us."

"What might that be, my protector count?"

I replied, "Human hammerhead sharks."

The happy hour was over. This was a country made for havoc, despite its golden, glittering, new glass towers. It was a study in contrasts, as it had a number of the most vicious hoods and cheapest executioners on the planet.

"Yes, my count. But first I believe we have overexposed ourselves," replied Isolde.

It made me check to see if my own clothes were in proper place.

"Why not take in a little bit of shade?" I suggested as protection.

We then got mutually inspired. So inspired that we whipped under one of the pastel pink beach umbrellas, and together ripped it up and through the first assailant's chops. He was in the pink of bad health, but his two other illiterates were just using him as an appetizer to distract us from their rear-guard movements.

The pincer was on, but General Ripper had nipped one, bringing the large lout to our attention. He took an evil liking to the dachshund. We had ducked as the general flew through the air with the face of an avenging angel. Some disguise. But at least he was not too lofty or stony faced.

Isolde cried out, "You beastly man!" She then *jujitsued* him into the exposed sharp nub of the umbrella.

The third carried a knife and a face that looked like the whetstone on which he had sharpened his instrument. He was, for sure, big-headed, which made it convenient. I kicked and boxed his large "observation tower," which seemed to rotate ever so slowly, like the Seattle Space Needle.

Unfortunately, he was more than a needle; he was as much innovation as I thought he could intellectually bring to bear. He hammered his bloody head into my gut, sending me wheezing into the water. He pressed me down into the ocean bottom. It was a distinction and conceivably my own innovation to be drowning and winded at the same time. I thought I was dead. But finally, with all my last strength, I blasted him with my fist into his temple.

As I was restored to consciousness, I saw beside me the gnarled, bloodstained, large body of what had once been something. Was I getting an OBE—out-of-body experience? Oh yes, I could more clearly recognize the battering ram-shaped head of our beach buddy. My hand stung, especially around my finger with its Yale graduation ring. Finally, for a brief moment, I recognized the wealth of my education.

"Oh, you poor darling! I thought it had been too late when I smashed that lovely umbrella into that very terrible man," Isolde said, with gentle sympathy that might have put Florence Nightingale to shame.

I did not like being in distress to a damsel. I wanted to tell her of my ring story, but thought it would just make a bad ending to a trilogy of her having saved the day by killing or maiming the number three son of a bitch. What could I say in such a case? I thought of the practical, not always easy for the egghead I sometimes could be when not switched fully into my mercenary personality.

"Help me up. Clean me up in your room. And when one or both of these thugs comes to, we are going to follow them and pay a visit to their paymaster."

Isolde looked mournful, but what was her problem? I had missed a funeral, and I hadn't thought that the other wrecks on the beach counted for much remorse.

"No more violence today," she said as she stroked my blood-soaked hair. She had had enough brutality for the day (so I thought). But as I increasingly composed myself, I was only getting whetted about what I wanted to do.

The "hammerheads" lying on the beach were about to become the bait.

*   *   *

I grinned into the mirror in Isolde's room. I never saw an uglier face that could be more beautiful. I was finally beginning to have true feelings for the story of "The Beauty and the Beast." Just as Isolde walked in, this beast expired into the netherworld of recovery. I was down for the count, but had not succumbed to the complete darkness. I had thankfully cheated it once again as the curtains closed down.

FIFTEEN

A thug from the beach, after a long tailing, was followed by Isolde to near proximity of the office of Jorgé Cassavates, who worked for a Panamanian lawyer. One too many Panamanian lawyers were considered to be rather seedy, putting their hands in the tills of their clients—and sometimes their skirts at times, too—and returning the money if they were lucky. But just in case things did not work out, a good Panamanian lawyer had strong friends.

Solicitor José Kartman truly believed that he could rely on the strength and permanent loyalty of Jorgé Cassavates. In fact, the word "permanent" was a very useful adjective to those who really pissed off José. It was no wonder that the solicitor delighted in his personal collection of stuffed sharks. For he had the moving ones, too, and with quite the legs, but certainly no skirts.

In Kartman's school was not only Jorgé, but also Carlos, a.k.a. "the Scissors."Jorgé's function was simple. He had the presence to clean up and ensure there was no physical presence of those who had been targeted for contract killing. He was like a vicious scavenger but whose habitat entailed the dark depths of depravity. He liked to share work with Carlos, who started at the feet. As a human shark, it came naturally.

Custom and police officials looked very pleased when Isolde had first briefed them with cash in her efforts to locate the man with the list, who had been Jorgé—unknown to her at the time. She had felt the need to make sure no one left the country with a piece of paper that was visibly distinct with its special Arabic print. The officials felt a wealth of obligation and looked forward to her making future deposits. Her case was not complicated, just full of cash used to ensure all went well in recovering the package.

To hunt down Jorgé by thrusting so much money that someone willingly or unwillingly would take her to his location—or at a minimum, provide useful hints—did not seem like a good short-term solution. But she had been desperate, given how screwed-up everything had gone. Unfortunately, the important package had been removed from the safety deposit box at the Banco San Diego, and there was no trace of the man through Kootoomba either. He had also been removed. Isolde decided immediately after learning about these two tragedies, to improvise to get it back using whatever underground or legitimate contacts she could quickly put into action.

She previously knew that a welcoming committee of *el senor sharkos* might be pulled out of their habitats to deal with all the attention she was giving to their master's stolen prize. She eventually discovered that the whole town seemed to know that Jorgé had something very special, if you forked over enough. But either no one knew or were too scared to tell her where he was.

For Jorgé, this was definitely not what he had wanted. He only wanted select customers to know about this "prize"—neither rival mafias nor any law enforcement agencies, including the omnipresent US Drug Enforcement Agency (DEA), which would have liked to nail him for anything given Jorgé's extensive dealings with the Mexican drug cartel. It was no wonder that he had sent his thugs to the beach to try and stop Isolde's prying about where he and the list were hidden.

All anybody was allowed to think about the document, if Isolde was pressed to describe its importance, was that it was simply a collection of unchangeable coded passwords to Middle East bearer bond accounts of millions of US dollars owned by an American multinational. But certainly not bearers of a world power conspiracy or terrorist plot.

At first, Jorgé's fellow sharks seemed like they were going to ground themselves and stay hidden at home. That was the case until Isolde, in her stakeout of the beached wonders, heard the phone ringing from their window, followed by the thugs rushing out the door. Her patient observations had proven fruitful—she had initially thought.

A failed execution without a good explanation could not only lead to termination of contract, but a permanent termination of these Panamanian hooligans once they were no longer trusted to do the job. But not returning or talking to their employer to explain why a job had been botched was automatic grounds for their own liquidation. Conceivably, they had word that their lives were no longer worth much. Isolde followed them all the way to the border, and then practically gave up.

Apparently, their employer had told them to get more than out of town. They were to get out of the country, and out of the universe if they could. However, Isolde found an alternative to discovering her real prey. The driver to the border, after letting off the two, had foolishly turned back after a few hours of temporarily disappearing into Costa Rica. Isolde was a true huntress, who would not give up if she thought there was any chance the prey was still in play. Jorgé had made a blunder in requesting that his car be returned to him. The driver had bungled by coming back through the same border crossing.

And by what the courier who had deposited the document at Banco San Diego had bled out under torture that left him not only toeless but speechless, Jorgé had prematurely begun to fantasize about the multimillion dollars he would get for the list. He felt he didn't need to tell rich Mr. Kartman that he had it. No, Mr. Kartman would be told that he was simply still trying to obtain it, and that maybe his sharks had blown it in trying to recover the list from us. That could have proven to be worrying. That could have put Isolde and me eventually into play with Mr. Kartman and his second string quartet.

Jorgé thought at the time that he was mature enough to go into business for himself and no longer needed the cunning or patronage of his boss. He had somehow also weaseled his way into the good graces of key mid-management at Banco San Diego, which his boss seemed to have trusted too much. He thought wrongly that he was in the big leagues, too. Dead wrong. Isolde practically triangulated onto him given how well her detective work succeeded. And, of course, given how sloppy Jorgé had been.

"It seems the whole school is out," said Isolde as she looked over her shoulder after she had plunged into his sad life. Jorgé's last words into his Palm phone were, "Get the bitch." It had been an expensive elimination.

Jorgé was dead, and could not know that the reflex motions of his body were as hopeless and final as the last actions that he had taken to become a top crime boss. Isolde had pierced the neck of his bloated body with a lead knife inscribed with a Wicca motif, overlaid by a large D. You could say, in a way, that it had been a ritual killing.

Somehow, Jorgé had not appreciated the religiosity of the moment. It was a book, a report, a bunch of papers, whatever—but holy Moses, worth up to two million dollars on the open market. The market had closed down on him with a crash as he fell on the floor.

Somewhere he had a mother, possibly a father, a brother or sister; he was a human being, after all. Would someone pity a hood, cry a tear, a poor sucker out of the slums trying to make it rich, who had pushed himself through a year of law school—even bribed his way with taxi money? Was this social justice? No, this was just Jorgé: unlucky, and not to forget a friend of a very questionable Panamanian lawyer.

For a moment, Isolde wondered if she should trust the package she had recovered from Jorgé in the hands of another Panamanian lawyer or banker. Or try to memorize the coded contents in the dead dialect of south Arabian, which she recognized as she had been a specialist in ancient dialects while attending Oxford. And then destroy it? It would be a mammoth challenge, but still theoretically possible. No, not even her photographic memory could process it all, certainly not there and then, she realized as she gave it a second thought.

She wondered and worried whether the papers contained anything within them beyond their visible messages in beautiful though deadly script. Thus, it might be imprudent both to destroy the document and certainly to leave it in Panama—especially after everything that had happened.

Isolde looked at Jorgé. The answer as to what to do with the document had become almost rhetorical. What had she needed: neon lights down the street swirling through the dumpy window and flashing the answer in her eyes with bells and whistles, trumpets, or even glockenspiels playing marching Prussian rhythms? After all, she had been ordered to bring it back to Z5 in Zürich. What had she been thinking?

It was, however, time to get the hell out as she goose-stepped over the body. It was not the stretching exercises she preferred so early in the morning.

Her ruthlessness had been surprising. Where had she learned such maneuvers and weaponry? It wasn't with the Austrian Girl Guides or Brownies. Had the Order withheld information about a special training location for assassination? They did go out to the English countryside in Althorp from time to time, and it wasn't for cookies and milk, or tea and crumpets.

Jorgé's organizational entrails spotted Isolde as she came out of the building. What they lacked in intestinal fortitude, they made up for in pure, fast-paced savagery. They were like the last breath of their master's call, sensing the fox was near.

But what they did not know was that Isolde was about to be the prey swallowing the predators. As they approached, the fox got bigger. It got so big it ran into them, over them, and around them like the force of a truck with the agility of a ballet dancer. It was Act II of the *Nutcracker* as Isolde turned on her high-definition audio and *Tchaikovskied* herself down to the airport. As the music blared out of the red vintage classic corvette, she thought how fitting the music was. It made her crack a smile. It made her crack up about the snap and crack of the past physical movements as she took in the entire movement.

I was on the plane waiting for her. A flight attendant handed me a note in a sealed envelope. It read *Destination, Sam Lord's Castle*. Where was that, I wondered. Possibly, I should have asked who Sam Lord was.

SIXTEEN

We successfully transited through Miami to Barbados, where we were going to hide out with the package until things cooled off. We expected a lot of the opposition would be waiting for us to come back to Europe. They would likely be by Heathrow or Zürich airports. Disappointing them without our presence, day in and day out for a while, might lead to shaking them off. We would still need Friegel of the Swiss police when we arrived back at our final destination in Zürich to further ensure our safety.

Barbados Customs and Immigration were generally relaxed with the kind of people we appeared to be—tourists, middle-aged, and professional looking, and booked into one of the finest hotels on the island. We got into our separate taxis, and we were off to the "castle." I let Isolde precede me by about a half hour.

The island had changed so many ways since my last visit. Had it been twenty years, or had it been longer? Barbados now had quite a network of reasonably wide highways, at least between the airport and the major towns. But the distinctive off-highway narrow lanes—even some with six crossroad intersections—were not so easy to negotiate. They were a constant source of vehicular mayhem and near misses.

The difference with Sarabia was that Barbadian drivers felt they could avoid going to the afterworld by having forethought of how to avoid a crash. While the wild sugarcane, growing so high and bending so easily to the pleasant rhythm of the soft, refreshing, off-water breezes, lent mystery, it provided important hidden dangers that were largely absent from highway driving in the desert. For the serious safety-minded driver, those island rhythms seemed to frustrate the desire for a very clear and predictable picture as to what was around the corner.

For the Bajans (the local dialect name for Barbadians), whatever the inconveniences of the rutted roads, the potholes, or the torrential-like rains in the afternoons, there was a calmness manifested in a blend of Welsh—and African-sounding accents. A dialect with its own easy rhythm of a "No problem, man" response when things got difficult.

Thus, the island for the tourist who had little agenda was a blessed land with its somewhat slow, relaxed, but very polite ways. That would be interrupted only by a hurricane or a major drug bust and only on a few occasions. Nothing much more happened, except for a billionaire or prime minister or *rock'n'roll* senior citizen celebrity coming in to relax for a spell.

Above its laid-back atmosphere but not backwardness, it was a fairly orderly island for the Caribbean, with a government that was generally free of corruption by regional standards. Somehow, that was reassuring to know. It felt like a large, floating safe house, another fine lady like the Schotland, but maybe with sugarcane fields and sugar smiles and offshore breezes as the protection. And oh yes, one of the Caribbean's finest constabularies.

After weaving in and out of the small lane connecting roads and bumping along a pothole or two, all of a sudden an old colonial-style, large mansion appeared at the end of the road. It had cannons about, ramparts, and wind-shutters looking thick enough to bounce any returning cannonballs if they ricocheted.

This was the impressive Sam Lord's Castle, with its million-dollar interior Italian moldings and a massive reconstruction. It was restored to look better than the original, which had mysteriously gone up in flames as a result of its previous owner, an insurance company that was unable to maintain its upkeep or dispose of it. The company's demise was theorized to have partially resulted from excessive purchases of troubled Wall Street and London repackaged investment instruments. There were interesting theories about its executive management, too. Fortunately, a partnership of trusts, including one based in the Island of Man, had bought it with newly injected offshore money from an Irish billionaire with enigmatic but highly profitable investments in Eastern Europe.

The hotel was named after a real nineteenth-century brigand, a pirate whose ship was *landlubbered* in the form of lanterns put out in back of the castle at night to con nearby ships into thinking that they were approaching the main harbor at Bridgetown. It had been a mystical light show with the deadly effect of a mythological siren of a Greek sailor tragedy. It was Medusa times two or times three. It would have even impressed the daredevilry of Somali pirates of today, who made their own huge fortunes, albeit with more modern artillery.

The schooners of that time were still made mostly of wooden hulls that would disintegrate upon hitting the coral reefs, no more than a few hundred meters from the castle. Sam Lord and his merry crew of brigands would then descend on the bounty. Those not dead would be slaughtered. He would have made banker Schmidt of Delaware very proud.

Although Sam Lord's was not the very best bastion this side of the Caribbean, only a full fort had been safer. With its massive thick walls and deep basement hideaways in the coral limestone bedrock, it was essentially the strongest deposit box in the region. And the hurricane-proof walls seemed to be a mere meter thick. Even Captain Morgan's descendants had deposited nearby some of his bounty in the secret limestone, bat-infested caves for a charge paid to Sam Lord. The building and the area around it, indeed, had an illustrious past.

I could not be absolutely sure if Isolde had arrived at the hotel when I reached it. And I certainly was not going to ask about her. Nevertheless, the clerk at the front desk registered me with the clockwork of a five-star hotel in the Caribbean. Just a very, very long minute or two short of the Swiss standard. Impressive for a southern clime.

"Welcome to Sam Lord's Castle, sir," a burly native receptionist said with a very pleasant and warm smile. One that looked a bit inherited from the British presence of three hundred years plus that had intimated that a warm smile was good and too big a smile was a con.

Bajans had learned to mimic the very polite British manners, but still managed to encapsulate around them the warmth, relaxation, and casualness so natural to the island, and so much a part of the currents of their African tribal ancestors.

"Thank you very much. I'd like to check in, though I have just a small bag so I'll manage it," I warmly responded, with seemingly buckets of sweat dripping on the counter due to all the humidity. Oh, not to forget all the running around in saving our scalps. Not to forget getting off too many airplanes worried and wondering whether anyone around us was going to shoot us or cut us open like a Bajan would do to a coconut. It was time to relax, but could I?

"Very good, sir, and what might be your name?" said the hotel clerk, insisting on asking for it cooperatively.

"I am . . .

"Yes, sir, your name."

I was caught wondering what identity and passport I would be using. Yes, of course, the one I had used foolishly at the airport.

"Pol Martin," I said. "Sorry, I was distracted for a moment."

The receptionist looked slightly taken aback, but in his professionalism he did not think to worry about whether I was in disguise or a mental case. He was after my credit card, as the final decider as to whether I would be politely escorted out or be simply considered as a mild eccentric.

"So, how many nights will you be staying, sir?"

"Three, I think, yes, that would be nice."

"And would you like an ocean view and a nonsmoking room?" he somewhat mechanically asked as he examined my completed form.

"Is there a quiet side?"

"Yes, sir, the top floor on the southeast corner so to speak. Actually, quite an interesting history to that room. The proprietor of a century and a half ago used to find he had the best view as he looked out for ships, a kind of interesting hobby you will read about in our brochures. We even have a telescope in that room that can scan a full one hundred and eighty degrees. Anyway, sorry to digress."

"Perfectly all right," I said, thinking how interesting that we would be staying at a former pirate's lair. Wondering why the clerk would be happy to be alluding to it.

"I expect you will be using your credit card. May I have it?"

"Oh, oh." Z5 had yet to renew my credit card for my Pol disguise, but fortunately I had plenty of American dollars.

"No, I'd simply like to leave a fairly nice-sized deposit, against which you can apply my charges. If I have to make a fast exit, you can credit the unused portion to my Real Holding bank account in Bridgetown, which I have kept as a souvenir since my last visit to your great island."

"Yes, sir, fifteen hundred Barbadian dollars will be fine. That's about seven hundred and fifty US by way of the current exchange rate. I will attach your note with its bank account number to it."

"Right—a receipt for that, please."

"Of course. Your money will be sealed in this envelope in your name, and put in our safe just around the corner. If you have any valuables you would like to accompany it, I'll be pleased at anytime and to your convenience to put them there. Excellent protection, but please read the terms of the agreement if you wish. We also have a few safety deposit boxes that I can give you. And your own key."

"No, that will be fine." I wondered whether Isolde had stashed the document in one of them. And if so, would it be truly safe?

"Here is your room number, 911," he said with a bit of a rolling laugh.

I had then gotten a queasy feeling. Was he in on our mission? Was our cover broken? Was it a setup, with a big Philistine, corrupt policeman about to step out and hammer me and take me away? Let's give it a shot, I thought, and keep with the Zürich protocol.

"You mean 119, of course."

"Oh yes, 119. Excuse me, I'm a bit dyslexic. It's a nice location. Funny, you just missed getting 911. By chance, a very nice lady just checked in and asked for it."

My head was spinning, tired and depleted and flashing a thousand fear alerts. Was this clerk playing with me? As well as Isolde—some cat-and-mouse game? I was maybe feeling mousy, but I was almost ready to be mouthy to the clerk. Too tired and fatigued for it in the end, drained by all the running around and the heightened paranoia.

"Is everything all right, Mr. Martin?" The front desk clerk looked at me with a slightly bemused smile.

"No, no, just something caught in my throat."

Out of the corner, a rather well-uniformed officer of the Royal Barbadian Constabulary greeted me. Well, not royal anymore, but looking in his very smart uniform as if he were still from those preindependence days.

"A very good day to you, Mr . . . ."

"Mr. Pol Martin, that is," I stated assertively. "It is a very nice hotel," I added.

"Might I have a word with you over in the lounge?" The politely polished policeman stated it almost casually. "Yes, that is all, Mr. Bird," he added. He then turned away from the front desk to lead me into the empty spacious room, where a nice offshore wind was blowing the white transparent curtain. It would have normally been a pleasant hypnotic feeling, with the rhythmic crashing of the waves against the reef in the near distance.

"Is your passport in order, Mr. Martin?" He said it with pursed lips of a smile.

I could not help but be a bit nervous. This was a favorite ploy by enforcement officials when they were a little uncertain about an individual's credentials. Hoping to catch the target off balance, leading to compromising or revealing behavior. I was too old a hand to be too bothered by this decoy. But then, if I did not look a bit nervous, it might make him suspicious that I was too much of a pro in the security business myself.

"I am sorry. Is there something wrong? I really do not have the foggiest idea what you are talking about."

"I do not know exactly what you are up to, Mr. Martin, but my instructions are to take you back to the airport."

"What! . . . You must be joking!"

"Do I look like a joking man?"

"For what reason?"

"I just received a message from my superior; I did not ask why. Your flight is leaving for London. It leaves in an hour. I suggest you be there. In fact, my sergeant here will drive you there now."

"Now, I just got here. After a very tiring journey. I'll want to talk to your superior, immediately."

"Oh, Mr. Martin, you will. We'll see you out in the front in five minutes. And you might want to use the lavatory. You seem to have quite a bit of perspiration on you—no offense, of course. Some of our visitors do occasionally find that the humidity lends itself to perspiration."

"Okay, okay." I knew it would be useless to argue, but I thought I would go up the stairs and knock on Isolde's room while on my way to make myself very British Barbadian proper. She would need to know that I was going.

"Mr. Martin going upstairs—any reason? We will ensure you do come along. There is no bathroom up there."

"Bathroom. Oh, right. I prefer the balcony up there, and I would like to at least see a full view of the sea before I depart. The breeze should cool me down, remove my sweat."

"Very well. But don't take all day to do it."

In my anxiety, I practically pranced upstairs and knocked on 911. Well, I moved as quickly as I could.

"Isolde, are you there? It's me."

I heard a voice that was groggy, a troubled voice. "J. C., is it you? Just leave me alone."

"I have got to get in and speak to you. Open the door."

"No, I can't," she said—or someone said in a muffled voice.

"Look, you have got to open the door!"

I could hear the police lieutenant along with another pair of feet quickly climbing the steps.

"Mr. Martin, what are you doing? Please do not disturb the guests. Come down with us, immediately and quietly." He sounded like he was almost at the top of the stairs.

I did not want to blow my cover or further draw their attention as to where I was directing my voice. I moved away to another door.

"Sorry, Lieutenant, I thought I heard someone in distress."

"You are having quite a peculiar day. Let's now be off. We do not want you to miss that plane."

"Oh, of course not—only business class this time," I said impishly. "I feel positively ravished for the first-class meal that I will be missing by not staying here."

The two kind gentlemen held me a little, directing me to the backseat of a bright blue Ford sedan.

The ride back to the airport was a lot more sultry and hotter than when I came in. Was it my nervousness? Maybe—or maybe I was getting hotter under the collar about the prospect of a bullet to my head in an abandoned cane field. I could not be fully sure as to these two being legitimate police officers.

But this was Barbados, not Sierra Leone. What was I thinking? I had a rush of regression back to my mercenary days of Frank Derenard's rescue from a pathetic hole of an African dungeon, after his merry mercenaries "screwed the pooch" as they say in American vernacular for a screwup.

After a half hour or so, thankfully, we finally arrived at the airport with me still in one piece, and the officers amazingly too. Was I losing my touch? But prudence called for more care than brutalizing what might very well be legitimate peace officers.

I was taken to the back of the main terminal building after being expedited through passport control. Most strangely, like a VIP persona non grata who practically needed to be physically seen as getting on the plane. Protocol in these parts had it that in dealing with criminals, they would usually be put on board well before the other passengers got on.

Before that, such visitors would be kept well out of sight. The only thing I felt missing from standard procedures was leg-irons, or more seriously handcuffs, for some reason.

Then an older Bajan gentleman in a very nice, creamy colored tailored suit stepped out from a car, possibly fifty meters away, near the edge of the runway that was out of sight of almost all passengers. He walked fairly quickly and with a determined purpose, but also with a very pleasant and controlled gait.

"Mr. Martin, I am Inspector Jones of the Criminal Branch here in Barbados," he said coolly and as a matter of fact. "Your departure from our sunny lovely island has now been confirmed, and possibly observed by not-so-nice locals working for devious offshore characters. Your controller at Interpol brought to my attention that some very nasty people followed you out of Panama and are about to be checked into the Sam Lord's in a manner of speaking. So we have provided you alternative housing at one of our finer private residences. Sorry to say, no pool and very inland. But a fine piece of old island architecture, if that matters."

"No, it does not. This is all a surprise to me. How do I know who you are?"

Jones quickly answered, "Your Interpol controller, I think, said you would be very suspicious. He told me to refer to 119 and pass on the message that a distinguished gentleman almost enjoyed the idea of being in the shed with you. He said something about you should be a trusting samurai. Is that enough? I could go on and say more. We don't usually get such important phone calls from Interpol every day. It was Interpol, wasn't it?" He coyly smiled.

"Okay, okay, Mr. Jones. You have made your point. Well, what about the lady, Mr. Jones?"

"She's fine, if you are speaking of the Countess."

"I possibly am."

"Oh, it was necessary to leave her there at the 'castle.' As the official word goes," he said with a bit of a mischievous wink.

"I knocked on her door, and she seemed sick, not well," I said with some alarm.

"Really? Lieutenant," said the Inspector, "get someone to go to the hotel to check on her. In fact, phone the hotel and check her status. Make sure that reception knows perfectly and clearly that he must keep everything hush, hush. And, Lieutenant, make clear its vital importance. This cannot go public."

"Yes, sir, I believe he is already aware."

"Meanwhile, Mr. Martin, step into my car and enjoy our ride through the countryside. The sun goes down early, and in a half hour or so it will begin to nicely cool off, especially as we get up to the highlands. A little coolness, not so bad."

"Where are we specifically going?"

"You'll see . . . . Oh yes, here is my identification. Would you care to show yours to me? Actually that will not be necessary," he said with a slightly smug grin.

I, of course, did not answer. The inspector was canny and probably knew my passport was a good fake, but was playful and a good sport about it.

"I don't know what you are up to, Mr. Martin . . . that is your name . . . but your friends are so high up that I am going to keep my mouth shut, and I know I can count on you doing the same. So if you want any information from me, all I can do is shoot the breeze with you about tourism, rum punch, and calypso music. If that isn't enough, then just sit back and enjoy the crickets and our other night-crawler sounds." Jones let out a very hearty laugh and patted me on the shoulder.

I worried that too many people on this small island would know about my presence, if not my mission. It would have probably been better if he had left me back at the plane. It was not like I felt as unwelcomed as when the lieutenant had greeted me. It was that strange, instinctive, bottom-gut feeling that I was not even safe in the hands of the top members of the police, who had instructed me to stay quiet.

I worried that the people who would want to sabotage Isolde's and my mission were unfortunately a cut above the expertise of this law enforcement bunch. Unless they were the leftovers of José Kartman—if there had been any. Then we might have had a chance. But Kartman would likely this time hire a more professional lot. And what if certain extremist elements in Sarabia were on to what had happened in Panama? Then we would all be screwed, including the Bajan police.

When we arrived at our destination, Drache Manor, the hurricane lamps seen through the windows burned with strange resonating and flickering lights, largely but not completely protected from the fairly strong evening breeze. A fresh breeze, which was so famous for its medicinal purposes that it had attracted over centuries the likes of George

Washington, who had brought his brother here in the hope of curing him from tuberculosis.

Barbados was indeed a place where many had gone for a cure, be it from disease or just the lamentable winters in northern Europe and the upper parts of North America. Was I going to get my own treatment for any of my ailments, whether of body or mind? I actually had to wonder what was in store.

Speaking of remedies, facing me was my cure for at least illness of heart as I entered the wide door that could have fitted a pair of wild beasts. Sitting very relaxed, with a big smile, was Isolde, looking very content and happy. What an incredible surprise! And how had she managed to beat the inspector and me here? It just was not possible unless . . .

"We did it," she called out and almost jumped me with a warm embrace like a girl meeting her date for the prom.

"What did we do?" I asked as I stretched out my arms to hold her. My first time, real physical contact with Isolde, ever.

"We've still got the package, even after being chased down by at least three gangs. The mob here in Barbados even thinks I am back at Sam Lord's. Didn't you, too?"

"Yes, even I did," I said as I coddled her embrace, yet more confused than enjoying enough of her warm bodily attention for the first time. Too much confusion relating to an embrace in my profession sometimes led to warm lead, instead. Whether after a surprise kiss, a pat on the back that was a mystery, or a hug from a thug, such warm tidings from those you didn't expect it from could be the prelude to a grand fateful delusion. What a sad profession to have to think too often this way, even as I melted looking at her gorgeous, welcoming eyes. Or were those deadly eyes?

Inspector Jones, who had entered the house with me, looked a little sheepishly guilty, with a quick smile—not too much so as not to look too content about the deception of pretending Isolde was back at Sam Lord's. That would have been very unsporting.

"Well, you'll enjoy the plantation house here." He added, "One of only three of its kind in all of the Americas—Jacobean. It was named for a famous British admiral, a man called Drache. *Drache* means *dragon*, so its nickname is Dragon Manor.

"Isn't this so interesting, Pol?" Isolde was acting like a schoolgirl on her first international vacation. She seemed out of character, this teenager girl personality. Was I beginning to get past her outward one to find a warmer, innocent, and youthful one on the interior? Or maybe there were two of her, too.

The fact that my Panamanian cover name was von Drax—a derivative of Drache—meant that this safe house could have been prepared weeks, if not months, before our arrival. And what about my Yorkshire friend and all that stuff about an obscure aristocratic name of "Drax" recovered from the ocean bottom? It seemed someone had a puckish sense of humor to assign it to me and place me in a house with something of the same name. Or was *macabre* the better word if all did not go well?

But seriously, did it matter if they called me Drake, Drone, or Druid, instead? Well, it could have shown a bit more imagination and deception if they had called me the latter, as I was with an Order that had its own rituals. It would have been a better confidence builder if the deceivers on my side had come up with something much different than what was close to the name of this old manor. And Z5 was supposed to represent top spies. Perhaps my suspicious mind had too tight a vice on my thinking.

Unfortunately, instead of enjoying my surroundings, it just made me worry that there was an inside traitor who was marking me out for a hit by labeling my cover name close to the name of this safe house. A cover name that could have been broken to a number of pretty ugly people in Panama, who could very well be on the island.

"We'll need the strength if not the fire of a dragon to defend us," I added wearily, to go with my concerns that this safe house might not be so safe.

"I think not," said Jones confidently. "You are surrounded by our very best, including even some of our commandos running around in the fields. But don't go too far afield—both of you."

"Why is that?" I twisted around in surprised worry.

"There are rats about, even in that windmill tower, a place you definitely do not want to venture forth to. The wooden-metal ladder is three hundred and fifty years old. You see, we have thoroughly checked the estate out. Even architectural drawings and historical references to it by a distinguished professor, knighted posthumously by the queen for advancing agriculture and pride in our island's history. Yes, professors are sometimes useful," added Jones chuckling.

"Very interesting reference to a professor. You do, do your research, Chief Inspector."

I now really wondered how much Zen, or likely Falcon, had told this guy about me. I wondered if I went down to the fish market in Oistens village, where the fishmongers flocked, whether someone would be calling me Adrian and asking for souvenirs from Agent 119. And maybe an autograph.

"Yes, Mr. Martin and Isolde," Jones continued, "vermin is your greatest threat. At least the four-leg kind for now."

Or the two-legged ones, I thought, even if they were only in my mind and in my recurring nightmares of my thrashing in Zürich. A nightmare that included my juvenile detractors with their rodent-tailed superiors in tuxedos at receptions.

"Do we get our own extermination kit?" I asked.

"No, we have let loose the dogs, and oh yes, an exterminator or two before your arrival, days ago—proverbially that is. Oh, we did know you were coming," said Jones with another smug little smile that got under my skin. "We knew days ago, but no real matter." (He probably meant weeks.)

"The owners do not use the mansion often. We have an arrangement to use it as a safe house. There will be two of my men in the grounds. I expect we are as far away as can be from those who are *loolooing* for you. Two of them, at the very least, who are professional assassins. Oh yes, I forgot to tell you . . ." He hesitated.

Yes, Jones was full of additionally delayed surprises—after-the-fact ones—stupendously important ones thought as an aside. He was a real interesting, mellow, and not very dramatic kind of fellow. He then added more.

"You will be taken tomorrow by boat to the Grenadine Islands. You'll be wrapped up in quite the disguises. And from the airport on the island of Mustique, flown by private jet to somewhere where I do not even know. So don't bother asking me. You won't find out unless your nifty little cell phone can be used to do so. But I advise a complete blackout—not even a telephone call."

"Inspector, I am surprised you are going to all this trouble!"

"Boy, you are important people. Do you know the Graceful Stones, too? If you see Mickey, the musician in Mustique, tell him we're sorry we arrested his friend last time she visited. We have had a sea change about her. A very influential woman, and so many of them!" he playfully effused as he turned to look at Isolde.

Jones laughed, but it was all a little bit over my head, and I had better things to do than try to figure out all of his jokes, mostly in dry wit and with somewhat old-style British airs. It was as if he had done advanced training at Sandhurst, or no . . . maybe RADA, the Royal Academy for Dramatic Art. The story of my life, trying to decode so many one-man acts with polished performances from foreign security people. Or their imposters.

Now, the whole inside of the manor looked as if occupied by an English country gentleman or lord, with very little reflecting the African-West Indies heritage. What it did was not flattering. There was a famous print of a member of the seventeenth-century *plantocracy* sitting in his planter's chair, making the natives run about for the most frivolous of requests. One could only describe this large glass framed sketching as distinctly bigoted.

There was also a small statue figure of a very large-looking lady, no doubt a side street seller of produce, looking like a kind of Aunt Jemima. Then, in opposite corners, were caricature wood carvings of a native woman and man, whose exaggerated smiles and clothes made them look almost infantile. There seemed to be few objects representing black Bajan life that could be remotely described as complimentary. Ah, the *plunderocracy*, one couldn't say enough about it—whichever version.

Then on a small table, I couldn't believe what I saw. There he was, a small portrait of Sam Lord, and above him a much larger one of William Dumbster, reportedly the purchaser and exporter of Sam Lord's bounty. Both "gentlemen" looked full in their cheeks, but it was their very cheeky business that was sadly an integral part of the island's economy in the nineteenth century. While they were simply land-based pirates, they were also publicly God-fearing men who regularly went to church and gave nice donations to the clergy. There were stories that they gave even bigger ones to custom officials and higher political authorities.

There were other oddities in the drawing room. Like the incredible oversized Ming vase, or the more interesting vase with a broken egg in porcelain stuck to it, which was perched with a bird on the side table. Did it all mean that the best-laid plans could crack up? For Sam Lord, such words and symbols had been signals to prosperity. But it made me wonder who would crack next—the pursuers or us?

There were also engravings of horses and the hunt in the English countryside that were all about, furthering the country as well as high-class feel. Then there was the dining room. Quite amazing, with its table made of the finest dark mahogany and enough places to seat a party of sixteen.

Under so much of the furniture were large tapestry-style carpets that were so fine they could have easily come from the best producers in Persia and Flanders. My, how well this God-fearing *plantocracy* had lived, while their subordinates used the whip to increase the harvest and shot up hundreds of revolting slaves throughout the centuries. And at very little expense or care.

There was also a bit of a musky smell, somewhat the same one I had sensed in Schmidt's vault of the depraved. The overall feel was of plantation and the creepy days of slavery, pirates, and even badly distilled rum. In fact, the Drache plantation had been one of the first ones on the island to have supplied the raw juice for rum manufacture.

The rum factory, in its broken-down state between huge walls of coral, odd rock, and mortar, was just behind the interior protecting woods that had been "transplanted" from Africa along with the indentured. Those indentured, by the way, also included the white slaves of Ireland who had taken up pitchfork against the imperial British. They could have done worse, like ending up permanently on a British navy vessel and lashed from time to time. Those who administered the cat-o'-nine-tails onboard those old navy ships made today's Sarabian authorities look gentle when they applied their own whips.

The dark history seemed trapped between the old walls of this fine piece of Jacobean architecture, no matter how large the windows, no matter how wide open they could be flung. Perhaps the trappings of its history—and that of some of the old Barbadian elites—were embedded in the mortar. The winds seemed to cry whispers of the slave ghost ancestors' torments that had cut through the cane, which had felled so many slaves in the backbreaking work of yesteryears.

Had the world changed so much over the centuries, no matter how any of us sensed our current freedoms or our civilizations, whether perceived as advanced, primitive, or plain ugly religious? There were the privileged few and the rest of us, and it would not change no matter what religion promised and no matter what our great American constitution beckoned. We could just hope our constitution could mitigate it, and retain the same hope that many descendants of the slaves anticipated. That promise was that Heaven would give them praise for tolerating so much suffering and so much barbaric domination.

It was now time for sleep, especially after all of these tiring thoughts of how most of us might still be shackled beyond my Scot's friend, who had refused to sing out praises to the police and the *Mootawa* after being so badly humiliated and chained in Sarabia. It was not only the Sarabian religious fanatics that I had always worried about. I was also concerned that I had been manipulated by Zen and Z5 higher-ups to protect those living high and mighty on the money of the exploited of the present or the Barbados past years.

We were both very weary. We were definitely overworked and underpaid for the risks we were taking, though Isolde was a well-off trooper. She would not mind and would complain much less about the deceit and manipulation of our work at times, and even the increasing violence of it all.

There would definitely be others at the very top who would always have it much better because of our sufferings and the high risks we were taking to defend civilization. But hopefully, there would be many on the bottom that would benefit as well from our endeavors to stop this destructive conspiracy emanating from the package we were holding. I was in danger of becoming an assassin with a conscience or a heart. Isolde and this island had put a spell on me, some kind of weird moral voodoo.

The soft lights flickered for reasons beyond me, as the wind had settled down. My hypnosis, along with the mild chirping of the tree frogs, was the tonic to cure my insomnia caused by my painful thoughts of imprisoned humanity, or perhaps by just my own physical pains. Or my thoughts of the ghosts that haunted this house. Or the ones that haunted our mission.

The House of Dragon, Drache Manor, had seemed indeed to have cast a spell on me. But that spell was not as strong as the sleep that was upon me. I rolled up onto my curtained bed and threw down the mosquito net, hoping it would protect me from all the possible stings and from the jungle out there. And hoping any possible large intruders in the bushes might get stung, instead of Isolde or me.

SEVENTEEN

There was no way to wake up after 7:00 a.m. in beautiful Barbados. Not with all the beauty and guffawing birds. Even a half hour past dawn, it was getting very warm; and especially where Drache Manor was, there was little breeze to abate the hot temperature during most of the day. Not even the curtains were dark enough to keep out the light known to be so strong as to bleach watercolors and wall paint to nothingness in a few years.

Yes, if you did not get up until much later, you had to be nothing, insensitive to temperature and light, insensitive of the welcoming paradise that beckoned. If you did not get up in Barbados by eight o'clock in the morning, it was time to send in the doctor to confirm whether a death certificate should be issued.

I was getting to feel very much alive on this island, even if I still felt a little pulverized from my Zürich mishap. So I had to get up. I got into a robe that had been left half-draped over a planter's chair, which stretched out so long and deep that it looked like it would swallow you. I then stepped out of the room.

And there was Isolde wrapping a towel around her head, looking almost like it was sculpted, based on one of the famous African heads in the more hidden corners of the manor. It was like a very noble one of ebony that spoke of dignity. That could have vicariously spoken of the possibility that an African princess—though defeated on the so-called Dark Continent—had frequented these chambers. Just like a mistress, which I wished Isolde could be for me, and as curvaceous and sensuous as the large hurricane lamps, which were missing one fine feature unlike that African sculpture or Isolde—their heads.

Fittingly, I could not help myself and blurted out amusingly, "Good morning, Highness, looking smashing for all the wear of yesterday."

184

"J. C., I wondered if you slept at all. Was it you, darling, who was up and about outside?" she said not intimately, but again with her coldness that reminded me something of Marlene Dietrich or Greta Garbo of the old film noir, though definitely shining more brightly.

"Strange. Where did you hear someone?"

"Just outside my room. Outside my window," replied Isolde.

"Possibly security checking on something." I said this attempting to assuage her, while actually knowing nothing of what it had been.

"Yes, you might be right about that."

"Anyway, how about breakfast? Jones didn't tell us about the meal plan, but surely nothing wrong with seeing if we can get a bite here," I added.

"I'll fix up my hair while you play house husband," Isolde said with a wink.

"How kind, your Majesty."

"Just Isolde is fine," she said playfully.

"You can count on me to defer to you as your royal subject. Okay, okay, I'll make myself scarce to the kitchen. And check out first the cockroaches—nothing less as your protector."

"Protector? I thought it was me protecting you," said Isolde in a bit of a play-acting huff.

"No, Mr. Martin—or whoever you call yourself—and Countess, I am your protection," said Inspector Jones stiffly. "Glad to see you are up and so eager to enjoy our sights."

"Yes, nice to see you, Inspector Jones. We were getting grumpy about the lack of breakfast service. Oh yes, there was a night crawler outside of Isolde's window last night."

"What do you mean?" said an astonished Jones, as if his daughter's virginity had been broken into before marriage.

"Yes," said Isolde, "I positively heard someone moving around outside my window."

"Snakes and mongooses?" I questioned.

Jones pulled out his walkie-talkie. "Excuse me," he muttered as he went outdoors, with a face faint with red and decidedly tense.

Jones returned with profuse apologies.

Meanwhile, I could hear my stomach rumble. It still had lots of company all over my body given how hard the bed was and how soft some of my bruises were still. God, I felt a model of imperfection before Isolde's perfectly immaculate, well-trimmed body, with not even a dimple or a pimple. And a grace that made me feel returned to Cro-Magnon form, though more upright now.

*   *   *

After consulting with his security team, Jones rushed us out of the manor into a Hummer. We were quickly taken down to a jetty. A small coast-guard boat had been secretly launched from a small cove known as Foul Bay. Known for being a redoubt for the most dubious pirates. Known as a favorite resting hole for Major Bonnet, Blackbeard's Barbados partner in crime. There, owning land, Squire Bonnet, who had separated from his henpecking wife for the life of a buccaneer, had awaited the long-bearded pirate from the top of a bluff that now housed a very successful, crime-fighting, real estate millionaire. The neighborhood had certainly experienced many changes over the years.

We, indeed, had a very nice coast-guard ride to Mustique, a small, seemingly inconsequential isle that had been popularized by such rock groups as the Graceful Stones and CO2 and Queen Elizabeth of England's late sister, who had all stayed there for winter vacations. Upon arriving on this paradise islet with seven-star hotels and the finest coral sand inlets anywhere, we were zipped over to the small, newly expanded airport. We wished that we could have stayed, but under the circumstances, Mustique would be left for another visit—if we survived, of course.

There it was, a Bombardier-class executive jet, X7 series, which could hold more than thirty. State-of-the-art, fastest of its line, and looking like a wide-bodied silver bullet. We were hurried onto it like someone was expecting the airport to be bombed, as if we had a transplant organ for a billionaire abroad who was close to dying, as if we were the world's last saviors of a planet that was about to die. As if we had a very special coded list that Z5 was so anxious to get, which was the truth, that they would be paying a ticket price for both of us of ten thousand big ones for the cost of this ride. I was impressed. And that was a rare word in my vocabulary.

The door was drawn up quickly by our flight attendant after she welcomed us on board. "Hi, I'm Patsy. Would you like your seat number, 911?"

God, not this routine again. I would give my phone number instead, to be cheeky.

"Yes, I'm Jean-Claude Carterone," I said with a kind of artistic flair that made her know I wasn't her type. "My number is 555-1212. What's yours? Please call me anytime."

At that moment, I got a nice quick punch of the elbow from Isolde.

The attendant smiled very invitingly. "J. C., that's your name. But that's not your proper numbered response. If you don't provide the code, we are instructed to have that very large gentleman here throw you out over the ocean, but not right away."

"Oh, that sounds relieving, given where we are. I always wanted to visit Mustique, with its six-star hotels and celebrities. I was so worried that we were in such a rush that we would not see it."

"No, that's seven-star hotels. You'll be visiting other stars from thirty thousand feet, our cruising height. And no parachute, by the way."

"You know, Patsy, I just provided my number as an invitation to a date, and now you tell me you're going to kill me if I don't also give you my secret number. What kind of girl are you?"

"J. C., stop that flirting. Give her the password," said Isolde in an embarrassing, yet bouncy tone. We needed relief from all the stress of safe houses, escape routes, and our varied deadly pursuers.

"Okay, you conspiracy of women to kill a man's adventurous self. No, I would prefer 911, but it's 119. I'll enjoy it as long as it doesn't give me a third-class seat on the outside. Or another request for a follow-up password."

It was a jibe at Isolde for having gotten a first-class transatlantic seat, while I had gotten far less. Isolde's eyes flashed hard and bright. She didn't like the insinuation of being treated better. But in my humble view she was better, so her getting better did not really bother me at all. Well, not much.

"You passed your flying test with colors," said youngish, attractive Patsy, knowing that we both knew that I was probably too old for her. Thankfully, Isolde was good-natured about it all. We began to lean back for a well-deserved sleep, after we collapsed into our seats without questioning the crew about anything, including our destination.

After all, we weren't paying for our ticket, and Inspector Jones seemed such a trustworthy travel agent. The comfy, deep plush, black leather seats had been well earned. Isolde had been kept awake into the late hours by the night crawlers outside her window. And I had been rather restless, tossing and turning in my bed in the early morning and then moving about in the house. That tossing was almost more than the bobbing of our coast-guard ship, which had run into rough waters around the reefs of Sam Lord's Castle.

Interestingly, the captain of our boat pointed out to us at the time a reef that had splintered pieces of what was left of a zodiac. It had broken up several hours earlier, along with rather dubious creatures the captain made only brief reference to.

Our skipper added after a bit of time had passed that it was fascinating that one of the dead men had been pierced by an arrow, seemingly from a partner's speargun. Which interestingly, Jones had no trouble not explaining.

We would feel safer, nevertheless, by what our honest boat captain was able to impart. Safer to know that in all likelihood the sharks, the real ones, must have had a feeding frenzy. If they had, then in a gruesome, humorous sense, the incident might have simply been reported by the coroner as death by cannibalism. But I learned later he had concluded death by misadventure, describing it as a ridiculously fluke sea-hunting accident with most of the evidence eaten away. Of course, the figurative references to cannibalism and to the Mafia would be left out of the newspapers. Simply another example of tourists losing all sense of where they were or the risks of their new recreational, tropical pleasures.

*   *   *

I finally woke up, which seemed hours after we had gotten on board the plane. The dull buzzing of the cabin was somehow a bit irritating. Probably I had just had enough of being in this conical pressurized cabin, which was now popping my ears as we began to descend. Where was that Patsy, or for that matter, the sumo wrestler to which there had been a possible promise of a last embrace. I still had not been told where we were going. Surely Patsy must have known.

I then looked out the window. Ah yes, I could recognize that peninsular arm known as Brittany, I speculated. Possibly we were getting ready for London, which was where we were to have originally gone on our way back from the Caribbean in our first plans. But that did not make sense, as London was only going to be a transit point for Zürich. Our flight path should now have been taking us farther south, directly to Zürich. Where was our Patsy, indeed?

I decided to get up and look around. There was no evidence of her. I knocked on the bathroom, opened the door. What did I find? Nothing. What about Isolde? Yes, still sleeping. I decided to leave her be. There was no good reason yet for waking up our Sleeping Beauty.

I then knocked on the cockpit door. An announcement came quickly after. A male voice. "This is the captain. Please put your seats in the upright position and fasten your seat belt. We will soon be landing."

There was a slight groan from our reviving beauty. "Ooh, J. C., what time is it? Are we near our destination, Zürich?"

"Bad news, Isolde. There is no Patsy. And they have given us no name as to where we are going. Though I think we are somewhere around northern France."

"Northern France! What—why are we going there? Weren't we supposed to be going to Zürich?" Isolde was as confused as me, and we had been just too happy to get on the plane and out of there. Very careless, but then did we have a choice?"

"Mmmmmmmmmmmm. What was that?" Isolde called out.

"Look, Isolde! The blinds to the windows are automatically going down!"

"What do you think, J. C.? Can we be sure our pilot is okay?"

"Let's see if we can reopen them by hand. No, firmly down. Locked!"

"J. C., they don't want us to know where we are going exactly. I'm worried. Do you think this plane is actually under the orders of Z5? Or has it been commandeered by who knows?"

"What did you say—Z what?"

"Oh my. Aah. Oh my . . ." Isolde was looking uncomfortable about what she had just said. Collecting herself after recognizing she had made a colossal mistake in the stupor of her awakening grogginess, she defensively added, "Something I heard you talk about in your sleep, when I woke up because of the noises of the night around the manor. You said, 'Z5 will save us.'"

"I doubt that, Isolde. You are sounding dangerously confusing."

"J. C., now you are sounding creepy!"

This lady did not know how eerie I would be if I didn't get clear answers when we arrived. Why had she known of Z5? Anyway, that was a real amateur move—just what a newly trained operative might do. Or was she playing me somehow? Did she have the faintest idea what I had to do to anyone who knew of Z5 who was not supposed to? I felt like I was ready to grab the barf bag. This was all becoming very worrisome and damn depressing.

One thing was for sure: if I didn't get some answers soon as to where we were going, I would probably cause cabin decompression from my mounting frustrations. My mood had gotten uglier by the minute.

"Okay, Isolde, let's just forget about it," I said. "I don't know about this Z5, which is what you said. But I feel you're holding out on me about something. We're friends, too. It's more than a job. You know what I mean."

"You're not angry, J. C., are you?"

I went silent. I knew I would likely have to kill her sometime after touching down. This whole operative business was becoming ridiculously tragic. I was beginning to understand, I think, why Zen had put my loyalty to the test at the shed. The bastard likely knew what was ahead. Having to knock off somebody I loved. Yes, that word was damn hard to say in my business.

The whole situation was beginning to make me feel threatened. I had to play dumb about Z5, in case she was just guessing and fishing for information for the opposition. Or worse, she could have been working with Patsy and whoever sponsored this plane—maybe the fanatics. God, they were good if that was the case. I had my own creepy feeling that Jones and his fine Barbados constabulary had been duped.

Then all of a sudden, the pilot's door popped open, and out came Patsy, dressed in a wickedly black Gothic, tight leather outfit. Sumo Joe, or whatever his nickname, was sitting in the copilot's chair facing away, but strangely not moving a twitch. Her clothing somehow drew flashbacks to my muggers on the Limmat in Zürich. She looked decidedly less friendly and more all business than when she had first greeted us.

"Put on these outfits—just like mine. Except don't forget to put on these hoods when you go back to your seats. I'll secure them. You are about to visit the Council, and they don't want you to know where they are for some reason."

"The Council. What's that?" I said, trying to act all innocent.

"You'll see," said Patsy. "By the way, what have you done, J. C.? Have you and the Countess been up to no good? Anyhow, I'm making too much small talk." Patsy was returning a bit more to her frisky self, but still looked deadly serious overall—with that kind of focus of mission and authority that I had seen from the British SAS special forces, or the former ones who had gone mercenary.

"There's the washroom for changing." Patsy pointed firmly to the obvious. "Mind your elbows in there. One person at a time, you lovers. You have about fifteen minutes to change, so be quick."

*   *   *

It was definitely a bumpy landing, almost like the landing strip had not been maintained that well and as if the pilot had not been too interested in his passengers' comfort. The reverse thrusters were put on powerfully, but for a fairly short period. In my mind, it indicated that the runway might not be that long. But I could not be sure. If it was, then it was likely that we were not at a major airport—and possibly, an old one at that. If not at a major place, then where?

"Just stand here near the front of the door," ordered our flight attendant transposed into a near master drill sergeant, right after we had taxied and moved to the hangar. I was the blind leading the blind with this headgear. Or did these two women have it over me? Was I about to be shot in the head and thrown out into a largely abandoned airfield? Or both of us could be.

"And upon my command, walk through until I tell you to stop." As the door was flung open, I could feel the cool salty breeze that told me that we were not inland. Maybe we had gone in circles around Mustique, I thought stupidly. No, the air was decidedly cooler, and so was I to a theory that we would be imminently assassinated. Nothing like cool fresh air to give one hope. Or to knock some sense into me from being so paranoid. They had had plenty of opportunity to throw us out the door over the ocean, if they had actually wanted to put us away and kill the evidence.

"Proceed now; watch your step," said Patsy. All I could say about Patsy was that if she could tell me whom I was meeting, she must have had a very high level of clearance. The Council, of whom I had feigned my ignorance, was more secretive and higher up than the Order. Well above the Z-bank that managed the finances of both organizations. And well above the secrecy of Z5, which was practically invisible in itself. God knows what else the Council managed or reported to. It made the Masons, including the Black Lodge, and other secret religious societies, look—comparatively speaking—like open houses by a realtor.

Zen had only mentioned the Council to me once. Possibly only to frighten me. In his defensive mind, to warn me that if I had any ideas of wiping out or seriously compromising Z5 or him, the Council had the power to completely obliterate me and anybody whom I told about Z5. And to start over a completely new operation altogether, well outside my knowledge. Zen was a shrewd operator who covered all the bases.

"Now be careful; you'll be lifted down to the ground," Patsy warned. ZZZZ . . . ZZZZ . . . ZZZZZ, as the winch lowered us as slowly as if we were delicate, fragile cargo. Why this was needed for a small executive jet plane was beyond me.

It was bizarre to be standing beside Isolde with both of us blackened out to what was surrounding us. The platform stopped. It shook a little. So did we. I had no idea what was ahead of us, and likely neither did Isolde, especially given that in her current status she had sanctioned herself to an execution. But first, the assassin had to focus on not getting himself assassinated.

"A right turn and a few steps. Please, step out gently, both of you. Now, hold my hand; I'll direct you to the Hummer. After twenty yards, perhaps more, we'll stop and get in." After a minute of careful walking, Patsy stopped. "Here, just get in carefully. I'll guide your heads. You first, Countess, and then move over to give space for the Professor."

We were off like a flash, and this time clearly not bothering with customs. Isolde had the package. I gathered it was somewhere on her person—I hoped. And speaking of packages, who knew where our luggage had gone? Conceivably for deep inspection.

The Hummer stopped abruptly after making a long curved drive around the airport and then a steep drive up a hill, followed by crossing a very short bridge. Drawbridge, possibly, given how short it was and how quick the stop was after it. There was all of a sudden a hard bounce on what seemed like very old cobblestone that echoed all about and off very thick walls.

The ride up the hill had taken no more than fifteen minutes, and we had been driven at quite a fast clip, for reasons I could only guess. To secure the document and protect the passengers. In that order. That might have meant that our hosts were still very worried about infiltration. That wasn't a good sign.

There was Patsy's voice again. But seemingly more urgent. "Come on, get out now. Come along, holding onto me at my sides." She guided us through a very long corridor from the way echoes of our feet resonated away for such a long period of time. And then seemingly we were maneuvered into a room. I gathered it was large by the distance to the voice at the other end.

"Thank you," said a rather baritone, male voice, around fiftyish. "Patsy, please remove our important guests' hoods. And that will be all. Oh yes, and close both outer and inner doors on the way out. And firmly, please. Please put on the electronic cloak fully."

"Yes, Mr. Stock."

There we were sitting in the main room of what looked like the inner keep of a Norman castle. Though I couldn't be sure it was Norman. All sorts of nice colorful pennants, no doubt relating to past ancient victories and possibly a few more recent ones. Were we in England? And who then was our new host, who turned dramatically around to greet us, right at the moment we could see?

"Professor Sands and Countess, you both look a little bemused. I don't blame you. Please, have one of these ports, Baron Forester vintage, vintage eighty-five, that's 1885. They'll be some good medicine, well, for what initially ails you—I hope.

"Right, thank you, but I somehow feel that your invitation was a trifle too formal." I was looking at our host tiredly when I said it. Fatigued about being incessantly left on a merry-go-round. However terrible I looked, I wanted to look a wee bit more abused.

"Sorry, old man and my lady, for all of this cloak-and-dagger, but you know how Zen is about protocol. And so am I."

"Oh yes," I nodded very knowingly and agreeably. I wasn't really too much in the arguing mood, as I still had a few bruises and bumps that I didn't want to be added to. I also sensed a somewhat friendly air on the part of our host. Isolde, though, was more interventionist and aggressive for answers.

"Why, pray tell, Mr . . . ."

"Yes, you can call me Mr. Stock. You heard correctly."

"Yes. Why, Mr. Stock, have you got us sequestered in this damp, dungeonlike facility? I am a little more used to friendlier and warmer environments, Renaissance castles with free access to the surroundings, even the outside ones. Ones without a shroud for their guests. Ones that don't make me feel, along with the surroundings, as if I'm soon to be a victim for the axe at the Tower of London."

"Yes, I assure you this is a much friendlier place, though interesting you noticed architectural similarities with that castle. Quite remarkable, Countess, given that we showed you so little on your first tour, so to speak."

"I certainly don't know why I was bundled up like general cargo. It's ridiculous," said Isolde with her nose in the air.

"Now, Countess, we know of your noble rank. That is why you will find your quarters make the best in the Condé Nast travel magazine look like trash. We also have a Cordon Bleu chef here who could put the best chefs in the world to shame. I hope things are looking up a bit more. We live a privileged life, as we are an off-balance sheet intelligence agency, generally free from taxpayer scrutiny."

Isolde and Stock laughed together like they were of the same breeding—tone, gastronomy, and hospitality so similar as to render any further apologies almost unnecessary. As an American brought up on the "wrong side of the tracks," I sometimes thought all these formalities and charm were ludicrous. And they were probably already great party buddies on the nobility circuit and playing me. Yes, I was tired.

"Now, Countess, can we speed you to your quarters so that you can get cleaned up and a bit rested? To make this all possible, I would simply ask you for the coded list. I would like to say on behalf of the intelligence community, we are truly appreciative of all the hard work you and Mr . . . . Or is it actually Professor Sands? Yes, it is hard to figure what to call you."

"J. C, please."

"Hmm, I have a difficult time with that as I am a devout Christian, and in fact descended from the very crusaders who built this castle."

"Then, why not call me Professor Sands, Mr. Stock?"

"Oh really now, just call me Sir Jonathan, both of you. No, just plain Jonathan. I think we're going to soon get along splendidly. I know you American chaps like informality, and so do I," he said unctuously.

"Right then. Adrian for me is okay."

"Let's make it a threesome. Call me Isolde." She laughed again. We were all making such good and fast social progress. How charming, but I still wasn't sure all was well. In fact, I still largely didn't know what the hell was going on, but I had a couple of aristocrats purring complimentary goodwill and gestures between them. How quaint.

However, good manners of the well-cultured were no substitute for good judgment. MI5 had been full of good breeding, lots of aristocrats, and yes, lots of leaks and traitors. And Stock was definitely very English. And sounding a bit old-fashioned and *MI5ish*.

"Splendid, yes, how witty, Countess . . . uh, I mean Isolde." Stock was still showing his old European refinement, or a pretty good act of it.

"Ah, Mr. Stock, and just a minute, Isolde, before you hand him the list. I'd like to make sure he is the real thing."

"Okay, Adrian, shoot away," said Jonathan with nonchalance, almost like he thought my comments were insignificant or a silly joke.

"I'm sorry, Jonathan; he is a suspicious American to anything that smells British and intelligence," said Isolde lightly apologetically.

"I quite understand. You chaps were rather let down by our side, but that was eons ago."

"Okay, Jonathan. What does Zen look like?" I could not help but get a bit testy with Jonathan, however juvenile I might sound with these questions. Strictly speaking, any questions about Z5 were out of order. But they would help me better understand how well connected and informed Jonathan was.

"Is this, old boy, like that Jeopardy game you have on TV? Do I get to choose my own subject categories?"

Isolde was looking downright embarrassed and almost giggling. Meanwhile, I was not amused.

"I can go one step further," said Stock, increasingly assured in his tone but also in his seriousness. "I can tell you what he recently said to you. He gave you a long lecture about the madness of Van Gogh, and to trust the virtue of our side. Didn't he?"

"Go on."

"And you should equally place that trust in us. Oh yes, you have a contact at Interpol whose name is Falcon. Zen has a birthmark on his right shoulder, or should I say a tattoo of a chrysanthemum, as you must have seen when you were taken out to the shed, proverbially speaking. Of course, you went there on your own at 4:30 p.m. I think your concierge contact is Nic at the Schotland. Do you want me to list your favorite colors or more intimate details?"

Isolde laughed. I didn't. For now I was wondering whether his dossier was so complete that it went to my bedroom.

"Okay, I get it." If I was being played, they were so good they deserved my partial cooperation.

"Adrian, let the man do his work. He doesn't have all day." Isolde handed him the list.

"Yes, thank you for the package. Hmm, this is quite a bizarre coded list. It looks like a list. But I'm not so sure of it. More like a poem, short couplets, who knows, given the length of the lines?" Stock was very intent as he looked at it with a worried frown.

"In southern Arabian, I believe," added Isolde. "A classical form that died out because of the spread of the Koran, which was in a northern Arabic dialect that became dominant through the Koran's spread."

"So I heard," said Stock disinterestedly as he focused intently on the list. "Now, Professor Sands, no, Adrian, I have a bit more embarrassing news for you."

"I'm used to it."

"Isolde has been with the Council—though only partially—for some time. The full Council includes me, whom she has met only today."

Isolde smiled somewhat bemusedly, I hoped, or was she hiding a kind of contempt for my lack of knowledge of her position? For some reason, at that moment, I could not help myself blurting out how I had been deceived—it had all been too much that I was not just going to merrily give a stiff upper lip and carry on and be a happy camper. I was going to be very un-British, and no doubt, disappointing to Jonathan, who was used to his top-down approach with little resistance, or at a minimum, the polite kind. I was going to be a delightfully pain-in-the-ass American who was not going to charge out for the Light Brigade, talking it up with cheerio.

"It's really amazing, Isolde, that you kept this from me. I'm a little hurt that you didn't confide in me. I wonder what was my purpose if, in fact, as I gathered from Panama and everything else, it is you who is very able to protect any of us from harm. Maybe I was just luggage."

Stock interrupted. "Oh yes, I heard, Adrian, that you were brilliantly muscular. I also heard you especially made a good imitation of a beached whale."

I wondered if he was getting in a jab, because so many English in the intelligent services still had this supremely confident feeling that they had invented the art, and that we Americans were a poor and amateur imitation of it. Or possibly, as an old-school British type, he might very well have not liked Americans because we talked back with a spice of insubordination. Oh yes, backed up by tons of resources, making us, I suppose, seem nouveau riche and a touch uncultivated.

I never felt an urge to terminate any of my higher-ups, but this rather smug, old Etonian, I guessed, could be a decent exception to the rule under the right circumstances. What indeed was I thinking? He was now probably my boss and supposed ally, irrespective that he was acting like a bit of an upper-class twit. Too bad I couldn't care that much about such nice-mannered conventions.

"Please, Adrian, don't look too out of kilter. Isolde was able to transmit from Panama a quick report on your mishaps and, more importantly, a few other more important details and even successes. And certainly you did have one. You survived and got away. Oh yes, excuse me, we could count that as two."

"Huh . . . Isolde filing reports. What was that about?" More news showing I had been played well out of the main loops.

"Yes, we might as well tell you that Isolde has been working a bit freelance off and on for us. May I say, keeping an eye on you too, and to keep you alive so as to protect the Order. You should feel very lucky not ending up in the Limmat. Oh yes, that rather eloquent tail was a member of Sarabian intelligence, just making sure you were not going to receive a second mugging. I quite assure you, he would have used his Beretta on anyone. You had a few agent angels looking over you, in fact, possibly one standing over you. Sorry, we only found out at the last minute from the Sarabians that you were going to be thumped. But may I add that we do feel grateful for your work too, nevertheless."

"What do you mean?" This was becoming a further nightmare. I felt dumb and getting dumber—like a very bad comedy that could have been called "Adrian the Buffoon," right out of a French, Louis de Funes police slapstick. Who were these people I was working for? They appeared to be a whole new breed that made the CIA and MI5 look like kindergarten.

"Anyway, Adrian, these are small details. But I wanted to thank you personally. Now, Adrian, I have a piece of paper for you."

I thought this was going to be my red letter or end of service check to say good-bye and good riddance in the polite parlance of supremely British management discourse.

"What is it?" I said. "Doesn't look like much more than a bunch of Arabic."

"Take a closer look," said Stock as he handed it completely over to me.

"Huh, this is, I think, the exact list that Isolde obtained with all that bloodshed we had to go through. How come you already had it before we even arrived?" I was actually feeling increasingly out of the loop. And a dork.

"I'm glad you are convinced that it is the same," responded Stock, now talking more officially like a law enforcement official than an aristocrat with putdown airs. "In reality, it is not. Isolde did Bluetooth a number of summarized details, but not too many in case it was intercepted. Just enough so we could fabricate a facsimile in a timely way. Incidentally Isolde will be further working on the original one to decipher," added Stock.

"Bloody amazing," I exclaimed. My head felt dented again from intense deception—or was that stupidity?

"But more importantly, my good man, Isolde is a cipher expert, as well as holding a doctorate specializing in ancient and current Semitic languages and linguistics."

"What does this exactly have to do with me? But I'm further amazed, Isolde. Do you work for the Cirque de Soleil or any other circus in between? A three-ring spy ring?"

Isolde now looked cannily smart and a little too happily smug for my liking.

Stock continued, "Now this is very important, Adrian. You are going to look like you are going to deliver it to Z5 in Zürich—and, should I say, look like it is extremely important to protect. This may prove to be one of the most important reasons we hired you. It's a very delicate and extremely important task."

"This is all news to me."

"No matter. Now, according to your original itinerary, your flight out of London is going to arrive at the gate in about two and a half hours in Zürich. Your name is on the passenger manifest, but don't ask how."

"Don't worry, Jonathan, I am all ears and growing impressed with your efficiency."

"You'll be on that flight with Patsy, who if you didn't notice has a sort of resemblance to Isolde, especially with wig and makeup. She has a pretty good karate chop too. Patsy is a highly trained operative who has studied

Isolde's voice and dossier. She was formerly the first woman commander with the British SAS.

"Really, Jonathan? Not even a request for me to help with the voice coaching?" Isolde said while looking at me, as if trying to give comfort that she had also not been enough in the inner circle.

"We expect leftovers of Mr. Kartman or his European contacts, plus possibly others, will be waiting to get their hot hands on your fake list. Oh officially, a real list, which by the way in its original form has supposedly the most comprehensive list of traitors to the very survival of Western civilization. You should possibly expect that there will be a major incident at the airport or elsewhere in Zürich to obtain it. I am telling you the basic nature of the document, so you know the extent of the danger that you will be in."

"Well, thank you," I said, trying to look like a ton of manure had been dropped on my foot—unwrapped. But Zen had already reminded me of the deadly stinking work that I had stepped into—in fact, countless times before, so I wondered why Jonathan was repeating it. But I initially played along.

"Don't worry, a heap of thanks will come your way if you follow instructions carefully and pull this off, which I have every confidence that you will."

"I'm obliged."

Jonathan continued in his serious professional tone, "Quite. Now to underscore how vital your mission is: those who are the intermediaries to delivering the list—after they steal it from you, or preferably the police—must think they are getting the original back. We believe, at the very least, its presence in Zürich could very well lead us to their high-level contacts. This in itself will help us put together more pieces of the puzzle as to who in the entirety are these traitors, conspirators."

"Conspirators, inside traitors?" queried Isolde. "Do you have any idea who might be the traitors? Are there traitors for certain?"

"We are not sure if anyone on this list is in our organization—though someone in Sarabia has given us indications that there could be. It was too hot for him to relay the specific information electronically. And it was very hard to decipher. And now he is dead."

"I see," Isolde said.

The Council and Z5 seemed to be near totally blind on knowing who might be the traitors. That wasn't good. It wasn't good at all—if that was the case. They could theoretically be in the castle, the plane, just about God damn anywhere, and with a knife looking for a fresh back.

"We have to also wonder, even as good as our cryptology team is, that we may not be able to decode enough of it or fast enough. So this is a two-way play to get critical answers," stated Jonathan.

"But the Kartman or other group may sell it to even a nonbelligerent Western intelligence organization," I said, with understated worry that this operation could be like finding a needle in a haystack with no haystacks on the horizon. And to be sure, given its importance, there could be a bevy of unsavory individuals, and even savory ones, who would have no compunction in removing me to get that list.

My chances of survival were getting very iffy. I was going to be one nice big piece of glowing fleshy bait in a pool of sharks. Was this dangerous operation, I wondered, just to get me dead?

"My guess, with cooperation from Interpol, which is increasingly in on the operation, is that the list is hands-off to their intervention and their members. So we don't expect any friendly fire."

"Oh, that's great, Jonathan. Interpol, with a number of those lunatic member countries, knowing more about what we're doing. Should I take my cyanide pill now?"

"Now really, Adrian, all the critical information is quarantined. They know to stay away from the airport—that is all the extra information we have provided. And if those so-called lunatic members show up, they are likely at some point going to deliver the list to those who are most worried about it being exposed. It may very well draw out those we need to know more about."

"Well, that sounds better," assuaged Isolde.

"I don't know. Perhaps they would just destroy it, along with me—and not to forget poor Patsy, too," I incredulously retorted.

"Nice that you're thinking like a team member," gleamed Jonathan. "No worry, Adrian. By the way, there is an incredible state-of-the-art bug that is nonmetallic, which is extremely unlikely in its microfiber content to be discovered. The paper is produced by a special security paper company based only in Switzerland, working with a highly confidential electronics contractor. It is well disguised in the paper."

"I'm impressed," I said but not feeling overimpressed about the entire operation.

"At least not until we follow it through several hands will we nab anybody. A number of agents will catalogue the locations and individuals getting their hands on it. Anyway, enough," said Jonathan.

"But what if they destroy it or recognize it as a fake before you get enough information?" Isolde queried.

"Then we'll simply give Isolde the real one, after it has been decoded. We would make it known that they were duped by an opportunist money-grubber, inside rogue element—meaning you, Adrian. It is very unlikely, given the amount of money at play, that those who first take it are going to have enough time or resources to figure out its authenticity for some time. Besides, would most of the initial people in contact with the list have the necessary expertise to decode or verify it? I doubt it. While they move the list closer to the original owners, we would hopefully learn about their outer networks at the minimum. We would round up as many as we could, unknown to the others, who would be in direct contact with the original owners by then."

"Well again, my fondest thanks to you, Jonathan."

"Yes, a swell job of using us," added Isolde.

"That's what you're here for, not a picnic."

"No, more like a rifle range, with us like sitting ducks with our wings clipped," I angrily added.

"Oh yes, something else," said Jonathan, not even registering Isolde's and my anxiety about whether the mission had been well thought out, including making our survival even a moderate possibility. "Don't rip it. The list, that is."

"Ah, your trust in me is growing by leaps and bounds," I laughed.

"Right, well, that's just about it. Ah yes . . . and good luck."

There was a knock at the door. In came Patsy, looking like a duplicate of Isolde. So good it made Isolde spin her head.

"Amazing, Adrian, isn't it?"

"You've been holding out again, Isolde. She's really your twin sister." It was finally my turn to make the jokes and the teases.

Patsy did an impressive twirl like she was on a catwalk. She was as cunning as a feline anywhere. And better looking than I had originally thought. Or the Isolde impression was turning me on.

"Now, again may I ask you, Adrian, to put the hood on?" Jonathan ordered diplomatically.

"Only if it comes with a spanking from Patsy."

Isolde laughed.

"You laugh, but I have had to deal with a bunch of banking sadists who are really into this stuff. Come on—is this all necessary?" I was sounding a little desperate, a little too demanding, like a kid asking for extra allowance from his dad. Yeah, under the complete control of this smooth-mannered fella, I was feeling infantile, feeling again like being pushed around as I had been in Sarabia. It never seemed to stop with me, no matter where I was or the year. "And where the heck are we?"

"Okay, Adrian, you win," said Jonathan, but with a voice that sounded more of frustration than genuineness. "Shall I give you a hint? Remember the cult TV series *The Prisoner*?"

"Really, Wales, you mean. That's where it was shot."

"Yes, we are going to put you in a village and call you number six until you confess that you have been working for the other side, given how dreadful a job you've been doing."

"What the hell? I have had it with you, Jonathan. Let's get on with it."

"Yes, indeed, I'm just messing with you, Adrian, and I'll do worse with you as we're beginning to run out of time. Just follow your controller's instructions. Patsy is your controller now."

Isolde, along with Patsy, was in a feast of laughter.

"More seriously, I wasn't going to tell you as it is quite off-putting, but in the spirit of openness . . ." Jonathan continued somewhat hesitantly. "Look, Zen had an accident with a gang of delinquents from what we've been able to piece together. He's in a coma."

"Jesus, how did that happen? There's more surprises happening here than at a Mason's Lodge in a year," I said.

"We don't know, but every resource we have available is into tracking down these fellows that we think also hit upon you. They seem for some reason to have very good and precise information on the movements of key Z5 people. Your repositioning to deliver the list here would have normally been a breach of security, or at least, of protocol."

I now wanted to take away some of my new confidence in this organization that I had initially expressed. God, if they had gotten to Zen, no wonder they had *hived* me off from Z5. Maybe they would close it. Our covers from top to bottom could be blown. But by whom?

"Patsy said you were the Council," I said. But not with a tone that indicated the information was very revealing, just that I wanted more information about it.

"Now that was a little too revealing at the time. I am the only one with authority to make such a revelation. But under the situation, it was inevitable, I suppose," said a rather put-off Jonathan, like one of his cute secrets had been too prematurely shown. I was like an actor abusing the script by jumping too far ahead of what the director wanted. Yeah, it all sounded a bit too scripted, and me taking the trouble to botch it.

"Thanks for throwing out an extra bone, Colonel," I facetiously tossed in. Confirming his former title in the military without knowing it.

"May I continue?"

"Yes, you're doing fine. You can see I'm a little beaten-up, as I think I said before."

"Well, you look better than Zen." Jonathan was reaffirming his lack of happiness with my peevishness, another sure sign I wasn't playing my role like the good old boy, Etonian style. I had certainly had enough of that formal total loyalty thing—like the freestyle American adolescent I had been, who coped badly with the British-style private school I had attended. But had I really had enough of this patronizing authority?

"Right you are, Colonel!" Yet, I still needed to show faith in somebody, even if I felt everything was at risk of falling down on us. No . . . I said the words, but I was losing confidence as fast as a snowball melting in an oven.

"Now, something I consider very uncomfortable. You will also be duping a very fine police team, headed by *Herr* Friegel, that is generally on our side," Jonathan continued. "You will deliver the fake list to them, and also retain a copy for delivery in case they are not able to deliver it so to speak. Swiss intelligence will be the only Swiss authorities to know how you have come in a private jet to Zürich."

"Jonathan, I can just see the face of *Herr* Friegel, if he were to ever find out he was excluded about how we are going to enter Switzerland and how fake the list is that I will be passing on."

"Oh yes, he is an inspector, I suppose." Jonathan responded to me as if Friegel were incidental. "Right. So don't even think of telling the inspector that you weren't on the commercial plane. Or anything else we have discussed here. I don't put much confidence into the police compared to the secret services in keeping anything important hush-hush."

"Did you know, Jonathan, we were going to Zürich by 'unconventional airlines' well before I arranged everything with Friegel to greet us at the gate? Even before Zen got clobbered?"

"Now, really, how efficient and devious do you think we are, Adrian?"

"I'm almost beginning to believe that I have had actually no idea as to what was going on overall. It's clearly your show, Jonathan, especially now that . . ."

"Continue—I am fascinated, though we are running a bit short," added Jonathan with an amused and curious look.

"Devious enough for you to give an undercover name for Panama that was just about the same as the safe house in Barbados. Devious enough to have a Bombardier jet waiting or on the way to Mustique way before I arrived at Sam Lord's. Devious and mischievous enough to give the coded words for recognizing me to the check-in clerk at Sam Lord's Castle to make sure of my identity. And devious enough to kill those Panama Mafiosi commandos who were about to storm the hotel, and make it look like they got killed because they had an accident with a reef and a 'bow and arrow.' And some sharks."

"Bravo, Adrian, you've demonstrated what a fine investigative and deductive mind you have after all. But how did you know about that motley Mafiosi crew storming Sam Lord's?"

"You kept an Isolde decoy there. I presume Patsy, who probably disposed of those attackers and then made off to Mustique. For all we know, she was made up to look like Isolde. Then, with the authorities' help, she dumped their bodies on the reef, along with their zodiac to make it look like an accident, no doubt. Oh, by the way, nice touch with the speargun or whatever."

"Touché. No, you're not so simpleminded. You have convinced me that our investment in you has been worth it."

"But you have forgotten something very important that I think you were supposed to learn in all your debriefings from Zen," I added. "Critically important."

"What might that be?" Jonathan queried, with such a high sense of confidence that he was practically purring it.

"Yes. We'll have to talk about my assassination orders for you," I added. "Is that what you wanted me to say?"

I was getting too nervous about how sly Jonathan had been and beginning to again lose my faith in this commander. I was now probably, to my further regret, about to regress into my insubordinate self of good old school and undergraduate days.

"Now really . . . how bizarre!" Stock looked uncharacteristically shocked and poured another glass of port, pretending to look cool and detached. "What do you mean?" He tried to sound flat, but his hand seemed to show a bit more nervousness than he would have liked it to have shown.

"Look, Jonathan, don't feel bad about it—it's just operational business, not personal. I am sure you can find convincing ways for me to break my orders. Or maybe not. After all, I don't know either you or Isolde as being officially in the loop about Z5 or Zen. Nobody told me that either of you were on the protection list. And you both have clearly shown you know about Z5."

I was looking for a little revenge for being played for a sucker, not too content with all this smugness at my expense. Oh yes, I was still not feeling a hundred percent about Jonathan, even after trying to convince myself, occasionally, of the merits of applying the *Führer* concept—obey and not question—to this new guy on the block. What a waste of time playing that game.

"What could you possibly mean, Adrian?" queried Jonathan.

"Adrian, what is this?" added Isolde. "Are you nuts?"

"Yes, I have been playing with that idea of whether I am insane. Insane to be in this job after all of the attempts to snuff me out. We are friends here. But we don't let anybody survive who knows about Z5 who is not in a need to know. Remember?"

"Oh yes," said Isolde, looking muffed that she had not recollected that important rule. Or that I was going to keep to it after all we had been through.

Jonathan was looking edgy and at his watch. "Look, we have clearly showed our good intentions, and I have demonstrated my identity with information that few could know about."

"How do I know that you're not the traitor inside, that you got Zen put into a coma? That Zen did not tell me about you for a good reason, so you wouldn't be put on the protection list if he became indisposed and you inevitably became my overseer?"

"Okay, Adrian, I've had enough of your many delusions. Here's a Colt fully loaded, which I could have used on you, by the way. If you doubt that any one of us is faithfully working for the right side, then shoot us. Time's just about up."

"What are you saying?" Isolde said as she jumped up. "This is preposterous!"

"Yes, it bloody is," I said as I took the gun.

"What are you going to do with that gun, Adrian?" inquired Isolde, alarmed.

"Well, shoot you, love, what else?"

"That would be a great mistake," said Jonathan. "You would have to go down in history as worse than Neville Chamberlain giving away next to the whole lot to Hitler."

"Are you now finished with your antics?" blared out Isolde.

"No more questions. Nobody is going to get shot unless you people shoot me." I then handed over the gun. "I'm quite satisfied now."

"Wise choice," sighed Jonathan. The man was not totally with ice in his veins.

"Let me explain a few more things to make things go easier," he continued. "I don't want to see such a charade ever repeated."

"Charade! It was both of you macho types with the charades!" Isolde screamed out. "There could have been a lot of useless dead bodies. A lot that would have done defending civilization from these traitors. You would have done the job for them."

"Okay, Colonel, everybody . . . Yeah, I kind of feel stupid. Though she is beautiful when angry, isn't she? I'm under a lot of pressure and quite confused. I probably should be on valium or God knows what. But glad nevertheless to get some answers, further evidence that you people are on my side," I said to diffuse the situation.

"Look, to further assuage you—the von Drax name was Zen's idea, and we know where Zen is—in a coma," added Jonathan. "I can show you the deciphered message as proof on that if you want. It would take a while, though, and we don't have so much time."

"Yes, okay, I assume you have it." I went along agreeably. It was getting pointless to try and generate any further trust. But Jonathan still felt the need to clarify, possibly as a precaution to me getting nervous feet.

"Now you're both probably wondering why we were quickly able to put another plan into play, I suppose. The plan at first was simply a backup plan in case things got too testy and we needed to smuggle you in through the airport's back door so to speak. We never knew that Zen's situation would lead us to having to bring the list here first, by way of Mustique. Finally, you are on the Island of Derby, under the protection so to speak of the Duchess of Normandy, for whatever that is worth, since you seem to want to know so much."

"Derby. Can I ask who she is really? Another female protector, how interesting."

Isolde chuckled, and Jonathan again looked smug and amused.

"Can we tell him that one, Patsy—that's top, top secret? We might have to . . . if we did."

"Come on, let's not play anymore, Jonathan. He might shoot us next time," said Patsy, looking actually bored.

"The Duchess of Normandy, my good man, is no other than Queen Elizabeth the Second. Or actually, the first for this island—but no matter. And by the way, she doesn't even know that I, you, and Isolde exist at all—officially. She is aware of the vital importance of our mission, I can tell you that."

"That's incredible; I thought she just lounged about and played with her corgis all day," I joked. I wasn't very good at this British thing.

"Really, Adrian. And we don't waste agents unnecessarily. I hope you fully understand that. You should, given your military record and being with Interpol . . . now for how many years?"

"Three, though only as a cover."

"Oh yes, yet I suppose we are a little unusual for our methods, and a lot has happened around you in the last weeks."

"Oh, we do understand, Colonel," added Isolde, looking like a school grader pining away for that extra gold star on her assignment.

"Another real problem was that Zen was going to reveal something important about the list to me in person, but only in person. Not long after that, he got mugged badly. Now, Adrian, I want you to sublimate your ego and hurt pride and stay cool and focused in the mission."

"And try to stay off the booze in flight or on the ground," added Isolde as she went all motherly on me.

Patsy added, "You now have twenty-five minutes to get to the plane so you arrive in enough time at Zürich, and be positioned to make it look like you are coming off that London flight."

Yeah, the concern by all around me made me feel like family.

"Good speed and make haste, but not too much haste. Hell, break a leg!" added Jonathan. He was encouraging, and this time not a condescending smile.

"See you, Isolde, my protecting countess," I said as I made a gentler wave in her direction, as if we were old flames.

Isolde laughed and choked up tears almost at the same time. Did she truly have real feelings for me? Her assassin to lover in one afternoon. Maybe that showed we were onto a great relationship. I wondered how much more bullshit I could take by working as a killer for these mobs. Not much more, I thought. But first, Isolde would stay and work herself almost to death if need be, to fully decipher the list.

"Oh, yes, one thing more, Jonathan."

"Oh, what is it?"

"Keep the hood definitely," I responded with a bit of a tease as I handed it to him almost forcefully. "Yeah, I like the Channel Islands, too—or the Norman Islands, as the French call them. One of my banks is down the hill from here. This would be Guernsey, not Derby. And she's Queen Elizabeth the Second of this rock if you study your history correctly."

I left some falling jaws behind with those comments. Yes, I very much wanted to leave Jonathan with his knowing that he should show a little respect to this ill-informed and rude American. All that upper-crust charm and supreme confidence made me worry that he might just get too up on himself, when Isolde's and my survival would be at stake.

I had seen these highly educated and so very noble types absolutely totally blowing it. With my apologies to the queen, who could have run the whole operation without an incident given everything she had been through, including fixing trucks in World War II and managing a highly interesting family. It was especially a few of the lower nobility and new nobility who worried me.

Meanwhile, I would be going from the frying pan into the fire. At least, I knew the full stakes, but poor old Friegel and his regular police detail didn't. I feared that they might be heading for a massacre, especially if I handed over the list to them. Friegel had known it was going to be trouble, but not a holocaust worth of it. And it might not be any easier for Patsy and me. Yeah, "patsy," that was a good name for what we both were. And for Friegel and his men, the name would be a lot less kind. That name would be *disposable*.

EIGHTEEN

Barney Rob was now essentially retired, living the good life in Panama that someone of his age and his health had to. At eighty, he was no Texas spring chicken. He needed to take it easy, which meant getting out of Texas during the *coolish* winters and being a bit more isolated from all those who pressed upon him in his home state to put on barbeque socials, given their great popularity.

He also had his own great sustaining popularity because of the wealth and charity he had spread around for decades, like a rich farmer spreading manure to make sure his next crops would present a full harvest. Barney deserved a bit of time out from the smell of it all. That was charity enough for the old wise geezer that he thought of himself as being.

His arthritis acted up during the Texas winters, which he proudly blamed on his rodeo days of branding cattle and lassoing wild horses that had sometimes gotten him twisted up and even stomped on. Barney might have been an arthritic, but he was someone with excellent financial health who still had his marbles. And most of the marbles were on his side in any good deal he still fashioned as an active billionaire. That huge wealth allowed him the unending pleasure of the best doctors and physiotherapists, and a whole lot of special treatment, including the most sophisticated smart-house contraptions. That involved having one high-tech device that precisely dehumidified each room depending upon who was in it—within his sprawling fifty-room beach house. All available to him, when he was not traveling during the humid sweltering heat of the Panama summer.

Living in Panama and having a Panamanian passport was not only healthy because of the better winter weather over Texas; it also helped him greatly reduce his income taxes and any future US death taxes. Barney was determined to escape what he called the "injustices of the

IRS motherfuckers" even if he could not be immortal. That was the only certainty he was going to allow. He would have liked to have sent the IRS to Sarabia for some purified Sarabian Abrahamic justice. In a moment of anger, he thought of writing in a codicil to his will requesting a hit on the IRS squad that had been specifically assigned to his dossier.

Barney did not know that someone might put his wishes into action only a continent away, and with a harsher, no-nonsense accent than his charming southerly drawl. Barney would not know a *Locarnetto* sanction if it walked up and whacked him. But he might have shaken its hand if it had been embodied, and especially if it was not specifically making a visit to him but rather to his so-called taxation oppressor.

There was a reason beyond just pure cash as to why MANCITC's top two had chosen Rob with Bashard's acceptance. This wily billionaire, whom Bashard had known since college days, was able to somehow crack through the prince's exterior and get him into a cheerful mood. To get him to talk about his riding ability and about his days in the desert when he was a small boy and Sarabia was full of debt and derision from the West. And when it had much less oil production.

Barney could only surmise that Bashard's lieutenants were here to reciprocate on that bit of congeniality with a few hundred or so millions—or a nice even billion bucks, if he was actually lucky. Bashard's deals were usually good. Well, they had been.

"Okay, gentlemen, nice to see you. Hope your ride into Panama was good. How were the Cubans, Chad?"

"What Cubans?" said Chad Pincer. He was wondering whether Barney was throwing a curveball just to put them off their game and maneuver into a better negotiating position. Chad pondered if Barney was on top of their new MANCITC initiatives with young Cuban Communist businessmen, knowledge of whom would make Barney Rob light up like a fireworks factory on fire just before the fourth of July. He feared the worst and Rob's wrath.

"Oh I don't know. I thought you guys were getting a bit desperate for cash so had visited good ole Castrato Junior. You were in Miami, weren't you? Heard he was secretly in town."

"Nope, not at all. Well, just the airport," said Chad. Pincer was not speaking for himself. But Jock, his CFO, had met a secret Cuban business delegation. Chad could have been a diplomat. Statecraft said only a poor diplomat ever had to lie. In other words, Chad was a first-class bullshitter.

Given the state of MANCITC's balance sheet, Chad felt he had to have a long invitation list to help bail MANCITC out, whether it was the Chinese Communist Mandarins, Cuban Marxists, Russian oligarchs, or "moderate" elements of the Taliban. People forgot the Taliban still had hundreds of millions from being paid off by an American pipeline company with operations in Waristan. The company had used its bank accounts in Delaware to pay their protection money to the Taliban, which then used the funds to buy arms and mines. And now that NATO was negotiating again with them, their money was almost good again.

"What a fucked-up world!" Barney thought, as he tried to make sense of it only when he counted his money at the bank.

"That's good to hear you're not too much directly in with Cuban commies, as much as I like Cuban hospitality," Barney said. "I'm still a little sore that a number of American bankers have now started double-dealing by making crazy agreements with Castrato. I lost a lot back in the *sisities* as I call the 1960s. Or should I say my granddad lost lots of concessions. No big meetings with commie Cubans—good."

"Ah, Barney, we need your help!"

"Okay, cut to the chase. Yeah, sorry about all that stuff with the Cubans. I'm getting screwed by a number of the Miami ones who are selling out to baby Castrato. Hmm, that younger generation, boy oh boy, they are sure flexible after everything we did to kill off Stalin's legacy, even in our own country. They are kissing the butts of the Chinese, who God damn it, practically own us—along with the Japanese and the Arabs. No disrespect to the prince, of course."

"Oh, of course not, we're with you all the way on patriotism," said Chad.

Barney, who had fought in the Korean War against the Chinese, looked at the young bankers with baited breath and disgust. He knew full well that the only war they would fight might be a rush up San Juan Hill to lend lucrative loans to Castrato, or storming Washington to kill new regulations to prevent them from getting their big fat bonus checks.

"Anyway, I thought we defeated all those people!" Barney continued, banging on the table and speaking loudly. "Well, I just want our family rum distilleries and ranches back. It's central to my mind before I pass away."

"Why, is there anything we can do for you on this Cuban matter? They have accounts with us—oh sorry, I wasn't supposed to tell you."

"Now, I like your thinking, Chad. At the right time, you can do something for me on that sore point. But what is it you want? Maybe we can help one another. Again, sorry about that Cuban shit."

"The prince needs, at a minimum, ten billion dollars as a start," said Chad without blinking an eye.

Barney was flabbergasted. He was so flabbergasted that he sprayed out his Jack Daniels on the rocks—he even looked like he was about to spit out his own rocks, if not his dentures. He then almost choked and looked in need of the Heimlich maneuver or a respirator.

"He wants what! Look, gentlemen, don't punish me for my lack of hospitality. Let's sit down in more comfort on my patio, and I'll get you gentlemen a drink. And if you don't mind, I'll get a refresher—like going for an ice-cold shower."

Chad and Jock very quietly sat down. Like two church mice not wanting to disturb a very large cat in the room, like a big old curmudgeon cougar that could rip your face off, or in this case, take a big bite out of your career with a quick call. They all went for Southern Comfort. The Jack Daniels had gone empty. Scared out of its bottle by Chad's request, Barney thought humorously to himself, and out of town if bourbon could have walked.

"Boy, that's really nasty—no Jack left. I'll phone up for some. That Southern Comfort is awful stuff to me—a gift from a New England lady with a lovely red ribbon and artsy card with a big "D" on the envelope for some reason. Made sense, I guess, as she was a dealer. An art dealer, that is. Bought me a *Van Goo* over there from her. 'Starry Lights'—cute, eh?"

"Wow, that must have cost you a mint," said Jock, who would have been more sincerely impressed if it had been a walled certificate instead, stating that under his direction he had negotiated a syndication loan of five billion dollars. That was as artsy as his office got for this younger Texan.

"Yeah, one hundred and fifty super-big *smakeroos*. I'll collateralize my whole collection and send you three hundred million, but the painting stays with me. Actually, I'm lending it to a big human rights do—my wife lassoed me into it. An exhibition in Switzerland."

"Oh, that thing," said Jock.

"Huh?" queried Barney.

"I heard about it. Rumors that they might be going to crap on Sarabian politics or something like that. Women's rights and that stuff."

"Oh shit, I don't want to be caught up in anything like that. I don't know, but between you and me, telling Mabel to stay away from those artsy-fartsy gals is like trying to get a wild horse under control."

"It's been done," said Jock, looking deadly serious.

"What do you mean by that comment?"

"I think you know."

"Implying what?" said Rob, beginning to look like his very eighty-plus years, as if all his sinews and veins were going to rupture and attack Jock.

"No, no . . . sorry, Barney!" Jock had realized his blunder. But hoped it wouldn't be too late to correct it. He had lost his diplomatic cool; he wanted nothing to interfere with Bashard wanting to go through with the deal to save MANCITC. The last thing he wanted was for Bashard to get upset with Barney's wife over Sarabian politics. He added, "Yeah, it could be good to have her feel like she's involved with something important. Only a rumor, Barney."

"Yeah, okay. Family stuff is separate anyway," he added a lot more calmly.

"Now, Barney, we just want you to funnel ten billion through your Panamanian foundations to help save MANCITC. If you want to throw in your own spare cash, I don't think there would be any problem with it, but we're not asking for it."

"Oh yeah, another one of those fancy New York banks run by mostly fancy-pansy Harvard and Princeton boys, with not much fancy money left. As you know, the prince and I go back a long way. I just don't know why there needs to be so much secrecy to making these investments. And the amounts. They are almost staggering!"

"Yes, Barney, I forgot to tell you, Prince Bashard extends a warm hello to you and can't wait for your next trip to Raddah in the spring. He promised to bring full air-conditioning to his tent next time. And only well-behaved camels."

Barney laughed. Chad knew he should have first broken the ice with some anecdotes. But he thought they were corny and too personal, more for the prince to recall himself.

Last time Barney visited Sarabia, his legs got so dry he had a contest with Bashard's camel to see who looked more leathery above the hoof. By a toss of the coin, the camel had won, only after the disgruntled female had given him a swift boot in the butt. She, indeed, was a real beauty, worth five hundred thousand dollars given how valuable her bloodlines were. It had been mating season, and yet Barney thought he would, under the advice of his friend, try to pet and make friends with her. But for the female camel, Barney had made a transformation to a real ugly male beast that this fat-lipped beauty had no time for. Or certainly did not want to have any progeny with. Bashard never let him forget that incident and reminded Rob of his endless poor luck with every kind of female, which went all the way back to a western square dance party decades ago, when Rob had been stood up by his second wife—who later divorced him.

"Look, Barney, the prince wants to ensure that MANCITC doesn't go bust," said Chad in a tone that would have been a frown if it had eyes.

"Oh right, throw more bad money to save face. More money than sense. I know it's important for the prince and his extended family there to save face, but I got to say with all respect this is crazy. Let the damn thing die or be picked up totally by the government. Or better, give it over to that buzzard, Willard Rose, who could breathe life back into a dead rattler full of venom or a rat with the plague. Again, no disrespect to the prince, maybe just time for it to go off to 'Bank of Euthanasia' bad bank paradise at the FDIC or at the hands of that prick, Rose. Though Rose is busy with politics these days."

Barney had seen a lot of Sarabian investors chasing much bad money with a lot more good money. But with oil having hit one hundred and fifty dollars a barrel at times, Rob could not argue with acting as a placement party—even putting up collateral to ensure his own significant presence in the deal. That is, as long as he got his nice 3 percent cut of the profits from the convertible bonds, and up to a 10 percent guarantee of the capital through a rights offering extended to him. Yes, on this one, he would put the brilliant Willard, a.k.a. "The Rat," to shame.

"Barney, let's face it, the authorities are not keen on Bashard owning too much of the bank. Last time, they practically turned him into the second coming of Oswald Al Harvee of 10/11 fame with so many investigations," stated Chad.

"Yeah, yeah, I know. These are big dominoes—MANCITC, Diamond Jamison, GAG, and Captain Morgan—I mean Jupiter Morgan. Pardon my humor: I'm not very high on 'easy' coast banks. Any one of them goes, we all go down with them. Yeah, yeah, yeah, I know the script."

"That's not only the news, it's the truth, Barney." Jock had finally spoken up after a long silence. But he still looked useless sitting there and eating ever more canapés, which a servant had brought out of sympathy for his idleness.

"So, you want little old Barney here to place some cash, billions or something like that, and seem like the owner or make it look like a Panamanian is the owner. Hell, you might want me to lie and say I'm the principal owner. Yes, now that I think about it more clearly, good idea to make it look like a non-Arab owns a big chunk of it."

"Now, Barney, the usual commissions. But I get to visit occasionally by way of Colombia, where I will be looking at oil and silver assets there anyway. I will also be delivering through an assistant, coded instructions, which you are to explicitly follow."

Barney shifted his disposition. He looked between stunned unhappy about all the clandestine necessities to this proposed operation, and stunned to the point of jubilation about the millions more he would be making. He conceivably thought that the FBI and CIA would loosen up about Sarabian investments if they saw a few, or even several, billions coming into the banking sector from that country to save the pillars of US capitalism—and all the well-positioned congressmen and senators who wanted to keep it upright.

He not only worried that the FBI and CIA might get sore at him. He also worried about the two-faced, well-bred Beacon Hill and Park Avenue cannibal crowd, who had shorted MANCITC stock and would be looking for blood—maybe his blood when they got ripped apart with their new major reversal of fortunes. He thought to himself that those pricks would short their own mothers to the point that the country would sink and they would be left on an island of only money, without even a pineapple or a coconut to eat. But he was used to the cut and thrust of pissing off enough well-bred sophisticated investors and regulators. He was in Panama, for God's sake!

He envied Bashard and the fact that Wadi Islam considered taxation to be a sin. Barney reflected that if income taxes were promised to be eliminated by a Muslim president, that man (or woman) might take the country by storm. That was the problem. Barney really had quite an imagination. He wondered sometimes where his imagination would lead him. If he wasn't careful, the MANCITC deal would more likely lead him all the way to jail, or worse. Like to a bullet in his head.

NINETEEN

There was Friegel at the executive jet hangar just as Patsy and I disembarked. "What the hell is he doing in this part of the Zürich airport?" I wondered to myself.

"Well, *Herr* Friegel. Surprise, surprise!" I had to think fast on my feet. No secret service. Or Christ, was he also the secret service, or was he close enough to it? I would start to play him like he was.

"Yes, Mr. Martin, let's keep it that way. We wouldn't like it if I was to get into trouble with your people. I'm a valuable asset—at least here and now. But let's keep it a secret between us." Friegel looked very bothered, with a frown wrapped up in a cloak and dagger of irony.

"Oh yes, your presence here confirms your immense value," I heartily agreed, with a quick, bright, welcoming grin. But I had no idea what I was talking about.

"Uh . . . Mr. Martin, what's happening here? This Friegel fella, is he our supposed contact?" said Patsy, a little unnerved.

"I am now, Ms. Isolde Wannabe," said Friegel.

Stunning-looking and supposedly well-camouflaged Patsy with Ray-Ban glasses looked stunned.

"Now, you two coming off an executive jet without any proper record of a detailed flight passenger list. Naughty, naughty. Always breaking protocol. Do you know, Ms . . . ."

"Okay, Patsy, if you will," said not-so-happy, not-so-confident Patsy.

"I feel privileged," Friegel chuckled. I chuckled. And Patsy rummaged around in her purse, possibly looking for pepper spray.

"Anything wrong, Patsy?"

"No, it's here. I thought I had left it on the plane."

"What?" I said.

"It's a woman's thing." What she meant to say was that it was a gun.

"Right, everyone, now that we have been introduced or reintroduced, let's move on," said Friegel.

"Quite," I said.

"Please get into the catering vehicle just inside the hangar gate."

"Ah . . . I still have to ask you, Friegel, what happened to our planned welcoming committee?"

"What, didn't you know? They were in a very bad traffic accident. They were hit as they rushed through a red light to get to the airport on time. The agents survived, but the couple in the other vehicle is dead. I was at the airport to do slightly different work. Remember?" There was still hostility in Friegel's tone.

"I see," I added eerily, as already this operation in Switzerland had begun ominously.

"Well, our special branch got a little desperate. But I don't look desperate, do I, Mr. Pol Martin? That is what you still call yourself?"

"Yes, Pol is fine, as usual."

"Considering all that's happened, you are quite cool about it," Patsy said.

"You didn't see my face when my supervisor gave me the last-minute details. And by the way, I am a police officer, and that's how I'm supposed to react—coolly, responsibly, and following orders strictly, but in a trusting way, with my official collaborators."

Friegel was like a dog not wanting to give up its bone when it came to the way he continually felt slighted by not being given the assignment to take me from the hangar to the regular flight. And not being given any information about it. But it was well beyond that. We had a history, the two of us, like an old marriage on love and hate lifeline, never knowing when it might just go so rotten into a divorce or recover into a second romance—or was that a third romance? What a disgusting idea. Married to someone whom you would always have to tell the complete truth to.

We were a few hundred meters away from the aircraft arrival gate when British Airways Flight 3119 from London Heathrow taxied into the gate for disembarking. I gathered Friegel would be briefing us on what the Swiss secret service had planned to get us onboard with the minimum of fuss and without anyone seeing us. But now I guessed Friegel was stuck with figuring it all out at the last minute—even with my help. It had felt like it was going to get a little messy.

"Now, Pol and Patsy, I want you to go to the back of this van and put yourselves inside the catering container once we have stopped. The elevator underneath will hoist you to the hole of the plane's kitchen hold. One of the flight attendants will direct you up and then into the passenger section. My men and I will get to the hallway leading to passport control and the baggage section and watch for your safety. There will be a bit of delay before the doors are opened and the passengers get out."

"Looks a little cramped, but I guess it will do."

Friegel smiled. "Do you want to know how you can comfortably fit yourselves in?"

"What do you mean?" I queried.

"Just play baron of beef. You're so good with disguises and aristocrats!" chuckled Friegel.

*　　*　　*

After going through the craft and exiting it like we were always on it, we went down a corridor to the interterminal shuttle. Between these terminals, the zippy modern Siemens-made cars mooed with German efficiency. The cow moos over the PA system went with the beautiful Alp visuals on the shuttle tunnel walls. They went well with the catered on-flight steak meal that I had gotten a whiff of—unless you were Indian or an animal rights activist.

After arriving at the central terminal, Friegel followed us not too far down the corridor at a safe distance on the way to passport control. I guess he had trusted the shuttle. With all that mooing onboard, along with the images of bucolic green fields, it was just too hard, or premature, to envisage someone being slaughtered. Or possibly, one of his men had been in our car.

As we moved farther toward passport control, I said, "Surprise, nice to see you, Inspector Friegel, but do you think coming directly out to greet us is so wise?" I was deliberately blowing our cover to make sure we were both marked. I had deliberately walked over to him. Jonathan wanted bait, and so he would get a fish farm worth of it.

"What are you doing?" said Friegel nervously. "I believe the point of the exercise today is to prevent us from getting noticed. Not to look like I have any real association or interest with you in the open, for God's sake."

"Oh, really. Touching that you care," I said.

"You're very welcome," he said sarcastically, as he shifted around ever so slightly to see who might be watching, but nobody seemed to be.

"By the way, how is the Countess?" Friegel asked. He simultaneously looked around as if he had misplaced something of the likes of a doggy-bag takeout.

"She is not quite looking herself. Yes, let's not leave her out of the equation since we're being so public." What Friegel did not know was that my job was to make the enemy think that Isolde was with me. To convince the enemy that the list was actually with us, if they were anywhere nearby.

"Yes, I'm fine, thank you for your concern," said Patsy as she quickly joined up after lagging a little behind. She put her sunglasses back on.

"By the way, do you have the real list?" asked Friegel as he moved away from me.

"Yes, Isolde has it," said Patsy.

"That's good if you mean you. Now I am sorry to say that my superiors insist that you provide it to me, and we shall give it back to you at the hotel. They are very concerned that we are protecting you for the wrong reasons."

"What the hell. Look, Friegel. We had a deal. Believe me, you don't want this list," I said a bit too loudly. This was as far as I could go with warning him. Personally, I would have rather eaten it than let him take it. But officially, Friegel was nicely fitting the preferred scenario to make it look very convincing to any observers that the list had such great value that Friegel would be seen taking possession of it in a demanding way. That's the way Jonathan said would be best for it to be played out, as Patsy had told me on the plane.

"I'm sorry. I'm going to have to insist. Now you don't want our Swiss customs to give you a thorough search. If you slide it off to me, I'll show both of you through. It's your call, my friend," said not-so-friendly Friegel.

"Okay, okay, Isolde," I said loudly. I told Patsy to take the list out again and make sure Friegel saw that it was clearly the document.

I grabbed it and waved it in his face to make sure. "See, Friegel, it's a coded package," I loudly barked out. "Your pals will have the hardest time deciphering it. We don't even know what's on it. You shouldn't have it. It'll hurt your head trying to figure it out."

"Just give it to me, and quit waving it," said Friegel, looking grave and irritated. Its waving about was providing a deliberate opportunity for our inevitable watchers to know that we had it. Or more importantly, that poor old Friegel was about to get it.

What Friegel did not know, and I was not going to caution him more directly about, was that the list in Zürich was practically a death sentence to anyone who held it. I had to warn him about it as best I could, given my respect for this usually straightforward, even if a bit of pain-in-the-ass, anti-American, cop. But the more I warned him publicly, the worse everything got. We were all screwed.

"Look, Friegel, I would be extremely careful with that."

"What do you exactly mean?"

"You feel secure enough. So be it."

"We have tremendous security. My men are everywhere. Nothing is going to happen. In fact, you have done a nice job making everyone—half of Zürich—think that you now no longer have it. Nicely protecting your asses, as you Americans would say. Not so nice for us, but we can deal with it."

"Friegel, if you're happy, then I'm happy. But please give us at a minimum one of your security detail, one of your best. Patsy and I are not out of the woods no matter how much safer you think we are. But in the spirit of mutual caring, actually you are going to need to retain your absolute top people around you."

"Yes, Pol, we can handle such serious matters, believe me. Anyway, Sergeant Schultz will take you to your hotel and stand guard there. With his replacement, you will be protected for twenty-four hours. Just in case unfriendly watchers think you might be playing them and keeping the real list or part of it. Or in case you are playing with us. Now, you wouldn't be doing such a foul thing to your favorite policeman, would you?"

"Right. Fine, if you say so." I avoided seriously registering his question, for the answer would be that we had duped him once again. Friegel was not somebody you wanted to mislead at all. I saw a price to pay for this deception, which might mean permanent divorce. Like his sitting back when something came across his table saying the Order and I might be getting firecrackers up our rear ends. And in ten minutes or less.

"That's the best I can do. I'll be visiting you a little later, Pol."

"But, Friegel, could you meet me away from where I'm staying?" Friegel would be like botulism with what he was carrying. Even if he ended up dropping it off, he could still be dropped out of the picture by a hit man, if not right away.

"Really, Pol, somewhat extra precautions. But so be it. I'll give you a call on your fancy mobile, later."

"Right, talk to you later, I hope." Friegel looked quixotically at me, then almost scoffed and laughed off my warnings. I had done my best. Schultz then took us to a bright blue, unmarked Mercedes outside the terminal. Patsy was smartly staying quiet.

"What hotel are you staying at?" Schultz inquired as we thought about getting in—and quickly. "And don't worry, we have your luggage."

"The Schotland."

"Oh yes, a nice choice, should be only a half-hour trip. Depends on traffic, of course."

"This time of day should not be too bad," I said.

"Any traffic is worrisome, if you understand what I mean," said Schultz, mysteriously failing at being mysterious.

"I suppose you're right on that one," said Patsy, not sounding like she had the greatest confidence in the exercise of getting us to the hotel in one piece.

"Mr. Martin and Ms. Patsy, we may have to speed up and do a few maneuvers. So please buckle up—it is the law, anyway."

"Sure, as long as we don't have to put on a veil or a hood," Patsy added with a laugh, followed by the subordinating silence of Schultz. I had my own enigmatic comments that I could have made, which he might have thought were made at his expense. But today, we were VIPs, so he just shut up like the good Schultz he was. He probably would have done so anyway, even if he had not been a Schultz.

The real problem was not whether or not we would be welcomed by those looking for the list. Not getting shot was the biggest real worry. It was a bit of a logistical challenge to avoid lead, as there were a thousand points between here and our hotel in Zürich where a person with a good rifle—or even a grenade—could get us. Or a bazooka or machine gun or maybe even a bow and arrow or who knows what else—possibly a Swiss knife, if they wanted to get messy and leave us to die slowly in a pool of blood. That is, if they didn't have any Swiss manners. And so far, my attackers on this trip had not shown any manners at all.

*   *   *

The Zürich airport is a small one by the overall standard of London's Heathrow airport or certainly by New York's Kennedy or Chicago's. But, like Switzerland, it packs a mighty punch. Though small, it hides the fact that it is one of continental Europe's top ten or so in terms of passenger traffic, with the number of bankers, passengers in transit, tourists, and officials passing through it equivalent to 80 percent of the traffic through Heathrow's Terminal 5. Because of that, it has the highest state-of-the-art security, with every possible sensor, though masked by the very quick manner in which customs processes its passengers with any major legitimate passport or visa. It would be very difficult for an assassin to get away cleanly and not be witnessed within or close outside.

Through the exit of smooth, wide, stainless steel, glistening, sliding gray doors of the terminal, you find a crosswalk that can take you immediately to the railway station, where one can catch the train to Paris, Frankfurt, or parts beyond in a hurry. It was too damn convenient for anyone coming in from areas unknown around Europe, such as hit persons, who would not have to go through security by taking the train. For this operation, I had definitely wanted to stay away from the trains, as well as the entranceway to them.

The crosswalks, after the airport exit, penetrate four lanes, separated by a meridian for picking up passengers by hotel buses going to luxury hotels. There was a reason for my reference to such road trivia. It came with support pillars to an airport roof overhang, with lots of angles to hide a gunman. A gunman who could be hidden in a fake or borrowed hotel bus, through which we could have been scoped. But as we had moved away from the terminal into the Mercedes skillfully, it was clear that was not how we were going to be taken out—at least on that day. Or should I have said at that moment.

The drive from the airport to downtown is quite regular and quick compared to most major European cities. Almost as fast as getting out of the airport from gate to final exit, which is swift enough. This was explained not only by Swiss efficiency, but by the fact that Zürich was a pint-size city for a major financial center. In fact, less than five hundred thousand people lived in the area.

After a few minutes on the airport terminal road, the car pulled out onto superhighway 51, which was the next category below the autobahn, permitting one to travel at speeds moving toward Formula One racing car standards. There appeared to be no turning back to go northward for quite some time. As if this road network were primarily made for express service to or from Zürich.

The next city you come to past the airport is Horerkann, a bit of a nasty surprise for those fully attached to Switzerland's peace-loving image. For Horerkann Corporation, which is located there, manufactures the kind of artillery and tanks that could have even launched this police vehicle practically into outer space, along with the rest of the nearby traffic. And all with only a burst of fire from a few of its armored vehicles.

It was, in fact, a very fine, modern, clean factory, with a sheen that made it almost look like a health complex rather than a tool production shop for the killing fields. It had a spa in it, and new age psychiatrists to assuage employees that they were doing a world of good. That Swiss sanitizing touch was everywhere, probably down to making bullets look like gleaming miniature peace negotiators. (No, sorry—it was Canada that made all the bullets, and had the peacekeepers.)

After you pass Horerkann, there is a well-engineered highway interchange with signs that prevent any directional confusion or, for that matter, any cracks irrespective of the cold winters that had gripped it over decades. Swiss highway engineering went along with impeccably modern factories, of which a number were so well put together that they didn't even need one worker, except for a few security guards. Because in terms of security, at every corner, there seemed to be CCTV cameras and other alarms.

Sometimes, the whole country felt as if it was that extensively covered by invasive devices—a kind of creepy security efficiency out of a bad science-fiction novel. I wondered how I might have looked on TV at the quay as I was getting pummeled in the shadows, but it would have been foolish to have asked for the movie. That might come quick enough with the book I was writing, unless the directors were put away for trying to make it.

Yes, things ran smoothly in this country outwardly, and so did this fine humming Mercedes built just next door in the other extension of Germania—otherwise known as Germany. Finally, after traveling several kilometers past Horerkann, one gets to route 11, which would then take us quickly to 17. And 17, in turn, would take us all the way down to Zürich Zee and then to the Schotland. At least in theory.

However you looked at it, whether it was the highways or not, there was a lot of numbering in Switzerland, probably because of so many turns, so many roads in the very densely populated country. Or was it part of a contagion from a country having so many secret-numbered bank accounts? To look at it more positively, it was nice to know that the highway engineering department wasn't run by the bankers, who might have kept the road numbers a complete secret to the general public. If they had, it might have helped to even out Swiss driving quality with the vehicular maneuvering horrors of Sarabia. I was suddenly jolted out of my marvelous diversions of highway reflections.

"What's the problem, Sergeant?" I asked, as he seemed distracted by his head weaving and bobbing around to better see an image in his rearview mirrors.

"We have company—nothing looking too major, given our horsepower and my defensive driving skills. They have been trailing us since around Horerkann."

It was clear that the opposition had come ready for all possibilities. But they had to know that Friegel was the prime hunt, as likely they would have seen me giving off the list. Or possibly they just had revenge on their mind. I sympathized.

The Alfa Romeo Spider with Locarno license plates was fast, too, and I could see from my own side mirror that it was approaching and gaining on us. It was dark black, and its front lights were flashing on and off, trying to get us to stop. Or to intimidate us. More messy amateur punks, I sadly thought.

"I think they are looking for *zu viel Freundsheep*," said Schultz in his first attempt at *Ginglish*—German English—which meant in quick translation that our pursuers were getting to be too intimate. Well, that was the more romantic version over the woolen one.

"Must be a bunch of lost diplomats—diplomatic, red license plates. Though strange out of Italian Switzerland—few diplomatic missions there. And it could be a stolen car to confuse us. I am truly going to screw them up. Hold tight."

Schultz put on the brakes so hard that it twisted us quickly with a thud, and moved us through the U-turn about as fast as any moving body could twist over one hundred and eighty degrees.

"Yes, Mr. Martin and Ms. Patsy," he smiled like one of my Sarabian students with his first car out for a drifting. "They have no real understanding that brakes can be precisely adjusted to get certain turning results on certain highway surfaces, under certain temperature and weather conditions—quite effective results. We Swiss do come well prepared to work with a sense of near-perfect timing. We're not so bad after all, Mr. Martin and Ms. Patsy. *Nicht so?*" He smiled again.

Patsy and I felt like we had been training for outer space, given how violently we had been pulled back and forward and sideways.

As we passed the black Spider in the opposite lane, Schultz yelled out, "Duck!"

A torch of machine-gun fire briefly poured out of the side window of the Spider. It took out our rear window in large parts. It was like a pane of defrosted ice from bottom end to top and side ends. It was, however, better than getting iced, I waxed poetically to myself as my hands could not stop shaking.

Yes, poetry came in handy at times. I could have also soothed on a soother, as I almost pissed in my pants. That was as poetic as I would get after that near-death experience—thinking of whining baby talk poems.

"Jesus, what was that? Hit the gas as if you want to put the pedal into the pavement," I said with enough acid reflux to put a Swiss pharmaceutical company into the big money.

"Geez, Pol, these guys are playing for real. And we don't have the bloody list," said Patsy in panic and victimhood that would have put Joan of Arc in a bad light.

Schultz phoned in the description, location, and license plate of the Spider, which looked like it had broken down trying to make the same maneuver.

*   *   *

After twenty minutes, Schultz turned the car around again, though this time more gently. Thank Heavens!

"Don't worry, we sent in a helicopter with a SWAT team after them. Or something or other. They have broken an absolute golden rule in Switzerland, so I doubt if they are going to survive. I have punched in a code alert on my Blackberry notifying my superiors of such a breach."

"What's that?" I also wanted to ask about the something or other, but thought it wasn't a good time to play twenty questions.

"Anyone who does an unauthorized shooting in public in Switzerland, is dead or to be jailed for eternity for all intents and porpoises."

"Yes, purposes, but I do like porpoises. Nice animals, good for the ecology," I said, not wanting to hurt the linguistic sensibilities too much of someone on whom our survival depended. There was something in the urgency and the quality of the moment that made him ignore my linguistic clarifications and environmental considerations.

"We make and sell all sorts of guns. That's one thing, but illegal use of them in neutral Switzerland—unpardonable!" said Schultz in partial response. "You know, Mr. Martin, we have a hang-up on privacy and good manners."

"I heard." Yes, I was beginning to like this Schultz, and see him more like management in training rather than a smart police puppet. That was a compliment—sort of. Schultz had more personality than I had credited him with, and more than I credited most Swiss as having. I think, in fact, I was bit of a Swiss "racist." I felt a little ashamed. Especially after that incredible driving. And after that silly remark about discriminating against the Swiss.

After five minutes, he turned around to us smiling, just after he had received a message into his earphone on his other apparatus—this time, a Google smartphone. He was a very modern fella, too, and well connected—electronically. However, there was a basic worry that didn't need electronic wizardry to figure out.

"Look," I said, "we could be going back for an ambush!"

"I don't think so," Schultz smiled coolly. "The problem has been taken care of!"

"Okay, I guess we'll see. Any bulletproof vests around in case things don't work out?"

Schultz didn't seem to like what he thought was my lack of confidence in him. But he really lacked sensitivity to my rather insensitive, ironic personality, which was kind of shameful. After all, I thought that I had been getting warmed up to "Mr. Chill."

I thought, too, that I would just leave him alone for a while, as much as you can leave anybody alone when you're in the same car, and in the front seat sharing the breeze from a machine-gunned back window. Then, after another few minutes, we saw a piece of scrap metal of a black car smashed into the rock cliff and on the shoulder. There were two stretchers with bodies being put into a helicopter. Nobody seemed in a hurry to do much with them.

Schultz piped up, "I hear from the news that some intoxicated truck driver accidentally got on the wrong side of the highway and totally creamed that car. A real shame. It was quite heavy, as it was carrying armaments from Horerkann. Headed for Sarabia, I think," Schultz added obtusely. Or was that humorously—as in dark humor? Schultz was definitely on a tear.

Yes, Schultz was talking again. Probably being very patriotic in demonstrating the positively destructive contributions of his country's defense industries. Circumstances of that black Spider tragedy had made him very proud, though he looked disappointed that I wasn't so impressed. He still didn't know me that well.

I decided, though, it would still be good to be friendly and add my own unctuous thanks to what Patsy had just said.

"You Swiss cops are impressive. No wonder the place is still tranquil despite your arming and financially backing almost everyone at war. And just about every kind of country."

Yes, Switzerland could be serene, I further thought to myself—despite all of its intrigues. And as I looked at Schultz and he looked back at me without saying a word, he finally let out a truly grand smile.

TWENTY

Sheik Suleiman Al Zayed of Sarabia, how could one describe him in terms that Westerners could understand? He was like a Robespierre of the French Revolution, who saw enemies everywhere and the need for purification of society through an executioner's steel. Added to this, he was the kindred spirit of a more modern-day Ayatollah Khomeini figure in the mounting theocratic revolution in Sarabia.

While the guillotine was the great purifier for Robespierre, for Zayed it was the famous thick curved Sarabian sword, the symbol of this chief's religious justice, at least outside of Raddah and beyond Joddah. And while Robespierre had his zealous judiciary of the Committee of Public Safety that had ordered the annihilation of the French aristocracy, Zayed had his Committee of Total Virtue. Like the threatened and eventually executed Bourbon King Louis and Queen Marie-Antoinette of France by Robespierre's minions, the parallels had become known to the Al Sarabs, who increasingly felt in danger. After all, they knew Zayed had bitter experiences with the royalty when he was young, just as Robespierre had. Zayed was not only full of good old Abrahamic revenge—it was personal too. He despised what he saw as the westernized and decadent Sarabian aristocracy.

To ensure this principle of revenge was not simply words, Zayed presided over many judicial decisions to put the accused to death. He also made sure the judges—as well as the executioners—did not go squeamish. He was not a big fan of having the accused released for blood money; while very traditional in Islamic terms, he personally saw it as undermining his sense of true justice, which he felt was a physical eye for an eye or a tooth for a tooth. Or a body bag for a body bag.

The sheik certainly got around, sometimes covering over three hundred kilometers in a week on the Sarabian roads. He saw them as his pathways to ensure salvation of the hundreds of communities he would pass through. More important to his pilgrimage for justice was that he brought along his own bloody panel of judges and executioners if he thought the locals were not up to the job. He also brought his own force of *Mootawa*, a personal guard in the hundreds in case things got out of control.

So far throughout the provinces, he had rallied ten thousand new *Mootawa* volunteers to his causes, including recently released former terrorists. A number had even volunteered as suicide bombers, but the key to their salvation had been their so-called profound public recanting and their promise not to repeat their violence. For Zayed, however, they were more importantly his arsenal of human grenades for when the moment was ripe. Though that moment was not quite there.

Yes, things had gotten proverbially hot, politically speaking, in the very conservative kingdom of Sarabia, with the sheik's Party of Virtue (PV) winning almost every municipal election. Democracy was a very convenient instrument for Zayed, even if there was little of it in the country. He would ban it if Sarabia became the pure and holy theocracy he envisaged for it, even more theocratic than Tyrania, from which he had picked up a few ideas. However, Tyrania was a little too morally decrepit for him. And worse for the sheik, the Tyranians were of the Shista sect, whose followers had been accused by the Sarabians of having bizarre sexual rituals.

I remember seeing one of these judicial hearings on live compressed video. For Zayed was not against the use of technology, even the high-definition digital kind. He used all sorts of it. His people had even developed special "blood tooth" software for a wide range of iPhones and the whole lot of other portable Western technology in order to channel his propaganda. His special *Mootawa* technology branch (MOOTEC) in the Ministry of Virtue had in fact led the development of Sarabia's own supercomputer server, called *Hallal,* with a built-in censoring program named *Haram.* Anyone not using it and the search engine called *Mootwow* could be disciplined. Anyone somehow tapping into Yahoo or Google would be lashed. And anyone using Facebook or Twitter would be imprisoned.

He was also in discussions with a Sarabian satellite TV network to get judicial hearings and executions televised through a number of European and North American-based communication networks owning satellite channels. They had categorically refused to show his TV program gore loosely translated into a reality show called *Justice Sarabian Style*. It was one of the most popular shows in the outer provinces—ever. It was not only a hugely effective propaganda tool, but had the highest ratings on Friday, which was execution day.

Before or sometimes following the killings, he would be interviewed, and a sample of families, including parents who brought their children to reinforce Sarabian justice, would also be asked questions. There would also be a charity fund-raiser phone-in for obtaining money for both the victim and family of the accused. I had recorded and translated one program with subtitles and narratives.

"Sheik, there are thousands at today's execution, which will take place fairly shortly. How do you see such a large turnout of so many families?" asked the sycophantic TV interviewer. "Is this another victory for the courts over decadence?"

The sheik produced his inspired response, which he had given a thousand times, but was happy nevertheless to repeat for any of the new TV audience—particularly the young, whom he was working to inspire. "It is Allah's providence. I am but a tool of that will. That will that Mohammed, peace be upon him, has also clearly expressed in the Hadiths. The will is that murder is one of the greatest offenses, and that the people need to know that the authorities will follow God's law—that murderers will receive dutiful punishment."

"Do you have any warnings for the criminals out there—and unbelievers?"

"We are a just and merciful society. But a new dawn has arisen. We are fully returning to our traditions and saying no to the greed and corruption of Sodom and Gomorrah. Youth has been soiled by outside ideas, though we welcome truly respectful outsiders who adopt or show respect for our religion. We encourage pilgrimage to the holy shrines to reinforce the faith."

"What do you mean, Sheik, by the return to the 'old traditions' and need for outsiders to be respectful?"

"We see here at this execution a foreigner who built an alcohol plant. We know that this taking of alcohol is a terrible habit. That our prophet rightfully banned it. We now see that it is a poison that is destroying nonfaithful countries around the world."

"And so foreigners are evil?"

"No. God loves all his children, even the heathen ones. But we are one of the very few countries that follow his laws obediently. However, we now have six million largely infidel foreigners, a good many of whom have been exposed to decadent behavior. Pornography, drugs, lack of respect for elders, harlotry, unsavory greed, and worship of mammon have reduced the pillars of their economy to rubble. Do we follow such rogue societies? Do we forsake the true seven pillars of our Islamic heritage, which are solid truths and make us firm, pure, and just?"

"No! No! No!" the crowd roared out as he yelled out the questions. There was almost a bloodlust in the air. The crowd was chanting, "Death to the criminal, death to the criminal."

There was no question about it. Zayed was a commanding speaker. A man of humble roots, he particularly inspired the trampled and poor masses, some of whom had little else but their faith. I wondered if Zayed's Robespierrist-style populism and demagoguery could be easily fed on, given that so much of his audience had such limited hope for economic progress and given his promise to help them at least achieve the pathway to Paradise. The sheik had almost full command to have them do practically anything. He made the Jonestown cult in Guyana look like a free-spirited open community. But his "Kool-Aid" was his talk, which was increasingly poisoning legions against the old establishment and the West.

Indeed, the royalty and Wadi sect elites based mostly in Raddah had to worry as to where this demagogue was going. But so far, he had made no direct public noises or specific plans against them. And so far, crime had gone down by 15 percent—including the political variety. Attendance at Wadi sect mosques and prayers had enjoyed a religious renewal. Even a few key princes had donated significant funds to Zayed, either in support or more like insurance against any possible future wrath. Further, the police minister tacitly showed approval at times by getting involved with his charities.

An example of how one of these Zayed executions had gone was the story of this small Bangladeshi man caught for being a distributor of alcohol. He was dragged out of a black van at a small square in the desert village of Hyenal, a very small, dusty town with a small date industry—and a force of migrant labor paid less than ten dollars a day for backbreaking work.

The windows of the van were blackened, as well as the paint, the tires, the hubcaps, and even the clothes, right down to the blindfold of the little man who was about to be executed.

Bootlegging in itself was not punishable by death. It was facilitated by the fact that this small penurious man from a country with an average individual yearly income of eight hundred dollars per worker had put together a very bad batch, which had gotten into the hands of some Sarabian youths. It had poisoned them to death given their uncontrolled drinking of it. To state the fairly obvious, there had been no information around to even discuss the possible idea of responsible drinking.

Zayed said that Islam valued all lives, including those of foreigners, equally. But the execution numbers in recent months read nonnationals four hundred, Sarabians twelve. And more discriminately, visible minorities 399 and whites one. Sarabian justice was largely blind to executing Westerners, but for Zayed, this was going to change, starting with less powerful countries. He had less worry of insulting them because of their weak geopolitical clout. He had a few in mind, some of whose citizens had been pushing drugs in different foreign compounds—and even beyond.

At most of the execution plazas, as well as the ones visited by the Sheik, the Sarabian police had a lot of weapons, as there was always the outside possibility that the accused family might commit a "heist." A theft to the Sarabians, but a recovery of a persecuted family member to those who pulled it off. It had happened before.

One Filipino falsely accused of drug smuggling had a bunch of machete-carrying, masked relatives and friends spirit him away to the Philippines' embassy, where the guards thought he was there for a visit to the library. The diplomatic furor had been terrible for the Philippine government, which was dependent on the huge remittances and their tax cut from the million-strong Filipino communities in Sarabia.

It had taken two months to work out an agreement, but Sheik Zayed had initially been histrionic about the need to execute the man. There had been a vigilance watch, as they called it, by the sheik's religious police. Before the agreement could be implemented that included no execution, though a fifteen-year prison term in the Philippines for the wrongfully accused, the man had been smuggled out through a cargo carrier to neighboring Borain.

It was, however, reported a few months later that this escapee had been killed in a bomb blast by terrorists in the southern Philippines island of Mindanao. Asked by a reporter about it, the sheik said little, but intoned the wisdom of the scholars and followers about the omnipotent presence of Allah. That had been one *Allah Akbar* too many for some of the royal family, as the sheik left the interview site with a smirk on his face.

After that day, the sheik swore to himself that there would be no escape for anyone from an execution. The guard had been doubled. And there were more plainclothes police well distributed through the crowd, as well as those in uniform, making for a sizable barrier for any of the public to get too close to the execution area.

This time, the sheik was present to additionally make sure there would be no screwups. He began by reading out the death order for the thin, shaking Bangladeshi man, who looked as if he would faint at any moment. The sheik wanted to show his followers that no job was too small for him. He had even personally amputated a thief's arm. This had been especially acceptable in Wadi sect Sharia law, as the thief had stolen a scooter from the *Mootowa* headquarters—supposedly about as sacrilegious as a theft could be.

Later, it was found out that the thief was simply retarded and had wanted to pretend to be one of the *Mootawa* he so admired. Even the sheik had been incensed when he found out the truth about the man's mental challenges and sent him off to the isolation of the Pharoahsan islands to become a gamekeeper of a dwarf variety of antelope. Yes, Sarabian justice was far from perfect and hard to make up for once the falsely accused had gotten the chop.

Nevertheless, the sheik would not let any imperfections of the system sway him away from brutally applying the death penalty if he thought it was warranted. He even applied the blade himself, with no exceptions if anyone in his extended family was killed. No one would ever wish to put Zayed to the test for his *blademanship*. Anyone disposing of any member of his inner circle could be sure of a most horrible revenge. And he made every move on or off television to convince his enemies that his vengeance would be total if they even picked up a pen against him and his crowd.

His movable feast of executions was seemingly unstoppable. Some of those in better economic and social positions far from the plight of the poor foreigners, also shuddered at night. They were a decidedly different lot: modern educators, liberal bureaucrats, well-traveled internationally, and those intimately tied in with Western finance and a lot of the Western establishment. But some, like Prince Waheed, considered the sheik as being temporarily lethal. Someone who would eventually be defeated by his own bloodthirsty colleagues, who the Prince hoped would turn on

Zayed the way others had turned on Robespierre. Nevertheless, Waheed participated in the sheik's charity fund-raiser as a way to keep the sheik off his back about all his connections to the West, including moderate Jewry, who had worked with him to improve his fortunes.

The executioner brought out a huge sword before the Bangladeshi man. It reminded me of the glitter of that very sword I had seen in Zürich in my delusions. It was like a replica I had also seen in a Louvre exhibition on Sarabia. It was bejeweled and inscribed in Arabic that translated into "God is great." And other descriptions that "God is merciful." With the appearance of the blade, the crowd looked excited.

There were not only fathers and sons in the crowd for so-called educational purposes. There were also lots of old hags, though covered head to foot in black. Their crooked, hunched bodies told their ages, as well as their dedication to old traditions of justice of their youth, which made today's execution numbers look paltry. The sheik to them was a resurrected hero from earlier days, when there had been more respect for elders. When drugs, barbiturates, and booze in the desert taken by truant youth would be unheard of; where relations outside of marriage would be near zero. And where not a single harlot would come a hundred miles near a shrine, and where homosexuals would be automatically stoned, buried, and disappeared without a trace for being a supposed shame to their families.

The old hags were also for a reinstatement of the ways of the very old days, a time so far back that they felt it in their bones. They had nostalgia for the simplicity of their younger days that made them want to get rid of TV altogether. With their knitting needles and cloth, they would have fitted nicely in before the guillotine stages of the French Revolution, albeit with modifications to their *abayas* and veils. As it was, these grandmothers were also used by the sheik as an information spy network, which made Stalin's neighborhood blocks monitored by good Communist Party members look relaxed and disorganized.

The policeman then tapped the accused. That was the signal for him to dutifully put his head literally onto the chopping block. That was the signal for the hags in the crowd, with the help of their family members, to push the foreigners and the young to the front. Foreigners, particularly infidel Westerners, along with the youth were considered especially in need of learning about the purifying power of Sarabian justice.

Then all of a sudden, the sheik more clearly intervened. He did a slight bow to the executioner, who did not need to be masked, given how positively society in general saw his job. Given how honored he was to do an important part of God's work, in his and the mind of almost all spectators. But Zayed always held the final decision to do the job himself. He took the sword and pointed it into the camera to reinforce that principle. Or was there more reason to his actions?

"Now, all ye who think our commitment to justice is not complete or thorough. In a true just world, all of us may be called upon one day to carry out the law by our judiciary and great leadership. To spill the blood of the horrible and the unfaithful when needed is glorious to Allah."

"Yes!" cried the crowd. "*Allah Akbar*." The cries became mesmerizing, sounding faster and faster into a swirling hypnotic frenzy. Then the sheik held up his hand to quiet the crowd.

"Though we hold the sword, we are merciful. So as to help this lost soul not go into Hell, let us ask him to recant."

The blindfolded accused then stood up on the cue of the executioner. He mouthed out a litany of terrible crimes he had committed. He invoked how he had been corrupted by foreign influences and welcomed his own death. He then bent down on his knees to the sheik to beg for forgiveness. This had all been well scripted by Zayed before, like a reality show would have been on Western TV. If there had been commercials, he could have made millions, given how many followed his live broadcasts. But it was a ridiculous statement to make anyway, as advertisements were largely banned. Under the sheik's leadership, commercial messages on billboards had been torn down. They had been replaced with important sayings of the Koran and proper rules for dress codes and neighborhood watch.

The sheik raised the sword to an even greater height, as if he were pointing it to the heavens for additional approval. Or was that for strength? His eyes lit up into what almost seemed like a fanatical delight, as if he were on a drug called "Fanatic." Then for dramatic effect, he looked at the crowd and the television camera and viciously swung the sword down onto the Bangladeshi man's thin neck.

A huge fountain of blood spread out and seemed to rain onto the feet of those closest to the execution. Zayed then looked solemn and clasped his hands nearly like a Buddhist giving greetings, though still holding the sword. There followed a pace of softer chants. Then the show was over, and the regular police made sure the crowd was dispersed. It seemed that not only had the foreigners been pushed forward at the beginning of this well-choreographed show. They had been equally pushed away after the execution, so as not to stay or mingle. Or possibly, not to have a chance to show their full repugnance, or even to regurgitate.

The sheik had developed his quality of showmanship through the application of modern marketing research, with the help of consultants from a small firm in Dallas called Market-Trick. Until the company figured out what their expertise had been actually used for. And until their company had been paid a million dollars for fulfilling the contract. He would still get a variety of computer printouts and analysis of the audience ratings, using every audience evaluation trick that Western expertise had taught his own marketing group. Details even on how his performance had been appreciated, or not. There was one overall audience, though, that he would not be getting the general approval of.

The senior members of the House of Sarab wondered where all the vulgarization of these judicial killings and the sheik's leading role were taking their country to. The royal family more and more feared that they might end up eventually on the block themselves. It was in some of their minds only a few minutes closer to eleven o'clock, if not midnight, for the House of Sarab as they saw the sheik's ratings go up, as well as the size of the mobs.

One prince, though, had not been so worried about Zayed. He had quietly disappeared up the stairs in the palace to watch the sheik's "freak" show. Another piece of the puzzle, he thought, was coming into place. Yes, it had been a good show, he had said to himself. And Zayed would be useful for a while.

But even the prince—in the order of how he saw the new Islamic universe unwinding—thought that Zayed's road show would eventually have to be scaled down a bit. But for now, the sheik was proving to be a very useful tool, indeed. So thought Prince Bashard bin Mustafa of and within the House of Sarab on that fateful day.

TWENTY-ONE

A stream of tears flowed from Isolde's eyes as she saw that the cover name in Sarabia of Adrian Sands was now fully on display. She had been working around the clock to decode the list and was exhausted, as well as being demoralized. She just could not believe who the traitor was within the Order. Spectacular events were now to unfold.

Adrian Sands was a name that only Smuts and Isolde knew among the ladies of the Order. Now, there seemed to be important evidence that the good ship Dianesis had become very leaky and that Sands was the principal one causing the damage. Yes, it had been good to put the names of key insiders into the computer, Isolde the scientist and cryptographer thought. Isolde the woman, though, felt totally depressed, followed by waves of feelings of self-idiocy, which were then smashed on the rocks by an emotional tsunami of absolute betrayal. Would an undertide of revenge be her next feeling?

In bold letters, the computer typed **Adrian Sands = sadirinan** again and again. Adrian Sands, it reaffirmed, no matter how many confirmations Isolde requested, directly or indirectly, about the possible involvement of anyone connected with the Order being involved in the conspiracy.

Isolde looked desperately around in her head for alternative answers that would provide an excuse for Adrian Sands not being the traitor; all rational evidence in the cryptology led to that dreadful conclusion.

Rationalization number one: there was an outside possibility that someone at the NSA end in Maryland was playing a very dangerous game and manipulating the outcomes. That an inside group in Washington knew Z5 or the Council would be eventually faced with the conundrum of having to use the NSA computer. Knowing that when Z5 or the Council entered critical information to find who the conspirators were, that the NSA "rogues" could use the opportunity to maximize the chaos on our side by producing bogus results—like the name of Adrian Sands. Possibly putting up names of people they wished to have killed, in hopes that the Council or Z5 might do their dirty work for them. If that were the case, then the size of the conspiracy was monumental, and no one of importance in field operations who was on the Z5 side could consider their lives safe.

Rationalization number two: another very worrisome thought sank into Isolde's head, which was now beginning to bulge with hopeful paranoia. What if the NSA had been effectively taken control of by a traitorous group loyal to the Brotherhood or elements of it? That would mean check, checkmate, and match—and championship for Al Quomini. Leaving the US president only with the task of pulling out the plug on the CIA and NSA, and turning out the last intelligence light. Not very likely, but the best conspiracy scenario that could have been generated for a smashing, antiterrorist, Hollywood movie. But one with little credibility in the intelligence community.

Isolde knew the chances of sabotage of the Council by someone in NSA were very small. Her own computer rated the conspiracy of the Al Quomini Brotherhood taking NSA over as having a .05 percent chance. And .000005 chance of Oswald Al Harvee and his people even being in Fort Meade and taking even minor control of the Big Bertha encryption computer.

Nevertheless, Isolde checked the lettering on the original list with a simple search. It was more probable that it had been too obvious the way the computer had so quickly spit out the name of Sands. All after the transliteration of the south Arabian from the irrelevant background noise and odd gibberish letters superimposed with the real ones.

The base algorithm for breaking the code was anagrammatic, usually with abbreviations for secret names. They were only partially represented, using a variety of repeated letters from the original lettering. Yes, it was a little clever, but not quite clever enough, based on abbreviated formations in more sophisticated codes that the Brotherhood had previously used. It looked a little too easy, indeed, the way the name Adrian had popped out.

Her code work assisted by the NSA computer was then widened to lead intelligence and Western politicians, ex-Nazis, neo-Nazis, Islamic fanatics, prominent international bankers, arms dealers, Muslim royalty, extremist youth, and a variety of terrorist names in the existing data banks and the Internet—even deep ecologists and cult leaders. A number of anagrammatic abbreviation-based algorithms, some highly sophisticated, were prioritized for use.

After about thirty minutes, the computer spat out a few dozen names. Only one called Frankenstein could not be fully deciphered. Maybe someone had a sick sense of humor, but then again, the 10/11 tragedy numerically spelled *peace memorial* in one of the Brotherhood's cryptograms. It was not beyond Al Quomini to embed such sick jokes.

The names deciphered from the list that sprung out were very troubling. The whole operation from within the Council and Z5 looked increasingly like it was totally blown. High-level notables, backers of the Zeel Foundation or Order in some cases, who were seen as friendly were on the list. Then further troubling, a whole list of groups that had recently not even been on the radar—mostly extremist groups—were listed beside certain staid establishment figures.

It just didn't make much sense, at least for a number of key politicians and officials friendly to the type of activities to which the Order was committed. Isolde asked the computer as to the present probability that such names could be wrong. There was less than 10 percent chance on the most improbable one. For the name Adrian, it still read .05 percent improbable that it had been a mistake. It was getting creepy, Isolde thought to herself.

Isolde decided to see if in any way using a further variety of algorithms, whether Jonathan—even by his different code names—could in any way be derived from the encrypted list. No, nothing even close came out. Putting Jonathan's name in the computer could get her into hell, as he could directly network to her screen. But she felt it was absolutely required.

Then she would confide in Jonathan with the names that had been spat out and deal with whatever backlash, if any, occurred for putting everyone she knew of in the Order, Z5, or the Council into the data. Which risked giving NSA too much information, and a reprimand from the Council if Jonathan refused to support her. But she could assuage him by saying he came up clean, and that she had even put her own name back into the data to further check the veracity of the list.

At the very least, Isolde was to ensure that none of the staff at the lab would get the list. The team was preoccupied with using more conventional programs while she worked separately with NSA and then had the list printed out on her own isolated printer.

After she got the final NSA-produced list, she deleted the electronic files. She did save them onto a special USB device customized for her top-secret work that ensured full decryption only when opened by a convoluted bizarre password she had memorized. Then, she thought again about destroying the printout. But Jonathan was of the old school, which liked hard copies. She would bring it.

This list was exceedingly worrisome for another reason. She thought to herself how amazing it was that Adrian had put the pressure on Jonathan and her to prove their legitimacy. What a charade! Some kind of evil genius he must be, that cunningly had made Jonathan and her look so brilliant. That made Adrian look so exploited, whining about being kept in the dark by Jonathan and her. It made her sick. It was the ultimate con and betrayal.

"Jonathan, I have to see you," said Isolde on the phone. "It's absolutely urgent." She had to immediately inform him of the bad news, especially about Adrian.

"Okay. Come right up."

She had to go through a long, damp, dungeon-looking corridor of a hundred meters, which seemed like an interminable trip to Isolde. If the world was hanging by a thread and only this list in the right hands could make it safe again, she had to consider herself, in a way, as being one of the most important beings on the planet. Isolde picked up the pace. She could hear echoing steps around the bend and behind. High heels, probably of her assistant, a hard-nosed young German who loved to go by protocol down to the dotted umlauts.

Isolde looked back around the corner, several seconds after the walking sounds had disappeared. To her amazement, there was Ingrid putting her shoes back on. She must have quietly crept up on her. "What's up, Ingrid?"

"You didn't file that last printout. We record how many pages are printed on every printer. And you know you have to log it."

"My, you have been a busybody. I thought you and the rest of the crew were busy on the deciphering work."

"Look, I just noticed you were gone without a note or explanation. So I followed up. I want to know what's going on."

"Nothing. Just an administrative meeting with Jonathan to discuss budget issues—actually, including your bonus."

"My bonus, really? Great. *Sehr gut.* I didn't know you were so happy with my work, Isolde."

"You've done a great job. But he's going to be quite busy, so I've got to get there soon."

Ingrid then went back to her cold self. "All right, but I need to see that the printout is properly filed or saved. It's my responsibility to catalogue all files properly and ensure their integrity. So please return the file."

"I've got to go, Ingrid. We'll talk about this more. But later."

Ingrid turned—and then quickly spun back to face Isolde. She was holding a Luger. "I'm sorry, but I am also security detail for the lab. Show me the list."

"What's all this?" Isolde said with a slight tremble. "Ah . . . Sorry, Ingrid. It's in my head. I put it through the shredder and down the chute. The only way you are going to know its contents is if you come to the meeting with me. It would be very foolish to use that," she added, motioning to the Luger.

"I can, you know," she said with feigned confidence, and hopefully a full lack of intention.

"Yes, come to the meeting. That'll be fine with me." Isolde had been rightfully rated as one of the coolest customers Jonathan had ever employed from either sex. But somewhere he had failed with his hiring of Ingrid, so it had seemed to Isolde. Or had he?

"Okay, let's go, Isolde."

"But I have to warn you, Ingrid, while I appreciate you may be carrying out functions unknown to me that are important, I find this situation very unnecessary. And frankly, bordering on the deadly farcical."

"Yes, I suppose, Isolde, you're right. But you must understand I have to do my job."

"Okay, but put that thing away." Isolde was trying to use the big supporting sister scenario. But she wondered how far she could go before big sister would become "huntress Diana," with depressing results for a subordinate she had treated almost like her own flesh and kin.

As Ingrid looked at the gun thinking maybe to put it away, Isolde flashed out her leg that ripped the gun out of Ingrid's hand.

"What!" screamed Ingrid, as Isolde had badly bruised her hand. Ingrid then looked vicious in the mouth, with an upturned nose that would have put a bulldog to shame. Yes, Ingrid wasn't the prettiest girl, but nobody was asking for good looks as a prerequisite to being hired for cryptology work.

She scrambled for the gun, but Isolde kicked it with her foot, forcing the gun back as Ingrid tried to get a grip on it. Isolde quickly maneuvered around a fallen Ingrid.

"That's enough, Ingrid!" Isolde grabbed the Luger an instant before Ingrid would have gotten it. And likely shot her with it.

"Look, Isolde, I didn't mean to make a big thing." She began to sob. "I just had to do my job. No, it's not my job. I've been threatened that if I didn't get that list, some very compromising photos would be released."

"You poor thing, Ingrid!" Isolde said with the full conviction of a Hollywood actress going through her lines. Speaking of conviction, Ingrid could spend years behind bars for what she had attempted to do. But Isolde had more important thoughts. Like thinking about the list, and the name on it that might have included an abbreviated anagram of Ingrid's family name that she had yet to test out. That's possibly why her nervous protégé had panicked. She was in on the conspiracy and on the list. Isolde began to think that Z5 and the Council weren't just fully penetrated as organizations—they were sieves.

Just after such flashing thoughts, Jonathan opened the door. He had probably heard the commotion or was getting impatient waiting for Isolde.

"What is happening out here? Why are you pointing that pistol at Ingrid? You . . ." Jonathan was abruptly cut off.

Ingrid jumped into the conversation. "Yes, Mr. Stock, I was trying to get a list of special names that our cryptology team was trying to uncover. But she destroyed the list and the file. All records need to be kept on file, and it is my duty to see it through."

"Really, is this true? Isolde, what do you have to say for yourself? These are serious charges."

"Do you believe any of it, Mr. Stock?" Isolde almost shook her head between disgust and amusement. Disgust that Jonathan would show any trust in Ingrid, her young protégé, over her, and amusement in Ingrid's little squeaky voice that had the false promise of a do-good Girl Scout.

Jonathan slowly reached his hand out. "Nevertheless, give me the gun, Isolde. I can take charge. Look, both of you come inside. We can't talk in the passage."

"Here, Jonathan, I have the printout with the decoding," said Isolde with a cool air.

"You lied to me. Give that to me!" said Ingrid, almost pouting.

"Look, young lady, I have just about had enough of you. You were to help with widening the database and some alterations to the decoding. You were not cleared to know what was on that list. Ms. *von* Leuvenstein knows what she is doing . . . I think." His voice trailed off on his last sentence, sounding a little lacking in confidence of his support for Isolde.

Behind Ingrid and unknown to her, one of the security people had slipped through the door that Jonathan had left open more than a crack. Jonathan had pressed an alarm device that he always kept with him.

"Aah," Ingrid cried out as she went for a knife in her blouse. She dropped it and then it was gone. She struggled to get away from the burly man who had been referred to as Sumo Joe. But it was like a babe being cradled by a grizzly.

"Sumo Joe, that's enough. Ingrid, I do not have the foggiest idea what you have been up to. You can now sit down, and let's just say Sumo Joe will be your protector . . . probably more against yourself. You seem to be your biggest enemy. Now what is this about?"

Ingrid started to sob, again. She finally stopped enough to explain herself. "There is a rumor in my father's *Kamaradenshaft* organization that there is a list and that his name is going to be on it."

"This is extraordinary! Your father knows of the list we have been working on here? How could that be?" said Jonathan almost melodramatically, almost not enough sincerity in his concern.

"I don't know. You have to ask him." She looked far from genuine in her reply and mildly defiant. Jonathan surmised that Ingrid had hacked into one of the dedicated terminals, accessed the file, seen its last decoded update, and conceivably recognized her father's name or something that looked like it.

"Look, come straight, Ingrid. You're in big trouble, young lady. Tell her how much, Isolde."

"You assaulted me, and I think Jonathan will be witness to it that you tried to murder us. Oh, twenty years in prison. And because of the security issues, probably no visitors."

"Yes, a Trappist monk's life would look jolly well a lot more exciting," added Jonathan. "And as possibly a terrorist, we could give you essentially *Habeas Corpus* for a long time until we extracted all the necessary information from you. Understand?"

"All right." Ingrid looked like she was about to crumble if it had not been for Sumo Joe. "I was curious about the list. I figured it was a list of traitors. I overhead one night when I was supposed to be asleep my father talking about the Berlin blast. And that he thought that there was a document about who did it."

"What?" said Isolde. "You know who was behind blowing up of the Holocaust Memorial?"

"Oh, really," said Jonathan.

"My father was saying what a nice job that was and describing the details of the ingredients and the chemicals and explosive devices."

"Ingrid, the information could have been gotten from certain police reports. And from them, there may have been leaks to the media, including speculation on the type of ingredients used. But as far as I know, it was strictly petrol and a kind of cyanide compound. Incidentally, where did you get the gun from?" asked Jonathan.

"I took it from my father's World War II trophy collection, which he has in the cellar. I think it's from my grandfather, who was a general close to Hitler."

"A what?" Isolde demanded from Ingrid.

"He was a general. Oh, I better tell you the whole story. He was a general of the S.S."

"Oh God! This is unbelievable. And you mentioned *Kamaradenshaft*. That's the veteran organization of ex-German soldiers, and there's even speculation that more than a few pro-Nazis are in it," added Isolde.

"Yes, I'm afraid that's true," said Ingrid, looking ashamed.

"Look," said Jonathan, "I am going to have to put you in the guesthouse under Sumo Joe's protection until we look into this whole matter. And get not only more of your story, but check it all out. I want you to promise never to do anything like this stunt again."

"Yes, Mr. Stock." Ingrid wept.

A highly trained young woman, supremely good as a code technician, had been rendered into a pool of total tears. Possibly highly irrational, too. A daughter to a father who sounded to be more an extreme right-wing nut or loser, rather than necessarily a top henchman in any elaborate conspiracy. Though he may have sympathized with the Holocaust Memorial Centre explosion, it did not necessarily mean that he was guilty of carrying it out or even planning it. But what list was he talking about? Maybe he was guessing. Who knew at the time? Maybe he was just trying to show a kind of false bravado to his *Kamaraden* brothers. Or possibly, Ingrid's father was more than what he seemed?

Isolde further thought about what a coincidence that Ingrid had gotten placed within the organization of the Council due to Zen's recommendation. Jonathan had to have been involved in vetting her selection, or he could have even nominated her. The question remained whether she was trying to protect her father or was she working for him? All of this seemed to further underscore the importance of the list and made Isolde increasingly suspicious that it was authentic. And that pro-Nazis were on it who had possibly leveraged Ingrid to report about any internal developments relating to them. Meanwhile, Sumo Joe took Ingrid to her quarantine.

"Now, Isolde, what do you have?" Jonathan grinned one of those lame smiles. The events of the last few days and all the pressure had turned him into not quite the unflappable self, as so well advertised by those in British senior intelligence who had staked their reputations on getting him selected for the job at the Council. Jonathan's eyes had the appearance of a very tired man, and his somewhat disheveled hair and grayed skin made him look much older than his years. He even sat slightly sunk in his chair, Isolde noticed. Uncharacteristic for him.

"Here's the list. I don't know whether any one of these German men is Ingrid's father or part of his *Kamaraden* group. Yes, one incompletely decrypted name looked close to Ingrid's. That will need more computer verification. But you will see one name on it that is clearly known to us."

"Adrian!" Jonathan jumped up. "No, it can't be! Go back to the computer and get it checked again."

"Of course, I have, as you well know, Jonathan. I've done that a few times. In fact, Adrian's name gets a very high probability rating—higher than any of the other names. Only Oswald Al Harvee gets a higher probability—that is, as not having infiltrated the NSA's computers and being physically in Maryland. There is no question that as far as cryptology shows, Adrian is guilty."

"I can't believe it. You remember he doubted our sincerity, especially mine. What a two-faced bugger! Making us look like we're holding out on him and treating him badly, considering him as a sort of amateur."

"I was thinking the very same thing," nodded Isolde.

"It just shows you in our business, one cannot trust just about anybody. Right, Isolde?"

"I couldn't concur with you more. No matter what elaborate precautions we take." Isolde had more than Adrian in mind when she said it. And she wondered if Jonathan would be questioning her loyalty, too, anytime soon. Things looked like they were beginning to fall apart badly. Extremely badly.

"What are you going to do, Colonel?" The seriousness of the situation seemed to make Isolde want to address Jonathan with his former ranking in the SAS.

"There is no question that my superiors will not want this mess left around. Now, Isolde, you are sure your contact in Sarabia got the real thing? This document is the real McCoy?"

"As sure as sure could be. For heaven's sake, my contact was executed in Panama for moving the package out. At least, I think so. After all, we were being chased halfway around the world for it."

"It's funny that Adrian didn't try to destroy it before you got it to us."

"He would have had to kill me to do that," responded Isolde.

"And why didn't he?"

"Can't you guess?"

"No."

"Adrian is in love with me, Jonathan. He said he was going to retire after this job. And he was making hints, I think, that he wanted me to come with him. Though I never responded—professional considerations, of course."

"Really!" said Jonathan, looking between disbelief and an expression that one gave when watching the insane babble nonsense.

"And maybe he is not all bad—just being compromised by something they are holding over him," added Isolde. "Or . . . that's why he let me bring the list back with him. Not all bad, Jonathan."

"Adrian mixing personal feelings with his job. Hard to believe. If that's the case, the Sarabian extremists may want to kill him more than we do. Or whoever he might be working for."

"Jonathan," said Isolde, "I had an eerie second thought. Adrian might have substituted a fake list for the real one, as I kept the actual one in my locked box that he might have accessed in Barbados. Then there would be no reason to kill me, particularly if he was so fond of me. If he had gotten what he wanted."

"I think that is ridiculous. After all, his name was on the list," said a peaked Jonathan, showing further strain in his face. "It's the real list, no question about it. Damn it, Isolde, you know it." Jonathan had never used that word to a female. Isolde had hit a raw nerve for some reason.

"Yes, that's . . . but what if his handlers put his name on the substitution list? Wanting to get rid of him, as they might have been losing trust in him or to cover their tracks?"

Isolde was looking very strained in her logic for the first time that Jonathan had known her. She was desperately trying to find an excuse to prevent Adrian from becoming practically public enemy number one to the Council.

"Yes, anything is possible, but not probable. However you look at it, he technically screwed up by letting you live because of his affections. I think I'll have him watched if we can locate him, and see if I can use him as a kind of bait. I am sure the list is genuine. That's the end of the discussion about it."

"But . . ."

Jonathan interrupted, looking testy. "I'm sorry, Isolde, you'll have to put your personal affections for Mr. Sands completely to the side. I'm thinking of taking you completely off the case now. But really, excellent . . . no, superb work, nevertheless, in decoding all this. Superb, indeed."

"Thank you for that. Yes, the work has been daunting at times."

"Meanwhile, yes . . . I'm going to assign you a few weeks of leave." The Department Executive Director (DED), Jonathan's official title, smiled as if he were Isolde's sugar daddy as well. Uncharacteristic of his usual hard-nosed position against leave.

"You can't do that to me, Jonathan!"

"I have enough information to have you grounded and put into the guestroom next to Ingrid. You're too emotionally involved. You are actually looking like you're coming unhinged . . . are you?"

"Certainly not. You know Heimlich has given me a good bill of health."

"Well, I have the right to wonder, with all the time that you have been together with Adrian that you didn't have some hint of his disloyalty. I could go with that in my report. But I won't, if you follow orders."

"That's preposterous given all the good work I've done."

"This is just two weeks out. I'll be good about it—with pay. Go to Tahiti or something, but bloody well stay out of the way. Very far out of the way."

Jonathan was beginning to look frazzled. It was he whose tone gave more than a hint of becoming unhinged. He awkwardly motioned for her to depart as a final sign that the decision about her having to take leave was final.

She left and slammed the door to his office. She then went down the hall to her room and prepared to pack. But that was not going to be the end of it.

Jonathan knew he had finally been provided enough evidence to order up a kill on good old Adrian, his faithful stooge turned traitor, as he would like so many to have believed him to be. A number of his agents had a license to murder, but he was in the unique situation of having a license to order it. It just had to be rubber-stamped by the Council. But he was permitted to order one in process under emergency as stipulated in the MOA—Manual of Action—that every member of the Council had in some vault; their copies provided no names of people.

Jonathan secretly ordered it on that fateful day by contracting it out. Using a very interesting assassin, who in a surprising coincidence was in Zürich on vacation. Yes, everything was nicely coming together, as Jonathan diabolically laughed to himself—trying to convince himself that all was well. Yet, he could not escape his worries that at any moment it could all fall apart. Somehow, Jonathan had known it—prepared the way for Isolde's vacation many days before. He could not help smiling at the time. He had just been getting warmed up for the big final party. However, he still had worries. Big ones.

Ingrid had played out her performance wonderfully and even thrown in her father and his *Kamaraden* club as decoys to convince Isolde of the veracity of the list. Jonathan now, with Isolde's unwitting contrivance as a highly respected cryptologist, had burning proof to liquidate a whole bunch of key people unfriendly to his grand plan and those of his fellow Islamic extremist-Nazi coconspirators. And to do so probably legally. As legally as any such shadowy organizations as the Council and Z5 could operate. Jonathan was a real piece of art—the espionage kind.

Yes, Adrian's liquidation would be done secretly—or if Jonathan was held responsible, retroactively to the Council's inevitable permission. Adrian had been brutally set up without any suspicion of it, at least initially. Isolde's assassination would be more complicated. Jonathan would put her out of the way sometime later. Only so many high-level bodies, including a number of whom heretofore had been well trusted by the Order or

Council, could be beaten up, put in a coma, or assassinated before the Council might order a special investigation under Article 13 that could possibly prove very damaging to Jonathan.

While there were too many on the Council board that had complete faith in Isolde, most had heard little about Adrian Sands. And if Isolde contacted others on the Council or in regular intelligence about the listed names, it would serve Jonathan's purpose of further giving credibility to the list and creating very useful diversions to the authorities away from stopping his master plan. It might drive additional complementary action, causing dissent and confusion in the mainstream intelligence communities. All at a critical time when together, Jonathan, Bashard, Schmidt, and Zayed began to open up their Pandora's Box. Yes, for Jonathan it would be good to keep Isolde alive. Well, at least for a while.

* * *

"Adrian . . ."

"Who's this on my private line? You are not listed as an authorized contact with this telephone number."

"This is Isolde; I have got to talk to you."

"Really?"

"Where are you, Adrian?"

I waited as my phone app tested to see if, in fact, the voice at the other end was Isolde's. It was confirmed. The polygraph software for telephone conversations, released by the CIA to Peach Corporation for commercial distribution, had worked its wonders.

"I'm in a hotel room. Possibly I'll have a coffee with Patsy. Almost ready to go to bed for a long one."

"Look, I'm not sure about Patsy. I'm having second thoughts about Jonathan. I'm also actually not fully sure about talking to you. You're in a lot of trouble, but . . ."

"Join the club," I said.

"I'm going to come to Zürich, to finally clear up this mess. After, we can meet if all goes well. You may be getting a birthday gift."

"Goes well? Gift?"

Isolde would not explain any further, but I could figure out that Jonathan was bad just by instinct. But now, it sounded from Isolde that my suspicions of him should have been worse. And my birthday was months away.

Isolde continued, "Actually, I think we had better meet outside somewhere. What about what we refer to as the B place? Again, if everything goes well."

"Look, that's going to be difficult. I'll leave a note with Nic in our special code as to the exact location, using codes for exact longitude and latitude. You know the password for the website that will decrypt it. I don't trust many of these telephone electronics. He'll give you instructions as to when we can meet. Probably during my bedtime, I would guess—nice time to slip out."

"Sounds good, Adrian. But make it a private hotel, not in the middle of a forest."

"Okay. Now, you must know that I'm a little famous right now and a little gun-shy. So we'll have to make our meeting reasonably clandestine—and quick."

"Right," Isolde said.

*   *   *

Kim Kil-Gun was amused by what he had picked up on the so-called private line of mine, which was supposed to be fully encrypted for discussions with members of the Order. With Kim's special intelligence apps on his Samsung smartphone, he was able to track up to nine supposed private and encrypted telephone conversations or chats, focusing in on the ones with frequent important key words that were popping up. And even translated into high-quality Korean if he wished.

Kim also possessed something even more useful to his work. He had a very long list of people whom he was supposed to assassinate. A number of whom he had managed to get their personal cell numbers. Interpol and Swiss police insiders had given them to Kim. Jonathan had special blackmail files on these police insider contacts that had proven very useful. Kim's extensive eavesdropping bore huge fruit.

The Korean hit man had never had so much business. It was getting ridiculous, he thought—a gang bang of assassinations. And a free-for-all where, if he was not careful, he could get into the crosshairs of one of his competitors. He had been told that there was, at a minimum, two or three other assassins who had the list, and he would get a bonus if he took down more than three listed targets. What he did not know was that he only had half of the full original and decoded list. That another three would be working on this "better half," and that his was the last name on it for execution. Kim's potential assignments were as follows:

1. Adrian Sands, Zürich, Hotel Schotland
2. Prince Waheed Al Sarab, Royal Yacht, Monaco
3. Johan Stihl, Swiss banker, Banque Swiss, Zürich
4. Julius and Caesar Julien, executives, Julien und Co. (Bring secretly to Grossmunster cathedral, gag and tie up, and hide in boarded-up tower.)
5. G. Smuts, Chairperson, Van der Roos Museum, Amsterdam
6. Prince Sarwawi bin Waleed Al Sarab (Sarabian intelligence chief)
7. Dionysus League, Athens, Greece (All five inner youth members to be liquidated. Photos attached.)
8. Fritz Konning, New Social People's Party and *Kamaradenshaft* (Berlin). And Ingrid Konning, his daughter (whereabouts unknown).
9. Frankenstein—True name unknown at this time. More information to be provided.
10. Pierre Shad-Bolt, Zürich CIA Station Chief (Also to be moved to Grossmunster cathedral and given same treatment as the Juliens.)
11. Galen Nickeroff, Real Holding Corporation, Toronto, Canada

The note added that he would be given the final instructions. These terminations were promised to have benediction from all significant Western government-connected law enforcement and intelligence authorities. Kim found that fascinating. The West was so messed up and decadent in his mind that they were even beginning to eat their own crusaders because of it. Poetic justice, he thought. And Kim loved poetry, which he wrote in *Hangul*, the very specific Korean lettering system, which he enjoyed writing in very thick dark brown calligraphy.

Kim quickly destroyed the cyber file with other instructions. He figured three or four kills, with no more than a few per week and over a wide geographical spread, would be all he or any competitors could get away with. He would watch the news closely, but worried that his competitors might get greedy and overly accelerate the pace of assassinations. But then, if his instructions were to be believed, authorities would be working to cover up where necessary to make the deaths of the above look like accidents. Why did he really care?

He remembered that assassination was an art for him, and he liked to explore sometimes not only how it was done, but how it was sometimes ingeniously covered up. Such an eye for latter detail had saved him many times from the revenge of the target's friends, lovers, and mothers. The list was just getting too long for Kim to want to think about it anymore. Nor did he want to calculate the odds of someone knocking him off.

Even if he messed up the whitewashing, by the time anyone started putting the puzzle together—including journalists, conspiracy-inspired computer geeks, and friends and relatives of the deceased—it would be too late. He would be in the clear to enjoy his prize money. Already a half million Swiss francs had been deposited by a mystery figure. He had electronically sourced it back to an offshore bank area off northern France, but got nothing more than the base number of an IP address. Kim, for the most part, did not want to know exactly where it came from.

Strangely and recently, he had more information from the Al Quomini Brotherhood to be ready to go to the Norman Islands soon and be ready to make a hit. There was actually way too much work. Conceivably he could subcontract it out—something he usually felt quite uncomfortable about doing, unless his good life began to compromise his blown balance sheet. Even an all-out Sicilian war between the Mafia looked tame compared to this bloodbath-to-be. It all was bordering on the ridiculous, unless it was a prelude to an actual war. Like a world war, where rapid assassinations would just all fit into the continued cry for intense havoc. And Kim had to admit that the global scene was increasingly looking like one big battlefront. So why was he uncomfortable with so much business? The world was quickly becoming tailor-made for the assassination trade. But something still did not quite seem right to this seasoned killer.

He had looked at the list carefully in his mind. He was not too excited about murdering anybody of his new Muslim faith, and he had already made a huge amount of money from doing rather delicate work for neo-Nazis, who promised more assignments. Then he thought about one very special name again, Adrian Sands. He thought to himself long and carefully. Was that the very same fucker known in the business as "The

Professor," who had stolen away a few of his very high price kills years ago? And who was at the top of the list. "Yes," he had muttered deliciously through his unique fusion food plate of raw beef *bulgogi a la tartare* and sour cabbage *kimchi*. "Sands will be the first to get it, and good."

TWENTY-TWO

The gift that Isolde had referred to in her last telephone conversation with me had arrived. It had been couriered to me by way of the Zürich central post office. I was instructed by her to bring it to the Z-bank vaults. I never quite knew why she had sent it that way—or initially, why she had sent it altogether. At one time, Amsterdam diamond merchants swore that it was safer to use the post office. Private couriers, including the ones in envelope form, sometimes drew much more unwanted attention than general delivery.

At the time, an anonymous text message as to what post office it was at had almost immediately disappeared as fast as I read it. And more importantly, it promised that the package would vanish in two hours if I did not get there on time and provide my usual password. That anyone else who showed up for it might be simply eliminated.

To deal with the problem of someone mugging me once more but this time upon fetching the package, I decided to do something dramatic that would definitely blunt any more youthful attacks on me. Yup, I rented a van full of stunningly attractive hookers, who would surround me right into the post office. I would change into a disguise of one of them in the nearest toilet. All, of course, after I had picked up the package. All, of course, after one of them changed into a disguise to look like me—even knowing the dangers of the mission which she felt was an attraction in itself. She along with the rest of the ladies had been paid well, too, which certainly helped.

*   *   *

In the package was *the* list, which was truly bizarre upon its initial inspection—not even in encrypted form, just made to look like an attached guest list to a party, as the covering letter indicated. Quite humorous in a strange way, as the reception it referred to was connected with the Van Gogh exposition.

There had been no references, of course, to the attached organizations of the conspirators, just a few creative misspellings of family names—supposedly to confuse anyone in customs or mail service who by chance or design might get a look at it. It would have been a *helluva* party and dance to have those on it in the same room. I would have given the event two minutes before the roof would have fallen in.

I had been told by Isolde that physically, just about anything was protected and secure in the Council's facilities in the Norman Islands. Only bunker buster bombs armed with tactical nuclear explosives, or cruise missiles equipped with megaton explosives, would have a chance to completely take out the underground vaults of the Council's Guernsey hideout. And that was a definite maybe. Still, why was she walking around with the original and sending a decoded variety of it to me?

I gathered later that the problem was that the enemy was truly throughout the Council directorate, so there was no going back to that bunker, especially with the likes of Jonathan being there. Yet all of these lists were too hot to handle anymore. They had to be returned—or appear to be returned. And to a more reliable source than the DED—and soon. One reason of which had nothing to do with pleasing Jonathan, whom I was still pretty pleased with displeasing. All to do about increasing our probabilities of survival, which may have gone down with the heavenly gift from Isolde. And even Friegel had returned his, though his was essentially valueless and with the bug missing.

Isolde had also wanted me to see if it was safe to go to Z-bank, as she wanted to make her own deposit—which, she had told me, was invaluable, even more so than mine. How, I wondered, could it be? I understood that what I had was no less than the same list that we had taken out of Panama. Actually worse, since it was decoded! All very confusing, indeed.

It would be the only copy that I knew of that other experts in her cryptography network would deem as verifying an apparent banking, neo-Nazi—and Sarabian-backed conspiracy. But considering the proof of Z5's extensive infiltration, as well, there was the possibility that this would be the last bank I would ever see, and the last bankers unless there was a kind of divine intervention. Not a bad deal if you had to go by being snuffed out in a plush Swiss bank, surrounded by all that glitter. And,

I suppose, not a bad arrangement if you were as putridly tired of Swiss bankers as I had become. If she did not hear back from me in a few hours after I had gone to the bank and dropped off her gift, she would know that I was likely done and that she would not be safe there—at all.

I wondered exactly what I would do with what I knew to be the first fake list, which Friegel had given back to me with a less-than-pleasant facial expression, followed by storming out without a single comment. I thought about putting it in the safety deposit box for Z papers, to confuse the hell out of anybody who had to go back and use them. I was beginning to get tired of all the deceit and games.

In fact, I decided to glue Isolde's gift together with the fake list given to Friegel and let Z-Bank and in turn Z5 and the Council deal with the mess. I really didn't know what Isolde was up to. I almost did not know at times what we were doing. It was getting crazier and crazier, this swirling, twisted conspiracy—or should one say conspiracies? The so-called Friegel list I liked at the time, as it distinctly did not have the one dummy on it that was very important to me—myself. I could not understand why I had been put on the decoded "gift" list, with Isolde penning in *tentative invitee* beside my name.

Nevertheless, as these lists played out, they were beginning to look like centers radiating more deadly subplots than a Roger Bedlum novel. I just wanted to get away from them and the whole disaster as fast as possible. I wanted that ticket to Tahiti that Isolde never got to use.

* * *

The Zeel Foundation, near Pelikanplatz in Zürich, is in one of those nondescript gray buildings with slight indentations to make the building look like a layered cake. The foundation's entrance is off the main street and almost hidden by a line of linden trees that look like they might have been planted years ago, rather than decades. The narrow alleyway and cobblestone walk up to it looks more like a service entrance. In fact, this is the back entrance and more concealed way to eventually get to Z-bank.

The foundation's bright brass sign *Zeel Stiftung*—under which reads in translation form, "charity for women"—is in small print and looks out of place, as it is in eyesight of the Zürich Bourse. This moderate-size stock market—but a modern one—can be seen not more than a few hundred meters through an immaculately tended park.

After buzzing the foundation and stating one's name and business, one passes through a darkened, small corridor that takes one to an elevator to the Z-bank. It could be described as a boutiquelike private wealth institution that the foundation established under the Council's instructions, but more tied to the Order and Z5 in terms of cash outflow. In reality, there was absolutely no paper trail from the Council to the bank.

Rather, the owners were mysteriously registered in Panama. This did not bother the Swiss government at all, as the previous owner was on the Swiss Federal Council and his political contacts were impeccable, right down to the banking and finance committee that they had been members of. The bank was small, too, and hence, did not show up much on the screen of regulators or protestors, who had the common denominator of being kept totally in the dark about its actual function.

The Council had decided that Z5 in its inception would have independent supporting financial structures, to reduce the risks that their efforts to stop sinister worldwide plots and terrorism would be compromised by probing eyes of bank regulators. These watchdogs, chiefly in those days following the *Big Melty*, were focused on large financial institutions adding considerably to systemic risk or with suspect connections to the Middle East. Certainly not small banks with establishment-type directors, collecting and managing money for high-society Swiss female do-gooders.

In fact, the cash assets of the foundation were less than ten million francs—on paper. The foundation had only a few social functions each year, and published a skimpy annual report that hid a lot of its wealth that had been kept off its balance sheets. In reality, it was worth one hundred million francs, with all of its assets financially managed by the bank. The bank also acted as the overall auditor to the Council and Z5.

The manager, a Z5 agent, and his staff of three were sworn to secrecy—their secrecy being guaranteed by a death sentence for whoever broke it, never mind the so-called strict Swiss banking laws to protect privacy of account holders. For the passerby public, they did not even know it was connected to a bank. The sign on the obscure door to the building said simply *ZFOR Holdings*. It was a financial riddle wrapped partly in a foundation riddle. But out of this bank was where Brother Biggart ran one of the most efficient financial networks for supporting high-level espionage. Oh yes, and a so-called "charity finance."

The board of directors of the bank were all nominees of the unknown individual owners. Some of Europe's most important, but low-profile philanthropists, joined by a dabbling few from Canada, America, and Japan. Two members of the board were unknown to the others except Brother Biggart. No references in any publications to them. They reserved the right to anonymously send in their votes on critical issues and provide advice. Finally, they reserved the right to be present at any board meeting should they choose, but in disguise. For the moment, they chose not. There were no records in vaults or files of the two. They were intertwined in the neurons of Brother Biggart and possibly Jonathan, as well as the oversight committee of the Council.

The board trusted Biggart that much. Such trust might prove to be very expensive one day. But as a former Trappist monk, who still liked to be referred to as Brother (maybe to give a feel of sanctity to his work), silence for him was more than an absolute necessity. It was his habit.

Biggart had even been an educator where the principal partner had demanded the use of the silent method of teaching. It was a standing joke for Biggart when he wanted to prove his silence was guaranteed: he just mentioned how taciturn he was, even when he taught for a California-based education organization steeped in retro-hippy methods, generally long forgotten and disused in the United States where it was headquartered. The board had chosen well. A former teacher and monk who had specialized in keeping his mouth shut. Adrian had hoped, though, that Biggart would not want to silence him, as Biggart also possessed a staff with silencers, and oh yes, hired guns too.

Isolde had not told anyone in the Z organizations that she was back in Zürich other than Adrian. She had certainly not told Jonathan that she had absconded with the list in its original form. Jonathan was getting sloppy, looking increasingly worn, she thought—and even looking a bit troubled. He definitely should have had her fully checked before she had gotten on the ferry to St. Malo, where she had connected to Paris for a quick TGV express to Zürich. Yes, why hadn't Jonathan checked her before she left? And more importantly, when would he find out that the original list had been taken? Maybe he still had residual faith in her—well, for no more than another day or two.

Isolde had been glad to get off the island in one piece, but still felt that she had been dodging shadowy figures. Why and by whom was she being followed? It had gotten difficult to completely shake them. They seemed to be as good as she had been when following the friends of José Kartman. A very disagreeable, hard-to-digest thought had rooted in her stomach. Were there any leftovers from the Kartman "fab four" still trying to get the list? Holding back to see to whom she might connect, so they could find the right moment to efficiently liquidate her and her coterie of associates in the Order? She could not forget what had happened to Zen. And grizzly revenge would be on their Panamanian minds—if it were they.

However, somehow she felt more secure after her arrival in the city, especially after the real document was safely put away at the university in the hands of her former quantum physics professor. She had left it overnight at the photon decryption unit of the Quantum Physics Laboratory at ZIT. It was the only one of its kind in Europe, able to discern highly complex, sophisticated coded messages in photonic bundles.

One of her old professors had arranged for the list's safekeeping and had gotten her clearance to use the facilities, given what she had told him in confidence about the importance of her mission. She knew what she had done could theoretically provide the Council every reason to sanction her. But she was no longer worried about a lot of bureaucratic rules that she often found contemptuous in the first place.

The new breakthroughs in this particular quantum decoding method were not supposed to be widely known to the public. In fact, officially only the University of Maryland and the California Institute of Technology were the two hubs in the process of developing the know-how. That was part of what little information the larger Western intelligence community had allowed to be published in the highly scientifically acclaimed and peer-reviewed periodicals, *Science* and *Nature*.

Yes, despite holding dozens of Nobel prizes in medicine and other sciences, the Swiss were a more discreet, and in a sense a more humble, lot when it came to getting their full share of credit in scientific discoveries. An incredible legacy for such a small country, in which Albert Einstein had done some of the first major pioneering work in quantum physics in Bern. And under whom her professor had been tutored and had been a young graduate student.

This was the last chance to check the document for any additional information that might be embedded in it. Isolde had heard about this photonic method, but had kept cannily quiet about it to Jonathan given her growing suspicions about him. Given the money Bashard and his people had, it would not be impossible for them to have arranged implanting evidence in it using this cutting-edge technology, with the outside list as a phony deadly distraction.

Perhaps she would not find anything else, but she owed herself a last chance to fully verify its authenticity. No, she owed it to humanity. And she thought she owed it to me. No . . . I considered myself to be just an undeserving, selfish, and aggressive male bastard. Separated from the common man by nothing more than a well-trained gun. But she remained dedicated to making every effort to save me and prove that I was not involved in the conspiracy.

Meanwhile, Isolde's hunch of using the new spectral quantum electron microscope to check for any photon patterns out of kilter was paying off. But she had no more than several hours before daybreak to discover whether there was another list within the document and exactly what was on it. After all, her use of the lab was not formally authorized, so it would be imprudent to use it during regular daylight hours. If there was anything in photonic form, it would signal the possibility that Bashard's people had illegally used this laboratory—or the two American ones. That was worrying, as it was unlikely that the American labs would have been accessible to Bashard's code workers, making Isolde worry about her safety.

It was also interesting that the list was on the highly specialized paper produced at Castle Papers. It was so advanced to prevent duplication that it was the sole paper producer for five hundred unit bills for many major European currencies. Making the money notes virtually impossible to counterfeit.

Finally, after several hours of tedious and technical work at the lab, she decided she could no longer stay away from the hotel. She was exhausted so it was time to leave. She had found most of what she was looking for.

She returned at 3:00 a.m. to her hotel, the Platanus, with its somewhat dull painted shades of gray and olive, with warblers painted onto her bedroom wallpaper. She decided to get in a few hours of sleep. She set the alarm clock for six o'clock, fully aware that there would be no need, as it would be next to impossible to get in even a few winks of sleep after what she had learned at the lab. Nevertheless, she would try. She trembled a little trying to set her old trusty Swiss-made clock. A clock that did not give the answer to what was another very real, major competing deadline. A deadline that was soon to be put into play by other craftsmen who had worked in a lab. The atomic bomb-maker kind.

*   *   *

Dr. Khalid Al Boom had always contended that building an atomic bomb was practically child's play once the enriched uranium was obtained. To convince himself of this, he had written an "Easy Man's Guide to Blowing the World Up," as he liked to call it. It had been a little humor against those in the West who had been convinced years ago that he wanted to store a nuclear bomb in every terrorist's family home or with his favorite rogue states.

At the time, he could only laugh as a half dozen states went nuclear or near nuclear with his direct but more wily indirect help, as his Swiss bank accounts got fatter by the millions each month. And more importantly, he looked with joy that his Waristan had gotten the bomb from the unselfish work of a small, well-chosen group of dedicated Muslims. They, like him, had been patriotic to their country, working day and night religiously to achieve this great accomplishment for Wadi Islam and his motherland. It had been the first Islamic atomic weapon for a small state, and his home one at that. So proud had the government been that they had awarded him a free luxury villa in a prized compound in the suburbs of Rorepuni, Waristan's unofficial capital.

But now, Waristan had sold out to the West, he thought. He could not give a damn what the retaliation would be on his government if he succeeded in getting a bomb put together in Zürich—a process that was taking much longer than he had hoped. He was in too much rage, too indoctrinated now with the faith that the bigger the jihad on the West, the more the majority of the faithful would cry out his name for hundreds of years as a sacred martyr.

Boom knew that if things did not turn around radically against the Western corrupt forces, as he saw them, permanent house arrest—or even possibly execution—would be his fate. With this serious reality staring him in his face and most of his money gone or inaccessible, he was content to not only hit a massive blow at the West, but to put a giant hole in the financial system that he felt had cheated not only him, but also millions of his Muslim brothers.

He remembered showing Zahed, who was overseeing the assemblage operations in Zürich, how easy it was to make a bomb. He had taken him and his colleague through the whole process. The main pieces had been assembled in practice, though they were scattered through ten medium-size boxes so as to better prevent Western security from becoming suspicious. Some of the crates had come through different ships, but all had ended up in a Norman island port for further transportation by a small plane to the final city of destination. "Or was that destinations?" he corrected himself mid-stream in destructive thoughts.

The enriched uranium, though, had not been put in the practice training area, which he had organized in a small shack. It had been slightly off-site from where Waristan had done its first research into building the bomb. He had never told his colleagues who were to assemble the bomb that it had not been enriched uranium used in the practice run. This was a final test of their loyalty, for in the small chance that they were agents working for Western interests, they would have had someone seize the material.

The concept was again simple. The enriched uranium had been molded into two pieces, but in a way that they would reach a supercritical stage. There was a need to position these sections of the uncommon metal so that a fire would not be started that would likely render it impossible to make a bomb. If this were to happen, the uranium would degrade into non-weapon producing material. Bringing the two pieces together too closely could also set off a nuclear explosion prematurely, though it was unlikely. More likely it would cause an overcritical reaction that would create excessive radioactivity, but no blast. Otherwise known as the dirty bomb, much less effective in creating damage than the real McCoy would do.

Zahed, with his colleagues, had to work tirelessly many times under the doctor's supervision to get the precise assemblage correct. K-Boom thought it had been fascinating that the practice work was being done near where the first Waristani bomb had been produced. The barracks were now largely abandoned, but he still had all the passes and codes that were still working, thankfully. The guards were accustomed to him coming and going with helpers in the overall area as naturally as the sun goes up in the morning and down at night. This trust that security still had in him at the time, given all his years of absolute loyalty to the state, was going to be cashed out before they ever thought of arresting him.

What concerned K-Boom was whether the detonator, with all the specs he had requested, would be able to fully create the effect of shoving one of the shaped, enriched uranium metal pieces into the other to create the critical reaction. If the trigger was even a bit faulty, he worried there might be no reaction at all.

He had also asked for a number of reflectors, which he had personally examined, that would further ensure that the neutrons would not escape and fizzle out the reaction. While the concept was simple, the exact timing and precision that would maximize the tonnage of explosion to take out more than a square kilometer of downtown Zürich was not so easy to get precisely right.

He also felt the need to have a second bomb-making team in another city if things went wrong. In fact, he had done so through direct procurement of most of his supplies by way of a Delaware bank account. A number of the restricted items had been smuggled in through a Mexican drug cartel, whose rank and numbers were being slaughtered by Mexican police in conjunction with advice from US authorities. They were up for massive revenge, too. Again, he had to ungraciously deal with what he considered to be certain "detestable Christians." Through these so-called new friends, he had to ship his equipment along with their *Haram* (forbidden) drugs.

The Mexicans had been loyal and had not asked questions once they found out that the good doctor had nothing to do with drugs at all. There was a reason they were called a cartel, which would probably in the end kill or mentally destroy more people in North America and Europe than a small-scale nuclear bomb.

It was considered a bit of a long shot to get the bomb assembled successfully and placed in New York City in good timing with the implementation of the full-blown conspiracy. Nevertheless, if the bomb pieces headed for New York were discovered by the authorities, he could use it as a diversion, as they would get much more preoccupied with focusing their resources on finding out where others might be placed in other US cities.

The Delaware accounts through which he had made the purchases belonged to a Mafia kingpin involved in ice cream and other refrigeration business. His only apparent illegal activities, if ever uncovered, would probably only be sourced back to the drug cartel. The US authorities would conclude that the potential nuclear device was payback for the extensive support DEA and other US agencies had provided for killing and rounding up hundreds of the cartel's members and seizing billions of dollars of illicit drug money.

Unfortunately, it was not outside the realm of possibility that the Zürich bomb might be found before it could be properly placed and exploded, or that it might not work satisfactorily, if at all. The doctor gave it a 30 percent chance that something might go wrong. Even the CIA intelligence theorists had ranked a terrorist nuclear bomb detonation as 95 percent unlikely in the next few years, but 95 percent likely in the average current life span of a middle-aged American or younger. However, these were the same office-ensconced experts who had told their president that it was very probable that Waristan would never have the sophistication to get the bomb, at least for another ten years at a minimum. It all made Boom laugh a bit about the odds of being stopped. It all gave him more confidence that he might pull it off, given his lack of confidence in the NATO intelligence community, who were unofficially short of the precision capabilities of Israeli and Swiss security services. Those last two had worryingly gone silent, like coiled eels hiding in the seabed, just waiting for the right time to strike. He would never cease to worry that these were the few who could be efficient enough to stop him.

Getting the weapons-grade uranium had been a little trickier for Boom. He had been dealing with Kalistan, a former Soviet republic with a large Muslim population. But more importantly, a country with a half dozen nuclear reactors that had a lot of spent fuel, never properly accounted for. And a few warheads were still missing since the fall of the Iron Curtain.

The Tyranians had been highly cooperative in brokering the deal with the Kalistani Muslim underground group known as the KAKE. Why not? He had provided enough equipment for Tyranian efforts to make their own bomb, which was now well underway though incomplete. The Tyranians knew that under the watchful eye of the international community, it would be next to impossible to import the enriched uranium without Western-imposed safeguards. So they continued to purify it with centrifuges, but this was a time-consuming process, even though K-Boom had already helped with procuring such vital equipment.

The highest-level imams didn't know in which Western city Boom was going to place his bombs. But the president of Tyrania, unknown to them, had paid a huge amount to have what he thought was the signal device to blow one. K-Boom had convinced the Tyranians that given the Patriot missile defense in Israel and the new American "Star War" defense umbrella, any Tyranian rocket with an atomic warhead might not make it through.

A greater problem was that intelligence showed that the Israelis were possibly weeks away from a massive strike against Tyranian nuclear facilities. A bomb in a downtown Western city would be the guarantor that a strike by their Israeli ally would be paid back with a thousand times of misery. Some of the Tyranian leadership did not care if K-Boom let off the bomb without their approval, as Israel would be blamed for creating the conditions that led to the devastating explosion. They would make sure of it. And a number of them might very well clap as they watched the mayhem and chaos from such a not only physically—but also psychologically—debilitating blast.

The International Atomic Energy Agency and various US agencies were appalled by the nuclear fuel booking of the Yeltsin regime in the immediate post-Soviet Union era. If they had known the actual story, that a good portion had been outright stolen through massive bribery during the initial collapsing days of the Communist Party-led regime, they would not have been shocked, given how riddled the country was with Mafia-run organizations and government corruption. The Russians partially "cooked" the fissile material books, as they knew if Washington had seen the actual accounting, they would have done their own imploding.

Fortunately, from the Western perspective, a number of combined Russian police and FBI sting-run operations subsequently resulted in getting most of the Russian enriched uranium and plutonium back. But there was a rumor, as K-Boom well knew, that fifty to sixty kilograms that were still unaccounted for, were in the hands of the Kalistan Muslim League (KML), which had buried and sat on it like an investor who stored his gold, waiting for its value to peak one day.

Yes, K-Boom realized there were many stories about where that uranium was. And they were all wrong. For it had finally gotten into his organization's possession, after having been successfully moved through the Bosporus straights of Istanbul and then onto an executive jet to Zürich from the Channel Islands.

It had been a little tricky, as he had to use a Sarabian to deliver the money in cash to, of all places, Nubia so as to pay for the uranium and the bomb's transportation. The courier who had gone through with the transaction had shown dissatisfaction with his payoff. But he was now dead, killed in Panama.

Worse for Boom, he had to borrow extensively from banker Schmidt in preparing for the financial aftershocks he foresaw after Zürich was nuked. Schmidt had simply been told that they would both make a killing on shorting weakened financial stocks, such as MANCITC and, of course, any major Swiss company. And to buy lots of gold. Schmidt was also to move as much of his gold as possible to either Hong Kong or Panama. Not to New York or London—or even Toronto.

Zürich was the third or fourth largest depositary for gold. And it provided much storage of silver and platinum, and a few other important precious materials whose names, such as tatadium, were totally unknown to the public. But not to the European defense establishment, which were in dire need of a number of these substances for their highly sophisticated command and control systems and structures. Not only would the so-called "Goldfinger effect" be put into play to radiate the gold and other precious metals to uselessness for decades to come, but the destruction or heavy radiation of the stored rare earths would put a hole in Western defenses for decades. The only others hoarding these very rare supplies were the Chinese, who even forbid export permits for them. Any "rare earth gap" could eventually help put the Chinese in the defense lead over the West within the century.

Possibly more important, the value of gold would almost triple as the West lost a third of its precious metal reserves if Zürich went up in smoke and people intensely grabbed for glitter as a result of a massive surge in risk. An atomic bomb explosion in the city would also create havoc in the stock market as 15 percent of Western European capital disappeared, which would be the temporary effect if the Zürich Bourse vanished.

Ironically, Bashard's other big bet besides gold would be on the American dollar, which would appreciate substantially as a safe haven currency, at least right after the first atomic bomb explosion. However, what Bashard did not know and K-Boom failed to tell him was that there was a second bomb that might be put into place. In America. Having a crushing effect on that nation's currency if the device detonated.

Bashard had promised as a total fee to K-Boom 10 percent of his nuclear mushrooming profits deposited into a Gulf Arab bank account, as well as a Hong Kong one, to reflect his appreciation for generating the conditions to create a new Islamic-extremist and neo-Nazi world order. Certainly for the bad doctor, that was enough to replace all the money that had been stolen by the CIA. After all, he considered that he deserved the premium for all the work and risks he would be taking. Yes, one billion dollars would be good.

There was one worry that Bashard had increasingly become aware of with his contacts in both Zürich and Raddah, and even Panama. There was a female that had a possible connection to one of his own people who had snooped around in certain important offices of his in Raddah and stolen part of his most important personal properties. It contained a list that had been put together that had his name on it and all his contacts crucial to bringing about the new caliphate order, his side of the new equation in the global division of power. It was a backup to his memory and would be used by his assistant if anything happened to him. He regretted keeping it, but he refused to let anyone else have a complete list of the whole operation and its key details while he was alive.

The weird thing was that a stolen item from inside a new customer's deposit box at his Banco San Diego had proven to be that very coded document, put there by one of his formerly trusted lieutenants. And some lowly Panamanian assassin had gotten hold of it. All the other information he got was that a blue-eyed, pretty blonde lady had killed the thief and was likely now in possession of the list. He was going to soon get more information about her and whether she had had any accomplices. He wanted that information then and now, like yesterday.

TWENTY-THREE

Picking up an anonymous taxi off the street would be safer. Certainly less risky than taking one of the crowded trams, from which she would have had to transfer at Bahnhofplatz. It was a favorite square of hers and included the fountain whose maintenance had been secretly sponsored by the Order. This fountain was a message drop for anyone who felt so seriously under threat that they could not use any electronic communication. The receptacle for any dispatch was placed up the silver dragon's ass.

After getting the original list back with her crucial notes from the ZIT labs that morning, Isolde indeed took a taxi. "Why not?" she said to herself. The cab was anonymous, but not without risks, especially given how gorgeous a woman she was. She would just hazard getting the usual stares in the rearview mirror, which she had never gotten fully used to. It almost made her envy those ladies who wore veils, though they too could get gazes even in Zürich, but more of the unfriendly ones. Yes, she could risk stares from a cabbie, easy enough compared to all the other unsafe actions she had taken.

That day's young taxi driver was initially more pleasant than the usual assortment that had collected her. She could still remember them—but not by face. This one was simply a lonely university student caught up on his thesis. It was a comparative analysis of the philosophical foundations of Friedrich Nietzsche and Franz Kafka as applied to modern Western institutions. "How exciting," she sarcastically said to herself.

He kept going on about how not only Western women, but Western men, were just cattle fodder to financial and government institutions, working hand-in-hand and largely no better than in the dark days of absolute monarchy and religious oppression. These institutions were generally designed to remove warm human emotions through senseless bureaucracies, so the new popes of banking could continue to exploit and divide the masses and stymie true individual creativity and freedom. All while preaching the virtue of their causes, and the need for the masses to conform to collective wants and mores that they had decided were right for society, through the engines of mass-marketing propaganda.

The cabbie continued like an irrepressible fountain of antiestablishment bile. He saw a good portion of the current elites as holy defenders of a kind of oppressive religion of neomonopolistic private wealth overly concentrated among the few, a rebellion against which had only begun to take root in a few states in the Middle East and the US Midwest America.

The only elites he had any time for were heads of Internet companies, such as Facebook, Google, and Twitter, and Internet hardware enablers like Apple, which furthered information freedom. He believed that the regular, old-style leaders wanted us to believe in a "virtue" based on a modern alliance of decaying financial temples of banking and crumbling government cathedrals. That was leading to an endgame of decadence, systemic bankruptcy, and finally, war.

In fact, he alleged that there was a powerful secret collusion to put the average man and woman back to near zero—as in zero control and zero financial power through increased levels of housing foreclosures, unemployment, stagflation, taxation, investment portfolio erosion, and just plain financial fear. With a manageable dose of political alienation thrown in for good measure.

For Isolde, it was kind of a Kafkaesque horror in itself to be stuck in traffic with her vehicular intellectual leader who could see little benefit in any system. For a bizarre reason, he asked her if she knew about BALS—an antibanking group. But Isolde's taxi experience that day could have been worse.

She recalled a trip in a Sydney, Australia, Jaguar cab, where she had been stripped of her dignity by a taxi driver who kept on going after her for supposed airs and snooty manners. Interestingly, she found out later from another cabbie that he had been a union steward, with his own hidden bank account in Monaco. The world, indeed, was very much in trouble, she thought to herself back then, after learning that even this "socialist" chauffeur and secret part owner of the small company had shipped out his own money from his own high-taxation country. And whose own Aussie dollar had temporarily collapsed to a fraction of a Swiss franc during the commodity bust that had unfolded after the second, or was that the third, economic collapse?

But in that cab, she had been more interested in the radio news about a final economic apocalyptic collapse that an inflation-fighting Swiss economist, called Dr. Gloom, had been discussing in a short interview. He had predicted it would happen five, or was that ten years, after the first big bust.

The Zürich taxi arrived without incident at 119 Pelikanplatz on Sankt-Johanstrasse. I had given Isolde the all-clear sign with the way I opened my newspaper to the headlines about the end of welfare in the United States. The address, which had mystified me, was irrelevant to her. She was intent on getting the package into Z-bank. The original list was just too hot a potato to want to be holding any longer. Isolde wanted to make sure that the relevant Z organizations and trusted individuals in the Council knew that she no longer had it. And she was counting on infiltrations to assure herself that the opposition would more and more know this too. That I had walked out of Z-bank unscathed, after depositing what I thought was my own deadly information, was a good sign.

She had attached a note to her document saying that further independent research had verified that the original list could not be fully authenticated nor dismissed as a fake. I later found out that she had falsified the report to leave the matter in confusion in case someone who was not genuinely on her side might access it. It would hopefully make them not feel further compelled to act. Or think that she might know anything definitive about its inner secrets if they were aware of them, which if they thought she did, might bring about a sanction against her. Or hurry it along.

However, it was now absolutely clear to her that the visible outer-layer list was a fraud. That those who were buried inside the paper in photon-cryptography would stay in her head and be given to me later to be presented to the proper authorities. I was in the clear with her, as I had not appeared on the actual list of conspirators. But knowing of Jonathan's guilt, as his name had shown up, she knew that both of us could be on a target list. He was not the kind of person to chance that she had not discovered its inner contents. Especially if—no, when he would find out that she had taken the original. Though, who knew for sure if Jonathan was aware that his name was on its inside? For the document had been prepared and coded in Sarabia, and not necessarily with his connivance. Our deposits would hopefully buy us extra time as the authorities went around arresting—or even terminating—our current or potential enemies. All after we passed on the details of the true inner contents to our trusted contacts, if everything worked out.

Isolde found the doors to the building almost too heavy to open. The door handles were of heavy brass. The actual door panels were painted black and decorated with what looked like gargoyle monsters in their cast-ironwork. Or they could have been other ancient beasts. A small message in German essentially read: "Ring and state your business." She pressed the largest of the six buttons.

"Madame Isolde *von* Leuvenstein."

"*Bitte kommen sie herein*," said a sharp perfunctory official in the voice of a senior madam.

"*Danke*," said Isolde with a formality and confidence that said she had real purpose.

Isolde pulled the door open and then walked to the elevator. No, not all bank operations occupied the first floor. There were other offices in the building: one was an importer of excruciatingly expensive wine spirits, and who knows what else. Another was a psychiatrist's office, with a plaque full of credentials in abbreviated form. It had a special consulting contract with Z organizations and Banque Suisse, as I later found out.

Isolde had once read that psychiatrists had one of the highest levels of suicide and social disorders. Her quoting this to Z5's psychiatrist had gotten her diagnosed as a manic depressive. The doctors provided her greater comfort by saying the new prognosis portended better, after she had acted more thankful and appreciative of their function. She was then falsely diagnosed as being only a paranoid schizophrenic, which they said was perfectly acceptable for her line of work.

She got out of the elevator directly connected to the posh receiving offices for officers of the bank to meet clients. Now, she would show her progress, psychologically. And in other less comfortable ways to her receiving hosts.

"Were you followed?" asked the assistant bank manager briskly to Isolde, yet somehow courtly, as she passed through the unguarded reception area. Surprising—"no guardian angels," there.

"No, not at all. I lost them," she said as she felt beads of sweat drip down on the bank counter, but only a few sad-looking ones. As a reformed manic-depressive according to Z5's own psychiatrist, but as a currently diagnosed paranoiac, she handled that very well. What she had not handled always satisfactorily was the manipulative tendencies of the psychiatric directorate to keep agents worried about their need for constant approval and treatment. All of which empowered the directorate to get more budget funds, as they manipulated the spies to provide glowing reviews of their work. She had actually been told that she was well-adjusted by a celebrated psychic-therapist far from the employ and influence of the directorate.

Isolde felt even more pressed to get rid of the original document, but wondered, in second thoughts, if it was crazy to leave it at the bank. She would inform the trusted heads of the Council and go over Jonathan's head to explain what she had truly done. That would not leave her in the position exposed to the Council as a thief of classified information. The time was ripe to tell the trustworthy members of the Council about the true list, as "ripe" as an apple beginning to go rotten to its core. If she waited any longer, she might soon become terminated from a DED sanction without even Council approval.

She figured Jonathan would be eventually consumed by his own rot, if he had not already been so. But possibly, his last ace would be to use her supposed theft of the original to get the Council onboard to get rid of her if he thought such "niceties" were needed. It was hard to know how long it would be before he realized that the high-quality copy of it that she had left behind was a fake. But surely, one or two in the Council would be told that she had returned it by way of the officers of Z-bank. That might be the final straw for Jonathan, after efforts to manipulate the Council against her.

The difference would be that the Council members she could trust would be specifically told that her note attached to it was bogus. They would have the actual inner contents revealed to them, hopefully before Jonathan could organize to put away anyone on the Council not totally loyal to him. But the question still remained as to whether the personnel at Z-bank could be fully trusted. This included the assistant manager, to eventually verify that Isolde had left the original document there. Jonathan's reach was long, and he was a cunning bastard who knew Isolde's capabilities at deception and self-protection. She would, nevertheless, have to trust this larger-than-life Swiss banker.

Frtiz Gerthing, her interlocutor, was no usual Swiss banker. He was a super Swiss banker with chocoholic tendencies, hence his girth. He was the paragon of consumption for the Lindt chocolate company, whose gift packaging house was coincidentally only a few doors down the street. It was said that Gerthing had advised the Council that the location of the bank was ideal after they had guaranteed him fresh daily delivery of his chocolate dosages.

Fritz liked a clean operation, right down to eradicating the individual tear of sweat on the counter, including Isolde's, which he had looked at with astonishment. Sweat marks, fingerprints, and footprints all had to be obliterated when necessary—even an odd body or body impression, given Gerthing's specialized banking services that Brother Biggart oversaw, but from a different floor. If it had not been too much of an effort, he would have bent down to get any residue off the flush green carpet.

Cleanliness was godliness for Gerthing, even if all the crisp snorts he made were not. Even if he was occasionally careless in not wiping away cleanly and summarily with his bland silk handkerchief any marks he, himself, had left behind. Unfortunately, he had. His less than pleasant-looking piggish nasal holes seemed to have expanded too much. In fact, he was a little too flaring and nervous that day.

"Please let me show you to the document safety deposit room," he said as his smoothly outstretched arm gave direction. Fritz truly had utilitarian manners—first safety and work, then pleasantries. Whether it was to give permission to go to the little girl's room, have a cup of coffee, or unlock the deep dark recesses of where he hid his five-star, Lindt chocolate bars, life had to be not only tidy, but also orderly.

Getting to his cognac cabinet, thought Isolde, was going to be the next big mission. She would vault into it without knocking anything out of place if she could. What a day it had been. She was in great need of a quick glass of *Schnapps*, though it would be too much to ask a man like Gerthing for even the smallest cigar, given his traditional views about women and sanitary and humorless manners.

"*Herr* Fritz, would you have *Schnapps* somewhere? It's been a very hard day," converted Isolde's imprudent thoughts to talk, though leaving out the cigar.

When Isolde looked reluctant to deposit the report into safekeeping to tease *Schnapps* out of Gerthing, there was something more rottweilerish rather than normal piggishness in Fritz's change of composure. He did manage to get hold of his less-than-charming self, though before it would have been too late.

"Oh yes, shocking of me, forgive me! Let me get you a bit of water from the fountain," he retorted. Fritz was just warming up and remembering his bead-swiping manners; it was clear that he was about to go for gold.

"*Bitte wann* all is done *vee* can have something more refreshing if you would like. But first, please, unburden yourself." Isolde felt like unburdening her incisors on Fritz's Rottweiler like charm.

Fritz conjured up all the sensitivity he could imagine as he sensed her discomfort. Isolde should have been even more uncomfortable about staying in that bank too long. At least, if I saw any strange bodies showing up in front of it, I would buzz her on her Blackberry to help her make as fast an exit as she could.

"Oh yes, please sit down in my office, and I will take care of this official document of our organization," added the roly-poly banker. "How impolite of me, though it would be customary for you to witness me putting it away into safekeeping. *Nicht?*"

By the time she was through with Fritz the banker, he would go through the ultimate transformation. The Swiss bankers she didn't like were especially good at this change if the deposit was right, giving her some worth of importance. Isolde thought to herself that Fritz would be whimpering like a Chihuahua on her way out.

Isolde's prima-donna airs reminded Fritz of how he could not stand operatives and how they figuratively smudged up his beautiful designer furniture. They left shadows and portrayed worse things to come. Like dirt stains on his carpet, with the outside possibility of a bloodstain, too.

The banker worried to himself that he might have to be the butcher, rather than just the banker. He worried that he might get skinned by this lady that Jonathan had previously warned him to treat with a bit of care, along with the other members of the Order who cashed out their expense accounts from him.

But Fritz was not named the "cleaner" simply for his sanitary manners and certainly not for money laundering. It was not only because he tried with great, but partly failed, effort to make his own offices as pristine clean as the best hospital. There was also no mistaking that he was simply the "janitor." Others under his coordination would do the actual dirty work if the customers, or those looking into his business from the outside, tried anything financially or otherwise untoward to the bank or to the foundation's finances they oversaw.

Rather, Fritz had his special nickname for supervising and implementing the "auditing standards" within the Council and Z organizations. Fritz was there to make sure that the corrupt got fully cleaned out of these organizations, as well as any threatening information or devices they and their associates might have that could likely be used against the bank.

Brother Biggart, his boss, could always be depended on to give a stamp of approval to generating the required silence in the right circumstances. No one fooled around with Z-bank, internally or externally. No one was allowed even to leave a tiny bit of a trail of dirty money or very dirty "manners" with this financial odd lot. Or to rip off a single franc.

After getting away from the bank in one piece and with one piece of Fritz's chocolate, it was clear that Isolde had managed to thwart some of her deadliest enemies. She had gotten the coordinates from Nic at the Schotland as to when and where I would be available at the B place after I had left my signatory newspaper position near the bank.

* * *

Later, she took the train, where she hid in the bicycle compartment, which a lot of the local trains had at this time of the year. She had put on a Swiss Bundesbahn employee uniform in one of the lavatories and bundled her hair under a cap.

But upon arrival in Baden, the so-called "B place," a short one-hour trip from Zürich, she still had that instinctive feeling that someone was still following her. So, she changed into another disguise with different clothing in the middle of an oak-forested area not far outside the city. Not far from where she had been let out by a taxi driver, this one thankfully only interested simply in fare and beer. Strangely, a male stag deer got sight of her and quickly ran off as if something had terrified it.

After Isolde had been let out in the woods, from behind a tree, she saw a large Korean-made, Chairman sedan swiftly pass by her, but the driver had certainly not seen her get out. Or had he? She had done it so quickly that the taxi had still been moving. It had been only five hundred meters to the path of the Aagen creek after the Countess had gotten out. It was coincidentally not far from the first ancestral castle of one of the main branches of the Leuvenstein family. She then traversed a small pedestrian bridge to the pink hotel famed for its bath springs.

Isolde felt at first that she would have a half hour or so with me before whoever followed her would have a chance to find out where she was—and me. She pitied the taxi driver, whom the assassin might have caught up to. She had instructed him to park in front of the police station and stay there until the Chairman car was well gone. She would look into his plight to see if he had survived. But much later. How Isolde frowned to herself about all the unnecessary collateral damage her Order created with innocent and decent people caught in the line of fire.

That was another reason she had to move fast. To avoid what might now be a Baden police force curious about her, if they had asked why the taxi driver had stopped in front of the police station and had not been too excited to move. Keeping the local law enforcement agency out of her work area was always a priority. Hopefully, there would be no collateral damage to the resident constabulary because of the presence of an assassin chasing her.

Isolde, after a quick walk, had gotten safely to the hotel without incident. I would spare her a meeting in the steam room or the sauna, though the thought was a lot more enticing than being reminded of all those weird meetings in the shed with what was now poor Zen. He was still in a coma, but his prognosis was getting better.

Isolde was somewhat breathless when I opened the door to her. She quickly handed the list to me. It had all the genuine names, which she had written at the last minute in the toilet in the train from Zürich to Baden. It was just another hi and bye, and not even a chance for a tender moment. She hurriedly got out of town, leaving in a suit and with a fake mustache. Nic had communicated to me that I should have those items ready at my new hotel room.

After she left the hotel, I had no idea where she went. But it was time for me to switch hotels and cities—and it would have almost been better, I thought momentarily, if I had reached that new "universe" I thought I was heading for on the bank of the Limmat that Friday evening. I had an increasingly unsettling feeling about my trade. That I was running out of options to keep myself safe, no matter what counteractions I would be taking.

But first things first to ensure survival. I would take a hike to get myself out of town without being located by that supposed assassin that Isolde had warned me about. That meant no rented cars, no use of credit cards. But leaving a forwarding address to Orficestan, that I hoped my pursuer would go to. But I kind of doubted it. I didn't think he was being paid enough to go there. He needed another five hundred thousand for that, but in euros.

There were countless numbers of these hiking trails in Switzerland marked by white crosses—kind of strangely painted on trees that did not always make it thoroughly clear as to what was the fastest or easiest way to your final destination. As it had been getting late, there was the worry that I would end up so deep undercover, I would have to sleep in the woods if I got lost.

However, there would be no Rambo scenario that evening. I finally found my way to the highway more than a few hours later with a backpack containing everything I had hurriedly taken with me from Baden. I then had to hitchhike to an out-of-the-way train station at a small town whose name I have forgotten by now. The gentleman who picked me up at the roadside wondered why I was there when it was so dark, without the chance of a Postal Bus coming until the next morning.

I went into my thickest US southern accent and acted like a disoriented hillbilly. Then he simply said, *"Ach so, ein Amerikaner"*—and then went quiet. I always loved that ruse to get the Europeans off my case, if I had done something stupid like not figuring out how to buy a subway ticket on the Vienna subway. Never mind trying to explain why I was lost in their neck of the woods. I would just cry out, "I'm an American!" and say I was confused and even lost. I did the same when the subway "Gestapo" in plainclothes began to check to see if everyone had paid for their ride. I never forgot that "American" experience that has kept on benefiting me even to this day.

After I got off the train just outside Kirchberg, I found some kilometers up the road a suitable bed-and-breakfast lodging on what is fashionably called "the Gold Coast" near Zürich. I registered myself with a seventh passport that I had not used for ages, provided to me by the Israelis for a small mission I had successfully done. It was in the name of Paul Furst, an eccentric hermit who thought he was the Phantom of the Madras Court in Chennai, India—in fact, still pretty well the largest judicial court of its kind. Furst, who thought all those who seriously criticized him were insane, was secretly locked up in isolation in an Australian asylum on Christmas Island and is not projected to get out until December 25, 2030.

I had chosen the B and B randomly, but only after doing a reconnaissance of the area. Hopefully, all these precautions would work, or I would be dead. Or more broadly, the whole house might be. Like incinerated by a grenade or two just so the assassin would be sure to get me. Or flush me out.

After settling in, I found an Internet cafe a few kilometers up the road from my new lodging. I was desperate to do some research on one of the very interesting names that was on the list Isolde had given me in Baden.

The name was Kurt (a.k.a. Ali) Schmidt, part of a political youth gang that was known for more than a few spats of bare-knuckle fighting. A further investigation using the Interpol website, to which I had special access, sourced him to Athens. A yet further investigation of him produced a photo, though a few years dated, that my Interpol contact provided me thorough a secret website.

I studied Kurt's file in my locked small room at the B and B. The first thing I discovered was that I had seen him before, but wondered initially where. I spent a few long seconds before figuring where it had been. The file also showed that he was a bit of a political pamphleteer under the pen name Dionysus. Those facts in themselves were not completely important. But I sat back and thought awhile whether Mr. Kurt Ali Schmidt had been one of the attackers who had clobbered me near Zürich's old city hall. I looked again at his photo and thought I was now pretty sure of it. It made me think a lot.

The pamphlet samples I had from looking at a pdf file stored on my Blackberry had the smell of neo-Nazi propaganda, borrowing rather bizarre allusions to Dionysus. There had, in fact, been a Dionysus Order, a kind of youth offshoot to Hitler's SS before and during World War II. It was a bizarre, highly secret society to screen and prepare young men for indoctrination into a Nazi cult. This included forcing any eugenically acceptable woman selected by their SS overseers to have sexual relations with these young men, between the ages of sixteen to twenty-one. This was an age range in which the Nazi doctors considered a male to be his most virile and with the healthiest of sperm.

The idea was not only to satisfy the desires of members in good standing, but also to produce healthy, so-called superior offspring that would improve the German race. As the young men and women were the fittest, partly given their young age, it was expected that very strong babies would be produced by the consummation of the relationship between these genetically matched pairs. A few older women, wives of senior Nazi party officials, also positioned themselves to get into the act for whatever they unofficially got out of it, especially when their husbands were out on maneuvers.

It was made clear to the young women that it was a privilege to be chosen. And their "superbabies" under the care of the "SS family" would disproportionately become the stock from which supreme leaders would be developed through a whole growing SS system. An organization that would mold them from cradle to grave. Albert Speer, Hitler's chief architect, even was asked to put the idea of SS supercities on the drawing board to make eugenic cities for these and similar offspring.

Now there was this sick offspring of this Nazi idea with the lower likes of people like Kurt Ali Schmidt, one of its chief members of supreme intercourse and battery. Who knew how many women he had forcefully impregnated and where the members of this newer Dionysus Order would all be going if the full conspiracy were successful? They would surely have enough financial support to guarantee their eventual high placements in business, politics, and the military. That is, if this conspiracy became successful.

The Dionysus Order's name was originally borrowed from a somewhat forced interpretation of Greek mythology related to the god Dionysus, associated with hedonistic tendencies. This cult worshipped the Dionysus classical concept that it was perfectly acceptable to manifest one's desires to take almost anything or anybody to feed even one's most base desires and pleasures, as members were part of the supreme group of chosen ones. They were like a superior supermen concept out of a Nietzsche book or titan demigods of Greek myth whose very exalted status defined their right to do what they willed.

The current Dionysus Order had eluded an Interpol investigation of their overall activities. The police had appeared at first to consider it to be of secondary importance, and it did not command the resources that it deserved. It had looked more like a youthful club of neo-Nazi delinquents and minor thugs, more akin to rejects from young brown shirts of Hitler's SA, which had preceded the much better organized and more ruthless SS.

Schmidt and his gang were referred to as the "Dionysus Order" in all of their coded file listings. But the label had been thought of by the Greek police as a sick juvenile joke. Just a bit of a silly group of the alienated, who occasionally got out of control—probably out of boredom and being unemployed. And there were lots of Greek-based young people without jobs or much of an immediate future. And too many for the Greek police to follow, as their funding began to shrink with deep government cutbacks.

True to its cultlike theatrics, the Dionysus Order was based in Athens, not far from the original Dionysus amphitheater, which was around two thousand years old and decaying. Their location was worrisome, given the grave economic situation that Greece was in the throes of. There was a growing second uprising of extremists, as the state was cutting back again, both on many social programs and on thousands of jobs, many of which had belonged to the youth.

A variety of political analysts were calling it the most protofascistic or totalitarian environment anywhere in Western Europe, and worse than the conditions that had led the Greek army generals to take over the country decades ago. With youth unemployment or underemployment rising to almost 45 percent, many young members of society were keen to join protests, even extremist groups, to vent their frustrations. It was a veritable garden for a rich harvest of young minds that could be twisted to neo-Nazi conspirator purposes. And they could be used as social and political detonators when their minders decided it. In that respect, it was curious that young Schmidt had a nickname that paralleled one of the heroes of the Al Quomini Brotherhood, a converted German who had taken out a school bus of innocent young children in Tel-Aviv.

Another worrying aspect about the Dionysus Order was that it could just be the center of the spider's web of a vast network of independent neo-Nazi youth cells. With enough momentum, they would be able to spread worldwide. There was even one rumor that the United Nations Youth Council had been infiltrated by them. This was a council with huge resources that had so worried the American government that it had made serious interventions in Ottawa to prevent it from being well established by a group of young Canadian idealists based in Montreal. The Swiss, decades later, had picked up the idea and had supported its establishment in Geneva. Would they regret it if people of the ilk of Schmidt began to take it over?

I had a distinct aversion for what Schmidt represented, but a greater aversion to not personally following up any leads that would take me to my muggers and ensure their merry band of delinquents would be put fully out of commission. That they would never be able again to do what they had done to me, and likely Zen—and who knows who else? It was all

I could do to return their favors, which still made me sore when going for a quick roll in the sack, even by myself.

Beyond getting whatever opportunities existed for revenge, I had to wonder whether this group might better lead me to whoever ran them in the adult netherworld of the organization. And whoever ran them might prove very useful in further helping us uncover increasingly important elements of what now seemed a worldwide conspiracy of incredible deceit and deception. We could not be totally sure that all the conspirators, including important minor ones, were on the authentic list.

I would speak to Falcon at Interpol as my last hope. He was clean. Besides, he needed to get the list of conspirators' names, which I would anonymously deliver to him after coding a signal that a very interesting gift was coming his way. And with his presumed blessings after I delivered this gift, I would hopefully get the mandate and resources in my Pol Martin manifestation to fly in with almost no one in Greek security knowing about my business. There was a more vital decision as to whether I should dispose of the whole Dionysus group.

I would meet Falcon by the Tiergarten, the Zürich zoo, by the giraffes in broad daylight before noon for the low-level conversation that was well beyond their and other elevated necks. We would make decisions about these dangerous youths. But it would be our necks on the line, I thought, if we fouled up any efforts to close down this sinister juvenile league. And Falcon would want to be as clandestine as possible in meeting me to avoid being their next victim. I was now too much bad news for too many in the inner police and spy circles to which I was associated. Maybe I was becoming like an undercover leper—even to my own friends.

*   *   *

K-Boom's team was working hard in a deep basement in Zürich behind a movable wall. They were having problems with their precision instruments in getting the uranium metal exactly placed, before being put into the large cylinder. But they were confident that it could be done. The krypton trigger device was looking good and pretested well. They had extras just in case. Finally, the two pieces of uranium, with one acting as the bullet to create the critical reaction, were finally put in place.

The assemblers looked at each other with great pride and went for Salah prayer. They were humbled by what they had done. Only a few more tests, as the booby trapping of the signal-receiving devices needed to be properly tested. Then it would be transported and put into the tower of the Grossmunster cathedral.

If all went well, the bomb would soon be ready and would be exploded about forty-eight hours after they left the house. This would also give them more than enough time to get to the airport to deal with any potential problems there. As Waristanis, they knew they would likely be profiled. There was also a chance that residual radiation on them might make detectors go off. They would meticulously wash down twenty times with a chemical shower that would probably make them merge with the normal background radiation. They had a device to make sure of it. They would, as well, dispose of their bomb-making clothes in the old furnace before leaving the house on Richterstasse. The furnace would be turned on automatically after their plane left. The incineration might cause a small release of radioactive substances that would alert monitoring devices placed on the main highways throughout the city.

If anything happened, they were promised by their contracts—of a sort—that their families would be provided millions and put into safe houses. They had been guaranteed this by K-Boom, who said he had very important banker friends in Switzerland who would make the arrangements in Borain. They only hoped that that banker would not be blown up, along with themselves if they got delayed and stuck at the airport—or worse, in traffic. Yes, they said to themselves, forty-eight hours should do it and provide enough time for their final prayers.

TWENTY-FOUR

The General, code-named "Falcon" and now at Interpol, was a graduate of Sandhurst, the British famed military college. He was quite pleased to see me. He was tall, with a mustache and pinkish cheeks. He had a swagger that he might have picked up either from that prestigious army officer academy or from having lived in Australia for too long. But he had neither the casualness of an Australian or a retiree, which he could have been at fifty-five when he left the British army.

Falcon had been so good at counterintelligence, and given his innumerable high-level security contacts, especially in Britain and the United States, he had been called up to serve at the very senior levels of Interpol. It was his turn to visit the shed, but fortunately this one was breezier and not so steamy. And not likely to involve any lectures, as Zen liked to give.

"Damn shame, that business about your controller—don't think I even knew him that well. Hope he pulls through, Pol, and yes, thank you for the list, and we'll take good care of it and are carefully checking it out. Yes, fine work by Isolde and Professor Myopis on it. He is, indeed, a bloody first rate expert on cryptology and quantum physics at ZIT. Too bad they'll never get a public commendation on it. You neither, come to think of it."

"No problem, General."

"Quite. That's the good public spirit that I see so little of in the new recruits, sorry to say. Yes, back to the main program, as they say in your parts."

"Yes, Zen was hit upon possibly by the very group that brutally mugged me," I added.

"Oh yes! Have you recovered from that bad spot of luck—same group you think?" probed the General.

"Hard to know one hundred percent—one of my superiors seems to think it's a possibility."

"Why is that? asked the General.

"Same methods, same numbers and age, from a witness account. And a picture of one of their pamphleteers seems remarkably like the face of one of my muggers—though it was somewhat dark."

"Right, happy to have gotten the photo to you, Pol. We shall call you Pol."

"And I had got pretty banged up by the time he came around and clanged me."

"How, for mother of Mary, did this young lot find out about your location—and Zen's? Sounds like you have a bit of a leaky ship. In fact, one of my bosses was not too keen on me meeting you. A number of bad vibrations in high circles now circulating about you," said the General, like he was dealing with a small matter of cleanup or some other rather picky detail.

"Yes, I can imagine where those rumors might be coming from. Like the polished, two-faced British bastard Jonathan. All due respect to you, General, to your fine training in England. And you're definitely not two-faced!"

"That's all right, and by the way, call me Falcon, or better yet, calling me nothing would be appropriate. You know, I'm Irish born. Anyway, never fully accepted by those British intelligence elites, though no problem with Interpol, who increasingly has to deal with intelligence matters as so much crime these days is mixed up with it. Indeed, the world has gotten very complicated."

"Yes, a lot of the great officers in the history of the British army came from Ireland. But I digress," I said.

"Oh yes, so do I, Pol. I find it sometimes relaxing before having to face various difficult troubles. I agree that some in British intelligence are a rather perfidious bunch, but don't quote me on that. I'll lose too many pub buddies if you do," said the General with a chuckle and the kind of British understated humor that reflected that he did have a kind of favorable disposition with the British spy elites.

"But remember, speaking of two-faced, I have definitely been following strange goings-on in our side."

"Convenient," said the General.

"Why's that?"

"We—or should I say, our inner circle—never liked your group and all its branches being set up outside of oversight. We may be quite bureaucratic—even leaky—but it's hard for anyone to go off and start earth-shattering operations without collective approval. And that's the worry that has happened with a full gumming up of the works."

"Okay, glad you still have some confidence in me. But the reason I called you in . . ."

"Yes, I know—Operation Dionysus."

"Operation? What, pardon me?"

"Yes, we are not letting those juveniles do any more strange business. The Greek police have been following their political activities for some time. But they had no idea that their jaunts to Zürich or other nearby areas for football matches, for example, were covers for group muggings of important spy officials and, in fact, even other criminal activities. It appears that they may have robbed a few banks, but no trace of their loot. Very disturbing. They may have a banker or financial advisor working with them in Switzerland to hide it in preparation of something even bigger."

"This Operation Dionysius, I'd like to be involved. I can possibly identify a number of these individuals who thrashed me, at the minimum."

"Oh, I think that might be good to let you on the loose to do some very dirty work for us. We do not even want to interrogate these chaps. And if you are familiar with the young offender laws—or even terrorist laws—we as an official and visible European-based agency could never be directly involved in any, shall we say, untidiness with so-called youths. Your organization does, indeed, come in handy at times."

"It will almost be my pleasure. I am used to it in a way."

"Oh yes, quite funny, as a professor known to be brutal to anyone who plagiarizes. And who is lethargic, let us say. But a little different than that now, my friend."

"Yes, time and the possible scale of this conspiracy necessitate it. This Dionysus Order seems to be the vicious attack dog on the streets for the opposition. If I understand what you are saying, it needs to be immediately put down."

"Oh, I'm not saying anything. I certainly did not meet you here, and pure coincidence if anybody says we did. A coincidental mutual fascination with giraffes in a zoo. One thing, as you look at that animal, they have a perspective over just about everybody, a knowledge sometimes far out of reach to the ordinary."

"What do you mean?"

"Let me say that I have a counterpart in the Middle East who is also busy on his side gazing for more than archaeological treasures. His code name, humorously, is 'Giraffe,' for the very description I just gave of that animal. So once you come back from Athens—I presume you will—I may have information treasures for you, as I expect you will have for me. A very healthy mutual exchange."

"You know things are so bad that every older teenager I see on the street at night, I have to look twice at. This little roving group of wolverines have scared the shit out of a lot of us. And I say that as a college professor, who knows what it is to be under siege from college kids after giving out more than a few nasty report cards."

Falcon laughed. "Pol, you have quite a reputation in Sarabia as being a kind of an assessment assassin. Your students should be happy that they are not your targets. All chiding aside, take great care."

"And so I will, as I certainly felt like it was touch and go after they piled on. So, how am I going to get the information as to where I can find these neo-Nazi brats?"

"I wouldn't call them that, as they have done more damage to you than what you experienced in your youthful days as a mercenary. And then, of course, poor Zen, though we can't be sure exactly who put him out."

"Clearly, I need to not underestimate these buggers again. But I'll need local muscle."

"When the time comes, contact Joseph Papagalopitis. When the steam gets high in your bathroom, this small handkerchief will show you his special contact number through which you can set up a meeting. The number will have to be memorized, as it will completely disappear without a trace after five seconds. Here is your flight itinerary, ticket, and a few rolls of bills. Now good luck, Pol—or whoever you are." He chuckled once again.

"Brilliant—everything is already prepared. Yes, I sometimes wonder myself as to who I am. Thank you, General." There was silence, and I waited as instructed, to allow him to exit the area by himself.

Then I heard a bit of a hearty laugh in the distance. He had already gone as I looked around at the giraffes, which seemed to be laughing too.

*   *   *

That very day, I flew directly to Athens from Zürich, this time in a full disguise as an Italian count named Crisco. I was not going to let the Dionysus Order get lucky and spot me in the street, whether by luck or from the tailing work I might have to do. I did not want to get too distracted with this smaller fry, given the more important players on the list that needed priority attention. However, these indoctrinated delinquents had been and still were very much part of the armory that the Islamic extremist-neo-Nazi nexus were all too willing to unleash. At least, that particular Zürich-Arabian axis represented an increasingly plausible theory. No, "theory" was too light a word after reading the entire genuine list of conspirators.

Tracking the Dionysus Order down and through Athens was a wonder in itself. Nevertheless, they actually overplayed their hand when they tried to rub out the patriarch of the Greek Orthodox Church, which was the current news. He was making the rounds through much of Greece and Eastern Europe, imploring the masses of unemployed youth not to attach themselves to the reemerging popularity of figures like Hitler and Mussolini. There had also been the breakaway General Constantine, who had even gone underground to fight the IMF-funded Greek government, which had massively slashed social programs down to the poorest pensioner and the destitute youth. Then, essentially went bankrupt, anyway.

The patriarch, in an interdenominational effort, had also been working with the Wiesenthal Foundation to uncover these final vestiges of neo-Nazi horrors—offspring in their full kaleidoscope of hatred.

It was a break to finally figure out exactly who and where these juvenile muggers were. Unfortunately these youths were well connected to a small but influential rump of right-wing parliamentarians. That explained in part why there had been little follow-up by the traditional enforcement agencies where a number of these legislative representatives had important contacts. It further explained why there had not been a swift capture of the culprits of the attempted assassination of this church patriarch, Andrus Philippoussis. He was left with a uranium-tipped bullet in his shoulder that had somehow failed to explode.

Fortunately, there were eyewitness accounts that were logged in with Interpol of this incident, which had occurred while I was traveling between Zürich and Athens. One of the apparent culprits fit the description of one of my Zürich assailants, but they had simply been running away and clearly not in the possession of any weapons that could have impacted with such force. There was also a recent note that other witnesses had seen them near the Acropolis on more than one occasion. I truly wondered why this group had become so publicly active that would, by all normal measures, lead to their arrest or annihilation by even their own senior minders. They seemed to be getting quite sloppy. It was almost like they were deliberately taunting the authorities, as if they thought they were untouchable. Maybe a sign of overconfidence? Or something worse?

* * *

I thought it could become a dull stakeout that night, walking around or perching myself on my hotel balcony. Looking out on the magnificent colossal ruins of the Parthenon, built over two thousand years ago. All on a flat top of what was essentially a fairly well-elevated, giant rock that had become center position to the city. Otherwise known as the Acropolis.

I didn't trust anybody at DED at this stage, so I had put in for a maximum two-week leave, nervous psychological stress (believable to a degree). To try and further get off their radar screen. Though I thought Jonathan would find it a bit farfetched, especially if the Z-bank reported back about my special deposit there. And who actually cared about Jonathan anyway? He was now getting special attention from the Council, courtesy of Isolde. Yet, it had still been prudent to get him to think that I might not be fully onto him. Whom was I fooling? Somehow, he seemed to have lost interest in me after I left the "Rock" in the Channel, other than a few messages asking where the hell I was after I had done my job with Friegel. And now he was giving me doctor's order on my Blackberry that I simply should enjoy myself and that my just rewards would eventually come. "Ominous generosity," I thought, particularly after I had avoided that date with the assassin-in-a-Chairman.

In the evening around eight o'clock, the primary suspect in my stakeout near the Acropolis did not show up. But more importantly, one of his dark soul colleagues did. I could recognize him as groin-kicker number two, with lightning strikes under his collar. No evidence of more of them through my telescopic glasses, of those who had given me such a shitkicking. That day of my beating on the Limmatquai in Zürich was etched in my memory forever.

I was going to stay a good distance from this one. I was not going to underestimate these guys again. For all I knew, they were already aware of my presence in town and were throwing out bait to draw me into a final ambush. I did need a weapon and thought justice demanded a modest addition to my own artillery toolbox of a small hammer that kind of looked like a judge's gavel. Well, at least in my mind. To be safe, I would holster to my lower leg a miniature pistol so it would not show, except through deep wound marks to the recipient of a bullet from it. I figured if I started with the hammer, they would figure I had nothing bigger than that. Letting down their defenses would be their mistake this time.

When I got to the Parthenon Park where the Acropolis was perched, it had gotten peaceful. So quiet that much of it had been locked for the night. But somehow, suspect number two was still around. I stayed near the railing, making sure no one saw me as I slipped into a shadow. Our scar-faced athlete seemed impatient. I guess he was waiting for dark—though with all the floodlights around about to go on, it seemed like an irrational conclusion. But no doubt here and there, he could hide in the shadows and do whatever he needed to.

Just then, he emerged from the dark again. He was circulating inside the park perimeter near the Dionysus amphitheater, which was below the cliffs of the Parthenon (a column lit-up beacon of glory for the founding fathers of democracy, so the story goes). What was he going to do, I wondered—put on a play? I was hoping for a big Greek tragedy, where the full cast would come out and drink hemlock. Too bad that it was not damn likely.

Then it struck me for some bizarre reason. Dionysus was almost pronounced as Dianesis; the players were playing us. Taking the name of a Greek god that had his fun with vengeance and despoiling women nymphs. It was this gang's counterstatement to the work of the ladies. No, I was getting a bit too cute with my thoughts in the dark, as I tried to stay well out of sight. Probably just so jumpy that my brain was now turning on extra-acute paranoia to prepare me for something that I would not really want to know about.

The number two son of a bitch all of a sudden looked like he was running away. I followed in pursuit. It was good to put my guard up, as let's call him "Fritzy" had circled around onto me and come hurtling through the woods, which had gotten very shadowy. I hammered him. I hammered him so badly it appeared he was carpentry work I had to nail. The other pricks, if they had been around, must have heard his screaming. I did not like his shrieking very much, as it was a nice neighborhood, which even complained that the building of a new museum so close to their backyards had been a grotesque and noisy distraction to their aesthetic tranquility. I actually felt intellectually ashamed about causing such an uncivilized disturbance in what was once the cradle of civilization.

Another hammering, and I knew some inconvenient police would show up, soon. Who would have hurt feelings that I had not called in to make the hammering official—or maybe, to prevent a hammering. That I seemed to have made it too personal on these poor downtrodden, Greek youths.

I thought sincerely. I thought constructively. I thought I would just shoot the next one in the face, but through the mouth to ensure maintenance of civilized quietude for this upscale neighborhood, which had the unfortunate situation of having at least two little young neo-Nazi trash about. But in the big picture, I wasn't finished, as hopefully four little *piggies* were still about somewhere, if my math was still good. I do believe so even if my vision had been badly blinded temporarily back in Zürich, in back of the old city hall on that near fatal Friday evening, which I would never forget. Which they would never forget.

Yes, there was a second and third one. They were escaping up the hill. Funny thing, they had gone straight up to the rock face and disappeared into it. What the hell was that by it? I soon gathered that it was a kind of hoist that had been removing precious antiquities, but from where? As I got closer to the base of the Acropolis, it became clear that they had entered a cave. I now remembered that there had been a chapel there, which had succeeded a worshiping area of some protogeometric period cult, known for human sacrifices. Did I dare go in? Fortunately, I had my night glasses, which worked on infrared and could zoom in for a better look. The coast seemed clear, so I decided to walk up the side of the hill to that chapel. Or whatever it was now, after all that construction around it.

Then strangely, there was a sound like a moving of rocks, a door, or something. Then, suddenly nothing. I stepped gingerly to the end of the cave, which was effectively at the back of the chapel. It was not a bad idea to go in, as I could hear at the time loud voices outside the cave and some distance behind me—no doubt the loud voices of the regular police, whom I would not want anything to do with. When I was ready, I would call up Papa's storm troopers. Unless they found me before I wanted to find them.

There were fresh footprints, from the work of the day. No, these were not workman boot prints. I cast around, seeing panoplies of beautiful geometric patterns well known from that period, but hard to make out after thousands of years of wear and tear. Conceivably, this was part of the official restoration project. Then, there was something I had not seen at first.

Ominous and foreboding. They were intermittently distributed through the cave on both sides: a swath of swastikas!

The swastikas arched up to a cross that was simple iron, almost looking in the shape of a cross of the Teutonic Order, which had been romanticized by the Nazis and the Prussian nobles before them. It was a bizarre crucifix, with two protruding rounded screws on the lateral axis toward each end. Were those welding spots, or were they simply to hold the cross onto the wall? They were not easy to see, but my night-vision glasses had helped me find them. I decided to move closer, and keep an eye out for anything that might strike out from the shadows.

It was now clear that black iron bars were superimposed over the cross, and looked as if parts of them could be swiveled around the screws into areas slightly indented in the walls. After the bars were moved on the horizontal axis, they created the oddest shape. Like a figurine, with one arm up and the other down. Was this a kind of clue? I scratched my head. Trying to remember the various key geometric shapes employed on artistic works and architecture during that period before the great classical Greek epoch, when Athens reigned as the center of a golden age and empire. I was clueless.

Wait. What about the other axis? I looked around frantically, as I had temporarily lost sight of it. There again, two thirds or so up the cross was a very small screw, almost invisible. I swiveled the bar to the right to fit it to the indentation in the wall. It was now evident that I had nearly formed a swastika. But where was the bottom part? I did not need to answer, for the bottom pushed out from the rock automatically and formed an unholy union with the rest. Next, a cavernous door opened. Was this the wolf lair of their pro-Nazi Order? Should I enter—knowing that I was very much in their territory, that they even could have some warning device to tell them who was coming? Well, at least, there was one less of them.

I wondered with curiosity, was this something newly created under the guise of restoration work or, in fact, a special passageway known to a small number of ancient Greeks that a few German archaeologists had stumbled upon. I remembered from historical readings that the Germans occupied Athens during World War II. It was rumored that Hitler had sent a special archaeological task force to discover truly spectacular artifacts that he thought would give him special supernatural powers.

It was beginning to feel creepy all around. What was hidden in these underground chambers? Would I be seeing ghosts and other nasty manifestations? Maybe there would be the phantoms of Borman, Himmler, and Hitler around the fire singing heroic pagan ballads with their youthful wonders. Perhaps I was out of my mind, and should pull out before I started hallucinating any further. Or before I got a knife in the back, or lead in my head.

I phoned Papa to tell them how to come for me if I wasn't back in a half hour. At first, they thought I was in a bar and had too much Ouzo; they were asking if they could drive me home. It took a while to sober them up, as they were clearly the ones doing the drinking.

I had to think that the odds were more in the punks' favor, as it was their home turf. Two or three of them against me was trouble. Nonetheless, I thought that I might have a fighting chance given how organized my vengeance was. I only felt sorry for the hammer, as it could have charged me with aggravated overuse of a clanging weapon. Yes, I just wasn't one of those touchy-feely professors who could sympathize enough with these wayward youths. I would have to do something about it, but certainly not at that moment.

I stepped fully beyond the door. There was some kind of spring release resulting from my weight, I think, that immediately closed the door behind me with such a snap that it reminded me that I should go on a diet. A little way inside of the entrance was what seemed to be a carving of Dionysus in the rock. I was now using my small flashlight to look around this veritable dungeon of evil.

But there! What was it? It looked like one of the most sinister scenes that I had seen in my life. It seemed to be an altar over which two young men were draped with the most horrible expressions on their blood-oozing, lifeless bodies. Upon closer inspection, it was like a scene of a joint suicide, with both of their brains shot out with a Luger, which was now between them. It was a grizzly sight. Possibly, a part of a reward program for not properly doing their job rites. Or maybe, they had previously thought of themselves as central figures to Nietzsche's concept of fully satisfying one's impulses if one attained the stature of a superior being—a kind of overkill to the ultimate commitment to hedonism. I could only hope for similar philosophical excesses for the remnants of this demented league, as I suddenly turned around . . .

TWENTY-FIVE

Given the countless family scheming, infighting, and maneuvers that he had to navigate, nothing much bothered King Abdul, at his age, short of the death of a loved one. But with this particular news, his face had gone white as the beaches on the Pharoahsan Islands. The head of Sarabian intelligence, who he had thought had too much time on his hands to imagine one too many regime-threatening schemes, actually had much to add. This time, the king would listen, and would be very much moved, though after some strong convincing.

"Your Highness, we are now totally sure of the plot. Reliable sources have confirmed it," said Sarwawi, his security chief, with full but nervous candor.

"How reliable?" the king asked.

"Even your own sister knows one of the undercover sources and, no doubt, would confirm that woman's credibility."

"A lady!" the king said with surprise. "They are using female spies now?"

"A male operative, too, but not someone of the faith or of our kingdom—nevertheless, he is likely reliable," stated Sarwawi.

"Is this man the main source of your information through the ladies?" The king was still skeptical of women agents and forbade any in the employ of the Sarabian intelligence services.

"Some of it, yes, but not all." Sarwawi continued after a slight pause to further gauge the king's reaction. "The crucial part especially directly affecting you has been fairly well corroborated through two other sources. And finally, Bashard has been in repeated contact with Boom, and has been shorting huge amounts of his own personal stocks, including betting against our prized MANCITC investments. As if he is expecting something terrible to happen. He has also intensified his meetings with Sheik Zayed."

The king looked a little bemused about his intelligence chief's last point and responded, "Zayed—everyone is talking to him. He's a TV celebrity with his ghoulish, though entertaining, Friday afternoon spectacle. A loudmouthed demagogue who'll fizzle out."

"I wish that were true, Highness, but Zayed has also been having quite serious meetings with the police head. That has not happened before."

The king straightened up and dismissed Sarwawi's concerns. "Well, so the sheik is getting to be too popular. No argument about it. The army is still under me, and the air force is under Nadel and he is loyal."

"May I play this conversation that Nadel's chief of staff had with the sheik?" asked the king's ever loyal intelligence head.

"Yes, that is your job to keep me informed, but officially I never heard it."

After a minute or so, the king was astounded that the chief of staff had been told by Sheik Zayed that he had heard loose rumors about a revolt. And that the air force chief had acted unperturbed and even nonchalant. The sheik had replied, "It is all God's will what happens." Normally, any such response in such a tone would involve serious sanctions, and the chief of staff, at a minimum, telling the crown prince of the troubling talk.

"All right, a number of ugly coincidences. But yes, more than worrying," replied the king, looking increasingly serious and focused on his intelligence briefing.

"I am worried that if something terrible happens to the economy in the West, they could be distracted at our expense" said the security chief very gravely.

"How so? What is expected? Out with it, Sarwawi. I hope this is not another one of your false alerts that will get one of my family members unnecessarily angry. There are enough of them already who would like to see me gone."

"If Boom is involved, we might expect the worst. A nuclear disaster that would do very well for Bashard's shorts. Between a serious hit on a major financial center again and a mobilization of the sheik's fanatical followers, the dynasty under your leadership would be put into risk. The police and army waiting in the wings or delaying action and response by the army would further threaten—should I even say, Highness—the very existence of your immediate family."

"Sarwawi! Have you been reading too many action thrillers? And what did you swallow when you were in Zürich?"

"I am very, very serious about this, your Highness. Why has Bashard massively shorted a stock he told you we had to buy and publicly advertise your support? And all supposedly key to propping up the American economy from falling apart? We believe that something ghastly is fairly imminent. Frankly, we're surprised he communicated directly with Boom to see if everything was in place as he described it. Maybe he is getting worried . . ."

The king interjected, "So Bashard is still talking with Boom—a very fishy fellow who brought the bomb to the control of Islam. Though what a tragedy that Waristan has it—that unstable camel dung heap."

"Yes, and also two more in North Korea and now possibly Tyrania, our enemy even if Muslim brothers."

The king nodded agreement and continued, "A few of those crazy people in the Tyranian cabinet are well outside the normal Islamic beliefs. Any country's leadership that thinks the total disintegration of Israel is the way to salvation is mad. Don't get me wrong. Giving Israel a quick kick like an uncooperative camel from time to time is not my worry. But some of the Tyranians are over the top."

"Well, Boom was helping Tyrania with their bomb-making activities. And rumors are even riper that Israel is now ready to bomb them because they have accumulated enough enriched uranium at the 80 percent enrichment level. A number of experts say they finished this enhancement months ago and are understating their capability. Just playing with us."

"Yes, yes, Sarwawi, I know all that. So what's going to be the damage in the West, you think? Worst possible scenario."

"We believe a nuclear bomb of possible megaton yield is being put in place that could take out a downtown area. The West won't want to know that Sarabian and Waristani nut cases were behind it, not you. They'll completely put this one on us, along with Tyrania and Waristan."

"So indeed, it all sounds like time is running out quickly, but we do not know precisely where to start, my loyal friend," said the king.

Sarwawi was beginning to make progress in convincing the king of the size of the conspiracy and was encouraged by the king to expand on the details, so the intelligence chief continued. "Bashard has made recent trips to London, New York, and one to Zürich—all major financial centers whose destruction would benefit him financially and destroy a significant part of the dynasty's investment wealth, thereby significantly reducing your leverage to react to any threats from within or even abroad."

"So you feel that . . ."

"We believe, Highness, Zürich is a high probability."

"That's where a lot of our gold is!"

"And Bashard has massively bought gold futures too."

"The bastard." The king had never used such profane language before to describe Bashard, who was a first cousin. It was almost unheard of to do in front of an official.

The intelligence chief smiled. He never liked Bashard, who he knew had become an extremist, but never had enough on him to make it worry the king. Bashard had also compromised the security chief on his requests to increase his budget on white-collar crime and financial laundering—investigations as part of a new cooperative effort with the West to fight terrorism.

The king pondered for a while as if wanting more proof. "I don't know if we should move against Bashard. All of this might just end up being a defensive play on finances. To help Tyranians get the bomb, which might be inevitable—not to light a fuse to a bomb in the West. After all, we need not overly polarize the Tyranians from the Islamic community, given that they are practically on our doorstep."

"Your Highness, a number of unsavory figures connected to him have provided us some vital information about Boom's labs in Waristan moving parts such as triggers and materials like beryllium, all with a destination in the British Norman islands. May I emphasize, Tyrania is not where our greatest risk is. These channel islands would likely be a transhipment point to a city, either in assembled or unassembled form."

"The Channel Islands! They are almost getting to the heart of Europe. It would be an unusual staging ground to send anything there from Tyrania," said the king, who had picked up very well on his chief's logic.

The king continued, "Yes, I have heard coincidentally that a rather independent agency of supposed do-gooders was run out of one of those islands. I occasionally wonder whose side they are on with their liberal ideas."

"Don't you know, Highness, that your sister is on its Council?"

"So she said, but it was charity work. Is it something else? Should I worry what she has gotten herself involved in?"

"This may come as a shock to you, but from what we have recently learned, it is a spy agency, supporting various activities independent to a large extent of government to fight Islamic extremists, at least in part."

"What! Whose permission gave her the right to be with such an organization?"

"I think you might want to take that up with her. I think you agreed to the charity work."

"Hmmm. I knew she should have been married," said the king like a concerned brother, but like the old-fashioned one his sister thought him to be. Well, he was in his eighties, so why shouldn't he be a bit old-fashioned, he thought a bit sadly to himself.

"Anyway, the operational head of that Council is a big worry," added Sarwawi dramatically.

"What do you mean by this?"

"He may be a main player in this conspiracy that Bashard is involved with, which will eventually lead to your removal."

"To overthrow me!"

"No, not yet, but fairly soon, very soon. But more importantly helping to deliver a nuclear bomb, operationally or otherwise, to a main European city. We have studied recent logs of ships going to and from a Channel island where the Council is based. There have been tourist ships, fishing boats, and one small cargo ship headed for Rotterdam. However, the only thing going in and out of there with the slightest radiation signature has been a small private jet leased to the Council. It made trips to London, New York, and Zürich. Because of its high-class security clearance arranged by MI5, it is only inspected on a limited basis. But a number of our people have investigated and found unusual radiation levels in its hangar. Though not excessively high, these are well beyond normal background radiation levels."

"So, Sarwawi, you are telling me that a nuclear bomb could very well be planted in a major European city by the support of one of my closest financial advisors, ready to go off at any time, along with a coup? And by my own direct cousin!"

There was silence. The intelligence chief knew if he made a final confirmation of this and it did not play out, his head would likely be placed on the chopping block and the king would be removed by the council of the royal family for being senile.

"Yes," confirmed the chief bluntly and without reservation.

"So, what do we do?"

"I suggest, your Highness that you go to Zürich."

"Are you crazy? Leaving the capital will give the traitors even more of a chance to organize against me."

"That may be so, but you will take Bashard with you, concerning a major financial concern that you will want his advice on."

"Will he not get suspicious?" worried the king.

"Of course, but he will know that refusing to go could look like he is guilty if he figures you have suspicions. And I think he knows it's too early to foment any uprising against you. Though, give it one more week or more, and I am very afraid, Highness, that you might be gone. We believe that the bomb is not operational quite yet, but once it is . . ."

"Unbelievable! Madness, pure madness, Sarwawi!"

"We figure that Bashard has enough influence that his other conspirators would not likely blow him up, as he will still be an important financial coordinator for accelerating the conspiracy after the bomb is blown. They might delay its explosion if he were in Zürich, and for all we know, he may have the trigger—though likely not the only one."

"What a full-scale conspiracy!" The king's eyes were rolling in horror.

"Yes, we are also piecing certain parts of it together with the help of Mossad."

"Mossad! What are we doing dealing with them? Surely through a third party."

"Yes, of course, Highness—in fact, through a reliable Swiss banker."

"Are there any left?" responded the king.

"So far this is what we are beginning to piece together, also with the help of Interpol and some freelance people, one of whom has actually been working in the kingdom—a Westerner, named Adrian Sands. He has been helpful, as he went around with his female colleague gathering information about the conspiracy."

"Adrian Sands, yes, that professor. Wasn't he working secretly on a controversial novel about our political inner workings—or was it an actual book about environmentalism and Islam? I cannot remember."

"No, just a ruse, I believe, to his so-called investigative activities against extremists."

"I see," said the king.

"What we understand from Sands and his colleague is that the opposition wishes to establish an Islamic caliphate under the titular head of Sheik Zayed beneath the financial management and direction of Bashard. Likely with Nadel and the head of the *Mootawa* and possibly the police taking on important supporting roles. With all the new resources and religious backing they would have, they would also start assisting the overthrow of moderate and 'pro-Western' Islamic countries. Islamic nations that don't fall in line with their political and religious interpretations could fall through internal intrigue, or would be eventually invaded by a so-called, new holy alliance of Muslim nations. Such a pact would be highly leveraged, once Tyrania got the bomb and began expanding its new nuclear arsenal."

"What about the West? They would support us—the House of Sarab." The king was now showing real nervousness in his voice.

"They are going to be in financial chaos, and their internal uprisings will be so great that the Islamic community will be convinced that Allah is behind Bashard's and Zayed's cause. Meanwhile, Israel might pull their own trigger, given their worries that they will be the next nuclear victim or be finally crushed by this new holy alliance, which will have much less resistance against it from the West. Such an aggressive action by Israel could cause or reinforce a major Islamic backlash. After all, the West's economy will be essentially blown apart with any Zürich bombing, as it is already fragile. This, in turn, will stir the masses even more against the West, especially if America makes their own strikes to defend Israel, even in the United States' more enfeebled predicament.

"However, any attack by the Americans may not happen if certain American politicians become further well positioned to reinforce the new administration's isolationist tendencies. Remember, your Highness, the West is tired from the wear and tear from being in Orficestan and Iraq for so long."

"Anything else?" the king said as he shook his head and pursed his lips in disgust. "Or should I ask?" the king added. He then looked at his security chief with eyes wide open as well as mouth. It had been a staggering revelation for the king.

"There is. There could be a pro-Nazi connection. Where they will mobilize the masses in an anti-Islam, anti-immigrant purge, blaming Muslim immigrants for assisting with the coordination of the bombing or having a set of religious values supportive of such. It's a kind of divide-the-world-up between opposites—something akin to the

Hitler-Stalin pact of World War II, but obviously more than just carving up a country like Poland."

The king wondered why he had not heard of all these potential threats before. But he had raked his intelligence chief so many times over the coals before his desert tent about noncorroborated concerns about Bashard, that it was probably no wonder that his chief had held back until everything had been well-corroborated. And on the brink.

"Yes, there has been a lot of stirring up by these neo-Nazis in Europe," the king acknowledged.

"Yes, Highness. Who knows if the Berlin bombing was a precursor to accelerating this anti-Islamic hysteria? The West, especially Germany, has been mobilized into martial law. In fact, a loose form of it has already been declared. The conspirators' intent is to create a new axis, as these right-wing leaders take on new positions at political, military, and other levels."

"This is bloody astonishing. How long have you known or have been highly suspicious about it?" asked the king.

"We have had a lot of bits and pieces, coded lists, strangely timed bombings, attacks by extremists on our more progressive colleges, neo-Nazi youth attacks on moderate intelligence agents and leaders, and increasingly more sharing of information from our Interpol source—though initially more slowly. It was the same with Mossad."

"Yes, of course, it has been difficult after 10/11 to rebuild those bridges with the Jewish community that Waheed had helped us with."

"Oh yes. About the female Order this report mentions. They have been working against Bashard. Maybe we should see if we can be helpful. To assist them in a concrete way. Bashard seems out to get them, though lacking a lot of the facts for now. I would gather that your sister probably would know something about them."

"And you are sure of all this?"

"There are too many coincidences. We are looking at a world going very, very ugly if we do not act fast. Your Highness, it is very much time to take action."

"Let me get Bashard on the line. Now, what do I say exactly?"

"Well, it's what you don't say. One, I'm not here. Your voice will be calm. You will be pleased to advise him that you are going on a European tour starting tomorrow to promote interfaith; the tour was planned quietly so as to not upset anyone. Also, you wish to check the gold deposits of

Sarabian holdings with him in Zürich. There has been a rumor that the Swiss bank that manages some of them has been illegally lending out our gold as collateral to fishy customers of theirs. You are not privy to tell the source, but it is of utmost national importance that he be there to back up the claims with urgency to correct the matter. And it is necessary to do a spot-check immediately, as you are worried billions may be missing. You are very upset about it and cannot tell him who your source is, as you are sworn to secrecy. And it must be done now."

"What if he says no?"

"You are the king. If he says no, he will be arrested, and our suspicions will be strengthened."

"And . . ."

"If he says yes, I suggest having him arrested anyway. Especially if he shows any unnecessary delay or unusual behavior on the way to the airport, like bringing his own squadron of security people."

"That sounds very risky, and why do we surely have to go to Zürich?"

"It is very difficult for me to tell you why."

"I'm getting an idea," said the king.

"If there is a bomb, to protect the image of Sarabia. Should it go off, your being in Zürich will show solidarity with the West, as it will all be documented before and deposited to Western leaders that you were there. No one classifies you as a suicide bomber given your reputation. That will show that at least most of the dynasty, the part you head, are still worthy of an alliance with America and what will be left of the West.

"I see. Well, I have lived a long life. If I must be martyred to save the reputation of my kingdom, the dynasty, and for world peace, so be it. It will be the will of Allah."

"Meanwhile, I'll quietly step up the patriot guard around you and your family, of course, with your approval."

"Yes, of course. When shall we go?"

"This late evening. In fact, as early as possible."

"So be it. I'll make it look like a quick routine trip, and keep it as low profile as possible by leaving just after prayers at dusk."

"I would suggest that you not liquidate stocks into US treasuries or do much short selling, as it would draw suspicions and could possibly be interpreted as collaboration with the conspirators."

"But this could be risky. A large part of the kingdom's wealth could be wiped out."

"Well, I'm not your financial or political adviser, but if they pull off this bomb, it may be immaterial how much wealth we lose. We'll all probably go on a list for assassination from the West or inside the country. And they'll want to be sure of it, if we made a lot of money out of it—the West, that is."

"Yes, let's get to it," the king said, looking upward, hoping that he would have the blessing of the highest authority. He felt he would need it more than ever before, as he went to his prayer room with worry beads in hand grinding furiously. And his teeth too.

TWENTY-SIX

She picked up the phone, knowing immediately who it was.

"Yes, Jonathan?" she said with dread in her mind, if not in her tone.

"I have word that Adrian left town. Why haven't you phoned me concerning his departure?" Jonathan's voice was ice-cold.

"What? He's down the passage in his room, isn't he? Last thing he said to me was that he was going to take heavy-duty sleeping pills after going for a bit of fresh air."

Cold silence followed—for a few brief but strongly punctuating seconds.

"What about Kim?" Jonathan inquired.

Silence, this time from Patsy. Jonathan, the DED to the Council, felt another vacuum sucking away at his authority.

"I hear noises that Adrian has disappeared to Athens," said the DED. "Did you see Kim at the hotel—and what about Adrian?"

Patsy said, "Never really saw Kim. No . . . sorry, he was in a desperate rush wondering where Adrian was yesterday afternoon, as he was not in the hotel at the time. Though he said he had a line on him—no matter, would find him. Said nothing further but to hold to electronic communication silence—emphasizing your orders to be maintained, sir."

"And Adrian?"

"Colonel, I thought he came back yesterday late evening after being out all day."

"Doing what? You were supposed to be his minder."

"He has had a do-not-disturb sign on his door and refused to take phone call messages. Left me a voice mail that he was very tired and said he took plenty of sleeping pills. Would see me around noon today, if up for it." Patsy was punching out information formally, the way a private

304

responded to a drill sergeant—too intimidated at that moment to use her more relaxed approach as a longtime subordinate to her boss.

"Bloody hell, Patsy! He's ditched you using the oldest trick in the book."

"I'll knock on his door, sir. If I don't get any response, I'll have management open it. I'm very sorry, sir."

"Don't bother," said Jonathan, too put out to be any more put out by Patsy's obvious failings to keep an eye on Adrian. Or had she already been getting nervous feet by then? The orders to maintain communication silence had possibly been her security blanket as she contemplated her next step.

"And are we supposed to be talking? This is a blackout period for the most part, isn't it, Jonathan?" She tried to soften her words of repeated protest against being made to break important protocol by being a bit chummy.

"Look, Patsy, I would not be calling if I wasn't worried. I'm thoroughly surprised that you don't know that he is very likely no longer in the hotel." Jonathan started doing something he seldom did, especially on the phone, particularly with a subordinate. He started showing a waning of self-confidence. "You know, we don't even know where Bashard is. Very concerning . . ."

"Again, should we be talking about him on the phone?"

"Forget the silence. Things are looking a little desperate. Get on with getting anything about Adrian—and Isolde, anything on her, too." Patsy had never heard his voice so strained.

"Okay, okay. I'll have the manager open the door and see if there are any clues as to where he went. I'll phone you back," Patsy lied. She was now desperate in her own way—to get the hell out of the hotel. She even worried that she might be Kim's next target. That is, if Jonathan contacted him again. Jonathan sounded like he was beginning to crack up, and his loss of confidence, she fearfully thought, might extend to her.

"Right, Patsy." Jonathan's voice faded off. He did not know whom to trust anymore. Even Schmidt had not picked up. It was all falling apart, he dreaded.

*   *   *

Patsy was planning her exit. She had initially thought this job was going to be her retirement party to make up for her slaughtered government pension. "Surely," Patsy thought out loud, "things cannot take a turn for the worse." However, they were about to. But first, her imagination would take over and do its own damage before the final damage was unleashed on her.

She visualized that good ole Kim would be showing up as room service with the extra towels she had requested. Or in another disguise. As she swore to herself, Patsy was beginning to believe how stupid she had been to take Jonathan's "fool's" gold that Schmidt had handed her almost violently. No, maybe instead of the cruel Korean, it would be Schmidt coming to take her to his bunker. The terror of the idea swelled up in her throat—before going down to her bowels. Patsy had killed herself in her mind before anyone would kill her body.

Then, the call came that she dreaded.

"Room service," but somehow said strangely and well after the knocks.

Patsy opened the door, but with a revolver in her back waist, in case things got ugly.

It was too late. A man unknown to her was holding a towel, which he then dropped on purpose. Patsy thought about picking it up—maybe just as a final act so as to be able to throw it in for surrender. She had had enough. As she picked it up, he went behind her and grabbed her gun. Patsy was well beaten. Her sordid work for Jonathan had become more than a game of chance to good retirement money winnings. It had become a forced invitation to a cage—no game in that at all. The man was a Swiss detective about to arrest her.

Behind him followed another detective, along with Friegel, who barked out an order for her to sit down and put away her damsel eyes of astonishment. She had played that poorly, too. In the end, Patsy was holding a full dunce against Friegel's flush of Schultzes. She was done for good.

*   *   *

As he put down the receiver ever so slowly, Jonathan's wrinkled forehead looked so creased that it seemed like he would have to take it to the dry cleaners if worse news showed up. And it did.

"Hello, Jonathan," said what he perfectly knew was the chief of the MI5 operations directorate.

"What the hell are you doing here unannounced? Oh sorry—startled, nice to see you, Smith."

"You plural, I think you mean, Jonathan. I hope you realize a number of my boys are outside, so let's keep our good old-school manners, shall we?"

"I'm quite confused. What is this really all about?"

"We need to have a chat. And don't do something like taking out a gun—unless it is to be used to commit suicide. But I am sorry; we shan't even let you do that unless we have squeezed everything out like a Panamanian shark—sound familiar?"

"What in God's name are you talking about, Smith?"

"Yes, let's do keep it formal."

"Again, why are you here?"

"You have been very naughty. We hesitated when your whole racket was set up separately, partly because too many very high-ups at the political end—whose names will go unsaid—thought we were becoming a cock-up. But what have we found here? It is real proof that my directorate isn't so bad after all. Quite a bit better comparatively speaking—though definitely not as well paid."

"Again, get to the point." Jonathan was now looking meaner in the mouth rather than innocent or confused.

"Indeed, so disloyal you make the Cambridge five look Boy *Scoutish*—a walk in the park."

"I don't know what the hell you're talking about, Smith."

"And very worrisome is that we have found all sorts of radiation traces around town, near the docks and the airport. We have very sophisticated equipment not all known to you at every port—even this measly one. But the data analysis can take some time. Clever how you tried to mask it."

"Yes, please go on, very fascinating story—I like it, real novel for a story. And that's all it is."

Smith had paused for air and for a reaction from Jonathan. Jonathan was beginning to look very itchy and sweaty under the collar. That radiation remark was making him feel sick.

"Okay, so what do you have? Nothing, right? You're trying to entrap me for some kind of failed operation I know nothing about. I'd like legal counsel."

"Forget it. No legal recourse for what you have done, Jonathan."

"This is all ridiculously unfair, baseless charges, and you effectively calling me a traitor. Scurrilous. It must be a setup by my detractors, who think I'm overpaid. Come on, Smith, it must be a joke."

"Sorry, Jonathan, you have been classified well out of bounds of getting counsel. The Official Secrets Act, which even applies to this miserable rock of a tax haven, and the Enemy Combatant Directive will deal nicely with putting you away for a very long time. With no public inquiries until maybe in five years if Amnesty International finds out about you. That is, if you are lucky."

"What indeed are you getting on about? You don't have jurisdiction at this facility."

"I am talking about the rosy scenario for being a traitor. I think even the human rights activists would be on our side to throw the key away."

The suspenseful warm-up was beginning to take its psychological toll on Jonathan, who feared he would be charged with every breach of the Official Secrets Act and if the bomb in Zürich went off, he might also be charged under the Crimes against Humanity laws no matter how well he defended himself.

"This is some ridiculous bureaucratic infighting that I am a victim of. I demand my rights. There will be an inquiry over this." Jonathan for the first time since Smith had known him began to have a wild, desperate look.

"But you are certainly no human rights arse, are you?" said Smith provocatively and with disgust. "By the time we strip you down for information, you'll really wish you were with Allah, if you even believe in that stuff, which I figure you don't."

"All right, I know when I'm licked." Jonathan quickly swung around and popped out the Luger that Ingrid had deposited by way of Isolde. He wondered at the moment where Ingrid was.

"A Luger? Nice touch that really says it all."

But the Luger was what Smith had deliberately instructed his insiders to ensure was not removed from the DED's office. A trap in fact—the gun deliberately left to see if Jonathan would use it, the so-called smoking gun before it was even shot, which no one would have been able to. Smith, before being at the point of the Luger, had not been fully convinced that his former colleague at MI5 had been thoroughly guilty—the man was, after all, a Knight of the Garter. But that automatic respect had changed, especially after Isolde had provided his contact on the Council information about the real list and whose names were on it.

"Look, Smith, we are going to go out of here together and onto that Council plane together—or die together." Jonathan was profusely sweating.

"Really!" said Smith, not looking like he was fully concerned. Saying it as if he were a teacher talking disappointment to a schoolchild.

Jonathan then blew his cool and let all his pretend ideology hang out.

"The whole lot of you are corrupt. You have let in dreadful rabble and riffraff into the country. The joke is just too much. London is now being called Londonstan. I would rather deal with people like the Brotherhood, who have no false ideals about mixing of opposites."

"So, Jonathan, all this *turncoatery* is because of your hatred toward Muslim minorities?"

"It's not hatred. It's a fact that there should be no mixing. Our culture is too fundamentally different from theirs. Let them have their caliphate, as long as they stay in their borders. To hell with them. It'll save us a huge amount of money and soldiers that we are using to fight them that could be better used."

"Very strong language, Jonathan, and not too civilized in terms of our core values. And all those innocent Westerners in Zürich, dead—or another city?"

"It's a small price to pay to stop this flood of immigrants and their taking over of our societies. Killing off our great Anglo Saxon, white male culture by the thousands every year is what you pricks are all about. You are gullible pawns to the *liberocracy*."

Jonathan was, in fact, playing for time and Smith knew it. Hoping his own troops would show up to deal with Smith's help.

"Well, I'd like to chat longer with you about your newborn fascism that wants to give half the world over to Islamic fanatics, but I just don't have the time—and I don't think Zürich does either. Or London, New York, or . . . Oh, by the way, thanks for the speech, but you know you largely did it for the money. Which we have now expropriated and partly given to a battered immigrant women's fund—and the Order."

"What? You shite, you can't take my money!"

"We did, and we are also going to use it in our further operations, as well as to fight bastards like you."

Jonathan was now getting vitriolic in the face. Smith had truly shot him, even if it was Jonathan who was armed. He now wanted to hit back hard.

"You're guessing. Any bomb could be in three or four cities that I have visited with the plane. And don't you need to be reminded of something very important?"

"What's that?"

"I'm holding the gun, Smith."

"What, you kidnapped a gunsmith? How funny!"

"There won't be anything funny about your shite sense of humor when I *fuckin'* blow you away." Jonathan was practically screaming—a tirade, maybe a sign that he was on the edge of a nervous breakdown.

"Before you do anything silly like shooting me, I want to ask you something . . ."

It was too late. Jonathan's delay tactics had backfired; he had hoped Ingrid might come to his rescue and take out Smith's men—but with what would have been a very appropriate question, as she no longer had a gun. But the screaming had been too much for two of Smith's so-called goons. They came crashing through the door.

Jonathan fired the gun once. Nothing happened. Then he fired it twice, and it jammed again. Before he could throw it, stab himself, look more stupid, or do anything else, the two grabbed him and shoved him down into his chair. They had not shot Jonathan, as they were told not to despite whatever happened. Only to come in if they heard fighting, screaming, or "loud bumps in the night."

All looked much better, until in came Ingrid with a set of sharp, silver steak knives looking ready to throw them at somebody. But Smith turned around and instinctively shot her, to his later chagrin.

Gerthing's janitors and cleaners, in the guise of auditors on behalf of the foundation, had recently visited and disarmed everything in Jonathan's office—but not Ingrid's set of knives in her room. It had been a major slipup by Gerthing's people that would figuratively lead to a whipping by Biggart of those responsible, and his own self-flagellation, too.

Smith was steaming mad about having killed Ingrid.

"Well, Jonathan, your good work has paid off. You recruited this young student to your warped aims. And she's dead, like a lot of other, more decent, innocent people are going to be. I hope you are actually proud of your stupid actions."

"You bloody bastard, Smith . . ."

"We want information. Now, before you look worse than—what is her name again?"

"You totally unfeeling bastard. My poor Ingrid," he almost screamed. "She was the love of my loves," said Jonathan, almost crying.

"No, I'm worse than a bastard. I knew exactly what she was to you." Smith lied to bait Jonathan about what was next in the program for him. Jonathan was snarling, but the rest of his body could not do anything but quiver in hatred. It was under restraining orders of two human gorillas, who were very pleased that they had missed getting a knife or two in their faces. But it was an experience that gave them a mean inclination to do anything that Smith would want inflicted on Jonathan.

"Now, where's the bomb? The city and exact location. We want it immediately and no fucking around!" Smith's demands were so pointed that they could have been their own set of knives had they been transformed into material. And what was material at that moment was getting an answer to the question, no matter what it would take.

"Forget it. What bomb? I'm just playing with you until you allow me my rights. I want my lawyer." Jonathan had few options to revenge the death of his loved one except to stiff Smith of vital information.

"Agents Novotny and Smothers. Did he call me a bum?"

"Yes, I think so," said Novotny.

"How about you break his nose a little?" added Smith.

Jonathan looked fearful. Like one of those cornered weasels that would get a last lick in at their prey given their dangerous teeth. But Jonathan, in fact, was not going to get even one vicious bite in. And if things worked out very badly, he would not even have a single tooth of a bite when it was over.

"Not going to tell?" Smith added in his interrogation.

"Nothing!" said Jonathan with clenched incisors.

"Novotny, have some fun with his nose before we get into the teeth of the matter. He has a face that looks like it's lived too good a life. Don't you think?"

Novotny had no sympathy. He came originally from a foreign orphanage—and had done a lot of boxing, which showed.

"Bam!" Novotny had good elbows. He liked hockey, for he was a Czech immigrant who, also unfortunately for Jonathan, had the patriotism that went with being one of those immigrants that Jonathan and his old crusty lot did not like very much.

"God, Smith. That's enough!" Jonathan gasped.

"No, I think Novotny is a perfectionist, and you've upset him too much by still having a nose that looks better than his. Mr. Novotny, please."

"My pleasure."

"Ahhhhhhhhhhhhhhhh shite! . . . You'll be investigated for this!"

"Are you stupid, Jonathan? What side of the nobility were you brought up on? Nobody will care a shite about a little two-faced shite like you. We're trying to find an atomic bomb, you moron. Now you want to play ball, or end up as a less-than-inspired piece of human gelatin—a new contemporary work for the ugly wing of the modern Tate. Or a very interesting gallery in Zürich, specializing in molten plastic kitsch."

"What do you mean?" Jonathan was just about crying—no, whimpering in agony and looking like he was getting warmed up for requesting a quick death.

"I'm thinking that since you're so fascinated with Nazism that a little display of Gestapo tactics would go a long way to impress you—though not me, as I really don't like this as a true English gentleman—which you are not, by the way."

"What are you going to do?" Jonathan was now panicking, looking dreadfully bloodier than bloody can be.

"How would you like to be a castrato? Singing high-pitched in Sing Sing, as the Americans would say. You would become quite an attraction for some of the more affectionate boys in those cells. We could sell tickets—you would be such a delightful attraction. Yes, we would send those funds to the Order, as well."

"Smith, you are really a bastard! How do I know you won't kill me if I tell you how to find it?"

"Jonathan, I don't need to lie. You should have the same view. Because I will kill you, but in a way that will be relatively painless if you give me the information."

"I'm thinking about it. Ahhhhhh, the pain . . . Okay, I'll tell you the city."

"Well, you just saved your teeth despite your nose," quipped Smith.

"It's Zürich."

"Okay. Novotny, give the man a glass of water. I need to step out and call someone. Now after I step out, I want you to think very hard about the address."

"Fuck you!"

"Not the right answer, Jonathan. But I live in optimism. You should be brave."

Smith phoned Falcon.

"Falcon!"

"S here."

"Right!" responded Falcon.

"Yes, the device is in Zürich."

"Ah. You're sure. We pretty well knew it," Falcon confirmed.

"Not completely. Our source does not have much to live for, except a quick demise. I suggest your people go to the hangar for executive jets at Zürich. Check to see what records they have about that airplane the Council has."

Falcon replied, "We have not taken any chances. We've checked out thoroughly international arrival areas in Zürich, after the Sarabians phoned us with the bad news before you chaps."

"That jet from the Council came in top secret," added Falcon. "But our service is trying to get all relevant records to it . . . which may not all be in electronic form. There could be an air cargo delivery address there, but maybe a fake one. So pump out any address from your so-called contact."

"Good to hear you're moving on things, and sorry if we were slower than the Sarabians—my apologies. We've been understaffed at MI5 since our restructuring. Fiscal insanity all about, too."

"Don't we know about it here. Okay, keep us posted, S—shall we say on further developments, which we wish are more bloody forthcoming."

Smith returned to his quarry. "Now, Jonathan, the real worry for you is that our agent in Zürich may not be able to find the exact location. He is a very impatient man, with an Irish temperament toward duplicitous English scumbags like you. In short, he wants answers now. To show our responsiveness to his inquiries, we have decided to speed things up. Smothers has very interesting pliers to work on you, one joint or tooth at a time."

"What will it be, governor?" Smothers said. "Rocks, scissors, or nuts?"

"Fuck you," Jonathan said, with wild eyes of hatred.

"Mr. Smith, I believe he gave us the wrong answer, sir," responded Smothers.

"Well, he did say nuts." Novotny had a cruel smile on his face.

"Now, Mr. Novotny," said Smith, "let's not be jealous—one at a time. Smothers first."

"Ahhhhhhhhhhhhhhhhhhhhhhhh. My God, no. Oh no, my God. No, please. I beg you."

"Look, Jonathan, I actually believe in the UN Covenant on Torture. You're fully pissing me off. If you have one iota of decency in you, you will spare me the pain of turning me into a full hot-blooded torturer—and my men, too. Somewhere in your British bones there must have been a mother, father—someone who brought you up to be better than this. This could be your epiphany." Smith changed his tactics by giving hope to a hopeless man, a page out of the unwritten book of torture.

"Look, I'll make a phone call and try to salvage your life. No guarantee, but as one gentleman to what was once a gentleman who got twisted around by God knows who. It happens; people lose it. We'll give you professional attention." Smith was now playing good cop, but he had to be the whole good cop given the kind of subordinates he had—one-way mean in two heads.

"God, Smith. How could you do this to me?" Jonathan was in a puddle of tears and blood, a totally broken man, who had been taught by MI5, his original employer—no, by himself—never to let himself be truly broken. At least, this quickly. "Okay, you promise not to kill me?"

"No full promise. You must work much harder for that. Promise to try and save your life, and if not, to make your exit from it as quick and painless as possible. Slow answers get the latter; faster answers a chance at the former. At the very best, you can turn around your situation and your image to your family. We'll give you an official funeral and put on record that you saved millions. Which would be the case."

"Okay. I just can't take it anymore. No, please, Mr. Novotny. Look, I only know it is somewhere near the Hôpital des Templiers in Zürich. Bashard, I think, or Boom may know the exact address. Yes, Richter or something place. The doctor was telling me how appropriate that it would be near some crusader icon. Look, I don't like these people either . . ."

"Okay, boys, get him cleaned up, shove him in that closet for now, and wait for further instructions."

"Yes, sir."

"I need to make another call."

Jonathan looked like a pitiful sight and a reminder that torture was a ghastly crime in itself.

*   *   *

"Yes, Smith, this is Falcon. We have located the apartment across from the hospital. Thanks for the confirmation. Hope not too much effort for it. Radiation levels indicate that it is the right place."

"Is it the real thing or a dirty bomb?" asked Smith.

"It depends on the craftsmanship. But if K-Boom is behind it with lots of Bashard's money, though the latter we don't know for sure, count on it being very dangerous."

*   *   *

I had just dropped in to Falcon's office, if you can say going through a gauntlet of detectors and security personnel is dropping in. I had gotten a blow-by-blow account of everything, by listening to Falcon on the phone with Smith and other security chiefs in the West.

I had come back from Athens after confirming Kim's assassination by Papagalopitis's men. The Korean had killed or maimed the rest of the Dionysus Order that I hadn't. The last ones were drooped over their ritual altar.

Kim had made a huge mistake—an assumption that mortals might make, but not what true gods of mythical Greek assassination would commit. He figured the Greek police would not be on top of the Acropolis after his handiwork of wiping out the greater half of the Dionysus Order. He also did not have the foggiest idea as to why their assassination had been ordered.

Kim had just escaped me minutes before through an ancient secret entrance, which next to no one knew about, except that last kid inside that block of rock who had revealed it under torture. (Though later, no one in on the autopsy report could initially figure out why the tortured member also had a large scar of an arrow wound on his leg.)

Kim, in fact, was shot on the spot where the original giant statue of the goddess Athena was said to have been placed—coincidentally, where the escape exit had been. And immediately beside where the construction crews on the top of the Acropolis had hoisted a new one of her.

If Kim's eyes had lit up anymore in surprise, I was told, while looking at his mortal wound, they would have made Christmas look dull. Or maybe simply, he had not been man enough to deal with a very tall lady towering over him. Especially with her concrete spear that he had bumped into. And a "noblewoman" with her lance that had distracted him into the gunsights of "No Escape Papa" Papagalopitis, whose men had shot Kim just outside the Temple of Athena. All because of wasted youths. The Greeks would have made theater of it, but no one in our agency would officially ever talk about Dionysus again.

Upon my return to Zürich, King Abdul had phoned me—providing a most distinguished mystery. I was astonished that he would contact me and had no idea why he decided to use me as a third party. He insisted that I arrange a meeting between Falcon and him. But that he needed to come in disguise as a woman—his sister, in fact, as a precaution strongly advised by his security chief. Falcon was to be told by me that the urgent meeting was pertaining to the bomb that the Sarabian king's eldest sister needed to talk to him about. It was described as a matter of vital importance. Falcon reluctantly agreed, waving off the face screening of the princess, considered a security breach. A protest about not following regular screening for her was made by one of the building security personnel supervisors, which was overridden with two quick, simple calls but not to simple persons—the lady president of Switzerland and the newly installed female head of Interpol.

* * *

Falcon continued with his office telephone discussions in my presence with security personnel. "That list is almost unbelievable," said Falcon who just could not get away from being so completely shocked with most of the names on it.

"Well, I have made it," Isolde said to Falcon as she stepped through the doorway while he was on the phone. She was in the office but was not talking to me. Maybe because I had glued up the works with putting the fake lists facing inward, pasting them, and depositing them at Z-bank. She described me as totally impertinent and irresponsible.

Falcon continued with an important call but briefly acknowledged Isolde's presence.

"Okay, right, things falling into place for a change," Falcon almost barked into his phone. "So I understand the bombers on Richterstrasse have now come out of the apartment, to leave or get a bite or whatever. We'll get them. But after they return or try to flee. We'll see if we can follow them and see what we can gain. Yes, start trying to defuse it."

"Yes, the list—unbelievable," Isolde stated after Falcon had put down the phone.

"Quite remarkable!" said Falcon. "It was actually inside the paper of the fake list. Though all of the original conspirators did not seem themselves to have the whole real list, except for Bashard and one of his lieutenants."

"Really?" I said, wondering how Falcon knew that—maybe just a strong supposition.

"One logical deduction why few knew of its content," said Falcon.

"Why's that?" I asked.

"Otherwise, you and Isolde might have been dead. If Jonathan had known that his name was on that list, for sure he would have hired a dozen people to kill you and Isolde. And quickly."

Isolde smiled—a tense but gratifying smile.

"Sophisticated operation," Isolde said. "I suppose Bashard was worried if something happened to him, there would be little chance for full coordination. So Bashard drew up this coded list with instructions to get it to his second-in-command—Schmidt or maybe . . ."

"But which scientists would have done the photonic code work?" I asked.

"Sorry to say, a few mercenary scientists from ZIT all disappeared last week. Most with relatives in Sarabia, or with Bashard having compromising files on them," said Falcon.

"Sad," I concluded. "By the way, how's Zen?" I inquired.

"Good news! He has come to, but is barely aware," said Falcon.

"Wonderful to hear. Can he talk?"

"No, but he scribbled Jonathan's name barely, with a big question mark."

"Don't we know," I confirmed with a touch of irony.

"Isolde, have you told the Order to go quiet?" asked Falcon.

"Yes, but there is no stopping them—or me, to be honest about it. We have our big Van Gogh gala tonight. Nothing would get them to move it forward."

"Look, Isolde, Zürich is a bloody, bloody dangerous place. I've asked my own family and those of highly positioned political people to move out as quickly as possible," said Falcon.

Falcon had something else on his mind. He was wondering when his Sarabian visiting dignitary was going to say anything. She had entered Falcon's office with me. He knew not to impose himself on such a high-level "princess," but to simply provide a customary welcome to this distinguished VIP. Even if one full of riddles more than answers at that moment. He looked over to me as to whether he should say something to "her."

It was then that the king took off his veil. "I have heard enough. Gentlemen and lady, I was never here as far as my royal subjects are concerned."

"Your Highness? What are you doing here?" asked Falcon, with eyes so full of surprise. Falcon had briefly met him a number of times at security conferences in Raddah.

"I am sorry to so spectacularly interrupt your delicate operations. But I have a request for you that my good chief intelligence officer also wishes."

"What is that?" asked Falcon, almost bedazzled that this woman was a man, and a king of one of the most important countries on Earth, who possessed a hundred times more money than the actual queen of England.

"I need to be by the bomb."

"What? No, not possible!" responded Falcon.

"It has to be." The king insisted and tried to continue. "Let me explain."

King Abdul's English, while more than basic, was not quite as good as the intelligence chief hoped for explaining the complexities of the matter. His security chief was now on the multivideo phone service that had been set up after 10/11 to better coordinate antiterrorism among G20 countries and beyond. Each head of intelligence had twenty or more monitors in their own so-called NTF situation room, which stood for Nuclear Terrorism and Fall-out. A full soundproof facility cloaked against eavesdropping. An office, which officially was just one of his regular ones until he pressed a button to open all screens and mechanically move a wall to expose a large boardroom table.

The Sarabian security chief spoke. "His Highness believes there has been too much publicity about terrorists who have come out of our country and who have done extreme destruction to the West."

"I see," said Falcon. "Please continue."

"If the bomb goes off, the world will more than likely think that the royal House of Sarab was behind it. Grave for the survival of our country, and may we say, of relations with the West."

"Yes, I see that. And Bashard is part of the royalty." As Falcon increasingly warmed to the king's request, he felt uncomfortable about such references to Bashard being a close relative to the king.

"We have Bashard," the king forcefully, almost defiantly, said, to prove that he had fully disassociated himself from his rogue cousin. "He is our prisoner. We will, with your help, leave him with the bomb, but completely shackled."

Falcon looked amazed. No, the word "spooked" would have been better. He was not accustomed to the way the House of Sarab cleaned up their internal dirt—or the external variety, either. I had almost gotten used to it—after four long years or more living in that country and listening to my royal students and all the rumors about palace intrigue.

"Where, Highness, is he?" I asked.

"Mr. Sands, he is at Zürich airport, crate xy11tObooMa."

"My lord, really!" said Falcon, looking astonished along with everybody else.

"Is he dead?" I asked.

"No, but I think in an hour his oxygen is going to run out. And about now, he has awakened and is feeling a little claustrophobic," added the king happily.

"Oh, I begin to see," said Falcon. "You Sarabians in a way have made things very convenient. Thank you for your help, Majesty."

Falcon then got a whole bunch of phone calls from security chiefs who could now see who the guests were in the NTF situation room. It was becoming a madhouse of monitors. So mad, that Isolde and I had not been able to follow all the communication. Nor had we been permitted to convey most of the vital information about the conspirators to everyone in the Order. Fortunately, I had convinced her to have the meeting with Falcon before talking to the Order—at least I thought I had.

A Swiss security official on one of the twenty screens then made a matter-of-fact proclamation. "Okay, we have the bomb."

Falcon looked radiant, for a bomb like that would kill outright a minimum of four hundred thousand people and spread carcinogenic radiation into five or six European states and beyond; it would make Chernobyl look like a picnic. Worse, strong Sirocco winds were predicted over the next days to be coming from the south. They would distribute any deadly radiation over Berlin, London, Paris, and other densely populated urban areas. It would poison critically important agricultural lands and further lead to food price hikes. Food riots would be exacerbated, both in Europe and around the world.

Twenty national security and intelligence chiefs and their assistants were now hooked up on a Cisco networking system in Falcon's office, which he had fully engaged. The Swiss security chief came on again, to better start the process more formally of what had been laid out in secret protocol NTF documents, not even fully discussed at NATO Headquarters.

"First, gentlemen and ladies, I want you to know that things are looking a bit more positive. I have to reiterate that we must keep all of this absolutely confidential so as not to cause a panic by the public. Such a panic could cause a huge loss of lives."

Herr Springer, from German SD, internal security, came on. "Falcon, I see you have some visitors in your office. Is that the Sarabian king?"

"Everyone here is cleared, though I know it looks strange. Dieter, let's not screw around. The Sarabians were first to give us many key details about the plot, which all of you have been briefed about partly through the Countess's and Professor Sands's work—two others who have been cleared by me."

"Okay, okay. *Ja* if you're sure. How are you going to handle this? Who should be the lead on this? Interpol is more for crime," added Springer.

"We have to do what's efficient and forget about our own internal issues," said Falcon, looking to make sure that Interpol remained as the central coordinating agency. Otherwise, a jurisdictional battle could break out.

"Clearly," said the *Deuxieme Bureau* chief from France. "So, Falcon, what have you come up with? And the Swiss, too? It's going to be their show operationally. Maybe the Austrians and Germans, too?"

"I don't know whether you are going to like this, but our technical branch already has on the drawing board our own provisions for this," the Swiss chief said anxiously.

"Yes, don't we all?" said the Italian chief as the Austrian chief nodded. These two bitter bureaucrat rivals at the European community meetings were now in fine agreement about something.

Falcon added, "We propose, as the Swiss and Germans have agreed, that the secret bunker in the Bavarian Alps be used."

"What bunker?" the French chief exclaimed. "I don't know of any bunker you speak of."

"But we know of it," said Springer.

"Yes, Dieter, continue," said Falcon.

"The bunker was built in the 1940s for Nazi V2 rockets."

"That was destroyed," said the Austrian.

Springer interjected, "Given the circumstances, I have to tell you that one of the bunkers was never found until decades after the war. But in more recent years . . ."

There were cries of astonishment from most of the mouths of the other chiefs. Not the happiest campers, to say the least, with Smith of MI5 literally looking as if someone had pulled his jaw off. The Germans had effectively remained equipped with rockets, offensive weapons that the terms of the surrender in World War II had forbade. The Germans weren't sure in 1980 when they uncovered the V2 bunker that NATO could fully defend them against the Russians, who had invaded Orficestan. These V2 rockets had become extra insurance against an East European and Russian attack, a very timely find.

"Shit, Springer, you were supposed to tell NATO about this," said the Dutch head of security, whose country was no stranger to invasions from its neighbor.

"I can go into why you were not told. It would, however, not seem to be a convenient time to do so. We will explain later. What is convenient, gentlemen, oh yes, and lady, is that bunker is so impregnable from bombs that we calculate that such a nuclear bomb as is now in Zürich would be muffled if it exploded in there."

Given that there was a chance that the bomb might be headed for Germany, it was clear why the head of the German SD wanted almost dominating control of the operations. But after that revelation about hiding the V2 rockets, there was not a chance in hell he would get it.

The Austrian chief interrupted. "Can you not defuse the bomb? This bomb, after all, will have to pass over a small amount of Austrian territory in a possible exit strategy for it. Highly worrisome. If it explodes prematurely, it could do extensive damage to the city of Bregenz."

Falcon came back in. "It is heavily booby-trapped. I am sorry to say, the two bomb assemblers we were to arrest have committed suicide, according to my text message from our men on the ground. Bizarre chewing gum, disguised as Wrigley Spearmint gum, set off some chemical reaction."

"Oh shit." The American CIA chief finally came in, looking like he had a crowd of fifty people sitting around him at the White House situation room, near ready to chew their own gum if things went much worse. "Look, it seems like the only course is to get that bomb the fuck out of town. The Treasury Secretary is worried about its impact on the global financial community."

"Of course, that is what we are doing," coolly stated the Swiss security chief. "Thank you very much. But we are bringing in special devices to prevent any vibrations, to reduce the risk it will go off."

Smith interjected, "Yes, and nobody says anything beyond their heads of state office, prime ministers, and relevant cabinet ministers or relevant officials, most of whom have a direct pipeline to our audio and these screens. No statement for sure until that bomb is well out of Zürich. We already have CNN asking about a reported kidnapping of a prince in Sarabia and no sightings of the king. And other increased security chatter."

"Not good," said Springer.

"It's okay," the American National Security Council chief stated. "We're used to ensuring cooperation from the top news directors on these matters—the freelancers can be a problem. We all need to keep an ear to the ground and on the Internet, as well. And provide our disinformation to important blogs and Twitter, Facebook, and such if rumors get out of control. We have our people as members in every major Facebook group that was active during the revolts promoting democracy in North Africa.

"Like we usually do," cynically stated the CSIS security chief of Canada, trying to look relevant and trying to add a bit of levity if that were possible. Not too happy about all the court cases he might have to face emanating from his country's Freedom of Information Law and Charter of Rights. If the world survived, he feared the worst—a legal nightmare from those he tried to prevent getting news information about the bomb.

It all made him almost forget that the nuclear terrorism of the day was a more important issue.

"Look, at some point this is going to get out. So we better have good news and fairly soon." The Brazilian security head was one of the most respected for his cold, hard examination of the facts, even if he was sometimes overly passionate about them.

"Gentlemen, we Swiss are an efficient lot. We will resolve this satisfactorily."

"Yeah, but that device got in," spat out the Chinese security chief, known for his ruthless efficiency and criticism of Western openness, which he equated with a major breach in a security wall.

Smith interjected, "Let the Swiss for crying out loud do their job. We'll take the blame if that makes you happy. Please go on."

Falcon came back in. "We propose—in fact, it's not a proposal. We are going to one way or another take this bomb out of Zürich. But the final destination should be south of Füssen in Bavaria. Please look at your monitors for the Google map showing the rail route."

"Looks goods so far," the SD Chief said, knowing full well it had already been approved by an emergency meeting of German cabinet ministers—so his Blackberry read.

The Swiss chief added, "We have a special railcar at this very moment being pulled into the station, but of course, far away from the passenger terminal so as to lessen public suspicion and curiosity."

"Right, *bon*," the French *Deuxieme Bureau* chief put in; his blood was slowly beginning to come back to his face.

The French, Germans, and Americans were maybe feeling a little bit guilty about having gone after Swiss banking, and in turn Switzerland's economy, with a buzz saw. They all knew the financial consequences of this bomb, which was a further reminder of what a destroyed Swiss economy would mean. In this case, a level of asset destruction that would make the 2008 Wall Street-inspired meltdown look *piddly*. The radiation waves, if not the pure force of the explosion, would have a high probability of wiping out priceless customer data, never mind the Goldfinger effect on precious metals.

Falcon then turned back to the subject of the real list of traitors that Isolde had uncovered. The names had shocked most of the security chiefs, who also resolved to keep them as much a secret for now as the disposal of the bomb. The list was a bomb in itself.

There was general agreement expressed in the meeting. Nobody wanted their dirty laundry to be exposed to the public about which key figures in their societies had joined up with Bashard and Schmidt. Each country would take responsibility for dealing with their own traitors or those noncountrymen on the list and in their own country. It was understood what would have to happen to these conspirators—including even a president or prime minister or two, never mind the high-flying bankers and political opposition leaders.

Smith had restrained himself at the meeting, as he thought the whole incident with Jonathan was downright embarrassing—a Brit being one of the leading three or four conspirators. Smith still wondered—like so many of those in the various countries' security branches—what was to be expected next. In his line of clandestine work of skulduggery, he knew one thing for sure: it was always the unexpected that should be expected. And the coming unexpected would worry him to no end—even if he had no idea what it might be.

TWENTY-SEVEN

Stihl was wondering what the hell was going on! His wife had just tried to kill him for being on some master list of top fascists and sadists. Accusing him of being heavy into murder, S and M, and female sexual slavery. His suspicion was that one of the members of the Schmidt, Bashard, K-Boom troika must have learned of his true motivations, leading to an all-out campaign against him turning those decent people around him into his mortal enemies. Stihl had left a long trail of false evidence to prove that he was on the same level of malevolence and debauchery as the Baron. Now, it had come home to haunt him. Fortunately, his wife had not been able to shoot straight before she collapsed into what seemed like an epileptic fit.

If that were not bad enough, Stihl had been requested under Swiss Federal Council emergency order 111 to organize an immediate transfer of all customer account information from his bank into a multigovernment trust data bank. It had been set up by the international bank clearinghouse in Basel just before World War II. This emergency directive was only to be used just prior to an imminent invasion of Switzerland or during a cataclysmic disaster to the nation. Or if a bank was under threat of a major computer virus attack against which it could not likely defend itself.

The authorities had hinted that there would be a potential Y2-like meltdown of computers throughout continental Europe. But none of his colleagues in France or Germany knew about it. It was all very confusing and worrisome. Stihl felt as if everything solid were crumbling underneath him. He phoned his kids, Bertha and Bertram, who were respectively at LCC and Eton, to see if the rest of his family bedrock was still intact. And so they were, for now. Though he could never manage to pull Bertha away from her athletic endeavors at the London Canoe Club.

A special so-called ultra-data vault had been recently developed by the Basel Security Settlements Agency. The cloud computers used as a final backup for most Western bank accounts had been transferred from Iceland, because of a mass volcanic explosion on the island. Such a location had been put into question by a number of its member state security specialists. They all belonged to the Quadrilateral Commission of States (QCOMS), which included Western Europe, North America, Japan, and China. Switzerland and a number of other tax havens, as well as emerging market countries, had initially opted out, due to worries about information leakage from the site.

This account information "safe house" had, in fact, been moved to Spitsbergen, some godforsaken island high in the Norwegian Arctic, where the cloud hardware had been built behind one-hundred-meter-thick granite walls, so as to withstand minus eight degree Celsius temperatures or bombings. The system was referred to as "BRICE—Banking Replication Information Centre Enterprise." Stihl had wondered whether the data would be literally frozen and not fully accessible for weeks, if not months, if anything went wrong with their own protocols and software for reverse data transfers back to the source. The system had never been fully tested under a major emergency.

Stihl had also wondered what he would tell his clients if there were any glitches in recovering all the information. Would they wonder what BRICE was, or would they even be allowed to know of BRICE's existence? If not, they might come to think that their bankers had been part of some elaborate collusion to steal their money—or report them to their home governments' tax authorities in the case of certain customers. The banker felt very uncomfortable under the collar about transferring data on a number of his Sarabian clients, who would have more than sharp tones in their criticism if all did not go smoothly with BRICE. Like sharp blades.

There was possibly a more critical question. To what extent could those in management operating BRICE be on the payrolls of the CIA and other Western intelligence services? It remained an interesting, if somewhat speculative, question that had further prevented the Swiss from buying into the scheme at first.

More immediately, Stihl, as chief risk officer, had to provide important advice that his board would have to swiftly act on. The principal question would be whether this was just a government scheme to compromise them once again and give in to American authorities, but under an emergency order guise. A big ploy of more American taxation on Swiss-held private wealth. Very worrisome—but consistent with the law. His bank had been given one hour to decide whether they would comply, all consistent under the terms of the national emergency power act that Bern had thrown down at them with a thud.

The protocol of schedules regarding each branch account's transfers and the time of completion would have to be provided quickly following the board's notarized agreements to proceed with posted pledges by each individual board member. Pledges to be personally paid out to the government if the order were not fully implemented on time. What was he to do?

Then further dramatic news came by way of TV 1. There was the briefest report about kidnapped bankers in the neighborhood around the Grossmunster, and an official from the American embassy who had been recovered from a boarded-up stairway to the cathedral tower. The American had not been identified. Stihl's ulcer just about went peptic upon hearing about these ominous, strange developments.

There was another news flash about a disposal unit that looked like they were wearing special uniforms for chemical disposal. However, they were reported to be WHO (World Health Organization) personnel and Swiss health department officials. They had been called in to organize several blocks of quarantine. Then, another urgent news flash. A warning was given about a breakout of a deadly form of flesh-eating disease in a ring around Richterstrasse, a long one-block street.

"*Sheisse*," he swore to himself. His wife had just been taken that morning to a hospital nearby with one of the best wards for epilepsy. None other than the Hôpital des Templiers. The world, thought Stihl, had gone totally mad. Though he had been warned by Z5 to soon expect the unexpected and to be cautious about his movements. As well, to be very careful as to whom he trusted, especially in his banking fraternity.

He phoned up Schmidt on his satellite telephone. He wanted to know if this son of a bitch was anywhere around to do him in after the reported kidnappings and so many poisoned surprises.

"*Ya*. Stihl. *Was gehts?*"

"Schmidt, have you been watching the news?"

"No, not at all. Everything's very peaceful here."

"Where are you, Schmidt?"

"I've gone away, am in Norway doing some salmon fishing."

"Oh, really?" Stihl was getting a very uneasy feeling.

"So, what's the news?"

"Oh, just a lot of shorting going on. A breakout of botulism or something in Zürich."

"Everyone . . . okay?" There was a sly insincere tone in his voice at first. Schmidt was not talking very much and seemingly not that interested in the emergency. And yet he seemed to have more than the usual nervousness in his tone as he trailed off.

"Hard to say . . ." Stihl was doing his own fishing to get a better idea as to what Schmidt might be up to and know already. Stihl was wondering whether Schmidt was in some manner involved in generating the news events.

"So, what's it all about? Anything important to us, Stihl?"

"No, just a major upswing in short selling, especially on the Zürich Bourse—normal, I guess, given the developments. Wondered if you knew why it was so steep?"

"Well, how much more?" As if Schmidt did not know, with his one hundred apps on his Apple iPhone to provide and analyze stock information, no matter where he was in Europe. Schmidt knew that Stihl must have pretty well known that he knew what was happening to the market. But he wanted to show distance, big distance from all the mayhem he was partly guilty in creating.

"Like a fifteen to thirty times spike in short sellers, especially showing up in London and New York and Chicago futures markets. A significant surprise, as a huge number of major call orders had been recently put through. Even MANCITC shares had been catapulting to new highs days before. But those short sellers who kept on buying are now making a killing. Know anything about them?"

"No, Stihl, except something about rising MANCITC shares may be now just a short-term phenomenon. Fishing is what it's all about for me." Schmidt chuckled to himself, as he had gone significantly short on all US banks for some time, even up to that day's trades. "Let me make a few phone calls on this one," added Schmidt.

"What do you think—we are missing something special? Not an anomaly or a virus getting into the computers?" said Stihl.

Schmidt chuckled to himself again. He thought Stihl was actually going to get screwed, given all the long positions he had recommended that he make on MANCITC—and that other brokers were advising.

Schmidt had placed huge bets against the market through his Panamanian accounts and even what was left in his Delaware ones. He had bet his whole house on a market meltdown. "Yes, a market meltdown!" he said out loud after he had closed his phone. He let out a hysterical and diabolical laugh that echoed about the small canyon, in which he let go another attempt to reel in the big one.

Stihl had his suspicions about Schmidt's involvement with what was now becoming evident to him as some sort of short-selling conspiracy—at a minimum. It was more not whether he was involved, but the extent of his involvement. And Stihl, no matter how much he had done to get into Schmidt's confidence, was still unclear about the precise extent of that participation. Nevertheless, he felt the Baron deserved whatever was coming his way, given the loathsome activities he had done to undermine Switzerland's international banking reputation. Stihl even felt sordid having to go along and get involved in Schmidt's various illegal deals to maintain the Baron's loyalty. And more importantly, to try and expose his vast dirty networks of laundering and criminal activities. It would take over a year of undercover work to make a proper case, the prosecutors had told him when he tried to advise them that he would be quitting and had had enough of being associated with Schmidt, FO's demented CEO.

Indeed, Stihl could not wait further for the prosecutors—it was getting too dangerous. So as to maximize damage to the unprosecuted sleazy banker, he had slipped a rumor through a trusted party to Schmidt's wife about the Baron's proclivities in S and M and other deviant behavior—and even torture. She had been satisfactorily vetted as someone who would not remain loyal to her husband. And someone who would be impassioned enough to commit violent revenge.

To Stihl's astonishment, he had been told that she had already recently found out his sordid actions. But too late, as he had left for Norway, a trip he had kept from everyone until now. Stihl had been impatient for the results. And they were unfortunately at the Hôpital des Templiers. Stihl had not worried that his wife would be violently turned on him by the FO head who had leaked information to her out about the supposed evil deeds that Stihl had been involved with. This had been Schmidt's revenge for Stihl having tried to undermine the relationship between Schmidt and his own wife. The incident had told him something important about the Baroness, however.

In a way, Stihl had hoped that Schmidt's wife would somehow more secretly deal with her husband, as a trial against Schmidt could prove too embarrassing, as well as possibly compromising to intelligence sources. Unknown to Stihl, getting rid of Schmidt using his wife would have been highly convenient to authorities, in light of this grotesque nobleman being on the master list of traitors.

Schmidt was, in fact, surprised that Stihl was still alive, not yet done in by his wife or by assassin Kim. That was why he had answered the call, to verify whether his old "buddy" was still standing. Well, no bother, Schmidt had thought to himself. By Schmidt's calculation, Stihl would be gone soon enough, as he looked at his salmon being roasted on the grill. Yes, Stihl would experience much worse than what this salmon was getting, pondered Schmidt, looking practically triumphant.

The Baron had kept his satellite Sirius radio channel open to be sure of the massive hit, as he expected the nuclear explosion to interfere with a lot of the medium and long-wave-emitting radio stations reporting out of Switzerland and the nearby area. And to think his foundations in Panama would collectively make three billion dollars out of that disaster if all went right, he further gloated to himself. Schmidt was happily smacking his lips as he felt everything in life was looking so delicious and grand.

As Schmidt pulled a big piece of salmon into his mouth from the small barbeque he had set up, he further thought how cunning he was. He would become one of the richest men in Europe. And on top of that, a mastermind behind the new political elite, to be the next principal puppet master of the new order and to reinvent a united Europe into what the *Führer* had set out decades ago in his secret, postwar blueprint. One that his grandfather had handed down to succeeding generations. That was Schmidt's last coherent string of thoughts, just before he had cause to choke on his food, which had a bit of a funny taste to it. Then out of nowhere, an arrow ripped through the side of his neck.

Isolde emerged out of the woods. Stihl looked more flabbergasted than worried about his pain as she moved forward to confront him. She was in a kind of bizarre hunting suit he must have thought—given its green and yellow camouflage in twirling patterns of Ds.

Schmidt crumpled down almost in a half-lotus position. He was now fully concerned with his wound and trying to dislodge what he now realized was a poison arrow sending waves of paralyzing pain through mostly his neck, but beginning to seize up and swell his throat.

"How did you? . . ."

Schmidt felt that he could not get another word out. He was slowing, losing the ability to breathe, as he choked out his last words, a force of absolute will against the massive toxins in his system, a kind of morbid defiance.

"Too late. See you in Hell."

Stihl's death would officially be death by suffocation on salmon, combined with an S and M hunting accident. As he started to die, he looked apocalyptic as he realized that it was a woman doing the damage. The D on her lapel was the last unsolved mystery for the Baron, so Isolde thought.

But the contraction of his throat had been his biggest mystery. It had been caused by a special Panamanian fruit derivative from a hills tribe. They had used it on their arrows for warfare, all the way back to the time of the European invasion, which had robbed them of so much of their gold and silver. Which had left them in so much of their current destitution.

As Isolde went around the campsite, she kept on talking to the limp, near-dead corpse as "Mr. Monster." She kept on referring to him out loud as she talked nervously to herself as she wiped her prints off everything as she toured the site. Before he expired, Isolde had told him that she knew of how he had bought his title from a struggling aristocratic family of German ancestry in Transylvania. And how he had wiped out the family by suffocating them one by one in the evening, to protect himself from future blackmail or being unmasked for being not of noble blood. Then, he had blamed it all on a visiting group of gypsies.

Mr. Monster, barely alive at the time, was only able to flash his eyes around like a cornered, sick badger desperately not knowing what to do and fearing the absolute worst. He kept struggling to spit something out like his tonsils, his thorax probably—his whole body convulsed as saliva and blood poured down his chin.

For Isolde, the final act was to take out a small bar of silver that Mr. Monster had used to kill her father with. She stuffed it into his throat, as if putting a muzzle to a dog. It had not only been a "sterling" performance, she thought, as he choked to death on it and his own puke. It was "sterling justice."

And yes, it was personal, including all the female slavery and sexual exploitation he had made possible through his various banks' financial schemes. Lady Ugly, or was that Madam Ugliest(?), would get the credit from police officials for his murder or perverted accident bordering on monsterslaughter. Lady Ugly unknowingly had gotten a free ticket to a funeral, thinking Schmidt was desperate to have her company. She would soon be arriving on the site from the airport with a little bit of added poison and arrows in her luggage.

It was time for Isolde to make her getaway. She wondered how Schmidt's death would be reported in the tabloid newspapers: "Swiss Banker Chokes on Silver?" The headlines, of course, would read differently.

TWENTY-EIGHT

The bomb disposal unit—though one with a nuclear bomb-making physicist—descended on the DBAM premises in an ambulance van that had come in quickly. The patient was going to be "Mr. Bomb" of megaton yield, who if they were lucky would be prevented from going into critical condition.

The neighborhood around the explosive was getting more official attention than it had ever had. That included the days when the nearby psychiatric and neurological hospital compound had seen its precursor building, a chapel completed in 1195 to commemorate a crusade involving the Templars, for which the hospital was later named and dedicated. The area near the old medical center, specifically around the DBAM premises, began to get floodlit, with men in full suits and goggles spraying the area down, all under the guise of a nasty germ breakout, but a containable one. The ghostly illuminating beams were there for another reason. To prevent any journalists or snoops from sneaking in and possibly uncovering the real truth.

After an hour or so, a large coffinlike box on a stretcher was taken out of the apartment building and carefully put into the van, which had had a special large set of straps put into it to minimize the movement of the patient, in this case, Mr. Bomb. The ambulance almost rocketed out to the train station by way of Schaffhauserstrasse and then to the Kornhaus Bridge, where it turned off its siren. It pulled up to a special train, with one passenger car and a sleek, modern freight wagon.

An interesting fact was that the joint Ahlstom and Siemens-manufactured locomotive was the fastest of its kind. It was so recent that it had been experimental up to the end of the previous year and only put into service in the last few months. There was none faster of its kind. However, it would only be able to reach its superspeed of four hundred and fifty kilometers per hour until it hit the Swiss-Austrian border near St. Margarethen, heading for its final destination near Füssen in the Bavarian Alps.

Fascinatingly, overlooking Füssen was a gingerbread-looking castle—which provided the architectural design concept to Disneyland—built under the patronage of the nineteenth-century monarch who had been referred to as "Mad" King Ludwig of Bavaria. He had died under strange circumstances. Some say murdered, for mortgaging his kingdom into bankruptcy by lavishly spending on the castle, which remains incomplete to this day. Some say he simply took his own life, as a part of the same psychosis that caused his fanatical desire to spend endlessly on his various luxury residences, of which giant Castle Neuschwanstein was only one.

Now, a bomb of apocalyptic destruction was to be deposited on the doorstep of what some believed to be the haunted hunting grounds of this famous so-called crazy king. In turn, to arrive at a final resting place in Hitler's V2 rocket bunker, another mass-scale inspiration of the insane. Ludwig's financial madness, relatively speaking, made the likes of Lanny Zeroche of GAG and Fole of Ripman look like pikers as raiders of a nation's treasury. As for Hitler—just the hundreds of rocket heads alone, left over from World War II, made all of Wall Street's hedge fund "weapons of mass destruction" seem pitiful. Coincidentally, the New York Philharmonic would be playing Wagner's *Twilights to the Gods* as the train passed by the castle's concert hall. Yes, there had been a total feel of lunacy to this journey even before it had entered "madman's land."

Mr. Bomb, who went under the further title of a "severely infected body with flesh-eating disease," was hoisted carefully up into the highly sealed and padded freight car, where the supposed coffin was attached to suspenders. The Swiss authorities had made it impossible for the bomb to be jarred even if the train were derailed.

There had been no time to stick around. The king and I and the volunteer locomotive driver and one slightly trembling Schultz were, in theory, to be the only ones on that train. A number of bomb disposal experts, including the best from the Swiss police, had largely, but not totally, given up trying to remove the highly sophisticated booby-trapped trigger devices and timers.

K-Boom had further done his dirty work by making absolutely sure that nothing could be done to defuse the bomb, and any serious attempts would lead to a catastrophe. The bomb disposal people would follow, but in different transport, working continuously on their satellite computer hookups for solutions to defusing it.

Schultz and I were there simply to provide protection to the king and to stop any possible tampering with the bomb. But by whom was the puzzling question. Troops were kept away to prevent any excessive drawing of attention to the train; nonetheless, they were in significant numbers at multiple locations along the route and in overhead helicopters. Incidentally, their positioning was hoped to minimize troop losses if the bomb went off. Though that was certainly not advertised to poor old Schultz or me.

There was one other coffin-size box in the car that had come in earlier by way of another ambulance. It held Prince Bashard on a respirator. The king had insisted that he be put onboard. There had been additional discussions with Falcon, who considered that it would be a further folly to let the Sarabian king travel with a nuclear weapon. But the king remained adamant about being on the train. Yes, a king from what many described as a mad state in a mad journey, with an atomic bomb, about to visit the former kingdom of a mad king. Why not? Anything for a few laughs for my grandchildren—that is, if I survived.

Given what the authorities had learned about how Bashard had managed the plan to destroy Zürich and beyond, nobody thought there was any way he should escape his own mad destiny with the bomb if it went off. The king, on the other hand, was eighty-three years old, after all, and ready to accept his nuclear form of martyrdom if it meant cleansing his country of Bashard's deeds.

There had been one worrisome request by the king that I had kept absolutely secret. Well before this express to Hell was set in motion, he had asked that I obtain one particular sword from the Berlin massacre. It was originally found out to have been in previous ownership of one of my students at the Sarabian college where I taught.

It had seemed like a nearly impossible request, yet one that his diplomatic and commercial contacts in Germany had made it possible to fulfill. This was one determined man for getting his way. He reiterated that I was simply to be a delivery boy and to pick it up at the Sarabian consul. The only other request was that I bring a camcorder that could instantly transmit his possibly last words.

The trip went fast, but a lot of passengers on various platforms looked perplexed and a little angry as the loudspeaker announced their trains would be delayed by several minutes due to a special cargo train. The Swiss, Austrian, and German army helicopters trailing it were not heard due to their advanced stealth rotary technology, which hid the sound of their vibrating blades.

As the train sped to the border, there was almost nothing to get in its way. The dispatchers had been informed to clear the tracks for a train that was then going so fast, it was almost like a runaway locomotive on fire. The news reports I picked up on my Blackberry tried to downplay the spread of the germ, and simply said that one body had to be taken to a special cremation site, given its highly contagious condition. There was no reference to its final destination. Most journalists cooperated for the sake of national security, but a few had been stopped blocks away from the train station on minor traffic or vehicular safety violations. The real story had not gotten out, but thankfully the bomb had. Well, at least it was clear of Zürich.

While the Swiss bomb experts could not stop its ticking down to its midnight deadline that they had determined upon the bomb's initial examination, they had successfully provided a signal blocking device around it to prevent anyone from triggering it prematurely by remote control. The experts thought it was a high probability that any signal to it would be jammed. All we could do at the time was to hope and pray along with the king, even if Schultz and I were more interested in our trajectory north than where Mecca was exactly.

*   *   *

K-Boom couldn't believe it. What had gone wrong? There had been no coded final messages to confirm that the bomb was ready; the messages were well overdue. He felt queasy and a great need to break silence to communicate with his people in Zürich. Nobody picked up. And when he tried to get Bashard, he couldn't get through either.

The bad doctor smelled a rat, though his high-level contacts might have been keeping strictly to protocol. He then looked at the TV news out of Europe, and what he heard got his undivided attention: about a deadly disease outbreak in a Zürich neighborhood. A few dead bodies, one taken out in a large coffin.

K-Boom furiously began to phone around to a few news agencies, but the lines were constantly busy. One he got through to, but only to a junior assistant who did not know the exact street, could only tell him that the outbreak had been in the area near Wunderseestrasse. He hurriedly took out his map and tried to find it, throwing the map all around desperate to find the location.

"Yes, there is Wunderseestrasse," he said to himself. Boom had only so many streets on this tourist map. That he could not any longer access his Internet system had reduced his options. And the president of Waristan had just phoned him to tell him not to go anywhere and that there were two secret service people outside his residence, supposedly for his protection. He felt cornered, isolated, and definitely out of the loop.

The mad doctor was sweating, even with his air-conditioner on at full blast. It was like he had the flesh-eating disease himself, as he feverishly thought what to do next. As every bone and muscle in his body started to swell and tighten up, the effect of Dengue Fever left over from a recent bout, he had imaginative thoughts, very insecure ones about what was happening.

Yes, it was possible that they had removed the bomb under the guise of this antigerm operation. If that was the case, he knew the scheme, principally of Bashard's and his, was just about dead. Or was it? Then he saw the news bulletin about kidnapped Zürich bankers being saved and pulled out of a church cathedral tower. He was furious, waving his fist, yelling and screaming that these banker bastards might not get their due along with the Zürich CIA station chief.

"These bastards!" he cried out aloud again and again. "Allah, have you let me down? What have I done to deserve this fate? Or is this a test?" He said to himself, "Yes, a great test to show that evil is not so easy to defeat. I need to pray harder and show more trust in our divine maker," he further said to himself.

Then, with full hatred on his face, he looked around to his painting of Mecca. He thought he had one ace up his sleeve. But the Tyranians might be livid if he now used it. He had agreed only to do it just before any possible Israeli bombing of Tyrania—especially if the Israelis dropped the big one on the country's new nuclear facilities containing its fully enriched uranium. The Tyranians would probably hunt him down for not giving them their maximum propaganda bang for their bucks if he let off the bomb prematurely and if the Israelis canceled their bombing run. The raid by the Israelis was rumored for midnight, the exact moment when the Tyranians wanted the bomb to go off if Israel carried out a massive aerial attack. He knew he would let it be blown anyway—with or without an Israeli bombing.

He took down the painting carefully. Then he opened up his vault after using a code and finger and retinal scans. He looked fanatically at the trigger device. He thought to himself that there was a chance the bomb was close enough to Zürich to make an impact. He then decided to put it away and call the boys from Locarno instead. It was a wiser move.

* * *

Prince Bashard had been revived from his box by Schultz, who had administered an injection. After twenty minutes, he was dragged into the passenger compartment. Meanwhile, a hidden camcorder had been set up at the king's request to record and feed the video and sound back to both the Sarabian embassy and Interpol's branch office. It would be in encrypted form only to be seen by the Sarabian security chief, now in Bern, and Interpol's top two people, one in Lyon and the other in Zürich—namely, Falcon. That had been the deal, which had been argued over endlessly between Sarabian and Western intelligence officials.

The king only wanted his security man at the embassy to get the feed. The final deal was that Interpol would destroy the recording if the train successfully carried out its mission. And there would be no Sarabian security people on the train. Unheard of, given that the king never went anywhere without his own personal protection. However, certain key national and Interpol department heads were not in a totally trusting mood to allow Sarabian agents to travel with an atomic bomb through Europe.

There had been no promise as to what the Sarabians would do with their recordings. Maybe, keep them to show what a scoundrel Bashard was if his people kept the pressure on to overthrow the Sarabian monarchy. I had no idea for sure. Who really knew if Bashard would ever say anything to indict himself in this conspiracy?

"Well, Bashard, what do you have to say for yourself?" said the king, as Bashard finally became cognizant of his surroundings.

"Your Majesty, I have nothing to say. Except I think you have been duped by the West into compromising yourself. This has all been staged to overthrow you and replace you by an extremist, whom they are getting ready to install to cause massive polarization. A perfect scenario for what they want."

"Enough of your lies, Bashard. Explain yourself fully to your king."

"I have no need to further clarify anything until I am properly returned to Sarabia. And I have to ask you where we are and what we are doing in this railcar. Why have I been kidnapped in this terrible way? Have you condoned this barbarous act?"

"You really do not know how difficult a situation you are in, Bashard." The king was gazing intensely into Bashard's eyes like burning lasers trying to penetrate the smoke screens that Bashard had unsuccessfully tried to put over a leader he knew was likely too wise to deceive anymore.

"And who are these Westerners? Where are your own bodyguards? This situation is outrageous, Highness!"

"It is you who are outrageous, Bashard. I have treated you practically like my own son, given over the jewel in our economic crown to manage for the good of our kingdom. And to the good image and good works of Islam. But what do I find?"

Bashard was now beginning to take on disrespectful and haughty airs. Beginning to show what he thought of a king whom he considered too much of a lackey to the West, with all his interdenominational efforts and his lending of billions to Europe and America.

"I do not have to say anything. I will now only recognize the sheiks."

"Which ones, I wonder?" the king said as he looked at Bashard half bemused.

The king was starting to have success on camera showing Bashard's disloyalty. To get final proof for the moderate leadership of the Wadi sect that Bashard had been out of control. And if lucky, the king thought he might goad or frighten Bashard into naming his key accomplices.

"There is not much to tell under these circumstances, or little time remaining," Bashard said under a snide smile.

"I think there is a lot. Mr. Schultz and Professor—if I may refer to you in the esteemed name we hold you in the kingdom—could you take the prince to Mr. Bomb?"

"Mr. Baum? You mean that lawyer friend of . . ."

"No, Bashard, we are not talking about P. M. Baum, the lawyer," said the king. "Something a bit more deadly than even a lawyer who defends such disgusting people as Nazi followers. Yes, we do not mention those sacrilegious tie-ups."

"I am not saying anything further."

"I think you should. But take him away to the freight car and give him a full briefing about Mr. Bomb."

"Yes, Highness," I replied. We took the handcuffs off but not the leg shackles. In the black suit Bashard had been dressed in as commanded by the king, somehow he did not look like a royal. We walked him to the freight car.

"What in the name of . . . is this?" Bashard shouted out.

"Prince Bashard," I stated, "let me make your acquaintance with Mr. Bomb." Schultz opened the coffin.

Bashard's face went ashen, and even his usual bright eyes became mere used-up embers barely glowing. He looked totally stunned, deflated like a punctured balloon.

"I see. I understand, yes. Gentlemen, to use your vernacular, I am screwed."

We returned to the passenger car, but Bashard seemed to have gone wobbly with fear, weighed down with what seemed like outright psychological trauma.

"Now, Bashard, do you see your position?" said the king.

"Yes, I see we are practically sitting on an atomic bomb and you have resigned yourself to this fact. Now, what do you want from me so I can get off this *fuckin'* train?" Bashard, possibly under the influence of my American presence, was regressing back to his old, Eastern Texas State University, rough days. King Abdul was not impressed or distressed with his language. There were bigger things to think about. Like mushrooming clouds on the horizon, total human incineration and meltdown, and how the world would perceive Sarabia's overall role in the whole mess if Bashard did not talk.

"I would like a confession from you into the camera up there, yes, that has recorded everything," said His Majesty, this time very calmly.

"All right, I understand," reflexed Bashard. He looked totally resigned and in a state of hopelessness beyond what he had experienced even when personally being subjected in his US college days to racism and ridicule by a group of drunken fraternity members. He was at his lowest moment, ever.

"I want you to confess and apologize to our people—and yes, even the world, about what you have done. And I want you to be explicit about it with your contriteness. This is the only way you can save your immediate tribe from political obliteration. Do you understand me, Bashard? I am not *fuckin'* around, to use your decadent Western language." The king barked out loudly that there was nothing left for Bashard to say but "yes" if he wanted to have a chance to get off the train in one piece.

"What about leaving this train right now? I have to tell you that K-Boom can trigger this device anytime. I suggest we all get off soon," said Bashard.

I was about to interrupt the king and tell him that it was not likely that K-Boom could trigger the bomb, but King Abdul prevented me from saying so with a forceful wave of his hand.

"Yes, Bashard, it would be a good idea to get cracking in making your confession, and then I can better guarantee you will get off this train."

"As one member of the royalty to another, I accept your promise in very good faith," said Bashard.

The prince then made a full declaration of guilt. It continued for some time, given how thorough and even convoluted the conspiracy had been.

* * *

K-Boom had finally gotten through to what he referred to as his infidel friends in Locarno.

"Can you stop that train?"

"Anything for you, Doc," the Mafia character replied in his sinister tone with a vernacular, New York Bronx accent. "Your money is usually good. But we'll need a down payment."

"That will be very difficult in my present circumstances, but you know my money has always been good."

"That's the problem. *Has* is the operative word, Doc. The boys here know you have been down on your luck, especially with the Julien Brothers. We're very sorry to hear that."

"That is no problem. I have other bank accounts," replied Boom.

"Okay, you're back in the money. Sounds good. Now, how are you planning to transfer . . . say, two million for this? It's an emergency job, going up against a lot of important people. In fact, our top boss could veto it unless you make him a very convincing offer."

"Two million! That is outrageous to simply take a coffin off a train and reroute it back to its origins."

"We were figuring, given what is happening on the stock market, that some kind of big disaster is expected. Could that coffin, with all the germs in it, be pretty deadly stuff? You get what I mean, Doc?"

"Yes, if you put it that way."

"Yes, we put it that way."

"Okay to the money," K-Boom gulped. Now he was down to a *piddly* half million, just as if he had spent his life as a schoolteacher in the American wilderness or abroad.

"How will you transfer it, Doc?"

"Mr. Carlos—if I may call you that, as you are a miserable man who reminds me of a jackal of a friend that I once knew . . ."

"Please, do not take it personally. It's just business."

"I cannot transfer any money. I am a little surrounded right now."

"You don't say," said the almost disinterested thug, who saw the "project," as he called it, as a bonus, not as a necessity, a bit of a risk. But the dons of Locarno had no intention of letting K-Boom open that box and spread its cargo. They would turn it in to the authorities and get more than chump change for it—and even time off for good behavior for some of their jailed friends. K-Boom knew this might be the case, but he thought to himself he would be the last man laughing as he pulled the trigger upon the bomb's rearrival in Zürich. Or maybe simply, Munich, but that just would not have the same financial punch to the Western economy.

"I have an idea, Doc. You give out a million-dollar down payment by giving us your bank account passwords to Banco San Diego. And pay the rest later."

"How do you know about my accounts there?"

"Relax. We all have accounts there." K-Boom could practically hear Carlos snicker. "We studiously follow as many offshore accounts as we can from our blackmail operation with your friends like the Baron. Lots of databases circulating around, a few with your accounts on them, but not many."

"You guys are something else." K-Boom gave all his account details, knowing that Carlos and his thugs would try to take a second tranche well before delivery.

*   *   *

Hours later, Schultz beckoned me over to inform me of some very bad news he had gotten from one of the circling helicopter pilots.

"There is a car stuck on the rail line up ahead. We are going to have to stop the train."

"Stop the train! We only have five hours before this thing goes off."

"Don't worry, Pol. Or should I call you Adrian? You know my traffic record," said Schultz smartly, still looking to get one up on me after my previous lack confidence and not so complimentary words about Swiss police.

Schultz went onto his iPhone. He turned around. "I have better news." Just as he said it, a large Sikorsky helicopter with German markings swept over us.

"What's the good news?"

"We Swiss, not to leave out our Austrian and German neighbors, are an efficient lot. We worried in the joint planning with various security arrangements about just such a possible hijack. We are going to be switched over to other tracks, if need be. Meanwhile, our troops in the helicopter are going to take a look at that distressed motorist. If he can be fully moved with no damage to the tracks, then we will continue to proceed on this main line."

"How long will this take?"

"How about fifteen minutes? The troops should be just about there. After a bit longer, we will resume our journey at regular speed."

I figured someone would be angry about our removing the bomb from Zürich. And my guess was that K-Boom might have had something to do with that motorist on the track, as an expression of that rage. Not surprisingly, the next thing I was told on my radio was that K-Boom had been arrested for treason against the Waristan state. It was clear that the president of Waristan had had his hands finally tied, isolating Boom completely. Pro-Boom elements in the Waristan intelligence services would be livid, as they considered the physicist a divinely inspired hero. What they might eventually do to cause revenge, given that Waristan had a nuclear arsenal, was too painful to even contemplate.

*　　*　　*

Two and a half hours after the car on the tracks had been successfully lifted away by the helicopter, we arrived in darkness on an old railway line to the top of a mountain quarry, or what had been camouflaged as such. Schultz and I stepped out to make sure all was clear before the German *Bundeswehr* (national military) showed up. It was a godsend to stretch our legs—and to anticipate the removal of the device by the army into a place that should protect us from radiation fallout.

King Abdul was content that we had arrived at this endpoint without injuring any of the farmers who he had seen harvesting crops or moving cattle between fields. He had thought how these hardworking, down-to-earth people might have appreciated his Bedouin people, at least of the old generations. They had kept to their honest virtue and pride in gaining small amounts of money from herding, rather than from the humungous petroleum wealth that he felt was distorting Sarabian youth from such finer virtues.

People like Bashard, he thought, had also lost touch with positive Bedouin traditions, with their coarse hungry ways for power and the need to dominate others using Sarabia's newfound oil and gas money. They had truly lost all that was important in the way he interpreted Islam. He felt ashamed to be sitting there, contemplating how such noblemen in his kingdom had gone so far astray. He felt he would have to assume full responsibility and personally make amends for this disaster that had befallen the House of Sarab. The king had looked for the sword with this in his mind.

As a matter of honor to his people and the royal family, he had one last important act to perform on this voyage. He had been ready many times before for the greater journey beyond Earth. Destiny called out, he thought. Allah's will would be carried out.

He went into the freight section and got the blade, the one that had been used by the Dionysus league, financed in part by Bashard. That had been used to kill that honorable Jewish guard at the Berlin Holocaust Memorial Centre. As the king emerged from the freight car, Bashard looked into the king's eyes and asked only that he be merciful and make it swift. Even Bashard knew that there was no other way out.

Bashard's last hope had been that he would be exchanged for the king's immediate family if Sheik Zayed was able to carry out a coup. There had been no information by his captors about any swap. He was done and knew it. A trial would be humiliating to many in his tribe and to the House of Sarab.

In one swift, hard rise followed by the heavy fall of the sword, Bashard was decapitated, and so was any chance of this prince becoming a public embarrassment. Sarabian justice had been served according to Wadi sect law. The king now felt he had thoroughly done his duty.

The force of Bashard's gushing arteries painted the windows in blood. And given the incline the train was on, the head of the prince rolled down into the freight car like a bowling ball looking for a strike. But the kingpin was not moved.

Schultz and I heard it as a terrible bouncing noise. We looked around in horror. Blood was splattered on the windows, and the corridor was smudged between pools of it. We wondered whether Bashard had escaped and killed the king.

As we reached the door of the passageway to the freight car, we were relieved. There was King Abdul, looking like a crumpled and sad man. He was looking over the decapitated body of Bashard, who had once been one of the great princes in the kingdom and the House of Sarab.

The official notice of his death would be that he was on a high-level royal secret mission to stop the mass evil of terrorists and to protect the good name of the kingdom. And sadly, his body had been blown to minute unrecoverable pieces in a bunker intended to contain the booby-trapped contagion, as he personally drove it in to protect others from getting in harm's way. Given the contamination and intense sterilizing heat of the bomb, it would be pointless to try and recover his body. For that moment, though, part of Bashard had bowled itself to its rightful resting ground, next to the nuclear bomb he had financially fathered. But happily without a strike.

TWENTY-NINE

The gala was spectacular. The Order had thought it would be cancelled because of the well-advertised breakout of the flesh-eating disease. But a WHO bulletin had given an all-clear for visits to the city. Except for a few blocks' radius around Richterstrasse, there was little problem accessing any part of Zürich. There was one exception to the rule. The Grossmunster cathedral had been cordoned off with throngs of police, including those from the bomb disposal unit.

Friegel and his colleagues were making sure there would be no more surprises over the released Swiss bankers from Julien and Company, who had been sedated, gagged, and tied up. Just a standard bomb scare would be the guise if any explanations were required as to why the immediate area had been barricaded. There would be a final check to make sure that there were no loose K-Boom packages left behind in the cathedral or environs.

Instead of bombs, only *Herr* Julius Julien, the bank's CEO, and his twin brother and bank chief operating officer, *Herr* Caesar Julien, had been found muzzled and tied in the boarded-up tower after the CIA station chief had been removed. They were informed upon their release that the nuclear bomb threats of their captor had all been a hoax and that, instead, the police had been busy dealing with a well-managed strain of deadly bacteria and there was a small chance of a standard bomb. The Juliens, upon hearing this news, looked pale, wondering whether they had been infected, but were relieved to hear that the germs were well away from both the cathedral and their bank depositaries.

Flesh-eating contaminated gold was a worry to their future business that they had never thought to hedge against. Thankfully, it was all immaterial. The Juliens were also clearly made aware that they would never speak of any nuclear menace. In fact, there would never be a public record of any nuclear bomb being placed in any urban center according to any official police force report. Unless, of course, it detonated. Mortgage bankers in certain urban real estate would be pleased with this government security strategy. In fact, European and Wall Street bank lobbyists had written it.

* * *

The gala was held at the spectacular law faculty library at the University of Zürich. It had the look of the future, with its glass transparent ceiling crisscrossed with small geometrical decorations, one of which looked like double Ds joined in reverse image to each other. The rumor was that funds had been used from the Diane de Poitiers Foundation to help build the spectacular structure. She not only had been a mistress to a French king, but had had great facility with property and finance.

The building was especially noted for its airy atrium, with wide stairs at each end to give a feel that all was possible. Which it seemed to be to a good number of the law graduates as they embarked on their own journey to what some might describe as the land of golden fleecing and excessive billing.

Van Gogh art was hung on the walls of the ground floor and along the open corridors overlooking the central atrium. A fashionable new emerging architecture of transparency for the centers of knowledge was supposed to steer humankind through the trials and tribulations of modern challenges. In this case, legal and human rights ones.

A final finishing touch, suspended from the ceiling, was a large Cyrillic-styled Z. It represented the Z for the Zeel Foundation. The Z could have also been for Zürich, for Z5, or for zip. But then it could have been zero, as in Ground Zero that night. But it was not going to be. The only question about Z was to be the number of zeroes on the final donation checks.

The cool, posh patrons of charities and most of the politicians, aristocrats, and bankers, including the "Wise Men club" of banker philanthropists and their junior acolytes, were circulating around. Few knew how close they had been to doomsday. And how their security forces once again, almost in a seamless manner, had prevented unparalleled public panic, which could have resulted in hundreds of needless deaths without even a firecracker going off.

Though they had confirmed the bomb had been isolated in the V2 bunker in Bavaria, Falcon was convinced there would likely be little thanks given to public health and security officials for preventing a near-catastrophic situation from developing. And if there were any, it would have to be seen as almost a surprise especially from the politicians. In fact, the city's police commissioner wanted a report from WHO on why it had not done a better job of containing the disease with less disruption to the good burghers of Zürich, with their pressing schedules and zeal for uninterrupted traffic flows.

The commissioner also wanted a word with Falcon on why the plot against the city seemed to have been stopped only at its last stages. He had a final question that had been passed on by his subordinate: "Who exactly was this so-called Order? And were they somehow mixed up with the tragic events at Richterstrasse and the Grossmunster?" The commissioner was highly thankful to *Herr* Friegel, who had passed on what the commissioner had referred to as his stellar preliminary research. He now wanted Falcon to come clean and show what he might be hiding from the Zürich police about these so-called dark ladies. Friegel had told the commissioner of his continual lack of success in getting much out of Interpol on their activities.

The outgoing mayor was the first speaker at the gala. (His term was coming to a close, and he was to be replaced by a female mayor.) He had shown outrage almost similar to the police commissioner's, but was now returning to his business as usual in politics as he glowed for the camera lights. It was now time at this international gala with a global media presence to assuage everyone on how fine a city Zürich was and to thank all the wonderful officials, including WHO, for cleaning up what had been a much smaller threat than originally thought. He radiated charm and efficiency, but he could have been radiating something else under different circumstances. What he failed to realize, or had been insensitive to, was that he was not even the appetizer, not even a minor snack, to the event of that evening. Instead, he was an irritating minor distraction.

What everyone had actually been waiting for was the unveiling of the mystery guest. The buzz was all about who this supposed undercover agent was. A guest who was now under threat for promoting women's rights. And what had been her projects in the very deadly country she had been working in. Or was it a he? The mayor, finally sensing his near-irrelevance happily truncated his speech to the applause of the audience. Applause toward him for having thankfully finished it.

*   *   *

The bomb was blown barely two hours after I had departed the area near the V2 bunker in a military convoy. I was left off at a minor train station linked on a short gauge to Füssen. All the time, I could not take my eyes off the lit-up fairy-tale castle of Neuschwanstein, where a Wagnerian concert had finally concluded on a piece called the "Ride of the Valkyries." And what a ride, indeed, it had been.

From Füssen, I would take a plane and arrive at the university library hall in time for the second half of the gala, which was to finish late in the night with a ballroom dance. Maybe I would even connect up with Isolde. However, what I did not know was that when I got to the airport near Füssen, I would be shown through as a VIP to the executive jet hangar. There, awaiting me on a Learjet, would be a special lady. I could not seem to escape her attention.

"Princess, what a coincidence!" I said. "To what do I owe this pleasure?" I smiled broadly in response to her puckish, upturned, and unctuous sensuous lips. Before anything else could be said, the king came out from the back. He had been previously spirited off by a *Bundeswehr* Hummer, leaving Schultz and myself to explain to the railway authorities the condition of their train when they arrived to retrieve the locomotive. I was simply told by Falcon to get to the airport near Füssen as soon as possible, and certainly nothing about the royal Sarabian treatment that awaited me.

"To what do I owe this double pleasure, Majesty, of you and the princess?" I asked.

"Oh, nothing important," the king said, looking nonplussed.

We all laughed.

"Another colorless day in the life of Sarabian royalty," he added. He looked worn. He looked his years. And if he had not been a king, I think he would have shown tears. On the other hand, Fatima was glowing as usual; she could not help doing so. She had a face of relief, but even she was showing a bit more wear and wrinkles from what appeared to be a lack of sleep and all the stress of the past events to which she must have been privy.

I then remembered my concerns about any remaining assassins on the loose that Boom might have called in. The Locarno-sponsored group that had tried to stop us in our tracks was one instance. I explained to the king my worries about his security.

"Not to worry, Professor; you should now take some well-earned rest," he said exhaustedly after we—including his bodyguards—took our seats. We then took off for Zürich.

As we accelerated into the night, Fatima just smiled like the so-called good obedient princess she would ensure she was considered to be, despite her maneuvering behind the scenes, as I would further learn about much later.

We all looked again at each other in a pleasant moment of contentment. A contentment that could be felt by few, or at least in few such equivalent historical circumstances. Maybe Churchill after the Battle of Britain, maybe George Washington after Yorktown, Jimmy Carter after signing the Israeli-Egyptian peace accord, or Nelson Mandela after his liberation and the throwing off of apartheid. Hundreds of thousands had been saved that day, and maybe millions might have been lost in outbreaks of hatred and war that would have likely resulted if there had been a nuclear blast in Zürich. But none of us would be able to walk through the Schotland with a Nobel Prize, nor would the king ever be given one.

Instead of stories to the press about hair-raising heroics saving humankind by the occupants in this plane, for instance, there might be stories that the king had been secretly flown out to a German clinic, if anyone figured out he had been in Europe. That Bashard had gone on a noble and highly secret mission under the king's reluctant acceptance to prove to the world that the Sarabian government had nothing to do with the terrorists' attempt to apply biological warfare. Indeed, that Bashard had been infected so badly that he decided to die in the blast in the V2 bunker caves. A great noble death and a great loss to the kingdom and the House of Sarab. Another demonstration of his love for the world, for peace, and for his people. Tears would flow, extra prayers would be said, and special portraits of Bashard commemorating his life would be put not only in the newspapers in the country, but also throughout the region on large billboards. At least that would be the official story if all went well.

The blast, given its size in the V2 bunker, would be hard to explain to seismologists, due to its magnitude of scale in an area not usually prone to major earthquakes. But it had been partly muffled by the thick granite walls. A further explanation would be that there had been a chain reaction initiated from a special bomb that was used to ensure the destruction of the canister of the deadly bacterial agent that had been booby-trapped. It would be further explained as having set off over a hundred V2 warheads, causing an enormous explosion. All necessary as an absolute precaution to ensure no further contamination and the isolation of the bomb before it went off at midnight, which gave no time for the removal of the V2 rockets.

The public would deal better with the idea of a plague, after all, which had visited the continent before over a period of more than several hundred years. It would be much easier to accept this notion, rather than the fact that a nuclear bomb had been fully armed and would have obliterated everyone in Zürich. Or contaminated everything right down to the old Roman foundations and every speck of gold, if it had gone off in the center of town as had been planned.

The summer season, when many good citizens of the Western world were on holiday, camping, or at the beach, and less interested in the news, would begin a season of special road accidents. These mishaps would be buried with statistics about much dangerous driving on the autobahns, interstate highways, and M-designated motorways in England and other countries. It would be a traffic season of mayhem, with well-known, extreme right-wing figures on the coded list slipping off Austrian mountain passes due to drunken driving, for example. And not to forget, some Islamic fanatics. A sheik or two in Sarabia getting sideswiped to infinity, due to the large presence of fatalistic road rage for which Sarabia was so well noted. There would also be heart attacks among certain Swiss and Delaware bankers, maybe even one dropped off in the Zürich Zee weighed down by "fool's" gold. That is, someone caught up in their glittering fishing tackle when they should never have been fishing.

Then there would be the more spectacular busts of deposed and exiled Third World dictators caught up in sex slavery, counterfeiting, drugs, and debauchery, all first exposed by cooperative "rats-eye" journalists who were no more paparazzi than popcorn, but disguised agents working for MI5 or MI6. It indeed would be a busy fall as well for global intelligence and their freelance assassins. But I would not be one of them. I would be hanging up my guns and looking for more worthy targets of interest. Like Isolde.

I began to doze off in the king's plane and into the heaven of contentment where we were riding below the constellation of Pleiades, the seven sisters, which I could see out of the window. Or maybe it was all another dream. We all then snoozed, except for Fatima, looking happy and reading some Norwegian fashion magazine. How bizarre. Yes, she was a cool customer, not only a fashionable one. And one with not only sensuous lips, but very tight ones too.

After landing and getting quickly back to my upgraded lodgings, which were now a hotel suite guarded by two of Friegel's finest, I prepared hurriedly for getting to the final activities of the gala. In fact, a Mercedes limousine had mysteriously shown up for me at the hotel. A voice on the phone said he was the officially designated chauffeur courtesy of King Abdul and that I should come down right away. There was a faint familiarity in the voice.

The Mercedes, a lovely stretch one, held something even lovelier all stretched out in the back. There in the corner as I opened the door was a stunning Isolde in a black chiffon dress, and yes, the best that Lady Oréal had offered to ladies like Fatima. She was gorgeous. She looked delicious enough to eat. My breath was taken away, but I managed to get out a few words.

"Isolde! Fancy meeting you here."

"Jean-Claude, or Adrian is it tonight?" She reached out with her broad warm smile, which was enough to smother me before I had even stepped in.

"For you, anything! Yes, Adrian will do."

As I sat down, she stretched over and gave me a kiss that melted me. It was really mostly a peck. But a peck from Isolde was like a kiss for eternity.

"Come here, you crazy blonde," I said in my persistent *Americanese*.

She moved over, and we embraced and kissed like there was no tomorrow, as if we were the last on Earth to have survived a blast.

"Yes, just call me lover. Forget all the other disguises."

She laughed. "Surely, more than that."

"Okay. How about Adrian Lover?" There, finally, a good name to blight all the dreary gray senior agents, who work endlessly to come up with cover names.

Before I could add something more impish, she had given me a nice elbow. We held hands, looking like kids on our prom date.

Then something felt wrong. We were not on the way to the gala. And then the window between us and the driver was electronically lowered.

"Shit . . . Isolde. Oh no!" I barked out. My happy face had gone from ecstasy to near asphyxiation. "That's Jackboot Herman. We're screwed," I exclaimed.

"Who?"

"That's right, little lady. Your driver has been indisposed. Picked up kind of a bug. A lot of that going around town," he sinisterly chuckled. Before I could get to the partition window, he looked at me with raw intense hatred.

"Naughty, naughty!" he said as he closed the window.

"Who is that, Adrian? What's happening?"

"That's Jackboot Herman, a Brit, but a secret direct descendent and admirer of Hermann Göring, Hitler's Reich Marshall. He tried to kill me. I was stopping him from making a sex slave deal with Armin and Kardiac."

"Oh no! How did he take charge of this car?"

"I think our operations are thoroughly compromised. And clearly, even after all those roundups of people on the list—or maybe, someone got angry because of them and is using Herman to get revenge."

"Can't we do something?"

"J. H. is not just anybody. Did you see the scar on his face? I gave it to him. The story gets worse. He was put in a jail in The Hague with Kardiac—maybe you've heard of him? The mad psychiatrist who coordinated the mass killings in Zarvia and was in on the human trafficking deal with Armin. Obviously, J. H. escaped. They're two guys I helped put away. Yes, that's what it is. This is Kardiac's revenge against me before he is put away for a very long time for his war crimes."

"What are we going to do, Adrian?"

"No idea, Isolde. There is no way we can fool around with these locks. And I was told explicitly to leave any firearms at home for the gala."

"Yes, I was, too."

The car pulled up to Banque Suisse's Zürich head office on the Bahnhofstrasse. While large, it looked like no more than a main branch. In fact, it included a retail branch. Underwhelming in size, when compared to GAG or Ripman Brodie of New York, its competitors.

"So, that's the final game. It's that banker bastard Stihl."

"What has he got in store for us?" asked Isolde.

"Silver bars up our . . . ," I replied politely by not completing the ugly word in front of a real lady. "No, he would go for gold for us. I am truly sorry, Isolde."

We hugged, thinking at the time that we could be minutes away from death.

As we got out and entered the vacuous reception hallway, Jackboot Herman could not help looking a little too contented.

"Just like old times, my friend. Except this time you'll be getting the scarring, with me holding the gun. You brilliant shit. What do they call you now . . . Professor? What a cover for such a dumbass."

Then out of the elevator, which I knew too well, from the catacombs of financial infamy, stepped out Johan Friedrich Stihl in black tie and tuxedo but without the tails, which would have been fitting for such a devilish character.

"Welcome to my own gala, Countess and Professor. Sorry, I will spare calling you a gentleman for now. Or a lady."

"So, you are the famous Mr. Stihl, banker to genocide and human trafficking." Isolde said it as if her words spat onto his face like saliva.

"No, my dear lady—banker simply. I do not associate myself with any labels except receivers of deposits, or in your case, final withdrawals. To the elevator, please."

After a slow-motion ride that seemingly took much longer than the few minutes, we got out. It was easy to know what to do, with Jackboot Herman holding a damn Nazi Lugar to my head and directing the traffic.

It was horrendous to think what a ricochet might do in the lucky case of a miss. But my thoughts were on the idea that it was the same Lugar that belonged to Ingrid. In that case, there was no reason to think that much hope was left. Jonathan himself—no, sorry, his ghost—might be lurking around orchestrating this show, including the props, steel-chambered or the two-footed kind.

"Please, to the vault," said Stihl.

My worst worries were that Stihl had picked up some not-too-nice techniques of torture from Schmidt and had his own packing operation. Those two bankers seemed to do everything in pairs.

"Yes, you are no doubt thinking about Baron Schmidt. Yes, you took care of him, didn't you, Madame Isolde," stated Stihl rather pointedly.

"What's this?" I queried.

"Nothing good, Adrian. Nothing good at all," added Isolde in a tone of embarrassment.

Jackboot Herman patted me on the back. "No hard feelings; all forgiven. Lighten up. I have been doing undercover work on Kardiac, Armin, and the lot, old man."

I began to ease up, but not altogether. "I don't believe it, Hermie!"

"Yeah, thanks for the scar. No, I should say thanks for not killing me. I am returning the compliment." He chuckled again.

To my continued astonishment, in the vault starting from the left was Princess Fatima. Beside her was what seemed to be an elderly lady in a veil and a very fashionable-looking Christian Dior *abaya*. In turn, beside her, was Brother Biggart from Z-bank and the Zeel Foundation. Then, past Falcon, was Zen—Zen of all people fully recovered, or had he been faking it all this time?

And was that the famous philanthropist with his wife, William P. Doors? Then there was Gal Nickeroff. "That fraud," I said to myself. How had he gotten in on this gig? And past him, Rabbi Jacob Stein, famous for his moderate views on interdenominational faith. And finally, sitting down beside him, was Johan Stihl, who had taken his place at what seemingly was the head of the table.

"The gentleman Adrian and the dear lady Isolde, please sit down across from us," Stihl commanded.

"What is this all about, Falcon?" I asked the only person whom I could have explicitly trusted, and who was standing to the side in the shadows.

"Yes, we'll get to that. But first, if you do not mind, we'll have brandies later," he said to Stihl, who was beginning to pour them. Brother Biggart nodded approval.

"First, I want to apologize for bringing you here this way," started off Falcon. "These meetings are held in absolute secrecy. We didn't know whether you had any electronics on you. We have also had a spate of eavesdropping, to say the least. We thought your conversation with Herman would confuse the heck out of the enemy if they were listening in. These vaults here are absolutely soundproof. And our special sensors in these Roman catacombs, so to speak, are further protective of our work. If you had had eavesdropping devices, our system would have detected them and led to their neutralization."

"Shall we get on with it," Stihl said with a certain authority that even Falcon looked as if he was about to bow to.

"Yes, what you are looking at is the Council—the complete one that not even you, Countess, have seen before. You only saw the subcommittee dealing with special operations."

"Really!" said Isolde, looking a bit skeptical.

"Yes, it is the real thing," Stihl confirmed. "I have been working undercover against Schmidt and his ignominious lot. Sorry, Professor, to have put you through all of those escapades."

"And so, what now?" I added almost impudently, taken aback that I had been so thoroughly deceived by Stihl.

"The Council has decided to make you both full members if that is acceptable to you," said this Swiss banker.

"What if we say no, Falcon?" I was indeed back to my insubordinate self, which just was not impressing Gal a bit.

"For heaven's sake, Adrian, get serious for once. After all, I nominated you," Gal threw in peevishly and to my surprise.

"Right, Gal. Sorry . . . forgot to say hello. Must have been that last body blow of an ice hockey check you gave me, after that "shitkicking" of your Morton friend I had dished out—what was it, more than thirty years ago?"

"Okay, so I see everybody knows each other—more or less," Stihl added coldly, immune to brutal, Canadian hockey talk.

"What will it be, Adrian—and Countess?" said Falcon.

Stihl turned those hard blue, icy eyes to me, looking as if any refusal of membership would be the immediate end of us—maybe taking us figuratively to the bottom of the Zürich Zee after a nice ride in his boat. Then he smiled, knowing what my reaction had been to such stares in the past. This group would be a regular carnival of carnivores under the wrong circumstances.

"*Kein problem*," Stihl said stiffly. "No problem at all, but I would have to . . ."

Falcon interrupted, "Be very disappointed. That's what you wanted to say, *Herr* Stihl—wasn't it?"

"Yes, of course, *Herr* Falcon," Stihl replied.

Princess Fatima interrupted. "Yes, I would be very sad." The lady with the veil nodded, too.

"I accept," I said.

Isolde nodded a yes as well.

"But under one condition," I continued. "As long as the seating order keeps me away from Mr. Zen." Zen looked put out by my comment as he proudly raised his head and pursed his lips.

I was giving a bit of payback to my boss. But as he was a man who had likely come out of a coma, I thought I lacked decent bedside manners.

"I'm sorry, but Mr. Zen is too intellectually and spiritually complex for me," I finally added.

Everyone—except the veiled lady—rolled out a wave of laughter, to which even Zen could not help but give a smile.

"Fine. That is all," Stihl stated with relief.

"Any document to sign?" I said foolishly like the bureaucrat I had occasionally turned into as a university professor.

Brother Biggart spoke up. "Your promise is as good as ours. We have almost no paper trails to this organization, as you know, Professor. We never met here, and we will go out different exits."

Brother Biggart then opened a special door to the back of the vault. "I heartily welcome your membership. And it is not good-bye, but *au revoir*." He closed the door after escorting out the lady with the veil.

"What was all that about?" asked Isolde.

"Oh, just an emergency escape route following an old Roman passageway. I do hope the lady does not hit herself—it is a little tight," replied Falcon.

"May I ask where in God's name does it go to?" Isolde queried.

"Yes, to the Grossmunster, where Brother Biggart incidentally has a small vestry office. It does occasionally get leaky as it passes under the Limmat. I actually wish there were another way to guide the elderly lady out."

"Those are her royal wishes," spoke up Princess Fatima. Bill nodded, with his Canadian buddy following suit.

"Who is she, the Queen of England or something?" I asked.

Fatima smiled widely but said no more. Meanwhile, Falcon could not help but shake his head and look up; he was wondering why protocol was being broken. As I found out later, nothing was to be said about the mysterious elderly lady.

"Really now, ladies and gentlemen, in the fullness of time all will be revealed to all of our members," added Falcon.

"When would that be?" I stupidly inquired.

"Yes," said Stihl. "I like that. We Swiss respect time and timeliness. And in this case, as Secretary to the Council, today I have to say—but not fatally, Professor—that time is up."

"Oh, *Herr* Stihl, I think you wanted to provide a special comment here," added Doors's wife, who also was a newspaper publisher for the *Washington Insight Post*.

"Oh yes. I just wanted to add a point, a little bit of a sensitivity, given some of the press I have had on this. That is beginning to affect my family. And certainly my wife does not need to see any more bad press on this matter." Stihl coughed and looked around nervously, as if he were about to say something dramatically embarrassing.

"Yes, it is true that I was an orphan, brought up by my aunt in Germany. My actual parents died under torture from the Gestapo for organizing an underground railway for political dissidents and Jews. I want it made clear, Mr. Doors and Mr. Nickeroff, that those rumors in the North American press about me being some superprogeny created from some SS camp breeding program are completely false. Furthermore, my bringing up and education were never funded by a secret numbered, Nazi-controlled account. Please help me put a stop to such innuendo that has been planted by one of those who was on the real list, involved with the extreme right media."

"Yes, yes, Herr Stihl, certain tabloids can sometimes go overboard, especially with all the efforts against Switzerland these days about tax havens," said Doors. Falcon and Gal seemed to nod, too.

"I am sure all of us will use our good offices to see what we can do. And I am sorry to hear about your wife, Johan," added Doors's wife.

"*Vielen Dank*. Very nice of you to say that. I am much relieved, gentlemen and ladies, about your care in this matter. As a banker, I consider it of absolute importance to have an honest reputation."

"Right . . . . Well, our best wishes for your wife's speedy recovery," added Stein.

"I hope that our work here in Zürich, my undercover work with dangerous people like Schmidt, will have some value with Washington," said Stihl.

"Yes," said Doors, with his wife, Belinda Kraftbrook, looking on sympathetically. "We can do something about that, can't we, dear?"

"Then, gentlemen and ladies, and with apologies to our two missing guests, a toast," stated Stihl. "Those who do not wish alcohol can have Sarabian champagne."

Then Stihl got up, stood rather rigidly, and waited for all to rise. A quick tribute was made.

"To the Council and all its bodies. And especially to the Order, another thousand years of good work," the redeemed Swiss banker said.

Afterward, everyone left for the gala after a quick swill of a few vintage, pressed grapes that had seen long rough travels in becoming a five-star brandy. It had not been a vintage journey for Isolde and me; we felt worse than pressed grapes. It had been one of intrigue and deception, which we hoped had mercifully come to a well-deserved end. We would be sadly mistaken.

THIRTY

Frau Smuts was looking particularly radiant. To go with her complexion, she had a peach-colored, long dress on that somehow looked both fashionable and ritualistic—as if she were a divinely stunning priestess. She would not, however, be performing any rites in Zürich that evening, but would be doing so elsewhere at the resting grounds of her patron lady. And not with anything resembling peach color, but more of medieval design and color approaching that of a Sarabian *abaya*. Tonight would be a different honoring, in a way, to a lady no less important than her patron. An evening dedication to one that had escaped being murdered by the very same people who had done in the Order's highest-ranking member.

Smut's dress for the night's gala contained a hint of black in the dress's margins, including where it modestly plunged. The dress was of a design specially put together for her by the well-known fashion designer Arveinian. He or she was an activist transsexual working out of the fashion center of Histeria in northern Italy and used only natural dye colors obtained from sacred trees. In fact, Arveinian was an escapee from the royal House of Borain. In reality, a direct descendant from the powerful Kholifloa family. Who had been banned to ever admit her or his orientation: he or she was under death threat from one of her or his brothers, if she or he did.

The dress, an evening gown, was also special beyond its material or design. For just below the plunge on her left side had been placed a diamond-studded seahorse pin. It had been a present from Isolde to her upon the former's return from Barbados. It had become almost iconic for beauty and survival from the lurking phantoms of the dark depths. In the case of Barbados, the ones left on the reef off Sam Lord's Castle. In the current case of Zürich, no one knew exactly what dangers remained, even as those on the true list were being rounded up or executed. The pin, however, was a poignant reminder to the ladies of the Order to remain prudent.

The events around the Van Gogh Ex sometimes looked more like a fashion convention than a gala. But due to the serious economic circumstances around the world, a lot of the ladies had asked their designers to not only give part of their proceeds from the dresses to the Foundation, but to scale them down somewhat in terms of expensive frills and details. The gowns themselves would be auctioned off to charity. Smuts, after a little bit of her own strutting about to show off her new fashion prize, turned around with class and shook the mayor's hand as he sat down to everyone's relief.

"Now, I have some special announcements to everyone here tonight," announced Smuts as she went behind the lectern that the mayor had thankfully abandoned. She was so well-known to the crowd that she had not bothered to introduce herself—unlike the mayor, who had had two people do so and in some nauseating detail.

"First, I want to talk about the film viewing tonight. I must warn you that this is not for the faint of heart. We have evidence of brutal applications of injustice against innocent women in Sarabia by none other than powerful sheiks in remote areas of the country. These are not just the regular stories of upset husbands. But of real, excessive torture, including women brought to near death or near physical ruin." After a short pause, Smuts continued.

"The reasons these women were so terribly brutalized were for the suspicion of standing up against the use of the lash. For asking for a divorce against their husband's wishes. For driving a car in a hospital emergency. For being girls without veils running out of their school on fire, forced to return by zealot *Mootowa*. And then perishing as a direct result. Being beaten for being young, single, and giving their phone numbers in paper balls to strangers. Being punished for trying to go to a foreign country without a brother's or father's permission. Even for being a businesswoman, accused by three cousins of being romantically involved with a Western stranger she had hardly seen in Paris."

Various projections of brutalized women were put onto a large screen behind Smuts. The corresponding slides read: *Punishment by death for changing religion* or *Hospitalized indefinitely due to 99 lashes* for talking to the Western media and showing her photo. And finally, *Died by Stoning.*

Smuts continued, "These are pictures of Sarabian women, almost no special VIPs, mostly decent, struggling Bedouin women. They have become center to a documentary narrative put together by our special guest. It focuses on them as mothers, daughters, members of the community, and just regular decent women trying to struggle, laugh, and love, like so many of their sisters around the world. Just trying to get on with their lives in the small, but heroic, ways that made their contributions to society so special."

One could hear a pin drop given how enraptured the audience was with what Smuts was saying. She continued after shedding her tears. After waiting for the audience to collect itself.

"Now, some of our guests tonight have been working undercover in Sarabia with the direct support of certain ladies in the audience in putting together this production through the last year. The brave young director of this film was working on this in Sarabia, knowing that her life was under threat constantly and that the Al Quomini Brotherhood would instantly annihilate her if they suspected her of making this film. I want to add that without the kind support of certain leadership in Sarabia, whose names cannot be mentioned, we would never have been able to put this movie together. Without further ado, please give a warm welcome to Theodina Van Gogh, the director of *Lost in Sarabia*."

The audience erupted in thunderous applause. Everyone stood up. The entire gala, largely of women, was beaming collectively from one end to every end of the room. The tears had changed to cheers. It was hard to figure if there had been a happier place on Earth. After more than five minutes of hoopla and applause, Smuts inveigled the audience to sit down, given how loud and long the standing ovation had been.

"Hello. Yes, my name is Theodina Van Gogh. Some of you may not know me, as I am a very small, independent moviemaker. I want to put my fingers together to show you how small that is. I want to thank the Zeel Foundation for making this work possible, and all the good people associated with this wonderful organization. The list of people to thank is too long, and I know they would like to remain unsung heroines and heroes—let's just say, because of their modesty. But to you, and through you, Madam Smuts, let me thank all the good women and, yes, good men, who have made the film possible."

There were more loud claps, deafening ones. Then the applause died down as Van Gogh looked to the audience with deeply sad seriousness and continued.

"As you may know, my uncle Theo Van Gogh was murdered by sympathizers of the Al Quomini Brotherhood for his own movie in collaboration with a feminist from the Sarabian religious sphere. His efforts strongly condemned Islamic fundamentalism. Whether one agreed or not with the full tone of that film, there was no reason that my uncle's life should have been taken."

Theodina then paused for dramatic effect. She then looked around trying it seemed to look like she truly wanted to connect to almost everyone in the room, and to prepare the audience for important information.

"What you might not know was that my great aunt and uncle were killed by the Gestapo. They, also, paid with their lives by standing up against extremists, Nazi ones in their case. They were also trying to make a better world for all of us here, and those well beyond here. Finally, of course, you know very well of the artist whose marvelous works are on display, Vincent Van Gogh—my great, great uncle, so to speak. They all pursued a bright new or distinct vision for the world, and because of it, paid with their lives. I guess certain traits are embedded in the family tree."

The members of the gala laughed a soft, affectionate, but short laugh.

"I want to dedicate this film not only to the suffering and abused women of the world—of whom we should be aware, but also to those on our own doorsteps. This dedication also goes to those relatives and friends who try to support them, as well as the many helpful organizations for battered women. They, and the many artists and human rights advocates at risk, never get enough of our support. Thank you. And please view the film, but you will forgive me if I cannot say, please enjoy it."

There was more applause.

Smuts then interjected, "We have a small little gift to give you from a secret admirer."

"Oh, that's not necessary," responded Van Gogh.

With considerable poise, in stepped Princess Fatima, who had been in the area and been invited by her king to represent Sarabia. It was a nonverbal commitment of the House of Sarab to try and push for more reforms, especially after everything that had happened in Zürich. The king had been moved by his sister's explanation of her work with the ladies of the Order. And after being totally sickened by the reactionary elements in the outer provinces, he had given his approval to the presentation. Fatima being at the gala was also to provide partial amends. Though not everyone was comfortable with her presence, as there were still some bitter feelings in the audience about Sarabia's remaining lack of progress on female rights.

The princess began her short speech with a kind but short complimentary smile that relayed to the audience that she would keep it politely short.

"I understand this is called the Dianesis Garland, a reproduction from a marble statue of 'Diana of the Hunt,' which is in a corner of the grounds to the Louvre. With its silver and gold branches intertwined by the best goldsmiths and silversmiths in Zürich, it will no doubt be a long-lasting permanent award for peace, good faith, and the rights of oppressed women everywhere in the world."

The princess twitched nervously a bit as she made the presentation, wondering whether she should place it on top of Theodina's head herself. But she knew better to let Smuts do it if she wanted to. Smuts smoothly moved over and lent a hand in placing the magnificent garland of twisted metallic twigs on Theodina's short-haired, classical-looking, dignified head.

There was further applause as the princess left the stage to the ladies. It had also been a very moving tribute to Isolde and different members of the Order. Some of them had been distributed throughout the audience. Baroness Schmidt, though, was indisposed, for she was being interrogated by Friegel. She had played a double-agent role, which had almost gotten Isolde and me killed. Friegel had found out about it. Bless him.

What came to be known in a very limited number of intelligence circles as the *ZUrabia* file, the code name for the Zürich-Sarabian joint conspiracy—including the Order's counterintelligence operations with Sarabian allies—was now closed. The conspiracy of criminal bankers, neo-Nazis, and Islamic extremists to produce a new malevolent world order was now over, I thought. Bless the ladies of the Order. Bless Isolde.

*　　*　　*

Six months later, I was invited to England for a fall ritual by the Order. Isolde had been providing me with books on all sorts of ancient societies, including female Masonic ones. I thought how bizarre, but extremely fascinating. I had assumed that the Masons had been strictly a closed shop for a rather conservative body of men—of no or little interest in getting female members or supporting human rights activists. I had been badly informed. Much of the propaganda that made all Masonic orders look dangerous or manipulative was simply bunkum for conspiracy hounds. It made great novels, but there was little of any wrong that I saw in the Order's rituals or in the overall work of Masons, including their hospital charities. At least, for the majority of the current-day ones.

We had been recently engaged, which she said made it important not to hold back any secrets from each other—or only a few significant ones. I had let it all hang out: the cruising with married women including those close to Isolde, the wild boozing, the fouled-up grizzly assassinations with their tragic results, my own minor double dealings with Schmidt including his giving me thirteen bars of silver every month to keep my mouth shut. And too many character flaws and disorders to list—even in a book.

The only things I think Isolde had initially held back were exactly how she had put Schmidt away in Norway and how her father had been killed and by whom. And exactly Fatima's contribution in having Schmidt rubbed out. (But she eventually told me about those, too.) She just smiled when I spoke to her about all of the women. She said simply that it was good that I had gotten beyond it and that she thought I would find no more reason for the excessive drinking. I replied with my own quiet smile into the bliss of now having a soul mate close-by to put me on the journey to spiritual rehabilitation. It would be a long muddy road, as the damage had been extensive, but not undoable.

We arrived on November 11 to a special country retreat in Althorp, England—another part of Isolde's coming clean with me about her secret life. I remembered references to the place, not only in Druid mythology, but in a small pamphlet mixed with everything that Isolde had given me about the history of the old Dianesis cult. It had been a Roman female sect that used to go there annually to celebrate under a very large oak tree on a small island in a lake. It was steeped in honoring nature, and the benevolent forces of femininity as epitomized by Goddess Diana. But it was also well beyond that.

The members of that very ancient Order were also repudiated to be female assassins, who would revenge gross injustices carried out against innocent women or their loved ones. They would secretly defend a variety of lost causes. The cult was further known for their hunting prowess, being some of the best bowpersons in the country, but unknown to their husbands. Better snipers, in fact, than anyone in the Roman legions, including the ones that were annihilated by the soldiers of Boadicea, the Celtic queen renowned for her warrior fame.

These highly unusual ladies of the first Order, circa 43 BC to around AD 380, were said to have worn very distinct rings. This all made me recall a story quite a few years back about ancient trinkets with the cameo figurines of Goddess Diana. They had been found near the foundation work in the building of the small temple, in which the remains of the People's Princess had been placed behind it in a grave.

Professor Apollo Mudd of Cambridge University, head of the dig and amateur soothsayer, was quoted in the *Guardian* in 1997 about the rings' aesthetic details and their great powers to forecast coming disasters when they were placed at the key points of a Zodiac chart on the Despensier Estate. The ritual had to be performed on the eleventh day of the eleventh month. As I remember from reading the clipping, it seemed the detail descriptions coincided with the rings on which the ladies of the Order had sworn their oaths of allegiance at the Rothirsh.

As Isolde drove me down a long driveway road to the ritual site in an old Silver Shadow Rolls-Royce, which had been repossessed from Schmidt's estate in Burnmouth, I began to get some strange tingling feeling of familiarity with the area. Yes, this site for the special annual ritual of the Dianesis Order was very exceptional, indeed. I remembered with a kind of sudden euphoria what this place was all about.

At the end of the long treed driveway, there was a small-scale replica of the Parthenon. All on a small oval island, so near but so far. Yes, of course, the Dianesis Order—it all made sense. How pathetic that I could not have put the pieces together. The patron lady of the Dianesis Order had been no less than Princess Di!

It all came back to me like a fast-moving motion film. MI5's "for eyes only" classified version of Diana's assassination—a version more confidential that the real function and members of Z5 and the Order. That file gave strong speculation to the view that she was murdered at the behest of Muslim extremists in Egypt connected to the Al Quomini Brotherhood—well, at least, emerging elements of it at the time. They could not accept what they saw as a woman icon from the West about to bring her liberalism and associated feminist charity works to Egypt—facilitated by her marrying one of the richest bachelors from that nation. Yes, indeed, the Al Quomini Brotherhood, in connivance with fascist elements in England, had her expunged, according to MI5 and MI6. The files were buried—no, burned—well before the inquest into her death. The fear was that if the information were ever released, it would practically cause a public revolt—no, more like a revolution.

The story, as it was told to me by Falcon, got worse. The plans for her assassination and money for the dirty-deed-to-be were exchanged at the Louvre during the fund-raising gala for the start-up of the Zeel Foundation. In fact, the exchange was done by the cheeky bastards right in front of the dark lead statue of the Goddess Diana holding a male stag by its antlers and grabbing an arrow from her quiver. As possibly a sick joke, a nearby window had a view of the roof almost to the highway where the tragic accident was to take place that subsequently led to Diana's death.

Jonathan, in his younger putrid incarnation, was the courier with the money. An unknown British agent brought the plans to him. Falcon never released that man's name, but seemed very saddened when he made reference to the unnamed conspirator. Had it been Falcon himself—now trying to make amends?

What Isolde told me regarding the further historical foundations of her Order beyond the Roman period was fascinating, but clearly not as moving as the Order's connection with its posthumous honorary patron. After the fall of Rome, information about the Covenant of Diana became sketchy. Documents in the Z-bank vaults that Isolde recovered indicated that it was revived during the Crusades in the subterranean passages below what is now the Masonic lodge in Zürich. Sponsored by the inheritance from three Masons referred to as the Wise Men, buried saints under the Grossmunster cathedral. They had been put there along with their gold, which had been dug up and used by the Order. The Wise Men were reputed to be the bankers of their time—a charity breakaway group to the Knights Templar.

Secretly, the noblewomen belonging to the Order in the subsequent Renaissance period raised millions of dollars in current-day money equivalent. The Z-bank documents confirmed that one of them was Diane de Poitier, mistress to King Francis I of France. It was as partial restitution for the massacres that Richard the Lionheart and other male crusading nobles of Europe perpetrated on Muslim women.

After this rather fascinating history lesson, Isolde looked at me with deep affection, but apparent sadness as she further revealed what would practically lift me off my feet—as if what had been just revealed before were not staggering enough.

"I have something more special I need to tell you, Adrian."

"Isolde, this has all been quite revealing enough. I am not sure I won't be totally projected into orbit if what you are about to tell me is more dramatic."

"No, something I surely need to get off my chest, but that you cannot tell anyone. Swear, absolutely to no one."

"Yes, of course, darling. My absolute sworn commitment until death do us part. What is it, my loved one?"

"I was the one who really killed Princess Diana!"

"What! . . . You are sounding delirious. I can't . . ."

"Well, it was my fault. I really believe it." Isolde broke down crying, more so than I had ever seen before. Her head was practically in her lap. Practically in line with the dashboard. Tears came to my own eyes, given how devastated she was.

"I did it, Adrian. I didn't want to do it. Forgive me."

She then took out a dagger with the famous D emblem on it. The kind she had stabbed the thief from Panama with—including its Wicca motif.

"I don't want to live."

"Give that to me. Let's sit close together." I took her hand.

"I started a project when I was younger. It was to give money to a women's charity in Cairo to seriously promote women's rights. The Brotherhood found out somehow that the princess was a huge fund-raiser for it. My God, Adrian, they arranged for her murder in Paris because of it!"

"It's okay, I heard about it. My sources have already told me very recently that the Brotherhood had targeted her before you initiated that project. Someone in the British intelligence community, a rogue element, paid the Brotherhood to coordinate it. Now dead—done in a most ghastly way. It's over, Isolde."

"It's never over for me."

"Now, Isolde, this is absolutely top secret. I should not be telling you this, but I will because I love you with all my heart. Please do not die after everything we have been through. I beg you not to."

"Who exactly then, Adrian? If not me."

"It was Jonathan who relayed the plans for her assassination. Paid for by a very small ring of extreme right-wing zealots in the British establishment, who had even supported Hitler in the War—or their fathers had. Teaming up with the Brotherhood—even back then. They let the Brotherhood oversee her assassination to cover the British group's involvement. Jonathan had been working for years in helping to mount this huge Islamic extremist-Nazi conspiracy."

"It was Jonathan! That's incredible, Adrian—so much destruction of the very best and good by that evil man. That bastard! All those years working with him and not knowing—how unbelievable. Though it's good to know that I wasn't the real cause." There was relief on Isolde's face, and a kind of embarrassment as well as she looked down.

"Yes, Isolde, let's get out of here and not talk anymore about this. How about going to my place and forgetting all of these sad things?" I held her hand tightly and looked as inviting as I could to convince her to get out of that place, where shadows of twisted tree branches and thickets seemed to evermore close in on us.

"No, Adrian. I have a ceremony to perform with the six sisters and our arch deaconesses."

"Oh, right . . . sure." It was no use to argue against this committed devotee, who was sworn once a year to carry out a complex ceremony involving a male stag that I did not wish to query more about.

"I think I should stay in the car. I feel I would be intruding if I were to attend—even to get close to your ceremonies. And, Isolde . . ."

"Yes, Adrian."

"Please, give me the dagger."

"I'll need it."

"You'll need it!"

"Yes, we use it to draw blood from an old stag, which we . . ."

"Okay, sure, fine. Will this take long?" I could not actually get into this part of her rituals, but it was so important to her there was no way I was going to restrain her from performing her Orderly duties.

"No, just an hour or so. Maybe longer, depending on how successful our hunt is."

"Okay, I'll just read the newspaper and wait, if you don't mind," I said rather *wimpishly,* even for someone who had become a reformed assassin.

"Okay, darling, I won't be long."

* * *

President Armandnogood of Tyrania had just received very bad news. A squadron of Israeli FI6 jets had been scrambled. They were over Sarabian airspace, as the Sarabians had just given them final clearance to enter their territory. This was it. What Shista scripture had predicted could be coming soon. The only problem was that the president never thought it would happen—at least in his lifetime. There had also been so many false alerts before, including a major one during the previous spring.

He felt nevertheless—no, he knew—he had no other choice. He went to the vault, where the device was that would send the signal to the nuclear weapon to explode it. His people abroad would monitor and report back as to whether the bomb had been successfully triggered. He had not heard from Boom recently, unsurprising as he had been put under house arrest and been kept totally incommunicado. And with what had transpired months before, Armandnogood was not all certain that the bomb would be operational. But no matter, the work had been done before, and Boom had guaranteed his work. His word to Armandnogood was as good as Zürich gold. As good as the hundreds of centrifuges that Boom had moved out of Belgium through payments by way of the First Commercial Bank of Delaware.

The president waited for word that the Israeli jets had made it through the air defenses to the nuclear site at Boozra or even the outskirts of the Tyranian capital. He still heard nothing on his receiver. He had, however, gotten a phone call from the secretary to the Grand Ayatollah, head of the Council of Theocracy, who demanded his presence almost immediately. He could feel sweat trickling onto his neck. A neck he thought might very well be on the line. Like the line of a chopping block, unless he was successful with what Boom used to bizarrely refer to as a last "Hail Mary for Islam." With apologies by Boom about his bizarre expression that had slipped out despite his devotion to Mary, mother of Prophet Jesus according to his faith.

The Tyranian air force commander was on the line. "I am sorry to say, your Excellency, that two Israeli jets got through and have destroyed much of our nuclear complex."

"Thank you, Commander. And may Allah protect all of your men."

The president knew what he had to do, with regret, as he recognized in his own mind that the Koran invoked serious revenge on anyone who critically compromised the people of his faith, especially if the attackers were infidels.

His people would demand a strong response, and his worry was that without one, his government would fall or might be the next country in the Middle East to be "obliterated" by the Americans. A massive response by the Tyranians would be a warning to the Americans and the Israelis to back off, as he would promise that another one could be triggered. His last thought said out loud was, "May Allah have mercy on their corrupt souls, who are soon to depart." He then pulled the pin of the device and fired the weapon, screaming out *Allah Akbar, Allah Akbar* as he slumped in his chair in despondency. He then got ready for the meeting with the Grand Ayatollah.

*   *   *

I turned on the car radio while waiting for Isolde, who was now already a half hour late. The news in the main pages of the paper seemed dull, which was good, but I felt like getting more up-to-date reports. There had been the spate of assassinations weeks before, which were still getting news but more in the back pages, as there had been so many reported car accidents of famous bankers, politicians, and industrialists over the last months. And oh yes, some bloodletting against Sheik Zayed and his men in Sarabia, who had all lost their heads not long after King Abdul returned home with his very much intact and wiser. All of which, I hated to read about. It just reminded me of my uncomfortable past of being a hit man.

After hearing at first little of interest on the radio, I picked up the business section of the newspaper. Strangely, underneath it, there seemed to be fresh blood on the seat. My stomach began to turn into knots as I confirmed that, indeed, it was blood! My growing panic—no, desperation—was interrupted by an urgent news flash on the radio.

We regret to tell our listeners that there has been a huge bomb blast in New York City. We should soon have more information about it.

"Oh, Jesus, God damn Boom and the Mexican drug cartel," I said to myself. "Their final revenge—they finally did it. I have to get to Isolde. We're all up shit creek, again," I said out loud to who knows who—maybe Caspar, the ghost of the oaks.

Meanwhile, in business news, markets are reacting dramatically to both the bomb blast and a coup by religious fundamentalists and other antimonarchy forces in Sarabia. Oil has reached two hundred dollars a barrel on the spot market.

On the home front, the famous billionaire Barney Rob has committed suicide with a gun, as his shares in MANCITC Bank "broke the buck." He and Sarabian Sovereign Holdings were purported to be the primary shareholders. Further on in today's business summary, Wall Street investment bankers Rich Fole of Ripman Brodie and Lanny Zeroche of GAG fled to Zürich, Switzerland, last night, escaping the bomb blast by only several hours. There are warrants for their arrests on the grounds of financial fraud and possibly treason. The Swiss are refusing to extradite them, as they have Swiss passports.

I looked to kick open the car door to run and find Isolde—there seemed to be nothing more worth listening to. This crazy, screwed-up world was not going to get between me and my love. There was a further urgent flash. I wished I could have thrown away the radio.

A special news bulletin. The president will be making an emergency announcement in the Oval Office any minute. There is speculation that President Rose will be making a declaration of war. And in other news about the blast in New York, it is now estimated that three million people . . .

KAAAA . . . BOOM!

*　　*　　*

K-Boom had planted a bomb in the Silver Shadow. His insurance against Schmidt turning on him—coverage that he had decided to exercise against us, after he found out how we had dashed his grand scheme and had been using Schmidt's vehicle.

But I had decided that Isolde was more important than the radio news about a dirty bomb explosion in New York that had slightly radiated millions. The radio broadcast had drifted away in the air as I had torn out of the car looking for Isolde. I had missed the explosion by seconds.

Instead of my being in pieces, there was an "angel" looking over me, pulling me out of the mud. She had a slightly bloody hand holding an arrow. But more importantly—an unveiled and loving smile and a promise to be my wife through eternity.

ABOUT THE AUTHOR

Peter Dash has been working throughout Asia as a school instructor, teacher trainer, university lecturer, and corporate trainer for over fifteen years. He has done extensive volunteer work to help youth. The author resided in Saudi Arabia for almost four years.

Peter graduated from Lower Canada College in Montreal and in forestry from the University of British Columbia. He was a researcher at Harvard University's Center for International Affairs and a freelance journalist. Additionally, he received the Master of Applied Linguistics from the University of Southern Queensland. As well, he took graduate business courses at McGill University and graduate courses in international affairs at Harvard University.

Currently, the author travels extensively throughout Europe and the Caribbean, and he is an avid investor. He is presently engaged with writing a follow-up novel.

Note: Fifteen percent of royalties from this publication will assist students in need at the institutions from which the author graduated.

CPSIA information can be obtained at www.ICGtesting.com
Printed in the USA
LVOW040139181111

255408LV00002B/63/P